NECESSARY CRUELTY

ASHLEY GEE

Necessary Cruelty

Will he save me or break me?

Vin Cortland is the crowned prince of Deception High. He is beloved by his subjects and ruthless with his enemies.

We used to be friends, once. Not anymore.

It's no secret that he hates me, but only the two of us will ever know why. And the guilt of what I've done makes me hate myself more than he ever could.
Except love and hate are two sides of the same coin and both will make you burn.

Then he comes to me with a proposition: one fake marriage in exchange for enough money to finally escape this town and leave the past behind me. The offer is hard to refuse and Vin is used to getting what he wants.

I want to know *why me*, but I won't ask for his secrets when it means revealing my own.

He is the best and worst thing that has ever happened to me.

My savior and my destruction.

It's a deal with the devil.

I'll let him take my hand in marriage.

The only question is whether or not he also gets my soul.

Playlist

"Heartbreak Hotel" — Alice Chater
"Tokyo Drifting" — Glass Animals
"Champagne Eyes" — Aluna George
"Daddy AF" — Slayyter
"My Name is Dark - Art Mix" — Grimes
"Bury Me Alive" — Kelvyn Cole
"Crossfire" — Stephen
"Own Me" — bülow

Nothing painful is there, nothing fraught with ruin, no shame, no dishonour, that I have not seen in thy woes and mine.

ANTIGONE

PROLOGUE

Zaya

Dark clouds swirl on the horizon. A distant storm rapidly approaches the shore. The crash of ocean waves is louder than ever as I walk down the deserted beach. I've spent my whole life with the world on mute, and now I'm hearing it all for the first time.

Silence has been my only defense against the world's cruelty for so long that the noise is more than I can bear.

My whole life has been driving toward this moment, forcing me closer and closer to the edge of the cliff until I don't have any choice but to jump.

I've never really felt like I belonged anywhere, certainly not here where I've never been more than the town trash. Even my family is only bits and pieces with no glue holding it together. My own mother couldn't bear to stay with me, not for any longer than she had to. Dementia has freed my grandfather of his bad memories and saved him from the pain of missing me. My brother is gone, and he won't be coming back.

No one left will miss me if I'm gone, at least not for long.

Shocking cold hits my toes as I step into the surf, a bitter mismatch for the warmth in the air. The water here is always frigid. It takes a brave soul to step into it without protection and hope to make it back out.

I've never been anything close to brave.

The idea of being done with all of it brings a surprising lightness to my step, a stark contrast to the crushing despair that has always been my more constant companion. In death, there won't be fear or pain.

There won't be anything at all.

I've always feared the ocean, a strange thing for someone who was born in spitting distance of the water. Growing up, trips to the beach were more frequent than visits to the grocery store. I'd never understood how anyone could look at the infinite water, the waves crashing hard enough to break bone, and see anything but death.

Just more evidence I was never meant to survive in this world.

As a kid, my mom used to tell me stories of people being washed out to sea by the tides, unable to make their way back to the shore. Even the strongest swimmers eventually grow exhausted fighting the undercurrent. She described in detail the lashing waves during a storm that could tear apart fishing boats in a matter of minutes and suck the pieces down to the bottom, too deep to be recovered.

Darkest ocean is the final frontier, harder to reach than walking on the moon.

I've dreamed about what it might be like to give my body over to the sea. I'd always called them nightmares until I realized the real nightmare began the moment I opened my eyes.

Water churns around my ankles like the phantom hands of death, so cold it burns my skin. I take another step forward, and the frigid surf splashes against my knees, weighing me down as water seeps into the long train of my dress.

Some girls gently pack their wedding dresses away like priceless antiques, mine will be a death shroud.

I shiver at the creeping chill, knowing it will only get worse. The most excruciating moment will come when the water rises to my chest, just above the level of my heart.

It's always the heart that can least take the cold.

My hand drifts down to touch the still flat plane of my belly. I imagine a touch of heat there, the tiniest spark of life, but it isn't enough to call me back. And I refuse to bring anyone else into this world who might experience the same pain I have.

A voice echoes through the distant canyon, familiar even over the sound of crashing waves that is so loud it's nearly deafening.

It's too late.

It has always been too late, even from the very beginning.

I force myself further into the water, because I'm running out of time. If my nerves give out now, I won't get this chance again. Padded restraints and the double locking doors of a psychiatric ward are all that await me. My supposed husband would rather leave me somewhere to rot than lose his meal ticket. I'll never be out of someone else's sight again.

This is my only opportunity.

"Don't do this, Zaya. Please!"

Vin is already on the beach, but far enough away I can't make out his face under the night sky. The only light out here is from a full moon hiding behind dark clouds. I don't need to be close to know it's him. No one else would stride down the sand of a public beach like he owns the entire world.

I turn away to face the endless black of a dark horizon. There may be distant lights from our small town behind me, but I can no longer see them. All I have to do is take a few final steps into oblivion, and it will all be over. I wade further into the water, licking cold creeping up my thighs and then my waist, forcing myself to take painful steps forward even as my heart pounds in my chest.

"Zaya," he calls again, voice sounding more desperate than I've ever heard it.

He can't see me in the dark, might even walk right past me and never know it, as long as I don't say a word. But that doesn't stop him from shouting his promises into the wind, begging me to give him another chance to prove himself.

Vin has never broken a promise to me, because I've never expected him to make any.

I don't want to believe it's possible for him to change. Belief requires hope. And hope forces you to pick yourself up so life can kick you right back down again.

I don't have the strength left to hope.

Eventually, he'll go away and I can finish this.

Except I underestimate both his vision and the flash of my off-white dress against the dark water. His feet slap on the shallow water as he starts toward me, but he still isn't close enough to reach me in time. I just have to force myself to move fast enough.

He shouts my name, screams it, until his throat sounds like it is going hoarse.

Soon he'll be on top of me, grabbing me, forcing me out of the water and back to the shore. If I'm going to choose, then it has to be right now. The time for indecision has long passed.

I have to make a choice.

Stay and fight, give him the chance to build me up so he can tear me down all over again.

Or let it all just float away with the tide, taking a lifetime of pain away with it.

I have to decide.

Vin

I pushed too hard and for way too long. There isn't any excuse except that I'm the biggest asshole who has ever lived.

Not to say that I haven't had my reasons. But it's hard to make the past matter when you're confronted with the reality of your future.

In the beginning, I convinced myself that keeping secrets would be the best thing for both of us. The less she knew, the easier it would be for me to control her. But I didn't understand what I stood to lose.

And now I've lost everything.

Waves crash around me with destructive force. The wind is so howling that it steals my voice and carries it away to the sky. I pray I'm not too late, even though I don't deserve to have any prayers answered at this point.

I don't deserve her. I don't deserve anything.

But I've never been one to worry too much about what I deserve. I've always taken what I want when I want it, regardless of the consequences. There isn't any reason to change my ways now, not when it means I have the chance to save her.

I'm going to save her.

From herself. From me. From the world, if I have to.

I'll tie her to the bed and keep her there for the rest of her life, if that is what it takes to keep her alive.

I'm barefoot because I kicked off my shiny loafers to run faster. Bits of coral and stone dig into my skin. Sharp enough to cut, but the physical pain is a distant thing. If I have to run a hundred miles across hot asphalt covered in broken glass to save her, then that is precisely what I'm going to do.

I scream her name again, even though I know she wouldn't hear it even if she was standing only a few feet away. The darkness and the angry sound of crashing waves are enough to hide any number of sins.

Hers and mine.

For the longest time, I wanted to break her. Tear her into bits so I could examine every piece until I figured out exactly what fascinated me so damn much. I succeeded, but she isn't the only one who has been broken.

In the beginning, this had mostly been about the money. And maybe a little about how much I got off on forcing her to be what I want. Everything seemed to make so much more sense back then, even the worst of what I've done seemed justifiable.

But now, I'm just disgusted with myself.

King of Deception.

Vice Lord.

The guy who has never heard the word no.

My reputation is as big as the waves crashing onto the beach and as powerful as the undertow threatening to pull us out to sea. I tell myself I'm more than the things people say about me, but I'm not convinced that's true.

Maybe it has never been.

I see a dark shadow in the meager light, and I fight through the water toward it, driven by instinct.

Everything about her is dark. Her hair. Her eyes. Her thoughts, at least the ones she shares with me. But that didn't stop her from becoming the only spot of light in my otherwise colorless world.

And I let all of my worst impulses nearly destroy her.

When I squint, there is the barest outline of a figure moving through the waves. The white dress is what gives her away. She has gone far enough out that the water has to be past her waist.

I'm running without a conscious awareness of what I'll do when I reach her. Like every other interaction we've ever had, I'm operating on an instinct I've never fully understood.

As I chase her into the water, I realize I would give anything to rewind the clock to a time before we became what we are.

Before tragedy robbed me of a real childhood.

Before I stole her voice.

Before fate and bad luck forced us together.

Before secrets and lies drove us apart.

Before it all went wrong.

I follow her into the sea like I'd follow her to the ends of the earth if that is where she leads me. Even if it is impossible to go back, I can move forward. Into tomorrow. Into the future. Whatever place she chooses to go.

Even death.

If she throws herself on the mercy of the gods, then I'll jump off the cliff after her.

At this point, it's only a question of who gets to her first.

Oblivion or me.

ONE

Zaya

Helen of Troy was the original basic bitch.

If she popped up in the twenty-first century, the chick would definitely have a skim pumpkin spice latte clutched in her hand with a stylishly oversized sweater hanging off her shoulder paired with skinny jeans and calf-skin ankle boots. Helen is the girl who orders food based on how good it will look on Instagram, knowing she isn't going to eat it anyway. She is *grateful* and *blessed* because the whole world is wrapped around her pinkie finger.

But Helen of Troy is long dead, which leaves me to deal with her spiritual successors, the fashionably scattered girls of Deception High School.

And the guys willing to go to war for them.

But it's one guy in particular that represents a key figure in the story of my life that puts Greek tragedy to shame. I try to avoid him like my life depends on it, because I often question whether it actually does. Keeping in mind that it's impossible to get away from anyone in a small, incestuous town like Deception, CA.

There isn't anywhere to hide where he can't find me.

My senior literature class is currently working its way through the Greek classics, and we get extra credit for dressing up like famous characters. So I'm drowning in a sea of Helens, assuming the aggressively blonde hair and tiaras made of gold leaf are any sign. Even the natural brunettes have gotten their hands on a wig or a box of dye for the occasion. Some fit the role better than others, but all of them try.

Except for me.

Because I am no Helen of Troy and never will be. If her face could launch a thousand ships, then mine isn't worthy of the old fishing boats anchored in Deception Harbor. I'm not ugly, at least I don't think I am, but Helen and I are a bit of a tonal mismatch.

Both on the outside and the inside.

The aspirational dress-up might be a measure of their optimism, the belief something better is waiting for them out there in the world. I can't share in that particular delusion, even in the moments when I give into the urge to try. My future seems written in stone, a stone that has been tied around my neck and then tossed into the ocean as I sink deeper and deeper beneath the California waves.

Hope is the easiest way to get your feelings hurt when life kicks you in the ass.

The hallways of Deception High are a prison for us all, and the same rules apply. Keep your head down and your business to yourself, and you just might survive. I'm counting down until graduation like an inmate scratching on the walls of their cell to mark the days, and with about the same amount of anticipation. This place is a minefield, and every step brings me that much closer to an explosion.

The school is divided so cleanly you'd almost think someone designed it that way. There are two very distinct groups walking the halls, and it's an established rule that a battlefield littered with bones lies between them. The rich kids, many of them descendants of our town's illustrious founders, live out on the Bluffs in their big fancy houses. They drive late-model imports to school and wear clothes that weren't fished out of a bargain bin. The rest of us live outside of the town proper in the Gulch, a dusty and unincorporated part of the valley that is full of broken storefronts and run-down offices for bail bondsmen.

Things might not have been so bad if I'd been born with a different last name, but that short combination of letters seems like the only thing that matter sometimes. Names are important when that is the only thing you have with any worth.

Mine is like tarnished gold. It used to shine, but any luster is hidden under years of neglect.

I walk through these halls like a ghost — no one acknowledges me, and I do my very best to return the favor. Sometimes, the loneliness is a weight on my chest, so heavy I can barely breathe. Other times, I try to think of it as a twisted sort of gift, because having no one to rely on means there isn't anyone to let me down.

An unfamiliar voice interrupts my brief moment of self-pity.

"Antigone, right?"

I look up into a face that is only vaguely familiar. The guy is generically cute: brown hair and brown eyes with no distracting flaws, but nothing much to recommend him except a disarming smile. It isn't normal to see an unfamiliar face around here.

Instead of responding, I just stare up at him with an expression that is deliberately blank. It's been so long that I don't think I could hold a civilized conversation if I tried. I don't bother to try, because that would be against the rules.

But the new guy tries his best to make up for my obvious deficits. "From the play...you're dressed up as Antigone, right? It's not like I thought that was your name. I'm Jake Tully, by the way. I just moved here from Los Angeles. And I clearly didn't get the memo about dressing up."

I almost forgot for a minute that I'm wearing this stupid costume.

"You shouldn't be talking to me," I whisper to him, my voice just loud enough to carry the handful of inches separating us. Regret colors my tone, because he seems nice. I wouldn't bother to warn him, otherwise.

There hasn't been any nice in my life for a long time.

Talking to him is a risk I shouldn't take, but I feel bad the way you do when a feeder fish is dropped into the shark tank at an aquarium. The guy hasn't been here long enough to learn how things work. When he does, it's going to be a hard lesson.

But the guy just laughs, which is more confirmation he doesn't understand the pile of shit he just stepped in. I would pity him if that weren't such a useless emotion.

"What are you talking about?"

I open my mouth to give him one last warning, but it's already too late.

The sound of a locker door slamming shut is our only warning.

Vin Cortland appears like some dark demon summoned from the ether by a single thought. His glare takes in both of us, but lingers on my face when I look away. The heat of it is like a fire on my skin.

Even though he hasn't spoken a word, the entire hallway falls silent around us. Standing behind him are the other members of his crew, who rule not only Deception High School but the entire town. They are the founding sons, descendants of the men who claimed this town from the wilderness a few hundred years ago.

The Vice Lords.

V.I.C.E.

Vin. Iain. Cal. Elliot.

The Lords of Deception, in every meaning of the phrase. Their wealth and status, combined with a ruthlessness rarely seen outside of prison yards, make them untouchable. The thought of it would infuriate me if I had the capacity for anything aside from an intense desire to stay the hell away from them.

Vin is the leader, the front man, the one who calls all the shots but almost never needs to get his hands dirty. The face of an angel and the soul of a sinner. If he wasn't such a monster, I might liken him to something out of a magazine spread. At an impressive 6'3", he towers over most of the other guys at school. But even though he might be the size of a Neanderthal, his face more closely resembles a Renaissance painting, almost too beautiful to be real.

An angry slash for a mouth that curls in perpetual sneer beneath eyes as hard as flint ruin the perfect image. Dark hair, so true black it is almost violet in certain lights, sets off turquoise eyes that look like a pristine lake when you can see all the way to the bottom. Except the only thing you'll see in the depths of his eyes is more darkness. Vin is dangerous, and not just because he is capable of anything.

You can get away with a lot when your dad is the richest guy in town and your uncle is the local district attorney. Vin Cortland is untouchable, and he knows it.

He pulls from the vape pen in his hand and exhales smoke from his nose directly into the new guy's face. Vaping, or smoking of any kind, isn't allowed on school grounds, but the rules have never applied to the Vice Lords and probably never will.

None of them waste time on conversation, because they just assume someone will explain it to poor Jake later. Iain, who moves so fast that he is little more than a shock of bright red hair and pale skin, rushes Jake and holds his hands behind his back as Elliot and Cal take turns delivering solid punches straight to his gut.

Vin watches it all with an unreadable expression, taking the occasional pull from his vape pen.

I don't beg them to leave the guy alone or put up any kind of protest at all. That would only make things worse for Jake. They don't stop until he collapses on the ground with tears streaming down his face, gasping for air. No one goes running for a teacher or tries to intervene. One person takes out their phone to record a video, but it will never be used as evidence. None of them would have been able to stop this.

Everyone who had been watching just as silently as I was turns away when Vin's narrow gaze sweeps the hallway.

Why paint a target on your own back?

Not for some new guy nobody even knows, and certainly not for me.

Vin catches me watching him, and his expression doesn't change. He says nothing, but reaches out to touch the noose I have looped around my neck. It's part of my costume, a symbol, because the character hanged herself. He pulls it hard enough that the breath catches in my throat as the rope tightens in the hollow of my throat. A faint smile touches his lips when I let out an involuntary gasp. It isn't a pleasant smile, but the kind that is prelude to a nightmare. He finally lets me go and walks away.

I don't take a deep breath until the Vice Lords disappear around the corner.

"You don't talk to her," Billy Harkniss says as he helps Jake to his feet. Billy has been in the same homeroom as me since freshman year, but doesn't even spare me a glance as he leads Jake down the hallway in the opposite direction of the Vice Lords. "Trust me, man. It's just not worth it."

The other students have already lost interest now that the show is over. None of them speak to me as they continue past me down the hallway. They'll clear a path, dodging out of the way and averting their eyes when they see me coming, but they won't speak. They never speak.

And neither do I.

I'll hear them chatting with each other as I round a corner, but they always fall quiet the moment I appear and avoid my gaze. So I spend my days at school surrounded by silence.

Silence so oppressive I could drown in it.

And if Vin Cortland ever gets his way, I will.

TWO

Zaya

I CHOKE DOWN MY LUNCH EVEN THOUGH I HATE cafeteria food. This is the only meal I'm likely to get between now and the end of the weekend. That is one of the few good things about coming to school, we're poor enough to qualify for the free lunch program, so at least I'm guaranteed a meal.

Only poor kids from the Gulch eat the food served at school. Everyone else has Paleo-inspired bento boxes packed by bored housekeepers while their society mothers sleep off a late-night liquid dinner. Lunches that wouldn't look out of place on the covers of culinary magazines and usually get dumped in the trashcan in favor of runs off campus, even though we're not supposed to leave during the lunch period.

The cafeteria is a hive of movement and noise, one of the few places where the cone of silence surrounding me is lifted. Nobody will talk to me, but I can bathe in the glow of their conversation and pretend for a bit that I'm still part of the real world. Sitting in my corner, alone at a table, people seem to forget that I'm even here.

My head is down as I study my battered copy of Antigone

over a cold grilled cheese sandwich and stale fries. We'd been given our choice of Greek tragedies to study for the unit and I'd chosen this one, although I already regretted dressing up. The extra credit had seemed worthwhile at the time, but now I'm walking around with a literal noose around my neck.

Antigone had seemed like an appropriate choice at the time. Better to be the woman who killed herself as a moral statement than a pretty bitch whose only purpose was to have men fight over her. At least, that was what I told myself when I picked the play. It's always easier to pretend you don't want the things you know you can't have.

The lunch period is almost over when someone slips into the seat across from me. I don't have to look up to know who it is. Only one person in this school is brave enough to sit across from me at lunch.

I look up and cast a steely-eyed gaze over my younger brother, Zion, trying to determine if he got high before coming to school. We don't speak, but words aren't necessary between us.

When I raise my eyebrows, the meaning is clear. I'm surprised that the administration let him back on campus after his last suspension. I think it was for drug possession this time. He was selling benzodiazepines, that he swears weren't stolen from Grandpa's medication drawer, outside of the gym between first and second period.

Zion grins and taps his watch. His most recent punishment must have ended today. He has spent more days out of school than he has inside the building, whether it's for fighting or truancy or any number of lesser crimes. Our family name is the only thing that keeps him from getting expelled completely, not that it carries much weight these days.

Deception High is the sort of school where fights break out between every class, weapons of all types are confiscated on a daily basis, and the administration is happy if everyone survives to the end of the day. No one is going to jam Zion up for cutting class and dealing a few prescription pills.

But when Principal Friedman needs to make a show of cleaning up the school, my brother always gets rounded up as one of the usual suspects. Living in the Gulch keeps a target on our backs, and it doesn't help that the two of us stand out like sore thumbs in a place like this.

Our skin is a few shades past the wrong side of tan, and our hair holds curls that are too tight, crossing the boundary line into kinks. We're the dark marks on this town's illustrious history. The Milbournes are a founding family, but the money dried up generations ago, and we look just like the cross-bred mutts everyone says we are.

Some people wonder why the rich families on the Bluffs don't send their kids to the fancy private school a few towns over or try to have the district lines redrawn so they can go to the much better county-run public school.

But I know the answer to that very stupid question:

It's better to rule in hell than to serve in heaven.

I can tell from the mischievous look in his eyes that my brother didn't come find me just to be social. His lunch tray only has a pack of cigarettes and a Dr. Pepper on it, so clearly he isn't here to eat.

He produces a neatly folded piece of paper and waves it under my nose as I just stare at him. Zion likes to play games, he always has. It's his way of coping with the devastation of our lives, pretending he doesn't take any of it seriously.

From Jake, he mouths and tosses the folded paper across the table so it lands on my tray.

I open the note, even though it would be a better idea to throw it away. If this Jake guy had even a bit of sense, he would have already forgotten that I exist, not use my brother to pass notes to me like we're in third grade.

It isn't exactly impressive that he figured out me and Zion's family connection so quickly. Not like anyone else in the school looks like us. Honestly, it bugs me anyone would assume that two people who happen to be the same skin color must also be related, even if it happens to be true.

I'm just like the drug dealer crying about profiling during a traffic stop, despite the pounds of drugs in my trunk.

Hypocrisy, thy name is Zaya Milbourne.

Cramped writing greets me as I flatten the paper on the table.

Is that asshole your boyfriend, or something?

I carefully refold the note before squeezing it in my fist. My gaze passes quickly over the sea of faces in the cafeteria, but I don't see Jake among them. He has balls, I'll give him that. Getting his ass kicked in the middle of the hallway wasn't near the deterrent I thought it would be.

I'd be flattered if I wasn't terrified.

When I hold out my hand with every intention of giving the note back to Zion unanswered, I see his eyes widen.

A shadow falls over the table.

Strong hands grip my wrist hard enough to leave a bruise, and I wince as the fine bones are ground together. I look up to see Vin's impassive face staring down at me. His crew of assholes flank him on either side, watching us with varying degrees of interest.

I squeeze my fingers into a hard fist, but I shouldn't have even bothered. He plucks the note from my hands as easily as picking a ripe apple from a tree. His expression doesn't change as he scans it and tosses it aside.

Vin's voice is mild and even-toned, but still carries over the din of conversation. "Lunch is over. Everybody out."

The room empties as quickly as it would if someone had pulled the fire alarm. Zion looks like he wants to argue when I subtly shake my head at him. This isn't worth the fight, especially with the odds so stacked against him. The Vice Lords obviously don't have a problem going four against one.

"Even for me?" Sophia Taylor sidles up to Vin's side, all simpering smile, baby-blue eyes, and wheedling voice. One of the few natural blondes, her hair is done in long ringlets beneath a gold signet woven through a crown of braided hair across the top of her head. Sophia is the only girl at school who pulls off the whole Helen of Troy look without seeming desperate for attention.

Don't get me wrong, she is absolutely desperate for attention. Just better at hiding it than the rest. And she seems to get a kick out of reminding me of my position at the bottom of the totem pole.

As if I need another reason to dislike her.

Now she stares down at me with a moue of distaste, like I'm a rat that's been caught in a trap. She is just waiting for someone to crush me under their boot heel.

He doesn't bother to look at her. "Pretty sure I said everybody."

"Boo, you never let me have any fun." Sophia makes a point of stroking her hand down Vin's arm, like a dog pissing on a tree to let the world know it's been claimed. "Don't forget to meet me by the bleachers before basketball practice."

Vin doesn't respond. She finally slinks away, brushing her long fall of curls over her shoulder in a wide arc so it hits the side of my face.

He still has a hold of my arm, raising it high enough that the muscles tingle painfully as the blood drains away from the appendage. But I don't speak a word of complaint, breaking the rules is never worth what comes after.

I've had to learn that the hard way.

Zion casts me one more look of concern as he rises, and I tip my head gently to the side as encouragement to leave. The Vice Lords have mostly left my brother alone over the years, and I don't want that to change. He blows out a sharp rush of air, but stomps out of the otherwise empty cafeteria.

Finally releasing my arm, Vin comes around the table and takes Zion's vacated seat. The surrounding silence is profound, even to me. This room is too large for so much empty air, and the pressure of it pushes against my skin, making it difficult to breathe.

Or maybe it's just that I know no one is coming to save me.

Vin picks up the note and taps it on the table. "This was a very bad idea."

I spread my arms wide and shrug. It isn't as if I wrote the damn thing.

"This new guy," Vin muses, playacting as if he doesn't know Jake's name. "Is today the first time he's talked to you?"

My head nods, even though I want to spit in his face. There isn't a point in pretending things are different than they are. Vin doesn't ask questions unless he already know the answers.

All of our families have been in Deception for generations. I don't have the luxury of secrets, not in a town where everyone's favorite pastime is getting into each other's business.

The forced silence is meant to hurt me, but it's done me the small favor of keeping my mouth from getting me into trouble. Because if I tell them what I'm actually thinking, there is no way I'd be walking out of here in one piece.

Vin feigns confusion as he leans forward and steeples his finger beneath his chin, regarding me steadily as if I'm the only thing that exists in the universe. "Have you forgotten the terms of our deal?"

I shake my head, heart fluttering in my chest. Not for the

first time, I wonder how far I could get if I decided to run. But that train of thought always derails when I realize there isn't anywhere for me to go.

But Vin just shakes his head, still wearing the expression of mock confusion. I know him well enough to recognize he is moments from laughing in my face. His voice turns low and dangerous. "You remember, right? The deal that says you aren't allowed to speak."

It's only then that I remember my earlier mistake. I had spoken to Jake, if just to tell him he shouldn't be talking to me. It was a dumb move, but I liked how sweet his smile had been, and I didn't want to see his teeth shattered.

Stupid.

Vin studies my face, lips twisting in a sneer as he watches the realization grow in my changed expression. He glances up at the rest of his crew still standing behind me.

"Hold her."

One of them wraps a belt around my chest and pulls it hard so I'm pressed against the chair, although I can't see which one of them is holding it. It doesn't matter. None of them will touch me with their bare hands, though that doesn't stop them from doing Vin's dirty work.

I only have eyes for the demon terrorizing my life as he comes around the table. A switchblade appears in his hand as if it materialized from thin air. The edge is always sharp and clean, like he takes care to make sure it's always ready to be used. I don't know where on his body he hides the thing or how he manages to get it past the metal detectors, but that doesn't matter either.

A ready blade has always been available when he needs it.

One of his hands holds down my wrist while the other presses the point against the sensitive skin on the inside of my upper arm, just below three rows of identical scars.

The pain is sharp and immediate, but I don't make a sound. My skin parts like butter, and I can only watch as blood beads at the bottom of the cut and then trails downward. They release me as soon as it's done, but I don't move from the chair.

I used to fight them, but nothing good ever came of that.

There aren't words to describe how I feel about Vincent Cortland.

Hate isn't evocative enough, and fear is too shallow, although that's usually the predominant emotion. Putting a name to any of the other things I feel would just give him more power over me than he already has.

Because it isn't fear that keeps me in line.

The worst thing the Vice Lords can do to me is deliver a little pain. And killing me would just be putting me out of my misery, so there is little threat there. No, it isn't fear or even hate that keeps me silent.

It's guilt.

THREE

Vin

Secondhand weed smoke fills the air like low-hanging fog. I inhale deeply as I lean back in my leather armchair and survey the room.

These weekend blow-out parties used to be something I did to annoy my parents. But the less they seem to give a shit, the more this all feels like a waste of time. There isn't any point in rebelling when no one bothers to pay attention.

Neither of them so much as commented on it when I moved out to the pool house a few years ago. I don't even make it back into the main house for meals most days.

My father has been preoccupied with some business deal lately, if all the time he spends locked in his office and speaking furtively into the phone is any indication. And my stepmother is as up her own ass as she has always been. I can only assume she likes the weather in there.

Chaos teems around me, and I sit at the center of it all like an indolent king on his throne. It isn't an accident that my chair is raised slightly higher than the others and angled so I can see everything happening around me. Let them think the power is an accident, and not something that has been carefully cultivated for me since birth.

The Cortlands have ruled Deception since the beginning, nothing will change that.

And I'm the heir to this petty little empire.

Lights from the pool shine through the sliding glass doors and cast everything in surreal blue and purple lights. It makes the writhing and overheated bodies look like something out of a fever dream.

People who don't get invites to these parties like to say it's always an all-out orgy. They're not entirely correct, but I let the rumor mill spin on its own. An invite to one of my parties is one of the most coveted things that exists at Deception High. Rumors abound about the secret society shit that must be happening here.

But the truth is that my friends like to get together and hang out with whatever girls they're in the mood for that week, imbibing on recreational substances and getting laid without too many hang-ups about privacy.

I've never been more bored in my fucking life.

Shitty trance music blasts from the Bluetooth speaker, and I turn in my chair to glare at whoever has the balls to mess with my sound system. "What the hell, Elliot? Turn that crap off."

One of my closest friends since middle school shrugs me off as he plays with the phone he has connected to the speakers. That asshole fancies himself a DJ and likes to force us to listen to dubstep, or whatever the fuck it is, whenever he gets the chance. With his long hair and Viking build, he looks like he should be into Norwegian death metal, not the electronic crap he puts on to assault our eardrums.

Someone's hand slides along my jean-covered thigh, momentarily distracting me from the shitty music. I look down to see Sophia coiled between my spread legs while she kneels on the floor. As I stare down at her, I wonder if she realizes that she picked the wrong lighting to do her makeup. Under the glare of the lamp behind me, her face and her neck are completely different shades of white girl. It's dried out honeybun vs. cancer ward beige, and I can't decide which color I like the least.

I could take out my dick and force it down her throat, or I could humiliate her in front of a room full of people by laughing in her face and shoving her away. Neither choice does anything for me as I stare down into her desperate face, feeling nothing but a keen sense of boredom with life in general.

Maybe I need fucking antidepressants.

"Go get me a drink," I command her, even though there is a nearly full beer on the table next to me.

"Of course, Vin," Sophia purrs in a voice I'm sure she thinks is sexy. She uses her hands on my thighs to lever herself up onto the sky-high heels that clack too loudly on my tile floor.

"An import. Check the fridge in the house."

I watch her go, partly because she has a semi-decent ass, but also because I'm secretly hoping one of those heels flies out from under her and she ends up crashing to the floor. *No such luck*, I think, as she tottles to the sliding glass door and pulls it open.

My stepmother doesn't compromise on her beauty sleep, so the the main house is locked down tighter than virgin pussy right now. It should buy me a few minutes of peace while Sophia figures that out. She knows better than to come back empty-handed.

"If you don't hit that soon, her head might shoot off into the stratosphere from all the built up pressure," Cal comments from the sofa a few feet away.

"She might need to find a different release valve. I'm not

into sloppy fifths, or is it sixths? I heard some rumors about the football team from Verdes Hills last fall."

Cal laughs, but it isn't a pleasant sound. "Maybe she really likes you."

Bullshit. If anybody but the other Vice Lords actually likes me, I'll suck my own dick. "She'd be the first."

"Poor little rich boy. People only want him for his money."

"Fuck off."

Hooking up with me is like climbing Everest. Something people do for the status, to say they did it, regardless if they think that they'll actually enjoy it.

I don't kid myself that there is some deeper connection going on here. If I didn't have the power and the status that comes with the Cortland name, none of the chicks at school would give me the time of day.

My bad attitude and general viciousness make sure of that.

"Maybe you need a few more hits, man. You look tense as hell."

The vape hangs loosely in my hand, and I realize I haven't taken a pull from it in several minutes. It's gone cold, so the heating element has probably shut off. I don't know where my head is right now, but it definitely isn't here.

I study the room through the haze of smoke, wondering how soon I can kick most of these assholes out of my place. There are even a few people I don't recognize, more evidence of how off my game I am tonight.

Maybe I should screw Sophia like she so desperately seems to want. If I make her do something depraved enough, I might actually feel something.

"You looking for anyone in particular?" Cal asks, following my gaze as it tracks around the room.

"Nope. I pride myself on keeping chicks interchangeable."

"You've always been all heart, Cortland."

That is the pot calling the kettle an asshole. Cal has been combing pussy out of his hair ever since he came back from a year abroad with his father's family in Italy talking with a slight accent. I guarantee he hasn't been keeping a catalogue of their names, and I'm almost certain he wouldn't recognize most of them on sight. "You're confusing my heart with my dick."

"Tell that to Sophia." Cal slouches further down on the couch as a random brunette straddles him. He brings a beer to his lips and takes a swig, barely looking at the girl on his lap. "You've had that fish on the hook for months, and you still haven't reeled it in. What's up with that?"

Girlfriends. Permanence. Commitment. Those might as well be four-letter words to us and a great way to mess up a good thing.

But it's all starting to feel empty.

I shake off the disturbing thoughts as Cal continues to stare me down. The look on his face might mean something to me if I hadn't smoked enough weed to kill off an acre of farmland, but I know I don't like it.

"I don't know what the fuck you're talking about."

"Yeah, okay."

His expression turns musing as he surveys me. I can tell from his expression that he's about to say something to get under my skin. Cal is one of the few people on planet Earth that I let give me shit, and he takes full advantage of the privilege. "Unless there is someone else that you're thinking about, like Zaya Milbourne maybe."

No one says her name. No one acknowledges her presence. No one so much as speaks to her without my permission. Those are the rules that have been in place since freshman year when the kids from the Gulch funnel their shitty middle school into Deception High.

Anyone else would be flying through the plate glass door, but Cal is one of my closest friends.

Instead, I pluck a still lit cigarette from the ashtray on the table. Moving fast enough that Cal doesn't have a chance to react, I press the end into the exposed skin of his knee just below the line of his shorts.

"Jesus Christ, man." Cal leaps back with a curse as he frantically brushes ash from his leg and inspects the mark on his skin. "This better not leave a scar, you psycho."

"Sorry, I didn't hear you." My voice is pleasant and easy as I take another pull from the vape and blow cool smoke out through my nose. I know I look like a raging bull from a cartoon strip, but deliberately keep my voice mild. "What was it you said?"

"Fuck, that hurts."

"Don't be a baby, it's just a little burn."

"Not all of us enjoy getting burnt up, or cut up."

Idly, I stroke the scars on the inside of my bicep. There are four of them, cut straight across in a row like hash marks scratched into the wall of a prison cell to mark the days passing. All but one are old enough that I barely feel anything as my fingers pass over the puckered skin. But I tease at the edge of the newest one, feeling it burn as my nail catches on the edge of a fresh scab.

I'll miss the pain when it heals. I'll think about the feel of a blade cutting into the sensitive skin, because I know what it represents, but I'll get another chance. Probably soon.

One for her, and one for me.

"Then watch your damn mouth next time," I say, no hint of an apology in my voice because there isn't one there. "It's out here making promises that you're sensitive skin doesn't want to keep."

My preoccupation with Zaya Milbourne is the stuff of local

legends, but no one knows the whole truth. Sometimes I wonder if I even know the truth, as if my mind has manufactured pieces of my own history to make them fit together, even though they're made for different puzzles. I know Cal likes to tell people the situation is complicated when he thinks I can't hear him, but my relationship with Zaya is the simplest thing in my life.

She gives, and I take.

It's been so many years that the stories people tell are indistinguishable from fantasy. People love to talk, but it's like the whole town is playing a game of telephone where they all speak different languages.

Everyone knows a piece of it, nobody knows it all.

I never bother to explain myself to anyone, not my friends, not my family, not even Zaya herself. Mostly, because I know I don't have to.

No matter what people want to think, I didn't create this particular cluster-fuck of a situation. I just react to it in the only messed up way I know.

Taking control and then burning it all to the ground.

If it's crazy to punish someone for something they did a decade ago, then I guess we all know what to call me.

But Zaya brought this all on herself. Some people might say that we were just kids, too young to know any better, but no one is ever that young.

She knows exactly what she did.

And what she has to do if she wants the torture to stop.

Sophia is at the sliding door, pulling on the handle that needs to be pushed. I watch her through the glass, trying to see something past the skirt dress barely long enough to cover her uterus and the hair teased up high enough to hide a full-sized raccoon.

Something that might be worth getting out of my chair.

The chick is pretty enough, I guess, but in a way that is generic and uninspired. This is the sort of girl that I'm supposed to be with, especially if you ask my father: lily-white, well-bred, and a perfect addition to the mantle of mediocrity lining the grand stairwell in the main house.

But nothing about Sophia Taylor excites me. And it's hard to respect someone who can't figure out how to a work a damn door.

Iain pushes himself off the floor where he's been playing a bloody first-person shooter on my massive flat-screen TV to let Sophia back in. He moves like a panther stalking its prey, all coiled muscle and barely restrained violence. But he barely spares her a glance as he pulls open the glass and then goes back to his game.

Girls hold no interest for him. Boys don't either, as far as I can tell. The only thing that keeps his attention for more than a few minutes is something aggressively destructive.

Dude is the only person I know who might be more intense than I am.

Sophia latches back on me as soon as she gets through the door. Her hands are empty, but I can't remember what nonsense thing I sent her looking for, so I let it go.

She presses her lips to my ear and bites gently on the lobe. "Let's find a place where we can be alone."

Her breath is swampy and hot on my skin, and I resist the urge to shove her away in disgust. There is no such thing as privacy in the pool house. It's basically one large space with a combined kitchen and living room, and a small bedroom area in the back separated from the rest by a thin wall that lets any and all sounds through as if it doesn't exist at all. Luckily, nobody here gives a shit about privacy. Even if I fucked Sophia up against a wall in the living room, nobody here would see anything they haven't seen my friends do a dozen times before.

When her hand glides over the soft bulge in my jeans, I realize I've had more than enough of this shit.

"Everybody get the fuck out," I say, coming to my feet. The room falls silent save for the low thrum of sub-bass and electronic rhythm coming from the speakers.

Elliot turns to face with me with a girl under each arm. "C'mon, Vin. The party's just getting started."

Except I can't be here for another minute without killing someone.

"Fine, fuck it. If any of my stuff is missing in the morning, I'm taking it out of your ass."

I'm out the door before anyone can say anything else. None of them come after me, not that I would have expected it. You don't get to be the unrepentant asshole one minute and the guy people go chasing after begging him to come back the next.

The party is probably better without my bad mood ruining it, anyway.

There is a decent chance none of them will even notice when I don't return for the night. Except for Sophia, but only because she's hoping to screw her way into the most powerful family in town.

Not exactly a compliment.

I don't let myself think about where I'm going as I get in my car and start the engine. What happens next won't be about thinking, or really anything requiring brain power.

This is all instinct.

FOUR

Zaya

I first met Vin Cortland when I was eight years old.

My mother worked for his family during that halcyon time when she actually managed to hold down a job, right before she abandoned us completely. The Cortlands even treated her well, for a nanny and housekeeper paid under the table. Like every other founding family in Deception, appearances mattered to them. They wouldn't ever be caught abusing their staff.

But Vin has always been the prince of the castle on the hill with me barely fit to clean up after him.

Once upon a time, my family could have been among the lucky few living on the Bluffs. We used to have money and status, but that was a long time ago. Long before I was born. Grandpa Milbourne talks about it sometimes, the glory days of Deception when there was still gold in the hills and fortunes to be made.

Nowadays, home for the Milbournes is in the Gulch, a stretch of barren land at the very bottom of the valley that floods in the summer and freezes in the winter. As much as anything can freeze in this part of California.

Zion and I live with our grandfather in one of the oldest houses still standing in the Gulch. The house was built back when there was still arable land here and it wasn't a dumping ground for society's rejects. According to Grandpa, the Milbournes used to own everything from one end of the valley to the other. Little by little, pieces were sold off until only the house remained.

My mother left a few years ago. The moment a random guy on a motorcycle blew through town who was willing to take her with him, she climbed up to ride bitch and didn't look back. Supposedly, our father was a jazz musician who hung around just long enough to give my mother two kids before going back on the road when both of us were still in diapers. I'm exactly nine months older than Zion, but our father left before I formed any memories of him. She never even told use his name.

"Zaya, is that you?" Grandpa says as I open the front door. He rarely leaves the living room these days because of his illness, but he tries his best to keep up with us. His mind goes a little more each day, making him scrambled and forgetful of things I told him only moments before.

I rap the wall with the side of my fist in response as I climb the stairs.

Vin Cortland isn't omniscient, and he doesn't have our dilapidated house bugged. But it's safer to play by his rules as much as humanly possible, even when he wouldn't know the difference. Otherwise, I might let something slip at the wrong moment and suffer for it.

Sometimes, it's just easier not to talk. It means that people don't ask the uncomfortable questions I see burning in their eyes. More than one social worker has made the trek out to the Gulch to check in on us, spurred by reports from the school or someone just wanting to be a crank. None of our close neighbors would call the authorities for any reason, much less something as pervasive as child neglect. But ultimately, Zion and I wouldn't be here if there were anywhere else to go. And any foster home willing to take us in would be significantly worse than this.

Zion won't be home tonight. I knew that from the moment he left the cafeteria today. He'll be off getting drunk or high, anything to forget that he walked away without putting up a fight. But I don't want him to fight, not when the odds are so heavily stacked against him. He'd only get himself hurt, and I'd still be in the same shitty situation I always have been.

That's guilt for you. It doesn't understand reason, all it wants is to eat you up from the inside out.

The stairs creak as I make my way up to my room. I grip the banister so I can skip the step with missing subfloor. The house is falling down around us, and eventually there will just be a wall or two holding up the leaking roof.

That's a concern for another day.

My room is at the far end of the hallway because it's furthest from the others. According to Grandpa, girls need their privacy. But my room also faces the back of the house, with a great view of the scraggly forest leading up the mountain. Anyone standing in our backyard has a clear view of my bed and wouldn't be visible from the street.

There isn't much in the way of decoration, some pink gossamer curtains I found at a thrift store and pictures cut from library magazines taped to the walls. I can clearly hear Grandpa snoring downstairs, and wind whistles through the siding, sometimes making it feel like there's a tornado inside the room with me.

My bag is heavy on my back. I sling it onto the rickety wooden desk in the corner.

I tell myself to get my schoolwork done. Decent grades and a scholarship to a state school are my only chance of finding a way out of this place. But there are days when even that modest dream feels as likely as winning the lottery when you've never even bought a ticket.

My stomach rumbles, the school lunch not enough to last an entire day. Emptiness gnaws at my spine and makes it difficult for me to think. The bed beckons me away from my work, slumber the only relief from the oppressive weight of my life.

In sleep, I can dream of something better.

At least until I open my eyes in the morning, back in the waking nightmare.

THORNS PRICK MY SKIN AS I PUSH MY WAY THROUGH THE tangle of old rose bushes, most of which stopped flowering years ago. It's Founders' Day, and the whole town has gathered to celebrate. Even the black sheep are invited, including us.

I don't always understand the whispers, but I know what the people in this town think of us. That we belong down in the Gulch with the day laborers and the riffraff.

But we're Milbournes, and we have as much a right to be here as anyone, that's what Grandpa always says.

Zion has wandered off to do God knows what with his friends and left me alone. I don't like the crowds — all the people make me nervous and edgy. So I'm searching for a place where things are quiet.

The ground is littered with large stones that dig into the sole of my too thin shoes, making my feet ache. Thorns catch in the fabric of my shirt, some deep enough to poke my skin. But I keep going, drawn inexorably forward and unwilling to turn back.

I don't mind pain when it serves a purpose

When I emerge from the thick patch of overgrown roses, I see a boy standing all alone at the edge of the cliff, staring down into the crashing waves below. He doesn't turn as I approach, but I know he must have heard me.

I come to a stop next to him, my toes just touching the edge of the cliff that is a hundred feet above the jagged rocks below. I've always been an anxious sort of kid, but in that moment I don't feel any fear. Wind blows against my back as if pushing me closer to the edge, but I won't take a step back, not until he does.

The boy finally turns to look at me, a mix of curiosity and respect in his gaze. I stare back as the wind picks up.

Something passes between us. Something that feels eternal and dangerous.

When he smiles, it's like the clouds parting to reveal a glorious sun.

I won't find out until later just how rare it is to see him smile.

He tells me his name, but it's chased away by the wind.

FIVE

Zaya

When I snap awake in the middle of the night, I immediately know I'm not alone.

The thin curtains covering the window let in enough of a glow from the floodlights outside that I can just make out the figure sitting at the desk chair in the corner of my room.

For a moment, fear tightens my throat and steals my breath as I reorient myself to the present instead of dreams about the past. The fear only lasts until my vision adjusts to the darkness enough that I can tell who it is sitting there.

As if there is more than one person that it could be.

Vin watches me come awake with an expression that isn't visible in the dark, but I know he has a scowl on his face. Wood creaks in the silence as he shifts his weight, but he doesn't say anything.

And neither do I.

Grandpa is long asleep, not that he would be capable of mounting the stairs to come to my rescue. And I know Zion hasn't returned from wherever he goes at night, because the noise he makes coming in the house would have woken me up.

Vin and I are never alone at school. He either has the other Vice Lords with him, or he avoids me like the plague. At least, it feels like he avoids me. But I can't ignore the fact that he always seems to be around anytime the rules are broken. One time, Liam Connelly grabbed my elbow and tried to pull me into a broom closet, knowing I probably wouldn't open my mouth to protest. Vin was there before Liam even had the chance to close the door behind us, breaking my would-be rapist's jaw badly enough that he required corrective surgery.

But that has always been one of the rules: no one else gets to touch me.

I see a flash of white in the darkness, and I know it's the note Jake had my brother pass me at lunch. Vin leaves it on the table as he stands, seeming to loom over me even though he is still across the room.

He circles the bed like a shark in the water, scenting blood. But it's his scent that permeates the room, a heady mix of woodsmoke and bergamot with just the barest hint of oleander. Always, with the fucking oleanders. I have the feeling he rubs himself down with them just to mess with me. That scent will stay here, tainting the air, long after he leaves.

It's been so long since the last time he showed up here like this that I almost had myself convinced we were done. But the two of us are like two meteors on a collision course in the darkness of space, destined to collide in a spectacular display of destruction.

In a moment of fancy, I wonder if it's jealousy or possession that has brought him here tonight, after months of staying away. Realistically, I know the reality is both simpler and more complicated than that. He is here because he can't stop himself from coming.

He wants me in a peculiar and twisted way, but he also might wrap his hands around my throat and squeeze the life from me, something he has threatened to do more than once in the past.

His presence here is inexplicable, because there isn't any explanation required.

Vincent Cortland does whatever he wants whenever he feels like doing it. That is the way it has always been.

Everybody talks about destiny like it's some wondrous thing that must be written in the stars. Really, destiny is just the inevitable result of your decisions rushing up from the future to blast you in the face. If you jump off a cliff, hitting the rocks below becomes your destiny. You're accelerating towards destiny in a free fall, and at that point there isn't any stopping what has to happen next.

Just because something is your destiny doesn't mean it won't destroy you.

I fold my legs in front of me and wrap my arms around my knees as my gaze tracks his movements in the dim light. He paces like a caged predator in a zoo, desperate for a way out. I don't say anything as I continue to watch him. This always plays out the same way, and I figured out it's better to be patient a long time ago.

Vin crawls into the bed without asking for permission, and I scoot over to make room for him. He lies on his side on top of the blankets behind me while one hand wraps around my waist to haul me back against him. His open hand rests heavily against my stomach, forcing me down with pressure that is just on the wrong side of too much.

Spooning is supposed to be a romantic thing, but he manages to turn it into a punishment. That has always been a talent of his, taking something good and twisting it into a thing that I both love and loathe.

We lie together in the dark until our breathing is in sync. I try to take slower and shallower breaths, because I hate that it is so easy for our bodies to become a perfect match. But there isn't any use trying to fight it. Our chests rise and fall together, his breath tickling the back of my neck as he exhales.

An hour passes in silence, but neither of us have fallen asleep. Every place his body touches mine burns. My muscles are clenched and taut as he forces me back against him, but his proximity compels me to relax even as I wish it wasn't the case.

Our hearts might be at war, but our bodies have a mind of their own.

I only wear a t-shirt to bed most nights, maybe throwing on a pair of sweatpants when it gets particularly cold. Pajamas are a luxury I simply do not understand. I can't imagine spending money on clothes that I never wear outside the house.

The hand that has been still on my stomach this entire time shifts to my hip, stroking down the bare skin of my exposed thigh. His lips touch the back of my neck, so softly it makes me want to cry.

But I won't call it a kiss, refuse to even think that word. Despite everything, despite my fear, the one thing we never do is kiss.

Vin Cortland doesn't kiss anyone.

When his mouth shifts away, it leaves a flash of heat across my skin, one that refuses to fade away. He rubs my thigh in small circles for long enough that it almost lulls me to sleep. When his fingers grip my skin hard, I let out an involuntary sound that isn't one of pain.

His hand finds the damp crotch of my panties, and he exhales sharply against my neck. Moments like this are the only time when he is ever gentle, touching me in a way that is slow and deliberate.

Almost reverent.

I could fight him off if I really wanted. If I screamed or said no and pushed him away, then he would leave. He isn't here to force me. It would almost be easier to deal with if he were. Knowing that I could end this, and I still don't, makes it so much worse.

I don't say yes, but I don't say no.

Because I don't say anything at all.

My silence is also my consent.

He pulls my underwear to the side. One thick finger pushes inside me, and my body uncoils until I sink into the mattress. The moment I've been anticipating since I first woke up with him in my room is finally here.

It's never as bad as I imagine it will be, as part of me hopes it will be. I think he does that on purpose, building up suspense until I can only focus on what he might do next.

A second finger joins the first. Vin works them in and out of me, curling just slightly on the downstroke to brush against the little ball of flesh inside of me that is so sensitive the pleasure borders on pain. He watches my face as he pulls out and uses the gathered wetness on his fingers to draw circles around my clit, sending sparks of painful pleasure down my spine.

I turn my head and squeeze my eyes shut so he won't see whatever emotion hides behind my gaze. He continues to tease me, using his fingers like implements of destruction as he strokes and thrusts. It is the most exquisite sort of torture.

I both love and hate it.

Similar to how I feel about him.

I keep my body still, even as my breathing comes faster and in sharp little gasps. God forbid I actually give him what he wants, a sign that I want this. He needs me to confirm that he doesn't climb into my window at night because he is some pervert who knows he can get away with abusing the girl that doesn't have anyone left to protect her.

He has to convince himself that I want this as much as he does.

Vin keeps going until I'm on the very edge of climax as stars burst behind my closed eyelids. Then his fingers slide away, leaving a trail of moisture on the inside of my thigh. He leans back, which leaves me feeling cold, like I'm standing next to a fire that just went out.

I hear the familiar sound of foil ripping, but I don't turn to look as he unwraps the condom. This is my last chance to raise a protest and make him stop. He moves more slowly than he needs to, almost leisurely as he pinches the center of the latex circle and then rolls it down himself.

Vin gives me plenty of time to protest, to react at all.

Like always, I don't say a word.

His hand comes back to my thigh to adjust the angle of my hips, and then the hard length of him pushes inside of me. He takes it slow, always does at first, with unhurried strokes. Pressure builds deep inside my belly as the pleasure overwhelms my ability to resist. When my nails dig into the heavy arm he has wrapped around my waist, it's a signal for him.

He thrusts inside me with the all the force of his strong hips, bottoming out until he fills me completely. I let out another gasp as my hands tighten on the only anchor I have as he pounds into me like he wants to drive both our bodies into the springs of my thin mattress. His name dances on the tip of my tongue, but I swallow it down until it feels like I might choke on it.

I won't give him the satisfaction.

Sex doesn't have to mean anything if you don't want it to, except part of me wishes it did. Even with all the negative emotions swirling between us, this becomes something greater. We're more than just two bodies illuminated by a streak of light from the low-hanging moon outside my window.

Anger. Hatred. The sins of the past. Things that connect us

in a way that transcends anything physical. Sex is an afterthought to what lies between us.

It's at moments like this, in the darkness when the whole world has gone quiet, that I can almost convince myself we've gone back to a time before. Before we lost faith in each other. Before the world conspired to destroy whatever precious thing once existed between us.

Before it all went wrong.

My beat-up copy of Antigone is on the nightstand, and I focus my gaze on it, willing myself to go somewhere else mentally. I try to remember the first line of the play as my mind descends into fog.

My mouth moves, even though no sound comes out. "*You would think that we had already suffered enough.*"

The arm around me shifts so his hand can worm its way between the thighs I try to keep clamped shut. His thumb flicks against my clit like he's thrumming a guitar, and then he presses down ever so slightly with the sharp edge of his nail.

I try to hide my reaction, but he pays too close attention. Orgasm hits me hard enough that my spine bows back against him as my mouth opens in a silent scream. Despite my attempts to keep still, my body turns boneless and loose as I collapse back against him.

Vin lets out a satisfied groan as he comes, gripping my hip hard enough that it will leave a bruised imprint of his fingers later. He chuckles darkly to himself as he rolls away, and I don't bother to ask him what he's laughing at.

I am always the butt of the joke.

He rises off the bed and flicks the blanket over me, knowing I won't move as long as he's here. The condom is tossed in the wastebasket, and I have to remind myself to take out the trash before Zion gets home, in case he comes in here looking for something. Only as Vin does up his pants do I realize he never took them off, screwing me with just his fly down and the waist of his pants around his hips. Somehow, that little detail makes me feel even worse than I already do.

He leaves a stack of crumpled bills on the table, and I know it will amount to exactly $125 without needing to get up and count it. That is the same amount of money my mother earned each day she worked for his family. In the past, I've thrown the money back in his face or tried to burn it with one of the lighters that is always lying around. But it's usually easier not to fight him, weak protests won't make him think any better of me.

My voice is hoarse with disuse when I finally recover enough breath to speak. I say the only thing guaranteed to get under his skin, the only thing that will hurt him in even a fraction of the way he hurts me.

"I forgive you."

His shoulders tense, so I know he heard me, but he doesn't turn back.

"I don't want your forgiveness," he says, voice a raspy whisper in the darkness. "Just your silence."

The door slams shut behind him with enough force to shake the walls, and a dusting of plaster falls from the ceiling to coat my bedspread.

Two meteors accelerating in the darkness of space.

It is only a matter of time before we crash and burst into a million tiny pieces.

SIX

I don't want your forgiveness, just your silence.

That's a lie, of course. Maybe not the first part. I have no doubts that the last thing on Vin's mind is reconciling even the smallest piece of our past. But he doesn't really want my silence. There is something very specific that he wants to spill from my lips, and I have spent the last ten years refusing to give it to him.

Which is why he decided I don't get to speak at all.

But secrets are like a cancer, eating away at you. In more fanciful moments, I tell myself that all the things I refuse to say have settled like acid on my vocal cords, burning them into dust.

At this point, I don't know what I would say if given the chance to speak freely.

It's easy to slip into melancholy, spend way too much time thinking about how things might have been. Who would I be if I'd been given the chance to grow up in the *before*, instead of the *after*. My family would still be poor, and I'd still live in the

Gulch, but maybe I wouldn't exist in perpetual isolation. Maybe I'd go out at night like other girls, even have a boyfriend.

The Milbournes have been here longer than the town limits. By rights, Zion and I should be running with the Vice Lords, not set up on the other side of this battle.

Like always, I wake up early in the morning to help get Grandpa situated. I don't remember the name of the disease that does it, but the same thing that messes with his memory makes his hands shake so he can't feed himself properly or stand too long on his own. His doctor wants him in a wheelchair full time, but that isn't something we can afford. Instead, he leans on me when he needs to get from one place to the other, and he doesn't get up at all when no one is around to help him.

Grandpa spends most of his days and all of his nights posted up in the old armchair by the window in our living room. He only leaves that spot when I take him on short walks around the house to keep his blood flowing and prevent bedsores.

I help him eat breakfast before I go to school. Meals on Wheels comes twice a week with a handful of trays I can stick in the freezer and then reheat for him, so at least he isn't in danger of starving to death.

As I spoon watery cream of wheat into his toothless mouth, I want to ask him for the dozenth time what happened to bring us here: to the Gulch, to the bottom of society, to a place where nobody cares what happens to us. But his memories of the past aren't much more than ramblings at this point, and I've never been able to get a straight answer out of him.

My mother always said that Grandpa's father made a business deal that went bad, but she didn't know much more than that. Although, everything she has ever said should be taken with a grain of salt the size of a sugar cube.

In contrast to our sorry state of affairs, Vin's family is one of the richest in the central valley. The Cortlands own more land than all the other founding families combined. He sits on a throne made of his family's legacy like an over-indulged prince.

It must be nice to have a future drenched in gold.

But there are some things in his past that vaguely resemble the tragedy of mine, not that anybody would figure that out by looking at him.

His real mother died in childbirth, and his father remarried so quickly that a whole year might not have passed before he had a stepmother. Giselle Cortland can't trace her lineage back to our town's founding, but she always seems happy to play like the queen of everything the light touches.

Vin should have thought of her as his mother — babies latch on to whatever maternal figure is available. But it never seemed to work out that way. As a kid, I could never figure out if the lack of bonding was his fault or hers. It didn't take long for me to understand that a darkness creeps over the majestic grounds of Cortland Manor.

A darkness that infects everything it touches.

Before I go to school, I take the money that Vin left on my desk and put it in the shoebox under my bed. I have several hundred dollars here, with no idea what to do with it. Even when there isn't any food in the house and my stomach aches from hunger, I still don't touch this cash.

I'm being paid for services rendered, just like mother was. That's all the Milbournes have ever been good for.

Vin is like a drug dealer who offers a first taste for free because he wants to get you hooked.

With the first dollar of this money I spend, he will own me.

Sometimes I dream about running away, escaping Deception and this broken existence. But five hundred dollars isn't enough for a new life, and I can't leave Grandpa to fend for himself. Zion would probably let him starve to death before remembering the man is stuck in his armchair.

Just like everything else in Deception, this money is tainted with the past, so dirty I still feel it on my skin even once I've put it away. There was one time that I tried giving it back to Vin, throwing it in his face. He just laughed and pinned me on the bed until I stopped struggling. When I woke up the next morning, the shoebox was back where it belonged and filled to the brim with cash.

Someday, I'll have enough strength to burn it.

And imagining what it might be like to douse Vin Cortland in gasoline and light a match is the happy thought that lets me fly away like Peter Pan into a dreamless sleep.

I MARCH INTO DECEPTION HIGH WITH A NEW PURPOSE. With the help of the recycled Hello Kitty calendar on my bedroom wall, I've calculated the exact number of days left until graduation when I can put this place and all the people here in my rearview mirror.

72 days and counting.

The day I leave this town, whether it's by bus or train or walking barefoot down the dusty highway, will be the best one of my life.

Sophia steps up behind me for the metal detectors with a group of other girls falling into line behind her like ducklings after a demented Mother Goose. She likes to fancy herself the queen bee of Deception High, but the Vice Lords are the only ones really in charge here. The founding families have always ruled this town, and it's hard to imagine that ever changing. Even though her father owns the largest dental practice in town and she has a beautiful house up on the Bluffs.

Money and power are like conjoined twins that would die if they ever got separated, but that doesn't make one the same as the other.

She might have her mindless little followers, but everyone knows who sits on the throne.

We all have our delusions. I don't begrudge Sophia her own, if that's what makes living through another day seem worth it.

Most days, the disdainful treatment she subjects me to isn't anything worse than what everyone else on the bottom of the social hierarchy gets. That happens to be one of the few positive aspects of being totally silent – sometimes people forget I'm here at all. There are always new targets for someone bent on teenage sociopathy. Her need to ensure the social pecking order stays intact almost makes some sort of twisted sense.

For someone to be on top, someone else has to be on the bottom.

Reinforcing the natural order of things by planting her flag at the mountain summit is all that keeps her from tumbling down to earth with the rest of us.

Sometimes I wonder if there might be at least a little misplaced jealousy there. Sophia doesn't know for certain what goes on between Vin and I, but she has to sense that what lies between us isn't fit for polite conversation. The true irony is that I would gladly switch places with her in a heartbeat, even if she'll never know it.

We have English together, and I've seen her notebooks. She writes *Mrs. Sophia Cortland* on them over and over again to practice her cursive.

"Did I tell you guys what happened after the party last weekend?" Her voice is high-pitched with the forced volume of someone who desperately wants to be overheard. "Vin and I were getting hot and heavy in his bedroom, and then I woke up the next day with all these curly hairs stuck in my teeth."

Another girl lets out a choked laugh, but I don't look back to see who it is. "That is so gross."

I put my bag on the little conveyer belt as I wait for the people ahead of me to slowly make their way through the metal detector. The guy ahead of me is being forced to remove every metal piercing in his body, including the ones that are covered by his clothes. I can only hope that the belly button ring is the southernmost piece as I wait for him to finish.

"I love the manly types, but I have to get him onboard with manscaping." Sophia laughs, the sound vaguely reminiscent of nails on a chalkboard. "It actually kind of reminded me of Zaya's little nappy hairs. Shaving her head would be better than whatever is going on there."

Sophia won't talk directly to me, even when the conversation is clearly meant for my ears. For all her bravado, she knows better than to do that. But she clearly has no problem talking *about* me loudly enough that anyone within twenty yards can hear her.

I tell myself that nothing these girls can think to say will bother me. The obvious ways that I'm different from them will always be a target for ridicule. If my hair looked like something out of a shampoo commercial, they'd still find a way to turn that into a negative.

Unfortunately for me, there aren't enough hot tools or styling products in the world that can make my messy riot of kinks and curls conform into anything like the perfect blonde waves framing Sophia's face.

I accepted who I am a long time ago. The only other choice was to curl up into a ball and die. My nappy hair. My unfashionably dark skin that dries out in unsightly white patches if I forget to moisturize. Full lips that Sophia likes to spitefully whisper are only good for sucking dick since I never speak. At least she didn't stoop to calling my mother a coonhound, a favorite insult among the smaller-minded residents of Deception in the last few years.

My gaze flicks over Sophia's face as I wait for my bag to slide into the X-ray machine. Our gazes meet, and the desperation in her eyes is obvious from a mile away to anyone looking for it. She needs all of our attention to distract herself from whatever is going on inside her head. No girl who chases after a guy like Vin Cortland is capable of loving herself.

If I can sympathize with anything, it's self-hatred.

For a moment, I wonder if a version of reality exists where we could have been friends.

"It's always a shame when good bloodlines end with mutts." Sophia stares into my face as she says it.

Yeah, friends will probably never be an option. *Not mortal enemies* might even be a bridge too far.

I pass through the metal detector and grab my bag without looking back at the girls behind me. In a different sort of life, I would have made a snarky comeback or tried to put them in their place. But they aren't worth it, not given the potential consequences.

In the past, I've risked Vin's wrath to give the bitches at school as good as I got. It didn't take long for me to realize that depriving them of any entertainment from my reaction is a far better strategy. After a while, my silence gets boring. Mocking me just isn't fun anymore.

Maybe it's maturity, or maybe I just don't want to give Vin another excuse to come after me.

It isn't until I look up again that I notice Elliot Spencer standing on the opposite side of the metal detector, arms crossed over his chest as he lounges against the wall. Elliot doesn't hold a candle to Vin when it comes to the danger factor, but his reputation as a brawler is well earned. He hangs around the Gulch sometimes when he's in the mood for a fight, something that can always be found in my neighborhood. Back in the days when Deception was just a mining settlement, his family's property was adjacent to mine.

Because of his size, he has a tendency to go after the bullies. Although if anyone is dumb enough to thank him for coming to their defense, he has no problem beating on the little guys, too.

Our gazes meet for a brief second before he looks past me.

"Hey, Soph," he says conversationally, light-green eyes glittering with menace. "What was it you were saying about Vin's hairy dick. I want to make sure I get it right when I tell him about it later."

Sophia makes a choking noise, her mouth moving like a fish that just got pulled out of the water. "I was just talking about Zaya's hair."

"I heard what you said." He taps his knuckles against the fullness of his lower lip. Leather creaks as he pushes off from the wall and stands to his full height. Elliot's style is full-on Rebel Without a Cause meets Rodeo Drive: black motorcycle jacket made of Italian leather, fitted jeans that have been tailored, and a white designer t-shirt that costs as much as some people's car payments. "Maybe you should take a page from Zaya's book. Hasn't anybody ever told you that silence is golden? It keeps our mouths from writing checks that our lily white asses can't cash."

Sophia isn't quite smart enough to keep the defiance out of her voice. "Why are you defending her, anyway? I thought all you Vice Lords had a hard-on for messing with her."

"I don't make the rules," Elliot replies with a careless shrug. "But Zaya is Founding, you should remember that."

He stalks away without sparing any of us another glance.

Elliot isn't exactly a white knight. The lesson is as much for me as it is for Sophia. Just because Vin has decided I have to suffer doesn't mean he is always willing to share the privilege. But if I'd spoken a word in my own defense, whatever the Vice Lords did to me would make Sophia Taylor look like a preschool teacher.

Like always, I'm on my own.

SEVEN

Zaya

Jake Tully finally works up the nerve to talk to me again while I'm hiding out in the library during lunch.

I want to be impressed with his persistence, then I remember he just moved here and doesn't understand the forces that are set up against him. It isn't the same thing as bravery when you're just too stupid to realize how afraid you should be.

Ignorance is bliss, I guess.

I notice him as soon as I walk in, because usually the librarian and I are the only ones who ever come here. Deception High isn't exactly at the forefront of technological innovations, so the computers are so ancient they might as well be bricks, and most of the books are moth-eaten or missing pages. Most students don't even bother trying to use the limited resources and opt for a drive out to the county library.

But Jake is here. He sits at a table in the very center of the rectangular room, an iPad with an attached keyboard set up in front of him. That cements for me he has to be living on the better side of town. No one from the Gulch would dare flash a piece of tech that expensive, assuming they could get their hands on it in the first place.

The sharp division between the haves and the have-nots makes Deception what it is. Anybody who wants to study the long-term of income inequality and economic stagnation should pay us a visit. Million-dollar mansions on the Bluffs are balanced by families living exclusively on food stamps in dilapidated trailers around the Gulch. The town's history made some of this inevitable — the children of the migrants brought in to work the mines or clean houses never climb out of the poverty trap. Social mobility is little more than a fantasy here — anybody who betters themselves does it by getting the hell out.

It's hard to imagine what this place must look like to an outsider.

I finally choose a spot as far from Jake as I can get, close to the reference section and a large bay window letting in dreary light from the overcast sky. Setting my bag on the table, I make a point of slowly removing each item I need from my bag one by one: textbook, binder, pencil, pen, calculator.

Too bad they don't allow pepper spray on campus.

When I finally look up, I'm not exactly surprised to see Jake hovering over the chair across from me, obviously trying to decide if he should sit down or not. I don't help him make the decision, simply staring up at him silently as he awkwardly stands there.

No one in this world has ever made things easy for me. I don't have a problem with paying that forward just a little bit.

"Hey," Jake murmurs, finally taking a seat.

A sharp rapping from the main desk silences whatever he might say next. The librarian, Mrs. Markel, glares at us over a pair of bifocals. Her wrinkled lips are pursed in extreme displeasure as she brings a withered finger to her lips.

Despite the general shabbiness, this is what I love most

about the school library. Silence isn't only acceptable, but encouraged practically on pain of death. Mrs. Markel has a reputation for eating disobedient students alive and then lecturing the remains about decorum. Even the Vice Lords know better than to tempt fate by getting on her bad side.

But Jake isn't that easily deterred. He reaches across the table and snags a page from my open binder, the ripping sound of paper echoing off the low ceiling as Mrs. Markel continues to glare.

If she ever figures out how to force choke like Darth Vader, we're all dead.

When he catches me watching, a slight smile curls his lips as he scrawls something with his pen before shoving the paper towards me so it skids across the table.

I glance down at it, because I can't help myself.

Will you go with me to the Founder's Ball?

Once a year, the Cortlands open up their magnificent home to the riffraff in celebration of our town's founding. It's a little bit debutante ball and a whole lot of showing off for the people in town trying and failing to keep up with the first family of Deception.

It's been years since I went to a Founder's Ball, and I hadn't planned on breaking that winning streak anytime soon. Zion will likely make an appearance, if just for the free booze, and stay exactly long enough to convince one of the girls from the Bluffs to slum it with him for the night before cutting out early.

Then I think about the look on Vin's face if he saw me walking into his house, his domain, on the arm of Jake Tully. That was almost enough to make whatever came next seem worth it.

I take the paper and hunch over it, hiding what I'm writing. Jake tries to peek, and I shift my arm up to block his view.

He eagerly leans forward to read what I've written when I slide the paper back.

Vin would either kill you or break every tooth in that pretty smile.

That same smile widens as he reads, seeming unbothered by the specter of threat represented by Vincent Renaldo Cortland. Or maybe some mild flirtation is enough to distract him from the fact that he risks serious pain over a girl he barely knows. For a surreal moment, I wonder if Jake might be the only sane person in Deception, like Alice right after she falls through the rabbit hole into Wonderland. The rest of us are operating under some shared delusion, that a senior in high school has the power to control an entire town.

Then I remind myself of the things Vin has done, and I go right back to believing.

Jake slides the paper back, and this time the writing is larger. I wonder if that's an unconscious signal of something.

But he isn't your boyfriend?

I quickly write back, any thoughts of actually getting my homework done forgotten. This is the most interaction I've had in days.

Fuck no.

When he passes the paper back to me, his fingers touch mine and stay for a beat too long before he pulls them away. It makes me feel sort of light and airy, like I'm flying.

I remind myself that the higher I go, the harder I'll hit the ground when I inevitably fall.

Then I read what Jake has written and feel the earth rushing up to meet me.

He acts like he's in love with you.

My hand shakes as I pick up the pen to write. It scares me to know what this looks like from the outside, this twisted dynamic between me and my greatest tormenter.

I don't have a word for what lies between us, but I know that love is the wrong one.

He loves to torture me. That's all. This is how it's always been.

I'm never this honest with anyone, not even Zion. Even talking about Vin gives me the fanciful idea that I'm ceding him even more power over me. I want to erase Vin from my brain, not spend my free time discussing him with a complete stranger.

I don't have a problem handling him then. Founder's Ball?

I remind myself that I can't let this piece of notepaper leave the library when we're done. Burning is the best way to destroy evidence, but I'll eat it if I have to. If Vin ever finds out that I had this conversation, even only in writing, he will make me regret it.

And my imagination isn't good enough to think of all the ways he might do that.

But I also don't want to live the rest of my life under someone's heel. Death would be more preferable than that. This life I have can't be forever, and the only way it will change is if I do.

And I don't give a fuck what Vin Cortland thinks about it.

Feeling suddenly defiant, even though I'll definitely be paying for it later, I take a gel pen and write **LET'S GO** in big block letters before holding it high enough for him to see.

Jake grins wide. He doesn't even seem to notice when I take the notepaper back, scrunch it up and shove it in the pocket of my oversized sweatshirt. He stands and murmurs something about getting the details from me later, voice low enough that even Mrs. Markel can't hear him.

I watch him go, already regretting my impulsiveness. Briefly, I consider running after him and trying to take it all back. As soon as I move to rise, Iain Hewitt steps out from behind a high bookcase and blocks my path.

My gaze follows Jake over Iain's shoulder as he pushes open the heavy doors and lets them slam shut loudly behind him. I don't say a word to call him back, and not just because of Mrs. Markel's laser-eyed attention.

The paper with our messages feels like it burns a hole in my pocket. Iain won't search me, because he knows as well as I do that he isn't allowed to touch me. But if he tells me to hand it over, I'm not convinced I'll refuse.

Iain is built like an MMA fighter, all lean muscle and explosive quickness, but he moves like a cat. I know exactly how much strength lies in the tightly corded muscles of his arms and just how fast he can move. He is the only one who can get around this school as silently as I do, probably why I didn't realize he was behind that bookcase until it was too late.

I give him a careless shrug as if I don't have any idea what he wants. One more small bright spot in the barren landscape of this situation.

You can't be caught in a lie when you never speak.

This will get back to Vin, eventually everything does. That shouldn't bother me when I'm planning to show up at the Founder's Ball with another guy, openly defying Vin for the whole town to see. But now I don't have the chance to change my mind.

There is only one way forward.

I try to shift past Iain, but he steps in to my path again, blocking the way.

With an angry huff of air, I hold my hands up in front of me as I step forward so he has to move out of the way or let me touch him. He dodges away with an annoyed sigh, but I still see the warning that burns in his gaze.

The hem of my sweatshirt brushes against his arm. Fear ratchets higher as I imagine him grabbing the fabric and choking me with it.

Relief rushes through me when I reach the doors of the library, far enough from Iain that I'm well out of reach. Then I push my hand into my pocket and realize there isn't anything there.

The note is gone.

I look back to see a folded paper in his hand, held between his index and middle finger like a magician about to perform a card trick.

He stole it out of my pocket with the skill of a seasoned thief.

I could go back and beg him to return it, but it wouldn't do any good. Iain's loyalty to Vin is absolute, and everyone knows it. All begging would do at this point is make the situation worse.

This will end badly.

It always does.

EIGHT

VIN

I HAVE A VERY BAD HABIT OF BREAKING THINGS, EVEN when I'm trying to do precisely the opposite. It's like I have the Midas touch, but instead of turning the things I covet into solid gold, I have to watch them disintegrate into a million pieces.

Does that make me a bad person?

Probably.

It started from the very day I was born. I destroyed my mother before I even managed to completely enter this world. My father thinks it's helpful to tell me that my face is the last thing she saw before she died, as if that somehow makes the fact she died in childbirth an easier pill to swallow.

And the sick thing is that sometimes I like breaking things, because if I can't have something, then I'd rather see it destroyed than given to someone else.

I didn't mean to break Zaya Milbourne, not at first. When I look at her now, all I want to do is pull her apart piece by piece so I can see what's hidden deep inside. And the overwhelming anger that rises in me when I see her face makes it feel good when I hurt her.

Even when I'm also hurting myself.

With every moment of weakness, I swear it has to be the last time. But I find myself climbing into her window in the middle of the night, like that shit is inevitable. I can never decide until I touch her whether I want to fuck her or wring her neck.

She doesn't know, either, which of the urges brings me to her door.

But she does know what she did.

My father sends me an oblique text on Saturday evening, making mention of the fact that he hasn't laid eyes on me in days. I wait as late as I can before finally venturing into the main house.

Silence greets me as I enter Cortland Manor. Silence and cold. This place is always freezing, as if none of the bright California sun is capable of penetrating the large picture windows of the entry hall that look out to the sea.

The only sound that echoes through my ears is the dull click of my heels on the tile floor, and if I could silence even that, I would.

Silence is the most precious sound known to man, if just because of how rare it is. Most of the time, I can't get anyone around me to just shut the fuck up.

A silver statue of a hawk taking off in flight greets me as I reach the stairs. Its claws clutch a large orb that has been etched to look like a miniature version of the earth, as if the hawk has laid claim to the entire world.

The hawk is a special symbol for the Cortlands. It is emblazoned on our family crest and represents the strength and cunning that are supposed to be our family's central values.

I remember hiding behind this same statue as my stepmother chased after me with a leather belt in her hand. When she was really angry, she would make sure to hold the end that didn't have a buckle so the metal would strike painfully against the bones of my skinny back.

I'm not a kid anymore, and she hasn't hit me in years, not since she realized how much bigger and stronger than her I am. But that doesn't stop the memory from coming, my shoulders stiffening like I'm anticipating another blow.

I refuse to call her my mother, even though she married my father when I was still in diapers. I don't remember a time before she was in my life, but I know this isn't the same as having an actual mother, and I refuse to pretend.

Giselle stands at the top of the elaborate stairwell, dressed in a long red evening gown. Her hair is done up in some crazy design that probably took hours to complete and enough hairspray to poke another hole in the ozone layer.

Think of the she-devil, and she doth appear.

Ridiculously long nails, also painted red, glide along the banister as she comes toward me. Those things look like bloody coffins stuck on her fingers, and I wonder how she wipes her ass without getting shit up under them.

Although she probably has one of the many servants she makes scurry around this place wipe her ass for her.

"Are you just getting home from school?" she asks, even though it's almost eleven o'clock at night.

And a Saturday.

I have no idea if she is just that vapid or simply doesn't give a shit.

"Something like that." I scrutinize her nipped and tucked face, marveling for a moment at how much her skin looks like plastic. "Looks like you're headed out."

"Just coming in, actually. Your father and I had the Junior Society Charity Auction. I swear, they always have their hands out for cash. Thank God ball gowns don't have pockets, because I'm sure someone's hand would have been in mine."

I want to point out that the money isn't hers to begin with. Giselle would still be a scheming social climber with a maxed-out credit card if my father hadn't plucked her from obscurity.

Forcing my attention away from my money-grubbing stepmother and back to the detested statue, I raise an eyebrow. As much as I hate the thing, facing your fears is the only way to keep them from owning you. "I'm sure you found a minimally acceptable number for the required donation."

"Of course I did, we're not here to be taken advantage of."

If my eyes roll any harder, they'll fly out of their sockets. I'm about to say something agreeable and make an excuse to get the fuck away from her, when I hear an annoyed shriek come from upstairs.

"Is Sophia still awake?" I ask incredulously.

Giselle makes a sound of annoyance. "This is the third nanny I've hired this year. There is no such thing as good help these days."

It's always the same shit, different day, at Cortland Manor.

Makes me wonder how I was ever young and dumb enough to think I could love my stepmother.

I'm already taking the stairs two at a time when her complaints filter through my ears. The nanny isn't the problem, and Giselle fucking knows it. Emma acts out because no one in this house pays any attention to her.

I push open the door of a bedroom that looks like it was decorated by a middle-aged man with a fetish for diaper play.

Pink walls clash with the lavender curtains on the window. Dead-eyed porcelain dolls dressed like princesses line up like dutiful little soldiers on a shelf beside the four-poster bed made of white wood and trimmed in gold. Every bit of decoration, from the lamp on the bedside table to the gold tiaras painted on the ceiling, is done in a princess theme.

Being in here is like overdosing on Pepto Bismol while trapped inside Disney Land.

Emma is thirteen going on thirty, and Giselle treats her like she is still in preschool. My little sister would much rather be on a baseball diamond practicing her fast pitch than playing pretty-pretty-princess with these creepy ass dolls.

But it's not like her own mother gives a shit.

Right now, Emma has a nanny standing over her that looks like an extra from an 80's movie about mental asylums. Giselle apparently has a thing for women who can double as line-backers.

When I walk in, they're arguing about whether ten o'clock is an appropriate bedtime for a middle schooler. Nurse Ratchet is obviously in the pro position. I'm inclined to take Emma's side, because that's always the case. But this screaming fit has got to stop.

I step completely into the room so they both see me and hold up a single hand. That's enough for both of them to go instantly quiet. This level of control, it's the same I hold over everyone in my life. I have to admit that I used to get off on it, but this isn't the kind of power that does good.

It's the kind that tricks you into doing bad.

By the time you realize just how bad you've gone, it's too late to stop.

"What the hell is going on here?"

The nanny, whose real name I can't remember for the life of me if I ever knew it at all, brings herself to her full height. "Miss Emma doesn't want to go to bed like she should."

Emma interrupts before I can say anything, her voice practically a screech. "No! Mom said that I could stay up to see her before going to bed, and she hasn't come in yet."

Giselle has been home long enough to say good night to her daughter, but obviously other priorities take precedence. I would say I'm surprised, but I'm not. I stopped keeping track of all the promises my stepmother makes without any intention of keeping them a long time ago.

Emma will have to learn eventually, but I'll try to protect her from the worst of it for as long as I can.

"I'll take care of this," I murmur, shrugging out of my jacket and tossing it into a puffed armchair covered in pale pink velvet. "You're relieved for the night."

Nurse Ratchet looks like she wants to argue. "But—"

I shoot her the look, the one I mastered years ago when I was just a snot-nosed kid who thought he ran the entire world. The look that doesn't brook any argument and promises swift retribution for any dissent. "Do I need to repeat myself?"

The nanny shakes her head, and wisely keeps her mouth clamped shut as she skirts past me and toward the door. I resist the urge to snap my teeth at her as she passes me. This is at least the dozenth nanny we've had since Emma was born, and not one of them have been younger than Methuselah. I can't help but wonder if Giselle keeps choosing these old battle axes to watch over Emma because she wants to make sure my father doesn't screw them.

God forbid her daughter's nurturing take precedence over irrational jealousy.

Emma crosses her arms over her chest, stubborn chin thrust forward, as I approach the bed and sit down on the end. "I'm not going to bed until Mom comes in to read to me like she said she would."

"Now I'm not good enough? You're killing me, kid." I bend over to rifle through the pile of books on the floor next to the bed. Not a single one of them has more words than pictures. "Is this what Giselle is reading to you?"

"No, that one."

I put down the book in my hand and pick up the one that looks like a jar of pink glitter exploded on the cover and read the title out loud. "*Little Princess Unicorn?* This is meant for toddlers."

Emma shrugs, but I catch the glare she levels at the purple comforter. "It's what Mom picked."

"Jesus." I rein in my temper with an effort, because I don't want Emma to see me angry. I glance at the bookshelf in the corner, but it's more of the same. There isn't even a copy of Harry Potter in here. "You know what, it's so late that maybe we should save story time for tomorrow night."

She pouts. "That's not fair. Mom promised me a story."

"Yeah, well. I got something better." I rifle in the pocket of my jacket for my phone and wave it in her face. "I'll let you listen to my newest playlist until you fall asleep. But you have to go to bed right now."

"Deal." Emma reaches for the phone with eager hands. "You always find the best stuff."

The smooth vocals of AlunaGeorge play from the tinny speaker. "Turn it down to low, and I'm coming back to get it in an hour, whether you're asleep or not."

"In an hour, *you* might be asleep."

"Not a chance," I reply with a grim smile, but she's already twisted onto her side and doesn't see it. I'll absolutely be awake, because I almost never sleep. It's a good night if I get an hour before waking up again. "Eyes closed, or I'm taking it back."

She positions the phone on the pillow next to her and then dutifully closes her eyes. "Night."

I lean forward to kiss her gently on the forehead. "Night, munchkin."

"Don't call me that," she grouses, voice already heavy with sleep. "I'm not a little kid anymore."

"You are as long as I have something to say about it."

Eventually, I'll break Emma just like I have everything else good that has been in my life.

But I'll put off the inevitable for as long as I possibly can.

NINE

VIN

When I come out into the hallway, Giselle is waiting for me with a sour expression on her face.

"What were you doing in there?" she asks, more demand than question.

"Tucking Emma into bed. You know, that thing you promised to do."

I have a secret suspicion that Giselle only gave birth to Emma as a way to secure her access to the Cortland family money. Even in the case of separation or divorce, the mother of an heir can still claim a piece of the pie.

The insecurity that wraps around her is as obvious as the over-the-top gown she hasn't taken off yet. Another one of my talents, seeing the things that people desperately try to hide.

Or maybe I'm being a little too uncharitable.

Giselle waves away her broken promise like a fly she can bat out of the air. "I'll make it up to her tomorrow."

Yeah, no.

"I don't give a shit what you do." I push past her, but her

hands come up to grip my arm, nails digging in just a touch too hard. "Get off me."

She lets me pull my arm away, likely because she doesn't want to ruin her manicure. "Your father wants to talk to you."

Duke Cortland isn't much for sleep, either, but unlike me he usually tries to get something constructive done in the wee hours of the night. The old man has always been focused almost exclusively on his work.

This town isn't going to run itself, after all.

But years of chronic insomnia are starting to show in the sagging lines of his face, the growing paunch around his middle and how much slower he moves compared with even just a few years ago.

My own bad habits haven't caught up with me. At least, not yet.

Duke is sitting at the desk in his study when I shove open the French doors. The room smells faintly of cigar smoke, but there isn't one in his hand when I step inside. He won't bring out the good stuff when Giselle is around, because she complains that his Cubans smell like dog fart. A decanter of brandy is on the table next to a full glass.

"What?" I drop into the armchair across from him without waiting to be invited. "I need to get to bed."

"Don't take that tone with me, boy. And lying in bed smoking a joint isn't the same thing as sleeping."

"Vaping, not smoking," I correct him, voice laconic as I lean back in the chair. "Gets the job done faster."

Duke just shakes his head as he shuffles the papers on his desk. "One of these days, something is going to come along to wipe that smirk off your face, and you're never going to see it coming."

"Doubt it." The relationship I have with my father is complicated, to say the least. For most of my childhood, there has been one form of benign neglect or another. I think he planned for Giselle to raise me after my mother died, but that's what happens when you don't know who you're marrying. "What did you need?"

"Something that you have to see." He pushes the sheaf of papers across the table, knowing my eyes will be drawn to the highlighted portion on the photocopied pages.

"What is this?"

"A copy of the prenuptial agreement I had with your mother. I've been trying to get my hands on the originals, but it's under lock and key at the only law firm in town I can't buy off."

"Wait a minute." I spread the pages across the table, trying to make sense of the legalese. "This makes it look like she brought the lion's share of the assets into your marriage. That doesn't make any sense."

"It does." Duke looks more tired than I've ever seen him. "This is something I'll deny if you ever breathe a word of it, but the Cortlands have been hemorrhaging money for years. Everything but the house was mortgaged to the hilt. Your grandfather made more than a few bad deals in his time, unfortunately. When your mother and I agreed to marry, her family's fortune saved us from bankruptcy. But the money came with conditions."

My real mother was born an Abbot, well-respected in Deception, but not one of the founding families. Like most of the social climbers in town, adding our last name to their family tree was worth a lot of money. Millions, in this case. Everyone knew Grandpa Abbot took a heavy hand in matching my parents together. I'd like to think it was a gentle touch for my mother's sake, but I had no idea this prenuptial agreement existed until now, so who the hell knows.

My mother's father died years ago, not so long after his own daughter, so there won't be any asking him about it now.

"This has been a fun history lesson and all, but I don't see the point of discussing it." I lean back from the desk and move to stand. "Goodnight."

"I refuse to believe that I was ever this stupid at your age." Duke jabs his finger into the stack of papers, sending a few pages flying off the desk. "Look at what I'm trying to show you before you destroy the rest of your life."

Tamping down on my mounting annoyance, I bend over the papers again, skimming the different paragraphs and codicils for whatever it is my father won't just spit out. "The majority of our money came from Mom's family and reverts back to the Abbot's in the case of divorce or separation, which isn't really an issue considering you can't divorce a dead woman. Something, something, *inheritance will pass on to any naturally born children of the union, but only in the event that the firstborn...*"

I cut myself off, convinced I'm not reading it right. The papers are out of order, and I flip through them, thinking I must have missed something. The last bit I read out loud, not because I'm stupid, but because whatever words are processing through my mind can't possibly be correct.

"*The firstborn of this union will marry a descendent of the Hewitt, McKinley, Bianchi, Spenser, Tackett, Avery, or Milbourne bloodlines, heretofore known as the Founding Families or all money and property aforementioned in this agreement shall revert to Abbott family holdings without lease or lien.* What the actual fuck does this mean?"

Duke looks at me with an expression that almost seems sympathetic. "It means that I can't pass any of our money onto you, because it doesn't actually belong to me. Old man Abbott played hardball, and I was too desperate to fight him on any of this. If we don't fulfill the contract, almost everything we have goes back to your mother's family. Unless you marry the descendent of a Founding family, you'll be penniless. Bristol Abbott was obsessed about the power of these last names, and he held the purse strings like a noose."

I note he doesn't say anything about being so in love with my mother that the money didn't matter, not that I'm surprised.

My father doesn't even sound like he blames Grandpa Abbott for being obsessed with status. Probably because no matter how much money you make, it never quite makes as much of a difference as having the right name does, especially in Deception. He wanted the one thing you can't buy.

I could respect someone else thinking that signing this prenup was a reasonable thing to do, but it's my life being screwed with now.

"This is bullshit."

"You missed the part that says you have to get married before your nineteenth birthday, and your wife has to conceive a child to carry on the family name within a year."

If it was possible to raise a man from the dead just to kill him all over again, in that moment I would happily do just that to my own grandfather.

"I'm not playing this game with you or anyone else. Nobody is going to make me get married before I'm ready, especially from beyond the grave."

My father sighed, the exhaustion clear in the set of his slumped shoulders. "Then we lose everything but the manor. And it takes six figures a year just to cover the property taxes on this place."

"There has to be a way to fight this." I slam my hands down on the table, ignoring the sharp sting in my palms. My voice sounds strained even to me. I wonder if this is what the bargaining stage of grief feels like. "Bring the lawyers in and let them handle it."

"I've already tried that and more. Your Abbott cousins are eager to see the money revert, for obvious reasons. They would give me a small stipend for the remainder of my life, but it won't be near like anything we're used to. Eventually, we would lose the house, and there certainly won't be enough for your college tuition."

"What about all the businesses and the land? Cortland Construction is booked out with jobs for the next six months."

"We're leveraged past the point of no return. My father, and his too, borrowed against everything more than a few times over. You don't want to know some of the people we owe money."

"Fortunes are lost and made every day," I argue, deciding his admission is something to deal with later. The desperation makes me crazed. "The construction company is doing well. We can focus on building up the business. We don't need dirty Abbott cash."

"You don't have any idea the kind of numbers we're talking about here." His voice is bleak, but accepting. It makes me wonder just how long he agonized before finally working up the nerve to tell me the truth. The vindictive part of me hopes that the guilt eats at him like acid in his gut. "There won't be enough money for private school tuition or tutors, so Emma will have to transfer to that Godforsaken high school full of every degenerate punk in town next year. We'll need to lay off all the staff. And that's just what has to happen immediately, while we prepare the house for sale. If we can act quickly enough to avoid a foreclosure, some of the equity might be salvaged."

He pauses for dramatic effect to let all of that sink in.

My father is desperate, no disputing that. But for the first time, I realize that I'm being manipulated. As much as I'd like to see the look on Giselle's face when she finds herself in the poorhouse, everyone who has ever met me knows I would rather chew broken glass than let Emma suffer so much as a hangnail.

I've seen the terrible things that go on at Deception High. Hell, a lot of it was instigated by me. I know what kinds of things people do when they're desperate for a better way of life.

Emma will get chewed up and spit right back out.

My father watches me with sad eyes, heavy with the weight of a terrible world. "There is only one real way to salvage this situation."

"Why would you sign this?"

"The codicil for your marriage only takes effect in the event of your mother's passing, if she died while any of her children were still young," Duke's voice breaks. With a shaking hand, he reaches for the brandy decanter and pours out a full glass. He drains the glass and pours another before speaking again. "I never thought she would die, not so soon. Not before me."

Pressure builds in my chest, a mix of anger and disquiet that momentarily robs me of the ability to breathe. A different sort of person might call it a panic attack, but I don't want to acknowledge the anxiety of a suddenly uncertain future.

Only the rage.

And a powerlessness so profound it makes me want to destroy everything in sight.

Power is the only thing that matters in a place like Deception. Money is the most important form of power there is. The Cortlands might have the right name, but without the money to back it up, any power we have left will dry up like an empty well.

A founding family without cash might as well be Gulch trash.

That is when the worst part of this all finally sinks in.

"There is only one founding family with a daughter old enough to get married." The Averys have a one-year-old daughter that Emma is always asking when she'll be old enough to babysit. There isn't enough money in the world to make literally robbing a cradle an option. "That only leaves..."

I trail off, because I don't know what my body's reaction will be if I continue.

Duke says her name softly like he fears what will happen when he says it out loud. It still feels like a bomb goes off inside my head.

"Zaya Milbourne."

The girl I love to hate, the one I've been torturing for years, is all that stands between my family and financial ruin.

My arm burns from the still healing cut, the one I'll keep hidden under the sleeve of my shirt until the scab falls off.

There are moments when you can say to yourself, *Someday I'll look back and realize this is the moment that defined my life.*

Then there are other moments, when you don't need the benefit of hindsight to know that fate is gleefully tearing your whole world apart.

"Well, fuck."

TEN

VIN

Fate is a sadistic bitch.

Or maybe this is karma finally giving me exactly what I deserve.

Either way, I'm not dealing with this shit lying down. I'd be lying if I said that Zaya Milbourne hadn't spent a considerable amount of time on my mind over the last few years, but not because I secretly hoped we'd get married someday.

Most days, I just want to wring her neck.

Or fuck her until we both cease to exist.

Depends on the day.

Yes, I sometimes find myself staring at her skin and trying to figure out why it looks so smooth. Or I study the bent curls in her hair, wondering how it's possible that every strand seems to follow a different pattern. She has always reminded me of those old school magic puzzles where you have to stare straight at them for several minutes before a picture finally emerges.

That's only because there isn't anyone else in Deception quite like her. She might as well be the only exotic animal at the local zoo.

None of that makes her a candidate for the next Mrs. Cortland.

The idea of getting married before I'm old enough to legally buy liquor is about as appealing as pulling off all my toenails and then dipping my feet in rubbing alcohol. And not having a choice about when or *who* is enough to send me completely over the edge.

This isn't fucking fair.

This isn't *right*.

And I really want to somehow blame this all on her, even though I know that's crazy.

But if I didn't find her so infuriatingly fascinating, if she didn't always manage to crawl under my skin and then claw her way back out again, the universe wouldn't have chosen her to punish me.

She has to take some of the blame.

I stride into the county courthouse like I own the building, displaying way more confidence than I actually feel like I always do. That is what it means to be a Cortland. If the mask slips for even a moment, everything falls apart.

On the outside, I maintain the facade. No one has ever cared what might be happening on the inside.

The overweight security guard operating the metal detector waves me through without even looking up from the screen in front of him. The state of California likes to hire five people for every one job, but his apparent inattentiveness isn't really my problem. It isn't as if I'm sneaking a bomb or a gun in here.

Although I might wish I were, depending on how this next conversation goes.

I mount the wooden staircase and take the steps two at a time, ignoring the loud slap of my shoes echoing off the high ceiling. Courthouses are in the same category as cathedrals or libraries. Silence reigns as an unspoken rule that most people innately follow without bothering to question. Even the lawyers who walk these halls every day communicate in hushed voices and respectful whispers, as if the wrath of God will strike them down if they raise their tone above the barely audible.

Personally, I couldn't give less of a shit.

A purse-lipped secretary glares at me as I stride past the entrance to the circuit court and toward the offices of the district attorney at the far end of the hall. Usually, I'd try to be a little less obnoxious, but I'm not in the mood for anyone's crap but my own at this point. I wink at her as I pass, making a point of pushing my hand through my messily styled hair. The austere look on her face immediately softens.

Women always love me until they get to know me.

Uncle West's office is in the far back, past several desks for assistants and paralegals, but no one says a word to stop me. Regardless of the metal detectors and the Night's Watch cosplay downstairs, it's a good thing I'm not here for anything more sinister than a tense conversation. If I was some bitter victim of the criminal justice system out for revenge, there wouldn't be much standing in my way.

West doesn't seem surprised when I burst into his office and slam the door shut hard enough behind me that it rattles in its frame.

"Did you know about this?" I growl as I toss a stack of photocopied papers onto the desk in front of him.

"Let me call you back," he says into the phone receiver in his hand before hanging up. My favorite uncle leans back in his chair, not bothering to look down at the papers on the desk. His voice is faintly chastising. "It's always nice to see you, nephew."

Without waiting to be invited, I yank a chair back from the desk and sink down into it as I glare at him. "I'll take that as a yes."

With a sigh, he picks up the top page and glances at it before tossing it back down. "I already know why you're here, and there is absolutely nothing I can do."

Bullshit.

"There's always something you can do. Aren't you the guy who never stops talking about how it was the IRS that took down Capone? *If there's a crime, there's a way,* that's always you when you're bragging about a case. Well, this isn't just a crime, it's a fucking travesty."

"And it's also ironclad." West leans back in the leather chair and drums his fingers on the African Blackwood desk that probably costs as much as the average paralegal's salary. He might pretend to be the morally upstanding assistant district attorney, but he enjoys the trappings of wealth as much as the next trust fund baby. "I've read over this thing at least a dozen times, and at least half of those were only because your father begged me to help him find a loophole. If you want to get pissy with anyone, it should be him for signing this damn thing in the first place."

The familiar anger rises in me. "Because he should have known my mother would die in childbirth and invoke the codicil?"

"Of course not." The look he casts me isn't without some empathy – we are talking about his sister, after all. "But the fact remains that your mother's portion will return to Abbott holdings in a year unless you fulfill the requirements. There isn't any way around it."

Leaning back in my chair, I lift my legs and rest my dirty heels on top of the immaculate desk. "And the fact that you're an Abbott doesn't have anything to do with your unwillingness to help. How much of that money will be going to you if I don't marry a Founding daughter, dear uncle?"

"Watch your tone with me, kid." West's steely-eyed gaze

makes it clear that he can only be pushed so far. "I don't need your money, but if you don't want my help, then feel free to let the door hit you in the ass on the way out."

It's eight in the morning, the earliest that the doors of the courthouse open. I know that because I had waited outside for the past hour or so. Way too early for this shit. Not like I ever actually get sleep, but my mind never races the way it has for the last few hours, ever since I got the news that the only person standing between me and the poorhouse is Zaya fucking Milbourne.

"Okay, you're right." I'm not going to apologize, but West knows better than to expect that from me. "Tell me what I need to do."

"Exactly what the agreement says: convince the girl to marry you and get her pregnant, ideally within a few months, but the contract gives you a year. Keep in mind, there only needs to be a confirmed pregnancy for the codicil to be fulfilled."

I raise a mocking eyebrow. "Does that mean what I think it does?"

"Miscarriage," West bites out. "My mother struggled with fertility issues, so the contract provides some allowances. Married by nineteen and pregnant at least once by age twenty, those are the requirements."

I wouldn't be able to think of a more ridiculous situation if I tried. "But why nineteen? I haven't even graduated from high school yet. Marriage can't wait for longer than the first semester of college?"

"Your Grandpa Abbott believed in marrying young. He met his wife when she was fifteen, and they had their first child only a year later. It's something of a family tradition."

Because the rich are allowed to have predilections that would be forbidden to anyone else.

"Except nobody forced you to get married when you were still in high school."

"I'm an Abbott, not a Cortland. Your father wanted a piece of our pie, and he knew what that might require. I don't know what else to tell you."

It's hard not to feel like someone is making a point of conspiring against me. Grandpa Abbott died when I was still a kid, but he had to have known the kind of chaos that would result from this stupid agreement.

This shouldn't be legal.

The basic mechanics of it could be manageable. Getting married so young isn't even really the problem – a quickie divorce after a few years should be relatively easy to brush under the rug. There are plenty of girls who'd be willing to visit a clinic, or at least take a settlement for child support and then be on their way.

It is the *who* that has become my major sticking point.

"What about this crap with the girl needing to be from a Founding family? The Abbotts aren't Founding."

"And that fact stuck in his craw until the day my father died." West lets out a rueful laugh, as if the insane ramblings of a demented old man are somehow humorous. "I'm not saying you have to like it, but if you want your inheritance, then you know what you have to do. Marry a Founding girl and get her pregnant, then the two of you can quietly divorce as if it was just a short and forgotten chapter in your lives. You don't even need custody of the baby to make this work."

I want to rip out every hair on my damn head. This is the most frustration I've felt in my entire life. "The only Founding daughter even remotely appropriate is Zaya Milbourne. I'm not exactly her favorite person in the world."

"Sounds like you've got some buttering up to do."

I've spent the majority of the last five years making her life a living hell. There isn't enough butter in the world to grease my way through Zaya's defenses. The minute she finds out that the my future is in the palm of her hand, she'll crush it into dust.

I grit my teeth. "Zaya hates me."

And I hate her.

"A year will go by before you know it." West's smile is grim. "Better get started changing her mind, and soon."

ELEVEN

VIN

I SPEND THE ENTIRE DRIVE INTO THE VALLEY TRYING TO convince myself to turn around.

My Maserati convertible takes the hairpin turns of the cliff-side road at reckless speed. Driving too fast on a road that has killed its fair share of people is an objectively bad idea, but I sometimes visualize what it might be like to blow through one of the barriers and go soaring into empty air.

I have no interest in dying, but I've always wondering what it might be like to fly.

You occasionally have to risk your life to remind yourself that it's still worth living. Some days, driving too fast works well enough.

Other days, it doesn't.

Today is the sort of day when my thoughts turn violently dramatic. Insane thoughts that don't have any business in the brain of a Cortland.

We have no use for weakness.

Those are the words my father would use if I ever shared anything with him aside from pleasantries and business discussions. I've spent enough years of my life being weak. There isn't any more room for it, not when I have a kingdom to rule.

A wheelchair is still gathering dust somewhere in Cortland Manor, locked away in my old room which is off limits even to the servants. I keep it as a relic of a time that would otherwise be forgotten, because I won't ever forget.

I've been born twice.

Once as an infant, innocent of sin and naive to the ways of the world.

Then I died. When they brought me back, I was reborn as something else.

Whatever it is that I've become.

But I'm not going to make any apologies, no one else ever has.

Driving into the Gulch is a visceral shock, especially when coming from the Bluffs. It's like jumping into frigidly cold water on a summer day — adjusting to it is similar to physical pain. But being in the Gulch is something one never really gets accustomed to.

Poverty like this shouldn't exist outside of charity infomercials, especially in a town with precious metals still buried in the dirt.

Entering the Gulch is like stepping into an old photograph from the Great Depression: everything is grainy and more than a little sad. I don't understand how people can stand to live here. Why don't they head to a bigger town or even to place like Los Angeles where at least there are opportunities for something better?

But I say that, even as I know the situation is never that simple. Most of the people who live here have been around since the beginning, and the newer transplants have their own reasons for staying. The mines and field work were the biggest draws, but the population stayed the same even when that work dried up.

Some of the older folks, like Zaya's grandfather, act like accepting the inevitable is the same as admitting defeat. They still remember the good old days and swear up and down they'll swing round again.

I say you should know when to cut your losses before things get worse.

But It's hard to tear a tree out by the roots, even if the ground around it is barren and dead.

That said, if Old Man Milbourne had left when he had the chance, then he probably would have tried to take his granddaughter with him.

I'm not going to let that happen.

That girl has a penance to pay, and this is the only place it can happen. This only ends where it began, and she knows it. The past is a debt to the future, and her bill is about to come due.

Even if she becomes Mrs. Vincent Cortland.

Even if it destroys us both.

I know where to find Zaya, just like I know everything else about her. Years of useless study and obsessive interest. I've known since the day we met that she would either destroy my life or save it. She already did the first one, I'm interested to see if she manages the second.

There is no way she'll agree to marry me willingly, and I still haven't decided if I'll try to force her. For someone who everyone thinks folds like a house of cards, Zaya Milbourne has a core of steel hiding underneath that silent exterior.

She was abandoned by a mother who had her way too young. It doesn't take a Rhodes Scholar to figure out that getting pregnant before the end of high school would be absolutely out of the question for her.

Anyone else I would just offer money.

I know from experience she'll just throw it back in my face.

But I like to think I can be charming when I want it to be. Everyone can be manipulated, you just need to know what buttons to push.

Everyone has a trigger, even someone as stubborn as Zaya.

Her stubbornness might be one of the few things worth liking about her. The girl never backs down from a challenge, even when it would be in her own best interests to keep her head down. The last few years are more than proof of that.

I would have given her voice back a long time ago if she had been willing to tell me what I need to know.

Our past is a concern for another time, I remind myself. Right now, I need something from her, and our history doesn't factor into it at all.

For this much money, I'm willing to forget about almost anything.

At least for a little while.

Smooth roadway turns cracked and jagged with potholes large enough to sink a lawnmower, which is how I know I'm almost to the boundary of the Gulch. Despite my desire for haste, I slow down to a snail's pace around the broken pieces of asphalt in the road, because I'm not reckless enough to risk blowing a tire in this neighborhood. My Maserati would be missing rims with a ripped out radio before I finished the call with roadside assistance.

This place is a cesspit full of scavengers and the dregs of society.

My luxury car catches more than one curious glance as I roll down the street, random assholes obviously scoping out what they think is an easy target. A group of hood guys on the corner, dressed in slouched jeans and gang colors, seem particularly interested. But I turn my head and boldly meet their gazes at a stop sign, daring them to try something. Once they realize who is sitting in the driver's seat, they immediately look away.

They need to remember who the fuck I am.

Even the gangbangers and petty thieves in the Gulch are smart enough to realize that messing with me isn't worth the fire my family would rain down on them.

I still watch them in the rearview mirror when I pull away from the light. There isn't a good reason to start a fight with odds this bad, but I'm not going to let anyone make me look like a punk. I'm not afraid of a fight, but I am alone.

What would they think if they knew I'm less than a year from being penniless, no better than the losers stocking shelves or laying roofing tiles? The power of the Cortland name is almost entirely based on the money backing it up. If we don't own this town, then who the fuck are we?

I stopped questioning the seemingly unlimited power of my name a long time ago. People treated me like I held the power of life and death in the palm of my hand early on, and so I acted like I believed it. Eventually, it became a cycle that no longer had a beginning or an end.

Which came first: the golden goose, or the asshole with a silver spoon in his mouth?

When people act like you're the center of the universe, that belief becomes indistinguishable from the truth.

They treat you like you're important, so you are.

Which came first: the chicken, the egg, or my inflated sense of self-worth?

So I started saying jump, just to see how high they would all go. And you know what they say about absolute power...

It's pretty fucking awesome most of the time.

Also empty.

Secretly, I've always wondered when everyone will finally

figure out that I'm not much more than a paper tiger. The emperor has no clothes and a slightly above average sized dick.

Okay, probably significantly above average, but still.

Zaya is the only one who saw through me from the very beginning. A lot of emotions crossed her face when she first looked at me, but fear wasn't one of them. Whatever exists between us is beyond something as simple as fear, and it only makes me want to drive her further into the ground.

Even when we were kids, I knew God had put Zaya Milbourne in my life to test me. I'm only now realizing that it might be a test I fail.

The parking lot of the Gas and Sip is barely worthy of the name, and I wince in sympathy with my car's suspension as I crawl over the broken pavement. The lot is to the side of the building and its windows face the street, so there isn't a place to park where I can still see my car from inside. I just have to take the risk that it will still be here when I get back.

If it's not, I'll just buy another before my inheritance becomes a figment of my imagination.

Zaya needs to come to the negotiating table, I remind myself. She has to put our past aside and deal with me, which means I have to reign in my tendency to turn malevolent whenever I see her face. This should be easy.

My hatred for her doesn't compare to half a billion dollars.

Her form is just barely visible through the steel bars that cover the dirty pane of glass at the front of the store. Like always, she is behind the counter, although I have to wonder how a girl who doesn't speak handles a job in customer service.

The orange smock she wears over her sweatshirt makes her look like a carrot that has just been pulled out of the ground, especially with the wild mop of dark hair flying loose around her head. The florescent polyester should make her look ridiculous, but I can't stop the way my body always reacts to the sight of her, whether she is dressed in her finest or drooling in her sleep.

I'm hard as a rock.

A smile twists her lips. Her smiles are rare, like a ray of sunshine breaking through storm clouds. Usually I'd feel an urge to wipe it off her face, but it isn't directed at me. My gaze moves to the other side of the counter and takes in the object of her obvious regard.

Jake Tully.

I tell myself to count to ten and calm down before I do something to sabotage my plan before it even starts.

One Mississipi.

This guy has been in town long enough to understand the rules of this game, but he clearly still needs a violent reminder.

Two Mississippi.

A *nice* guy who doesn't have a decade's worth of backage, like a weed growing in a garden that doesn't belong to him.

Three Mississippi.

And he makes her smile. The only smiles I ever see are the ones she gives other people when she thinks I'm not watching.

Four Mississippi.

My gaze shifts away from their faces as the fuckboy hands her a crisp twenty, their fingers touching for way longer than necessary.

A haze settles over my vision, casting everything in red.

Fucking ten.

The door is already slamming open in front of me, before I've even realized I'm moving. They don't seem to notice me, which just ratchets my rage higher.

I should have known playing it cool wouldn't be an option.

TWELVE

Zaya

Two days a week, I work as a cashier at the Gas and Sip on Main Street. Even though it barely qualifies as a convenience store, the Gas and Sip is the only place to get food in the Gulch that isn't served under golden arches or out of a truck that stinks of pork and barbecue sauce. There is a fancy grocery store in the nicer part of town close to the Bluffs, full of organic produce and bulk foods that shoppers can measure out themselves. No one from the Gulch ever shops there, because not only is the store overpriced, but none of the bus routes go there. Even if you have a car, it takes half a tank of gas to make it up the steep roads of the valley

I walk to work, just like I walk most places, past broken storefronts and houses with boarded up windows. Low-hanging fog always descends on the valley in the afternoons, making everything seem like it has been painted in grayscale. Sometimes, the fog is thick enough that I can't see someone coming straight toward me until their almost on top of me. I used to imagine myself as the heroine of some Gothic romance, pages from being spirited away to something better than her dreary and broken existence.

Then I remind myself how often those stories end in tragedy.

Anti-heroes are completely overrated. I've met my Heathcliff, and I need to stay as far away from him as possible.

Wind whips through my hair and casts a chill over my skin. The air smells like coming rain, and I pray it will hold off until I reach the Gas and Sip. It's one thing to end up soaked on my way home, but I really don't want to spend my entire shift at work soaking wet and shivering behind the counter like a drowned rat.

The sky is obscured by the fog, but I look up anyway. I imagine I can distinguish the outline of the tall ridge that marks the edge of the Bluffs, even though I know it's impossible to see from here. If I could see the clouds, I know they'd be the threatening gray of my mood, oppressive and a signal of what might be coming next.

Cortland Manor would be just there, at the furthest point of the cliffs as if thrusting itself forward into the universe. Their private road is long and winding, dangerous even in good weather. My mother used to take the turns so slowly it was a wonder we didn't go rolling backwards, but that didn't stop me from gripping the door with both hands, imagining the catastrophic fate if we slipped just an inch off the paved road where sheer cliff awaited.

But thoughts of the manor only lead to reminders of its most notorious occupant.

Vin is the last thing I should be thinking about. He can torture me all he wants at school, but I refuse to let his shadow follow me everywhere else I go.

I pass a house, one of the few still occupied on this block. A bunch of guys I recognize from school are sitting on lawn chairs in the scrubby front lawn that is more dirt than grass. Empty beer cans litter the ground and will probably stay there until someone desperate for cash picks them up to recycle.

One guy, it's hard to see who it is from the sidewalk, raises the can in his hand like a greeting but immediately lowers it when he catches sight of my face. Once he recognizes me, whatever adolescent mating ritual he had planned is abruptly curtailed. He knows better than to so much as catcall me.

There is no shortage of guys in the Gulch, but none of them are my type, and most don't bother to briefly acknowledge my existence.

I used to wonder how it was possible that the influence of one guy still in high school could expand to cover the entire town. But then I remembered how many of the men in the Gulch are employed by Cortland Construction. Even the ones that don't work could have charges laid or dropped on the whim of a county prosecutor who also happens to be Vin's uncle.

The cone of silence that usually surrounds me is so much worse when I see how wary other people are of me.

It would be better if they didn't notice me at all.

But Vin won't let me go unnoticed, not for as long as I have the nerve to show my face in his town.

I enter the Gas and Sip just in time for an orange apron to be tossed in my face that I catch on reflex. Kathy, who works the early shift on the same days I do, isn't trying to be rude, but she has four kids to get back to and a babysitter who charges for every minute she runs late. That woman is pretty much always in a hurry.

The wooden bowl on the counter next to me has half a bunch of brown spotted bananas and a few apples, which likely accounts for the entirety of the fresh produce available in the Gulch.

Everyone who lives in the Gulch filters through here. I know all of them by sight and most by name. From the drug dealers who think nobody knows about the stash houses they have along the train tracks to the migrant families who work the fields in the rural part of the county an hour away but live here because it's the only place with houses they can afford. I know all the kids with reddened skin and pinched faces from living too close to the abandoned gold mine, because chronic exposure to heavy metals in the dirt leaves a visible mark.

Splashing water hits the window at the front of the store which is so close to the street that only the sidewalk separates the door from the cars speeding down the road.

"Fuckers!"

Amelia Makepeace slams into the store, soaking wet and fuming. Her long-waisted, ankle-length dress has a muddy stain down the front, and the blue checkered fabric is heavy from street water so it tangles around her legs as she tries to kick it away. She dresses like something out of Little House on the Prairie, but judging from the way she acts, that isn't by choice.

"God, people drive like they have their heads up their assholes."

It isn't raining outside anymore, but there is almost always water in the streets that pools in the deep potholes that never get repaired. When a car drives too fast down the road, like all of them do, whoever happens to be on the sidewalk at the time is going to get soaked.

The Makepeaces don't let Amelia drive, even though she is more than old enough to get her license. I'm not sure if it's a financial thing or something to do with their beliefs.

For obvious reasons, I can't exactly ask.

Not that I should be throwing stones. I have a license but

no ability to use it, because Grandpa's ancient Buick broke down over a year ago and there isn't any money to get it fixed.

Amelia's father is the preacher at the tiny little church in the Gulch, although you'd never know it from listening to her. She is a chain-smoking, curse spitting dynamo, but only when her parents are out of earshot. She doesn't attend Deception High, so I can only assume they homeschool her, but we see each other around town all the time.

I get the feeling she saves up all the snarky things she isn't allowed to say at home and then unleashes them all at once the moment that she leaves the house. She curses like a sailor and doesn't seem to fear the consequences when word of it inevitably gets back to her father. Whatever punishment she gets is something she clearly is willing to deal with if it means she can be herself.

That only makes me like her more.

The Makepeaces have a dozen children, although it's difficult for me to remember which of them are adopted and which aren't. She likes to say that her parents found her by answering a classified ad while on a mission trip to Korea, but I assume that's a joke. Amelia is the oldest girl, but the youngest Makepeace kid is still in diapers. Every Sunday, I see them walking past my house and down the dusky road toward the little church house. Amelia is always out front like a mother duck who wouldn't mind so much if one of her mismatched ducklings wandered away.

She is one of the few people who also understands what it's like to stand out like a sore thumb in this town.

I gesture at the roll of shop towels at the end of the counter that we use to clean up food spills, but she waves me away.

"It'll dry on its own," she gripes. "And there's no getting this stain out."

Amelia is one of the few people in the Gulch who won't

comment on the fact that I never speak, if she notices at all. Sometimes, I wonder if she has even figured out that I never hold up my end of the conversation. Typically, she says enough for the both of us, which I appreciate. Most people treat me like a circus freak or make a game out of trying to get me to slip up, like tourists who try to make the guards at Buckingham Palace break their forced silence.

Because most people are assholes.

Amelia just prattles on like she's happy just to have someone listening.

"Are there any hot dogs left?"

She doesn't bother to wait for a response and heads for the machine where pale hot dogs spin on rollers, beads of sweat dripping off them to sizzle on the heating element underneath. The smell of it used to bother me on the days when I came to work hungry. Even with my employee discount, it's an indulgence I can rarely afford.

Now I barely think of the things as food. Imagining the slurried flesh being forced into casings of skin helps it seem less appetizing. I watch her slather a bun with mustard and take a gigantic bite in a detached way. When I think about my empty stomach, I try to imagine that the gnawing feeling at the pit of my belly is a superpower. Other people need sustenance to live, but I gain strength from the emptiness.

Sometimes, I almost believe it.

Amelia doesn't know that I'm literally starving, because I've never told her. Our lives have bounced off each other like the lines of two parabolas briefly touching before turning away, but they don't intersect or overlap. She knows as little about what goes on behind the closed door of my house as I do about hers.

Amelia comes back to the counter and plunks down a few crumpled bills and some coins.

"You here alone again?" she asks, mouth still nearly full of hot dog. "That's not safe. Anyone could come in here and hold you at gunpoint, or something,"

I shrug in answer. The owner's son is supposed to work with me in the afternoons but he only shows up when he feels like it. And it isn't a blue moon tonight, so I'm on my own. And I'm not scared of armed robbery. Even someone from the Gulch wouldn't bother with the tiny amount of money in the register, and I wouldn't be afraid even if they did.

You have to value your life to be afraid of losing it.

Amelia pays and even drops her change in the tip jar that no one else ever seems to notice is there. I'm handing her a receipt when the bell dings above the door.

I look up to see Jake Tully walk into the Gas and Sip.

Amelia catches sight of my jaw-dropped expression and follows the direction of my gaze. When she glances back at me, a mischievous smile teases along her lips.

"And who are you?" she drawls, leaning back on the counter. Despite the too long and too loose dress and a face that is entirely free of makeup, Amelia has all the confidence of a model walking down the catwalk. "I know all the boys around here."

"I'm Jake," he says, an open smile on his face. "I just moved here from Los Angeles. What's your name?"

"Amelia," she purrs, batting at his shoulder like a playful kitten. "Well, aren't you just a big piece of man meat."

She always acts like this. Only people like me, who pay attention, realize it's an act. These moments when she manages to get away from her family, as brief as they are, bring out the urge in her to act out. If her father were to walk through the door, God forbid, Amelia would immediately revert to the shy and retiring pastor's daughter that she has to be during every other moment in her life. I wonder if Jake notices the unease in her narrowed eyes.

It makes me wonder what goes on behind the closed doors of the Makepeace house.

But for right now, I find myself staring at Jake in fascination. Everything about him seems genuine, uncomplicated, and I have no idea what to make of it. No one around here behaves like this, walking around introducing themselves and acting like they don't have anything to hide.

He seems so...normal.

Like someone who isn't doomed.

It's weird.

Jake doesn't seem surprised to see me standing behind the counter, which is noteworthy because I never told him I work here. Or where I live, for that matter.

People who don't live in the Gulch, don't hang around here just for fun.

Catching me watching him, Jake's smile widens. He gestures behind me to the wall of tobacco products locked up in a case. "I need a pack of Newports."

I wrinkle my nose as I turn to unlock the case. Smoking might be the most disgusting habit I can think of, aside from maybe taking dumps in public spaces.

"They're not for me," he adds, obviously reading the expression on my face. "I'm making an art project about consumerism under late stage capitalism. How the things we consume to relieve ourselves of the stress of society lead to even more anxiety that keeps up beholden to our own oppression. We're all cogs in the machine."

Grandpa would have said that Jake sounds like a damn hippy. I have no idea what I would say if I had a voice, even mentally I'm at a loss for words.

"Sorry," Jake murmurs with a small shrug. "That was a little much."

"You're an artist, huh?" Amelia sidles closer with half of a hotdog still in her hand. "That's cool. Most of the guys around here want to be drug dealers when they grow up." She catches the expression on my face, and her eyes widen. "But you don't live around here, do you?"

"Not exactly, my family bought a house off El Dorado, I think you guys call that area..."

"The Bluffs," Amelia finishes, the curiosity on her face shifting to something more wary, although it doesn't stop her from asking questions. "What brings you all the way out here? You had to drive by a Whole Foods and the Rite Aid."

Jake blushes. He actually blushes. "I was just driving."

"And you thought you'd stop here? At this crappy little convenience store that doesn't even have a gas station attached because the pumps stopped working years ago and the owner never bothered to get them fixed. The parking lot is so wrecked that grass is growing through the pavement. They really should call it the Keep Walking and Sip."

He holds up the pack of cigarettes that I just placed on the counter. "They don't sell Newports at the Whole Foods."

She leans forward to rest her elbow on the counter, her chin propped up on her hand. It's as close to him as she can possibly get without climbing into his lap. "Still seems like a long way to go."

But Jake just shakes his head with a rueful laugh. "You sure are persistent."

It's a weird sensation to not be part of a conversation that is clearly for my benefit. Amelia obviously wants to assuage her curiosity, but she is making a choice to hold this little interrogation here at the counter

And it's an even stranger realization that someone can be your closest friend when they never hear your voice.

I ring up the cigarettes and loudly tap the display before Amelia can say anything else. As much as I want to hear Jake admit that he came all this way just to see me, the whole exchange is a little bit excruciating. If Amelia embarrasses him enough, he might not try again next time.

Then I remember that he asked me to the Founder's Ball and I said yes, which makes my heart beat a little too fast. I can't decide which I'm more worried about, Jake figuring out that I'm not worth the hassle, or what Vin will do when he finds out.

When Jake holds out a crisp twenty-dollar bill, I reach for it, but he doesn't immediately let go. The tips of our fingers touch, and I stare up into his friendly eyes for a moment that seems outside of time. I can't decide if I feel drawn to him because I genuinely like him, or because he is the first normal guy who has ever taken an interest in me.

I make his change, the coins in the drawer clanging loudly together because my hands are shaking. When I hand the money to him, I ensure our skin doesn't come in contact again because I don't trust my own body's reactions.

Amelia watches the interaction with obvious interest, her gaze passing back and forth between us. "Did you know my girl here can sing?"

It usually isn't this hard to maintain the imposed silence, but at the moment all I want to do is yell at her to *shut the hell up*. I restrain myself to just glaring, an obvious cue she chooses to ignore.

"I mean, it's been years, but our church choir has never been the same." Amelia ignores my rapid head shake of negation and smiles brightly up at Jake. "Maybe you can help me coax her back sometime."

If a hole wants to open up in the earth and swallow a person whole, this would be a great time for it.

"That's something I'd love to see, or hear, I guess," he says, smiling until he sees the look on my face. "If you want to, I mean."

I definitely don't, and not just because Vin has robbed me of a voice. Neither Zion or I have stepped foot inside the church since our mother left. She was always the one who seemed to think that showing up for a few hours every Sunday could make up for a week's worth of sins.

Judging by the way we live, all of us risk bursting into flame the moment that we cross the threshold.

I just shake my head at Jake as I tap the smiley face sticker on the register that says *Have a Great Day!* It's not quite the same thing as a dismissal, but I can't take much more of this conversation, even if I'm not exactly participating in it.

Amelia slips her arm through Jake's after giving me a conspiratorial wink. If it were anyone else, I'd think they were messing with me, but she's doing what she does best: getting information out of people that they don't necessarily want to give up.

I turn back to the register with a small smile as I finish up the transaction.

"I'll walk you out, new guy," she says airily. "And on the way, you can tell me why you'd come all the way out here of all places."

"I'm wondering the same damn thing."

The familiar voice raises the hair on the back of my neck, making me shiver like a piece of ice is sliding down my spine. It can't be him. He would never be caught in the Gulch unless it's the middle of the night and he's about to sneak into my window. And it isn't as if he would let anyone catch him doing that.

It isn't him.
It isn't him.
It isn't him.
But then I look up and meet the cool gaze of Vin Cortland.

THIRTEEN

VIN

My hand is already moving to turn the open sign on the door to *Closed* as I address Jake and the other girl whose name I don't try hard enough to remember.

"You both have about five seconds to decide if you're staying or going. I know what I'd recommend, but I consider it only fair to give people enough rope to hang themselves."

The stubborn look on Jake's face doesn't bode well for the rest of it remaining intact. He has the nerve to turn to Zaya, who just shakes her head quickly, obviously recommending the smarter choice.

Amber, Ashley, Alaska — whatever her damn name is — grabs Jake's arm and pulls him toward the door. Like the true coward he is, he lets the tiny Asian chick who looks like she is roleplaying as a pioneer woman propel him toward the door, but not before asking Zaya if she'll be okay.

Zaya waves him away, but the glare she levels at me is hot enough to burn.

We're both burning, baby.

The other girl stops just short of the door and spares a

glance at me. "Always nice to see you out and about, Vin. I assume the weather in hell isn't favorable enough for you this time of year and you're planning for a summer there."

Inwardly, I appreciate the attempt to grow a backbone, but the stony look on my face doesn't change. "Two seconds left. Last warning, Allison."

"It's Amelia, actually." She rolls her eyes, but still yanks open the door and pulls Jake toward it. He hesitates, but takes another step away from the counter, gaze still on the girl he'll only have over my lifeless body.

Dude wants to play big man on campus but still does what he's told. If anything, I'm doing Zaya a favor by making sure she sees how easy it is to make him back down.

But then Jake shakes off Amelia's hand on his arm and turns to face me. "I'm not leaving you alone with her."

My head tilts to the side as I stare him down. I'm taller, something I relish even though it wouldn't matter if he was on the starting line of an NBA team.

I own this town and everyone in it.

"Jake Tully." My voice has taken on the lazy quality that will be his only warning, assuming he's smart enough to hear it. "Your dad is trying to open that new medical practice downtown, right? I heard the remodel has been seriously delayed, though. Getting those permits straightened out can be a real bitch."

My father owns the only construction company in town worth working with, and it's pretty much impossible to get any permitted work done in this town without going through Cortland Construction.

We snipe all the best labor and ruthlessly suppress the competition. I should feel bad about that, but I don't. If the building contract isn't with us, then the work doesn't get done.

I see the wheels turning in the idiot's head while he tries to decide if I'm bluffing.

Spoiler alert: I'm not.

One phone call, and his daddy's precious medical practice will never get off the ground, at least not in Deception. The family will probably have to go right back to whatever basic bitch place they came from.

It's tempting to do it anyway, whether he happens to be smart enough to leave or not.

But I play fair, even when it seems like I don't. It's not my fault that I'm the only one who knows the rules of this particular game.

"What's it going to be?" I ask, voice a low murmur. "Daddy's dreams go up in smoke in five...four...three...two...."

"I'll be right outside waiting for you." Jake says it to Zaya, but he doesn't look at her as he slips through the door after Amelia and lets it slam shut behind him.

I turn the lock with a decisive click before crossing my arms over my chest and turning to face the girl that I'm strongly considering throwing through a plate glass window. The fact that I'm even here, about to beg her to help me keep what already belongs to me, is frankly infuriating.

My imagination is already running wild thinking of all the different ways I could make her suffer.

Zaya isn't cowed when I turn my glare back on her. The annoyed look on her face says more than words. *Happy now?*

This is a first, even for us. Me showing up in the Gulch and in broad daylight. I wouldn't normally leave my kitchen garbage in this part of town, much less my Maserati. But desperate times call for desperate measures and all that.

This close to her, her work apron looks even more ridiculous. The thing is at least four sizes two big and makes her look like she's wrapped in a bright orange tarp. On anybody else the get-up would look like a bright orange sack, but her slim form gives it an almost endearing quality, like a kid playing dress-up in their mother's closet.

It's too bad that her mother skipped town years ago and that slim form is a result of skipping every other meal. Nothing against ten-year-old boys, but she shouldn't have a body like one.

I don't realize how long I've been staring until Zaya drums her fingers on the dirty countertop and makes a hurrying motion with her hand.

It takes all my self-control not to take that hand and shove it down the waistband of my jeans.

"I have a business proposition for you," I tell her, meeting her watchful gaze with a penetrating one of my own. It only makes sense to offer the carrot before I use the stick. "I'm willing to call a moratorium on the forced mutism and all the other shit. Do one thing for me, and you'll never have a problem with me, or anyone else, ever again."

Her interest is obviously piqued even as she tries to hide the subtle reaction of her body, catching herself when she shifts forward slightly across the counter. Stepping back, Zaya leans against the shelf of charger cords and vape pens behind her as she continues to stare at me.

The girl isn't going to give an inch.

And if her recalcitrance were standing in anyone else's way, I might feel a little proud of her, but this is *my* life about to be screwed six ways to Sunday.

"You aren't going to ask me what the favor is?"

She taps her mouth with the tip of one finger and raises an eyebrow. Stubborn brat is going to act like answering me is a violation, when she usually has no problem telling me what's on her mind if we're alone, even when she knows it's not anything I want to hear.

"Speak, damnit."

Her stony-faced expression gives nothing away as she glares at me from behind the counter. But she twists her fingers at the corner of her lips and then flicks her hand as if locking them and throwing away the key.

Little bitch.

"I'm also offering you fifty thousand dollars, free and clear, when the thing is done."

Her gaze bores into mine, but the wariness hasn't left her eyes. If anything, Zaya seems even more alert to danger than she was when I walked in. Her need for money won't ever trump her ability to recognize a devil's bargain when she hears one.

Unlike everyone else in this town, Zaya isn't for sale.

She takes the barest second to consider it. Then she just shakes her head and gestures toward the door, obviously a request for me to leave.

But I'm not going anywhere until I have what I need.

"Let's make it one hundred thousand then," I tell her, voice casual as if I'm throwing out numbers that are barely more than pocket change. They will be, as long as I get to keep my inheritance. "And I'll make sure your grandfather and that delinquent brother of yours are taken care of for as long as they live in Deception. That old rickety house won't ever fall down around their ears if you agree to help me."

It's mentioning her family that makes Zaya hesitate. Her loyalty to them has always been absolute, even when they didn't deserve it. But I can't think about that right now, because then the old familiar anger will get the best of me.

And I need her to say yes.

Her mouth opens and closes, as if she has to practice forming the words when she has gotten so used to other methods of communicating.

"What would I have to do?"

The sound of her voice sends a shock of awareness over my skin.

Relief shoots through me when I realize I've finally convinced her to speak. Forcing her to be silent had started as an angry pronouncement that then morphed into a way of life. I pushed a boulder downhill and then got surprised when it flew off without me.

Sometimes what's done can't be undone.

Her voice is like liquid sugar: thick, sweet, and addictive. I hadn't taken it away just as a punishment but because it was something I didn't want shared with the rest of the world when it was being withheld from me.

Surprise, I'm a selfish asshole.

Nice to meet you, and what rock have you been hiding under until now?

The look she casts me is expectant as she waits for an answer, an explanation for why I decided to drive all the way out here and confront her at work. Not that she has insisted on an explanation for anything I've done.

Maybe part of her realizes she deserves it.

"I need you to marry me." My voice is airy, like I'm asking her to help me move or pick up groceries. "And soon, next week maybe."

She has the nerve to laugh in my face. The sound is unexpected but lyrical, like church bells ringing on a clear morning.

And then she realizes I'm serious.

The response is visceral. Zaya looks like she's going to be sick or pass out. The thought of being married to me obviously so disgusts her that she can't stop herself from visibly recoiling.

I'd be more insulted if I didn't know how easy it is for me to make her wet, but the response still stings.

She stares at me like I have a second head growing out of my neck. "Are you serious?"

"As the grave."

"You're insane."

I let the smallest hint of truth shine through. "Not insane, just desperate. It only has to be for a year, not even a day more. Thank Christ."

"Why?"

I give her the barest detail, hopefully enough to convince her the offer is legit without giving everything away. She can't know the kind of power she potentially holds over me. "It's a requirement if I ever want access to my sizable inheritance."

Her dark eyes flare with heat, sucking me in with the gravity of twin black holes. "Why me?"

"Because I know you'll agree to a prenup without complaint and be just as interested in signing the divorce papers as I will be. Day 365 on the dot. When it's done, we never have to see each other again."

For a moment, I have myself convinced that she's considering it. I see her doing mental calculations in her head, tabulating just how far the money I'm offering would take her. Or maybe she's thinking about the prospect of never needing to be in the same room with me again when it's all over.

I'm taking a calculated risk not telling her about the requirement for a baby, although I like to think it's only a lie by omission.

She would never agree to this otherwise.

Baby steps. I'll get what I need eventually.

"No," she says, finally. "I won't do it."

My hands ball into fists, but I do my level best to respond calmly. "You drive a hard bargain. What if I throw in college tuition at the over-hyped and overpriced private school of your choice?"

"This isn't a negotiation. It's not about the money. Even a million dollars wouldn't be worth it." She shakes her head violently enough that hanks of hair fly into her face, and she bats them away in annoyance. "I would rather never speak again."

I tell myself I don't care about the clear rejection, — I'm mostly just annoyed at not getting my way. Who does this girl think she is? After everything that's happened, the things she's done, that she won't even do me the courtesy of considering my offer is infuriating.

"That might also be an option." I stride toward the counter and lean across it, forcing my face into her personal space. The aisle is narrow enough behind the counter that there isn't any room for her to lean away. "The things I've done to you are nothing compared to what I can think of if I'm feeling creative."

"Then do it," she says boldly, despite the flash of unease in the dark depths of her eyes. Those eyes are always a touch too wide, like something you'd see on a porcelain doll or a cartoon character. It should make her face ridiculous, but the effect is precisely the opposite. "I don't care anymore, Vin. Do your worst."

I want to tell her that she has never seen my worst. She has no idea what happens when I decide to make it my life's mission to tear apart someone's psyche brick-by-motherfucking-brick. Up to this point, I've been riding her ass with training wheels on. "This is the only time I'm going to ask nicely. Next time, the deal won't be anywhere near as good."

Zaya squares her shoulders like a prize fighter readying for another round. "My answer isn't going to change."

So I let every bit of darkness into my smile and watch with satisfaction as the bravado slowly dies from her expression and fear takes its place.

I smile when a shiver works its way down her spin.

"Game on."

I SLAM THE SLIDING GLASS DOOR SHUT HARD ENOUGH THAT the pane rattles dangerously in its frame. Part of me is disappointed when the thing doesn't fall and shatter into a million fucking pieces.

Just like the rest of my life.

"I assume things went as well as you hoped they would?" Iain asks from his lounging position on the floor in front of my flat screen, barely sparing a glance from Call of Duty. "Although I don't see a ring on your finger, so maybe we'll wait to alert the papers."

Iain is the only person I let in my space when I'm not around, mostly because I know how much he hates being in his own house. The Hewitts have a sparkly mansion on the Bluffs just like the rest of us, but it's as dead on the inside as it is pretty on the outside.

Sometimes the prettiest places hide the dirtiest secrets.

But I don't ask him about shit like that, and he doesn't volunteer any information. Mutually assured silence is part of why we've always gotten along so well.

He is also the only other person, aside from my father and uncle, who knows the full truth about that prenuptial agreement tying up my inheritance. Partly because I need to talk to somebody about it who isn't going to lecture me, but mostly because I know his moral compass points as true north as mine.

That little needle is just spinning around in circles at this point.

"I just wasted two hours I can't ever get back."

Thankfully, my Maserati was still intact when I stomped out of the Gas and Sip. At least it was until I kicked a dent in the front bumper out of sheer frustration, compounded by the fact that I'm nearly positive Jake was still hanging around and saw the whole thing.

If anybody is on the top of my shitlist, it's that fuck.

Iain pushes to his feet and watches me make a beeline for the bar. "So she said no?"

"In about a dozen different ways." I reach for a bottle of Jameson's and pull out the cork with my teeth before filling two tumblers. Sobriety and this conversation do not go hand in hand. "Pretty much any inducement short of pain of death won't do the trick."

"Are you planning a kidnapping?" Iain picks up one of the nearly full glasses and takes a swig from it, blowing out a breath of air that smells like pine needles and hard liquor. "Say the word, and I'll clear out my basement. The parental figures never go down there."

The fact that I'm not entirely sure whether he is serious stops me from ready agreement. I might be a total asshole, but sometimes I wonder if Iain is diagnosable.

"I'll let you know. For now, I'm planning a campaign of terror that will turn her into a quivering mess. I can marry whatever pieces are left."

He shrugs and sets the empty glass back down on the bar. "If you're sure that's the best idea."

His tone is enough to make the words a lie.

"You have a better idea?"

"*The supreme art of war is to subdue the enemy without fighting. The greatest victory is that which requires no battle.*" He slumps back down on the couch and picks of the controller, smiling when something to his left explodes and angry yells come from the headset lying on the floor by his feet. "Fuck, I love the graphics on this game. Every headshot is a blood geyser.

This motherfucker is really going to sit here and quote the Art of War. "Did you get into my weed, because that sounds like something a person who is high as hell would say?"

"Or kill her with kindness, if you prefer. Zaya has gotten used to fighting with you, that's all the two of you have done for years. Giving her something else might provide the advantage you need."

Encouraging me to be kind is like gently recommending a fish avoid water. It's just not going to work, no matter how hard you try. "I sincerely doubt a bouquet of flowers and a mariachi band are going to cut it."

"I'm sure you'll think of something suitably insidious and deceptive." Iain smashes some buttons, a feral smile on his face. I don't need to look at the screen to know someone just got sniped. "Find out what she really needs, or wants, and then show her you're the only who can provide it."

"That's manipulative as hell." I drain my glass and pour myself another. "I like it."

"Happy to be of service."

My phone is already in my hand, and I'm scrolling through all my contacts at Cortland Construction until I find the name of one of the foreman. This is the kind of thing that money was designed to do, buy things that can't be procured in any other way. And for the time being, I still have funds to throw around.

Zaya Milbourne wants to believe she can't be bought. We're going to test that little theory right fucking now.

FOURTEEN

The asshole wants me to marry him.

It would be funny if it weren't so completely insane. I'd say it has to be some sort of joke he's playing on me, but Vin Cortland doesn't have a sense of humor. At least not one I've ever seen. The only thing that brings a smile to his face is watching someone else suffer.

The more I think on the ridiculous offer, the harder it is to decide if I should be flattered or enraged. What was it he said?

I know you'll agree to a prenup without complaint and just as interested in signing the divorce papers as I will be.

He chose me for this crazy plan because he thinks he can control me, just like he has always tried to control me. And that fact alone wants me to tell him exactly where he can shove his half-assed proposal.

I'm not the kind of girl who spent her entire childhood imagining a perfect wedding. I don't have a hope chest or a Pinterest Board full of expensive dresses and over the top wedding venues.

I still didn't expect the lamest proposal in the universe when the time finally came.

Hey, here's enough blood money to make you forget your conscience. Now just say I do.

I wouldn't marry Vin if he had the last working dick on planet Earth. I'd rather shackle myself to a particularly curvy piece of driftwood for all of eternity.

All of that would be well and good if I wasn't excruciatingly aware of the fact that it's been almost an entire day since I last laid eyes on Vin. I hate to admit to myself that I've been waiting for him, anticipating whatever awful thing he might do next. I half expect him to meet me on the steps of the school ready to deliver some new form of torture.

It worries me more that he has been missing in action.

As far as I can tell, he didn't even show up for school today. I wonder if he's embarrassed. When Jake came back into the Gas and Sip after Vin finally unlocked the door and shoved out past him, he told me that he definitely saw Vin kicking the shit out of his car like it had personally wronged him.

As if it actually mattered to him that I had said no.

I find myself searching the crowd in the nearly full hallways, looking for the face that rises above the rest by several inches and always has a scowl plastered across it. Each time that I don't see him, I have to remind myself that his absence is a reprieve and not something to be worried about.

But I am worried, because Vin is dangerous when everything is going his way.

If he gets pissed off enough, all hell might break lose.

He can marry someone else, I remind myself. Someone like Sophia who would lap up all the shit he dishes out like it's bacon-flavored. She has the ability to ignore her emotional pain in a way that makes her way more immune to Vin's cruelty than I ever will be.

Pride cometh before the fall, and all that.

A sense of foreboding permeates my entire day, to the point that it's impossible for me to focus during any of my classes. At one point, when I happen to meet the cold gaze of Iain Hewitt, I considered breaking my cone of silence. If just to see whether or not Vin then descends on me like some angry and vengeful god.

I manage that impulse, just barely.

It helps that Iain is just as scary as Vin, if in a completely different way. Vin rages hot like an exploding sun, but Iain is so cold that he seems practically reptilian.

With about the same level of humanity.

He was the sort of child who burned ants with a magnifying glass just to watch them fry. It's as likely his mother gave birth to him as it is that she hatched him from an egg.

Speaking would also draw his attention, which is the last thing I want.

I move through my day in the same way I always do, completely silently and without any attention from a breathing person. But the entire time, I'm secretly waiting for the hammer to fall and Vin to show me what terrible fate awaits for rejecting him so completely.

It isn't until I get home that I realize Vin has been playing an entirely different game.

The first thing I notice is the fleet of black F-150s lined up on the road with *Cortland Construction* painted on them in gold letters. I've seen them around town before, because the Cortland's company handles pretty much every building or renovation project in the county. But they never do business in the Gulch.

Nothing ever gets built or renovated here.

I'm halfway down the block before I realize the gigantic trash bin they use for construction debris is parked in my front lawn. Disgusted, I step over the planks of wood laid out on the sidewalk and make my way to the front door. If Vin thinks that using my house as a dump is going to get under my skin, then he has no idea what it's like to live in the Gulch.

That feeling of smug satisfaction lasts as long as it takes to open my front door.

Controlled chaos is the only word for it. Two workers with tool belts strapped around their waists are on the stairs, hammering down fresh pieces of wood to replace the steps that have been rotted and broken my entire life. Another one slips past me with an armful of tile, headed for the tiny bathroom that all three of us share.

What in the hell are they doing here?

A balding man with a paunchy midsection, dressed in a cheap button-down shirt and khaki pants approaches me with a clipboard in his hand. "Are you Zaya Milbourne?"

I nod more out of shock than anything else.

"You need to sign this work order and then initial there." He thrusts the clipboard under my face. Obviously sensing my hesitation, he clears his throat. "Everything is already paid for, but without a signature from the homeowner, we can't guarantee the work."

I wave him away and the man just shrugs and walks off, like it doesn't make a difference to him.

My house is being renovated.

Vin set this up, all of it.

It has to be just another form of manipulation, and I refuse to accept it. I tell the nearest workman to stop what he's doing and take it all away, and he just ignores me. But as I hurry through the house, it quickly becomes clear this isn't the sort of thing that can just be undone.

There is new flooring in the living room, and the last of the wallpaper has been scraped off so the walls could be painted a soft gray. In addition to the stairs being reinforced, workmen carry wooden timbers into the unfinished basement to reinforce the sagging floor. Grandpa's sleeping chair has been replaced with a hospital bed that elevates nearly into a sitting position.

I wouldn't believe it was possible to do all this in one day if I wasn't seeing it for myself.

Zion strolls past with a sandwich dangling from his mouth and a bag of chips in his hand.

My mouth falls open before I can stop it. "Where did you get that food?"

He raises his eyebrows, speaking with his mouth still full. "Kitchen."

Of course, he got food from the kitchen. The kitchen that hasn't had anything but expired cans of green beans and frozen trays from Meals on Wheels for the last year. I stomp down the hallway, noting with some aggravation that the floorboards no longer creak.

Our dingy kitchen has been scrubbed to within an inch of its life, although that isn't enough to hide the decades of neglect and wear. But if the new countertops and appliances lining the hallway just waiting to be installed are any indication, an even greater transformation is to come.

And I want to tear my fucking hair out.

Zion comes up behind me, slurping on a can of soda that definitely wasn't here a few hours ago. "Nice, isn't it?"

The glare I cast him speaks volumes. The loudest thing it says is that we can't trust charity from Vin Cortland.

"Let's just enjoy it while it lasts," Zion says with a shrug. "There was even a nurse in here earlier giving Grandpa a sponge bath."

I also hadn't missed the brand new hospital bed in the living room and a row of oxygen tanks that the insurance usually only paid to replace every other month that Grandpa needed it.

You can look a gift horse in the mouth when it's attached to more strings than would choke a marionette. Nothing in this world comes for free, especially not from a guy like Vin Cortland.

If Vin is trying to get under my skin, he succeeded.

I hate that.

He isn't even here overseeing all the work he ordered. I search every inch of the house, ostensibly to catalogue all the invasive changes, but don't catch so much as a glimpse of his characteristically smug face so I can throw something at it. It's somehow even more annoying that he would do this and not even give me a chance to refuse it.

Because I realize as I tour the house that not all of this can be taken back. The walls can't be unpainted, it isn't possible to un-repair the foundation or replace the wooden stair steps with the broken pieces in that trash container outside. Some of this is permanent, the labor paid for, the work signed, sealed, and delivered.

Which means I'm in Vin Cortland's debt.

That bastard.

The men wrap up for the day pretty quickly after I get home, although I wonder if they've received some kind of signal. None of them will look me in the eye as they file out to their trucks, except for the apparent foreman who holds the clipboard out to me again with a hopeful look on his face. My glare chases him out the door.

To my relief, the crew hasn't had time to do much upstairs. The long hallway still has the same depressingly dingy wallpaper, little yellow flowers on a green background that have faded so much I can barely make out the pattern. The door of my room is closed, and I push it open slowly, dreading what I might find on the other side.

Everything looks the same. The same cut out pictures on the wall and ratty comforter on the bed. Then my gaze shifts to the far corner, and I let out a weary sigh.

A shiny new iPhone sits on top of my desk with the film still covering its dark glass surface. The thing looks like it came straight off the factory line, but when I pick it up the screen lights up as if it's already been activated.

I used to have a cell phone, one of those prepaid deals you can buy without needing credit. We sell a few different ones at the Gas and Sip. But I ran out of minutes months ago and couldn't afford to buy more, so the phone stopped working completely.

But this is the latest model and nothing like what you can buy from a gas station. And I don't have to guess who is paying for the plan.

As soon as I pick it, the phone pings with a new message that pops up on the screen.

Vin: More where this came from. Just say yes.

My gaze moves to the closed window that looks out onto the scrabbly trees and far off cliffs. The sky here is thick with fog and smog, nothing like the beautiful views up in the Bluffs. Nothing moves out in the distance, and it's still broad daylight. I just hope it's a coincidence this message came at the exact same moment I picked up the phone. I tell myself he can't be out there, only a coincidence.

Vin isn't out there somewhere watching me right now.

He doesn't need to see me to know exactly what I'm doing. He has been able to see right through me from the very day we met.

It takes everything I have not to throw the very expensive piece of tech across the room so it shatters against the wall. It's only my aversion to destroying something so expensive that keeps the thing in my hand and not in the nearest trash can.

I don't bother to respond and close down the messaging app. Instead, I open up the list of contacts. Vin's number is the only one that is programmed in, of course. I wouldn't even be surprised if Vin figured out a way to keep me from calling anyone else with this thing.

This is a Faustian bargain if I ever heard one, except Vin won't be happy with just my soul.

FIFTEEN

Zaya

It takes a day or two of ignoring the elephant in my house before I finally get around to playing with the iPhone. Vin hasn't approached me at all, no more messages and no following me around at school, almost as if he's trying to bide his time.

Every so often a new text from the only contact pops up on the screen, always saying the same thing.

Say yes

Say yes

Say yes

But I haven't so much as laid eyes on him in the hallway. There hasn't been any sneaking into my room in the middle of the night, or otherwise pestering me. My days are as silent as they've ever been. Even my usual tormentors, like Sophia, have mostly been ignoring me.

Zion has been spending more and more of his time cutting class and hanging out with his Gulch friends, most of whom had already dropped out by sophomore year. Grandpa is doing better than he has in years, but he is still usually asleep by the time I get home from school.

Jake still smiles at me when our path's cross at school, but he learned his lesson the last time and hasn't spoken a word to me. He risked passing me one note during AP Government to confirm that we were still on for the Founder's Ball.

It makes me wonder if he only wants to take me at this point to prove something to Vin.

That would be pointless, taking on Vin Cortland doesn't make you brave. Just stupid.

But even the possibility of going to the Founder's Ball with the person who will piss Vin off most isn't enough to overrule the isolation that suffuses every moment.

I have never felt so alone in my entire life.

But maybe that's the point.

When I finally force myself to ask him, it turns out that Zion has Amelia's phone number.

I've never asked him how he always manages to have a phone on him despite our extreme poverty, but I can only assume it involves petty theft of some kind.

The night before the Founder's Ball, I finally decide to reach out to her. Amelia is the closest thing I have to a girl friend. I can trust her not to spread stories, because she has as few people to talk to as I do.

It's Zaya. I have an iPhone, a fridge full of food, and I don't know what to do.

Be there in 15.

"This looks like something out of Extreme Makeover - Trailer Park Edition," Amelia exclaims as she walks through the door. "What in the name of Adam's shiny elbow happened to your house?"

Amelia isn't cursing, even though it really seems like she wants to. It makes me wonder what the hell must have happened for her not to let a damn or hell slip out of her mouth.

I hold up the phone so she can see the picture of Vin that has been set on the home screen. There is some kind of parental lock that prevents me from changing it. It's been days, and I still haven't cracked it.

Amelia lets out a low whistle as she looks around the transformed living room. "Is this what all that posturing at the Gas and Sip was about? I thought Cortland was going to strangle you, not remodel your house."

If given the two options, I know which one I'd have preferred. I gesture for her to follow me upstairs so we don't disturb Grandpa, who is still sleeping.

He sleeps a lot these days. I doubt he has even noticed all of the changes in the house.

"Are you going to explain?" she asks expectantly as I close the bedroom door behind us and sit down on the bed.

Instead of answering, my thumbs move along the phone's screen. Moments later her crappy flip phone vibrates with the message.

He wants me to marry him.

I like her even more when, instead of screaming for joy or telling me how lucky I am, her mouth drops open and she just stares at me.

"Why?"

I text her again.

He has to get married to get his inheritance.

"That's not really an answer to my question." Amelia sits gingerly on the edge of my bed and crosses her legs at the ankle. Today she wears a calico-patterned dress that has short sleeves but bunches of ruffles down the front. I catch the hint of a bright pink bra strap before she pulls the ruffled neckline back into place. "There are a hundred girls who would take that deal, even if there was nothing coming on their end but the name. Why would he pick you?"

I shrug, even though it isn't just confusion swirling through my head. Amelia doesn't know anything about the history between Vin and I, nobody really does. But nothing from the past would explain this bizarre turn of events.

And I don't want to speculate on the whims of Vin Cortland, because that is the best way I know of to get my feelings hurt. He either chose me because torturing me has been a favorite pastime of his for years, or because he thought I would be easy to control.

Neither of those options is particularly flattering.

It should tell me something that I still have his gift in my hand, an expensive phone that I should have pawned at the first opportunity.

I think I'm going to get rid of this thing. Hammer maybe?

"Don't you dare!" Amelia snatches the phone out of my hand and turns it over to inspect the back. "This is some top-of-the-line crap. Sell it if you have to, but trashing it would just be a waste. Then you'll only have something else to feel bad about."

I hate that she's right.

It makes me want to share a thing with her that nobody but me knows, if just to see what her reaction will be. I need to know just how far from sanity I've let myself go.

When I pull the shoebox out from under the bed and drop it in her lap, Amelia looks at me like she thinks there might be a bomb in there. I nod at her to open it when she hesitates.

Her face is gratifying, because clearly I'm not the only one going crazy here.

"Where did you get this?" She gasps the question as she thumbs quickly through the bills, clearly doing a mental calculation. Then she catches the look on my face, and her eyebrows shoot up. "From Vin?"

I nod as she hands the shoebox back, gaze lingering only for a moment on the pile of cash before she lets the lid fall shut.

"That's wild."

Picking up my new phone, I text her again.

I don't know what I'm going to do with it.

"Well, don't throw it away," she insists with a laugh. "In fact, if you're ever feeling generous just make sure to keep me in mind."

I know Amelia well enough that I don't think she'd come back here with a crew and try to roll us over. She isn't like that, and not just because her family is religious. Amelia is a straight shooter. If she was thinking about robbing me, she would give me fair warning to keep my belongings locked up.

Which is why she is the only person I feel comfortable coming to for help. I trust her to tell me precisely what she's thinking, just because I asked.

Jake is taking me to the Founder's Ball. I need you to help me get ready. Like really ready.

"Sounds like you're hoping to turn heads," she comments. "Or maybe just one head in particular."

I shrug as I gesture toward my closet. Even though I rarely have more than two quarters to rub together, my closet is full to bursting. My mother didn't take much with her when she blew out of town. Initially, I told myself that meant she had to be planning to come back eventually. But with each passing year, it seemed more and more likely that she just didn't want to waste the time it would have taken to pack up her stuff.

So I still have everything. From the "lucky" jean shorts she'd always wear on Saturday nights at the bar to the wrinkled uniform the Cortlands gave her that is still covered in grass stains and smells like glass cleaner.

Amelia lets out a surprised gasp when she opens the door and a cascade of fabrics in every possible color burst from the closet. Julia Milbourne's tastes trended toward the cheap and flashy, but nobody could fault the variety of her wardrobe.

"Holy forking shirt balls. I feel like I'm in the wardrobe department at the theatre. The only thing missing is a space man costume." She sifts through the hangers so quickly that dresses move like flashes of colored light. "You should have told me to bring my sewing machine so we could alter some of this stuff. Although, I do love a good vintage item."

I already knew Amelia makes her own clothes. Her father buys yards of plain fabric from the farming supply store with the only instruction to cover everything below her neck and above her ankles. The way she eyes the mini-skirts and slinky tops in the closet, I wonder what she would do if given free reign.

Amelia pulls out a flaming red dress, so bright that it practically glows stoplight. It's low-cut, lower than anything I've ever worn outside of the house before, with a slit up the side that stops at mid-thigh. She holds it up to herself and lets out a low whistle. It's one of the few dresses in the closet that is classic instead of dated. "If you want to make a statement, this one will get the job done."

I take it from her with shaking fingers, unsure why I suddenly feel so nervous. She turns her back as I pull off my sweatshirt. It isn't necessary to try the dress on to know it will be a perfect fit, but I do anyway. I inherited my build from my mother, curves that don't disappear even when I don't get enough to eat and wide hips that I've always hated.

My body always seems like an invitation thrown out to the world for all the wrong things.

"Wow."

That's all Amelia can say when she turns back around and

sees me standing in front of the mirror. My reflection is that of a fully-realized woman with the world in the palm of her hand, not a little girl who won't speak up for anything, including herself. The dress hugs my hips, which only highlights the gentle taper of my waist. Even without a bra, the bust creates enough cleavage to be sexy without crossing the line into the obscene.

I look amazing in this dress, not something I'm used to saying about myself.

Amelia comes up from behind, her gaze meeting mine in our reflection. "I hope you know what you're doing."

My motives still aren't completely clear, even to me. But I know that I when I step foot inside of Cortland Manor for the first time in years, I have to be ready for battle.

Maybe it's not fair to Jake, but tonight he'll be my shield.

A flattering dress will be my armor.

Makeup will be my war paint.

And like always, Vin will choose our weapons.

SIXTEEN

VIN

Friday morning finds me sitting in a full cafeteria wishing I could make everyone inside of it disappear, including my closest damn friends.

I had made it clear with as few words as possible that Zaya was completely off limits. Most people probably assume I'm planning something truly diabolical, but none would dare ask me that directly.

Cal won't stop giving me a shit-eating grin from across the lunch table as he shoves way more food than any one person should consume down his throat. From the way Iain refuses to meet my gaze as he stares meditatively down at his phone screen, I can only assume the news about my inheritance has already been shared.

I'd be pissed if not for the fact that we're the Vice Lords.

We don't keep secrets from each other, especially not about something like this.

But that doesn't mean I won't wipe the knowing smile off Cal's face if he lets anything annoying come out of his damn mouth. Just because I've decided to accept the inevitable, doesn't mean I want to hear anything from the peanut gallery about it.

Seriously, fuck Cal for thinking anything about this situation is funny.

And fuck Iain for telling him about it in the first place.

Elliot is the only one who displays anything approaching sympathy, and it isn't even for me.

"That poor girl," he says, taking a meditative bite of his sandwich. "She must have really corked things up in a previous life."

My voice is caustic. "Cork? That's not even a fucking word."

"You know what I mean, whatever the opposite of a guardian angel is must have a hand in this. Guardian demon, maybe. Nobody deserves to be forced into marrying you." Elliot dodges the carrot stick I throw at him with ease and takes another bite. His mouth is completely full, which does nothing to stop him from continuing. "If I were her, I'd tell you exactly where to shove your marriage proposal."

"That's just because you have a thing for ass play," Iain comments wryly.

I have to remind myself that my anger should be directed at Zaya for being so stubborn. Girl doesn't know a good thing when she sees it. There are about a dozen girls in this school who would be on their knees by the time my mouth formed the *M* in *marry me.*

But not Zaya.

Never her.

I could push and push her, but when I hit that wall she has erected around herself there won't be getting any further. It would be easy to admire her if I didn't hate her so much.

As if sensing the direction of my thoughts, Elliot watches me with a pensive expression.

"Most people would wonder why you let all that shit in the past mess with you so many years later."

I glare at him. "You don't have any idea what the fuck you're talking about."

"I would if you ever let us in on this big secret. I heard about how her mom used to bring Zaya to your house and shit. Then one day, you hate each other. What gives?"

Only two people in the entire world know the true story of what happened between Zaya and me. And one of us prefers never speaking again to telling the damn truth.

And a deal is a deal.

"Does it have anything to do with—"

I wing a thick plastic plate at Elliot's head. He dodges and it bangs against the wall behind him. "If you really want to know, we can take this conversation outside. You know how I feel about gossiping in public spaces."

A raised eyebrow is his only response. He knows if we go outside that we won't be talking about anything. Would I beat the shit out of a good friend for asking the wrong questions?

Absolutely, I fucking would.

Elliot just gives me a crooked smile, because he relishes a fight as much as I do. We don't need an excuse to pummel each other — sometimes you just need to drive your fists into someone. Catharsis, and all that.

"I'm not sure who I should feel more pity for," Iain murmurs, gaze not rising from handheld gaming device that has suddenly appeared in his hands. "Zaya, or you."

"That's easy since you're not capable of feeling pity for anyone," Cal says, leaning over Iain's shoulder to see the screen and wincing as some fantasy character gets beheaded or worse.

Iain only plays games rated for extreme violence.

"True," he says with a careless shrug.

Elliot turns back to me. "So what are you going to do about this inheritance thing?"

He is like a pit bull with its jaws clamped, just refusing to let shit go. "None of your damn business."

"It is if you're going to be all poor and sad in a few months. My family still has some property in the Gulch if you're going to need a place to crash. But you'll have to deal with the crackheads on your own."

"You can fuck right off." I know it's a joke, but that doesn't stop a full body shudder. The thought of living in the Gulch, after a lifetime with a golden spoon in my mouth, has to be the highest form of dramatic irony. If God has a sense of humor, then he is laughing hard enough to give himself a coronary at this point. I would rather leave town and never come back than deal with the shame of it. "That isn't going to happen."

"It is, if Zaya Milbourne has anything to say about it. Or not say in her case. Have you even tried being nice to the chick?"

If being *nice* includes spending a small fortune on renovating her house so it won't fall down around her ears in the near future. Although, I have no idea if Zaya sees it that way, since she seems to be refusing to communicate with me.

I've sent her maybe a dozen text messages on the brand new phone I picked out, but she didn't bother to respond. The damn thing is even the same color as the lavender gel pens she always uses in class, because I assume that's her favorite color.

If that isn't nice, then what the fuck is?

For some reason, her continued silence annoys me more than anything else has up to this point. It isn't like I necessarily expected obvious gratitude after everything that has gone on between us, but some acknowledgement would be nice.

I tell myself that the hot feeling burning in my chest is simple rage, because anger is an emotion I'm familiar with. It's practically my comfort animal at this point. I don't want to explore the possibility that the emotion I'm feeling might be anything else.

"You could always sneak into her room in the middle of the night, assuming you can get drunk enough for it to seem like a good idea without passing out first," Iain comments, tone droll.

Cal laughs, but immediately sobers when he sees the look on my face.

I'm going to murder them, take us all out in a blaze of glory. That has to be preferable to dealing with Zaya Milbourne right now.

The more I think about it, the more anger becomes the dominant emotion churning in my gut. Who does the girl think she is to just refuse a deal that will benefit both of us? Without my help, there is no way she will ever rise out of the muck of the Gulch, not with all the forces conspiring to hold her back. But she would rather be poor for the rest of her life than deal with me for a year.

That realization burns just like rage, but with a dark edge of something else.

Iain lets the game system drop to the table with a clatter and opens his lunch bag. "Just so you know, Zaya is going to the Founder's Ball with Jake Tully."

Ice slides through my veins, painfully cold. "How the fuck do you know that?"

He pulls a crumpled paper out of his pocket and tosses it at me. I unfold the thing and quickly scan it. One set of handwriting is immediately recognizable, it definitely belongs to Zaya. And the icy cold inside me quickly turns to heat as I read the flirtatious banter that turns into an invitation.

An invitation that is accepted.

It feels good to be angry, like an embrace from an old friend.

"How long have you had this?" The paper crumples into a ball in my fist.

Iain shrugs and takes a bite of his apple. "A few days."

"And you didn't think to tell me about it until now?"

"Forgot."

"Your mom forgot not to drop you on your head as a baby." I want to blame him for this, but getting mad at Iain is like spitting into the wind. The loogie is just coming back to land in your face. "Fucking Jake."

Iain raises a sardonic eyebrow. "You want us to drive him out to the cliffs and toss him off?"

I don't really think Iain is serious, but he says everything in the same bored monotone, so I can never be completely sure. He describes brutal murders with the same inflection as plans for dinner.

"So Zaya can cry crocodile tears at this dick's funeral? No thanks. I'll figure out a way to deal with Jake, apparently violence isn't going to do the trick."

I'm going to destroy him, grind him into the dirt until there isn't anything left to mourn.

This isn't about jealousy.

This is about ownership.

Zaya Milbourne is mine. Her pain is mine. Her voice is mine.

She owes me a debt, and only I get to decide when it finally gets paid.

Both of them are going to learn that lesson in as complete a way as possible.

The only question is how.

With the same impeccable timing as always, Sophia sidles up behind me and covers my eyes with her clammy hands.

"Guess who?" she trills, voice pitched just a few notes too high.

I already know who it is, because nobody else wears the same perfume she does, likely because she issued some sort of threat to the other girls to keep it exclusive. She smells like a knock-off Ariana Grande with the cloying combination of baby powder and cucumber-melon body spray.

It's suffocating.

The easy thing would be to turn my anger and frustration on her. Sophia makes a good target. I think of her like one of those blow-up clowns that eagerly pops right back up every time you punch it down.

But as much fun as it would be to make her cry for the hell of it, I'm playing a longer game.

"Nurse Reynolds? I don't need my temperature checked again, thanks."

"You're so bad." Sophia giggles and slaps me lightly on the arm as she comes around to wedge herself between me and Elliot on the bench seat. "And you haven't asked anyone to the Founder's Ball yet. If you wait much longer, there won't be any girls left."

This particular girl couldn't be more obvious if she tried — sometimes I find her obvious desperation a bit charming. From what I've heard, she already turned down half a dozen invitations to the Founder's Ball in the hopes that I'll finally get around to asking her.

I don't do dates. It's hard to see the point. If a girl is willing to lay down and spread her legs regardless, then why waste time with dinner and roses? Even if I show up alone to the Founder's Ball, that doesn't mean I'm going to leave that way.

Then I remember what I've just learned about Jake and how he has been sniffing around Zaya since the moment he showed up in town. I haven't decided how to handle that he had the nerve to ask her to the Founder's Ball.

My Founder's Ball.

The one my family has been throwing every year for the past hundred. Just thinking about them strolling into my house together, arm in arm, makes my blood boil.

So an idea forms.

"You want to go?" I ask Sophia. Casual, like it doesn't matter to me one way or the other.

Elliot makes a choking sound from behind her that I choose to ignore. I don't need to hear his opinion on this clusterfuck of a situation.

Her squeal is loud enough to burst ear drums, and I let her hug me even though it makes my skin crawl. Sophia is a pretty girl, even I notice that, but her looks don't do anything for me. Sometimes I wish they did, if just because it would make things easier.

"Come by early and you can stand in the receiving line with me," I tell her. The more this idea percolates in my brain, the more I like it.

Sophia's eyes are so bright they're practically strobe lights. She says something appropriately fawning and enthusiastic, but I've already stopped listening. I hold my hand up to stop her when she starts prattling about matching her gown to my cummerbund. The details don't matter to me.

Every year, my family stands at the entrance of Cortland Manor to welcome each guest personally to our mausoleum of a home.

Every single person who comes to the ball has to walk the receiving line. It's tradition. That means the entire town will see Sophia at my side, playing queen of the manor.

Standing up there with me is an honor, communicating something significantly more than status as a fuck buddy, and Sophia knows it.

Zaya will, too.

Iain and Cal just look on in mild amusement as Sophia

peppers me with questions about what time she should arrive and if she should bring a gift for my *mother*. Elliot watches me with obvious disapproval, but I don't have time for his crap right now.

I didn't start this game, but I will be the one who wins it.

SEVENTEEN

VIN

I PULL AT MY BOWTIE, FIGHTING THE URGE TO RIP THE stupid thing off my neck and throw it across the room. Wearing a tuxedo feels about as binding as a straightjacket and puts me in a similar frame of mind.

You'd have to be a little crazy to get any pleasure out of this shit.

The last thing I want to do is throw open the doors of Cortland Manor and let every knuckle dragger in Deception wander through our house, but it isn't as if I have a choice.

Sophia is just happy to be here, if the dozens of text messages she sent over the last few hours are any indication. Her excitement is naïve and might even be flattering under different circumstances.

I remind myself that she doesn't want me because I'm *me*. Everybody wants Vincent Renaldo Cortland, prince of Deception. Twirling on my arm in a ball gown while the whole town watches with envy is just part of the fantasy. She wouldn't be so excited to sit out front of a shanty house in the Gulch and drink light beer.

If my inheritance disappeared, so would she.

That makes it easier to take advantage of her with a clear conscience, or at least one that has gone mercifully quiet. The angel and devil on my shoulder went to war years ago, and it doesn't take an idiot to figure out which side won that battle.

I stand sandwiched between my little sister and Sophia in the receiving line. Emma keeps casting curious, if reserved, glances Sophia's way, but doesn't say anything until a few dozen people have gone past us.

"She is wearing really tall shoes," Emma whispers to me during a break in the flow of people, because she hasn't learned what stripper heels are yet. "I hope she doesn't tip over, because then everyone will see up her skirt."

I just shake my head and try not to laugh.

Or cry.

My father seems surprised to see me with a date, but he doesn't say anything, either. He knows better than to comment on how I handle this situation, especially considering his terrible decision making got me here in the first place. Giselle doesn't even seem to notice anything is different. Her focus is exclusively on all the effusive compliments as people marvel over *that dramatic crystal chandelier* or the *original wood paneling*.

Sophia's hand tightens on my arm whenever a girl from our school moves through the receiving line, nails practically digging into the skin. I'm sure she has already told anyone who will listen that she has officially staked a claim. At some point, I assume she'll raise her dress and piss on my leg, just to make it clear to anyone in smelling distance that I belong to her.

At any other point, I'd feel the need to put her back in her place. But even standing right next to me, Sophia is barely on my radar right now.

Zaya hasn't shown up yet, and neither has Jake. I can't help but wonder if they've decided to skip the ball completely. Maybe they're holed up somewhere together, engaging in other forms of entertainment.

The thought makes my blood boil.

The crowd of arrivals eventually thins until there is only a trickle of late arrivals. My father and Giselle wander off to mingle while Emma is dragged back upstairs by her nanny.

"Do you want to dance?" Sophia asks, trailing her fingers up and down my arm in a way she must think is flirtatious but is mostly just annoying.

"In a minute."

My gaze stays trained on the massive front doors, willing them to open again. Almost everyone I've ever met has wandered past us at this point. If Zaya and Jake aren't here, then they have to be alone because Deception is basically a ghost town at this point.

Sophia shifts closer to me, her hand moving down the front of my pants. "Or we could do something else if you want."

My hands rise to her shoulders with every intention of pushing her away.

Then the door opens again.

Zaya appears first, peeking her head furtively through the opening as if afraid someone might slam it in her face. Her gaze takes in the empty entryway as she slowly enters the house with Jake right behind her, his hand on the small of her back.

I wait for her attention to shift across the room. She visibly startles to find me standing there and staring her down. She stops short and freezes, gaze lingering on where my hands rest over Sophia's shoulders.

In a spark of inspiration, I pull Sophia close with an arm around her waist. Like the response is Pavlovian, her body melts against mine.

Zaya won't know that Sophia isn't in on the trick.

Some mysterious emotion blooms in her eyes before they narrow and she lets Jake hustle her away.

The moment Zaya is out of sight, I step away from Sophia. Zaya's gaze is burned onto my retinas.

What emotion flared in her eyes?

Jealousy or disgust?

The only way to know is to keep pushing until she snaps.

Or breaks.

And if I'm feeling generous, maybe I'll put her back together again.

Sophia tries to push her hand down the waistband of my pants and I grip her wrist harder than is strictly necessary to shove it away. She makes a mewling sound that sets my teeth on edge, but I do my best to ignore it. For now, I still need her.

"Let's go dance," I suggest, not waiting for a response as I use the leverage on her wrist to pull her after me. We're heading in the same direction Zaya and Jake just went.

People make a point of trying to talk to me as I stride past with Sophia in tow. I ignore most of them, giving a brief smile that probably looks more like a grimace here and a nod there, but it should be obvious to anyone watching that I don't give a shit. Each and every one of these people could disappear off the face of the planet, and I wouldn't care.

I'm only here for one reason.

Zaya is dancing with Jake. The song is slow, but the arm he has at her waist is stiff and a little awkward, like he isn't sure how much pressure to use. There is enough space between their bodies that a determined person could easily push in between them.

Obviously, they haven't screwed yet.

The sense of relief I feel just annoys me even more.

Swinging Sophia into my arms like a rag doll, I glide us

close enough that Zaya would have to be blindfolded not to notice us coming closer.

Hopefully, selective mutism doesn't go along with selective blindness. I stole her voice, not her goddamn eyes.

Zaya makes a point of ignoring me, going as far as turning her head away when I get close. But I'm too attuned to her to miss the tension that tightens her shoulders and raises the little hairs on her arms. She is as aware of me as she always is.

I know, because I'm just as aware of her.

The music changes as the band picks up speed for a faster song. I watch the way Zaya moves out of the corner of my eye, her body swaying with the beat in a way that is unlike any other girl here.

I tell myself I'm watching her for a sign of weakness, some hint that it's finally time to move in for the kill. But I try and fail to tear my gaze away.

"What's with you?" Sophia bites out in annoyance as she follows my gaze. "I thought you were here with me."

I swing her around, the movement fast enough that she stumbles and ends up facing away from where Zaya and Jake are dancing. "Shut up."

I'm not surprised when she clamps her mouth shut, but just a little disappointed. Sophia has never been a challenge. If I say jump, she'll already be in the air when she asks how high. I could tell her to suck my dick right now, and she probably wouldn't hesitate, even with most of the town here for the show.

It's boring. This has always been boring, but that bothers me more now than it ever has.

Maybe the problem is that everyone always assumes Sophia and I will end up together, including her. People treat us like a foregone conclusion, as if I don't have any real choice in the matter. She thinks I don't know that she warns other girls away from me and writes my name all over her notebooks like a lovesick idiot.

I don't do anything because I've never cared enough to address it.

Maybe I saw ending up with her as a necessary eventuality, too. It wouldn't be a terrible match, all things considered. Her family is wealthy and well-placed. She might be a vapid and vindictive idiot, but that describes most people in this town. And she isn't too terrible to look at if you're into that hair bleach seeping into the brain look.

But I'd never made us official, and not just because I was putting it off. I keep Sophia hanging on the hook because she makes things easy, but I've never really wanted her.

At least, not in any way that matters.

Whatever I feel for Zaya is too complicated to dwell on for long stretches of time. I like to focus on the simple parts. She owes me a debt, and I own her ass until it's paid.

But now the bitch is standing in between me and my damn inheritance.

Remembering that infuriating little fact makes me want to stride across the ballroom and wrap my hands around her throat. But I don't have to worry about that urge. When I glare over Sophia's shoulder, there is only an empty space on the dance floor where Zaya and Jake had been.

They're both gone.

EIGHTEEN

"This house is ridiculous. Why does one family need all this space?"

Jake shakes his head in disbelief as we walk down a deserted upstairs hallway, his question obviously rhetorical. He stops at an impressive portrait of some Cortland ancestor from a hundred years ago that stares imperiously down at us from the wall. "My dad makes good money, but this is something else. How rich are these people?"

I shrug in answer. Not just because of the cone of silence, but I also don't have an answer to his question. I've wondered, myself, just how much the Cortlands are actually worth. Grandpa used to say they were all cheats and fakes, but I don't know how much of that was the dementia talking.

Regardless, the Cortlands have ruled like kings on the mountain since our town was founded. It really doesn't matter how much money is actually in the bank when no one ever denies them anything.

Jake turns a corner, but I don't immediately follow him. I

recognize this part of the house. We're about to enter the wing where the family has their bedrooms.

We definitely shouldn't be here.

It was one thing when Jake asked if I wanted to find some place quiet. Maybe I even hoped he wanted to make out a little. But I don't have any interest in snooping around Cortland Manor when I would never live it down if we were caught.

I've seen enough of this house to last a lifetime.

Jake turns back to me with a question in his eyes. I shake my head and gesture in the direction we just came, back to the party.

His smile teases me. "Aren't you even a little bit curious?"

I just shake my head again, more resolutely this time.

But Jake doesn't take the hint. Or if he does, he makes a conscious decision to ignore it. Grabbing my wrist, he pulls me down the hallway. "Just a few more minutes. I want to see as much of this freakshow as I can while we have the chance. Don't worry, I'll take the blame if someone catches us."

I don't actually want to go back to the party, not with Vin staring daggers at me whenever our gazes meet. We can't leave this early without some sort of explanation to Jake. At least hiding out like this, I won't have to deal with anyone but him.

Against my better judgment, I let Jake guide me down the hallway and toward a familiar set of rooms. I'm surprised we were able to get this far past the roaming staff and into a part of the house I know is supposed to be very off limits. The staff assigned to keep everyone corralled probably assumed nobody would be stupid enough to duck under the *Do Not Enter!* sign. No one in this town would dare sneak around Cortland Manor during the Founder's Ball and risk never being invited onto the property again.

I think that might be what I like most about Jake. He doesn't care about breaking the rigid and unspoken set of rules that the rest of us are forced to live by, because he doesn't have any idea how important they are. As soon as he does, I'll probably never see him again, so I should appreciate his ignorance while I can.

I still haven't quite figured out what Jake wants from me.

He can't be putting up with all this — the muteness, the threats from Vin, the general unpleasantness — because I'm the most interesting girl at Deception High. If anything, the opposite of true. My silence practically makes me a blank slate — people fill in my margins with whatever colors they want. I don't need to have low self-esteem to know that nothing about me is worth all this hassle, not when we've only just met.

Maybe he just likes the idea of getting under Vin's skin.

It was impossible not to notice Vin's death glare when we walked into the house together. The grand entrance I hoped to make into the Founder's Ball had been curtailed by just how long it had taken to tame my hair. I never straighten it, but tonight I did my best to turn the kinky curls into something approaching sleek. The entire time I was picturing Sophia's perfectly styled waves and wishing that hair transplants were a real thing. Jake's appreciative reaction when I finally came downstairs made me happy I'd made the herculean effort.

I want to feel fabulous and strong, that is the only defense I have left against Vin.

He asked me to fucking marry him.

I still can't shake the feeling I'll wake up and realize the last few days never happened, just feverish imaginings from the strangest dream I've ever had. Last night was the first time I didn't wake up to the sound of my house creaking from rotten wood. There was enough food in the house that it actually tempted Zion to stay in for the night instead of running around the streets. I hate that money is my greatest weakness, but I can't ignore that it wouldn't take much to completely change my life.

It just can't come from him.

Saying yes isn't an option.

Vin has spent his entire life getting everything he wants without needing to lift a finger. I refuse to add myself to the long list of his personal possessions.

No matter what he might be offering.

"I wonder what's in here?" Jake murmurs as he pushes open a door that creaks on its hinges.

Too many years have passed, which is my only excuse. I spent more time in the gardens and grounds of Cortland Manor, rarely coming inside. The layout is vaguely familiar, but I didn't realize just how far we've ventured from the ballroom.

A blast of frigidly cold air blows over my skin as the door swings open, like opening a freezer door in the summer. The manor is always cold, but I don't understand how anyone can stand this. Giselle keeps the air-conditioning running pretty much every day of the year. She told my mother once that sweating prematurely ages the skin.

"This place is like the Addam's Family mansion, I swear." Jake rustles one of the sheets that cover all the furniture, even the bed. "I bet there are a dozen bedrooms in this place that nobody even uses."

A strange note has entered Jake's voice, as if he finds something personally insulting about this house. I want to ask him about the disgust in his tone. We're alone, and Vin would never know.

But I decide I don't want to know the answer.

"What do we have here?"

It's only when Jake pushes a rusted metal wheelchair out of

the shadows that I realize our mistake. This isn't some random guest room.

This is Vin's old bedroom, the one he slept in as a child because it's located on the first floor.

We have to get out of here.

I yank at Jake's arm, but he ignores me and pulls the wheelchair further out into the light. Dried leaves and petals are stuck in the spokes, crumbling to bits at our feet as the wheels turn.

That wheelchair is a relic from another life. Vin would kill us both if he found us here with it. Memories are long in a town like this, but they don't beat carefully cultivated lies. Few people know that Vin didn't spend his elementary years away at boarding school, but closed up inside Cortland Manor like the beast from a fairytale. No pictures exist from that time in his life, at least none I've ever seen.

He erased those years so completely that it's as if they never existed.

There is no telling what he might do to keep the past hidden.

"This is creepy as hell," Jake says with a wide grin. "You think some old relative died in here, or something?"

I loop my arm through his again and try to lead him back toward the door, but he resists. He turns to face me with a wide smile on his face. "Even with the creepy aesthetics, I'm glad we finally have the chance to be alone."

Maybe it's that my only other significant interaction with the opposite sex has been with a sociopath, but it hadn't occurred to me that there was an ulterior motive to Jake's invitation to *get some air*.

I've gone off alone with a boy that I barely know.

I was so concerned with Vin, I didn't stop to think that I

might be throwing myself out of the frying pan and into an open flame.

So stupid.

Jake stares down at me with an eager smile and expectation in his gaze. If he was a bad guy, there had been plenty of opportunity for him to prove it before now. But a shiver of awareness runs down my spine as he steps closer, eating up the small amount of space separating us.

Before I can convey to him that we should be anywhere but here right now, he bends his head and kisses me.

It's a nice kiss, just enough pressure and not too much tongue. Pleasant like floating on your back in the ocean on a day when the waves are calm and the sky is clear. He tastes like sunshine, salt air and all things purely good.

But I still feel a stab of disappointment.

Jake is barely a glowing ember next to Vin's raging inferno.

The kiss is good, but not even close to being the same.

He pulls away to look down at me with that same half-smile on his face, but now uncertainty lingers in his gaze. "Are you okay?"

"She's probably just bored. That was about as hot as sponge-bathing your grandmother."

My heart stops.

Vin steps into the dark room, his cold gaze lowering the already frigid temperature by several degrees. The door slams shut behind him, and he watches us like a fox who has cornered shivering rabbits in the grass.

To his credit, Jake shifts to stand in front of me as if his body isn't something Vin would tear apart to get to me. "Look, man. I don't want a problem."

"You should have learned a long time ago that you don't always get what you want." Vin's gaze shifts to the rusted wheelchair behind me, and his eyes narrow before flashing to my face. If looks could kill, I'd be dead and buried. "But today is your lucky day, because I'm giving you a choice. You can go out this door — alone — or I can send you out through the window."

Jake's shoulders tense. "And Zaya?"

"She'll be going out the window right behind you."

I want to believe he isn't serious. But staring into his eyes, I don't see anything aside from dark intent. My lips burn with awareness as his gaze lingers there with hyper-focused attention, a manic twist to his lips.

In a mood like this, Vin is capable of anything.

"You can't just go around threatening people," Jake insists, even as his weight shifts uncomfortably from one foot to the other. "Just let it go, and we can forget about all this."

Vin tilts his head to the side, regarding the other guy like a particularly interesting specimen under a microscope. His gaze flicks up and down, assessing even as his body coils with tension like a snake about to strike. "You can't go around playing with other people's toys and think something won't get broken."

I want to tell Jake that he should leave. I also want to beg him to stay as if he might actually be able to save me from whatever Vin is planning to do. But I don't say anything at all, because even now I allow Vin to make the rules of this game we've been playing since we were kids.

My hands push at Jake's back, urging him toward the door. He spins to face me with surprise and what almost looks like betrayal in his eyes.

"You want me to leave you with him?" he asks, voice incredulous.

"Maybe not too stupid to live, after all," Vin murmurs with a sardonic smile. "Run along and leave a girl to fight your battles for you, just like last time. You'll cover more ground if you split up."

Because my life is a horror movie, right?

Jake sucks in his breath, obviously preparing to say something scathing. I just shake my head furiously, trying to tell Jake without words that this isn't his fight. Even if it were, it's not one he can win. Perversely, I hope he fights me on it. I want him to insist on rescuing me, promise to take me away from this awful place even though you can't run from what is inside you.

Just because I refuse to be a damsel-in-distress, doesn't mean I don't wish there was someone willing to be my knight-in-shining-armor.

But I can't expect that from Jake, who rode into town in a late-model luxury sedan and not a white horse. His gaze searches mine, looking for something he obviously doesn't find. Anger twists his features before he turns away and strides toward the door.

"You two deserve each other."

I wince as the door slams shut behind him.

Vin has the nerve to smirk at me. "My, people do come and go quickly here."

My heart skips more than a few beats as I glare at him. Silence be damned. Clearly, all of the rules have changed.

"What the hell do you want?"

"You mean, aside from world peace?"

"Aside from torturing me. Aside from making my life a living hell. What. Do. You. Want. Vin?"

He pushes off the wall and takes a step closer to me. I fight the urge to back away, even as every fiber of my being urges me to run. Everybody knows if you run from a predator, it won't be able to stop itself from chasing you.

"You seem on edge. Must be the sexual frustration. From the looks of it, Jakey-boy has a hard time getting the job done.

He seems like the type to ask *is this okay* about a dozen times before he even gets inside of you."

God, he is gross. The satisfied smirk he makes says he thinks a few talents in the bedroom make up for the shittiest personality that has ever existed.

"There isn't anything wrong with affirmative consent," I snap, wishing I could wipe that mocking smile off his face. Now that the floodgates are open, I feel almost a decade of things left unsaid welling up in me like a rising tide. The people at school call me weak, but they have no idea I've just been biding my fucking time. "Although, you are the kind of guy that the #Metoo crowd practically salivates over. Fast forward a few years from now, and you'll be wondering why nobody cares about your side of the story when all your former secretaries start coming forward."

He has the nerve to chuckle at that, instead of getting angry. "Rape doesn't do anything for me, but I think you've already figured that out by now."

I want to strangle him, even as my hands fist uselessly at my sides. "Fuck you."

His smile widens. "Exactly."

We never speak to each other like this. We almost never talk at all, haven't had anything resembling a real conversation in years.

But something has fundamentally changed between us. Part of it is probably the arrival of Jake, a guy at least a little willing to push back against Vin's bullying. But I didn't realize until this moment how much his misguided wedding proposal has tipped the scales in my favor.

If not for the undercurrent of violence in the air, you could almost call it bantering.

He wants something from me, and that gives me power over him. It's not much, but it's more than I've ever had.

"Says the guy who has to break into people's houses to get laid."

"But consent isn't Jakey's problem, is it?" Vin muses, ignoring my barb. "His problem is that kissing him felt like doing a favor for your sad friend. Something you do out of pity because you feel bad saying no."

Despite all the things we've done, the things I've let him do, Vin and I have never kissed. That always felt like a line that couldn't be crossed, an intimacy neither of us wanted to share with the other.

There was one time when he showed up drunk enough to try, but he didn't force the issue when I turned away. He didn't seem to remember anything about it the next day, and I sure as hell wasn't going to remind him.

Vin is guilty of a lot of things, but he has always listened when I said no.

Too bad there can't be redemption for the devil. Some people are past saving.

I force myself to laugh derisively, hating that he isn't entirely wrong. "You don't just sound like you have no idea what you're talking about. You sound jealous."

"And you sound like a liar," Vin laughs, but chaos swirls in his eyes. He takes a menacing step closer. "Tell me the truth. Tell me he lit you up, set you on fire. Make me believe it, and I'll let you walk out of here right now."

If I was scared before, then I don't have words for whatever it is I'm feeling now. "I don't have to tell you anything."

"We're not leaving this room until you tell me the truth. And the longer you wait, the more time I have to think of creative ways to torture you. Maybe I'll start by tying you to that wheelchair, see what you think of being trapped in it like I was."

I've never been able to lie to Vin, not when we were children, and not now. Even though I've made pathetic attempts in the past, he has always been able to see right through it. I have to make the choice between speaking truth and not speaking at all.

Up until now, he let me have that choice.

But things have changed.

"Jake Tully is the most amazing kisser on the planet," I say defiantly. "Kissing him was all shooting stars and fireworks. If I could spend the rest of my life tongue fighting him, I would."

"Liar. Although, it's cute you care enough about Jake's feelings to try."

Vin takes another step forward, pushing firmly into my personal space until the front of our bodies almost touch. The space between us is full of electricity and heat.

"What did your grandfather think about his new bed?"

The abrupt change in subject knocks me off balance, which is precisely what he wants.

"Anything is better than a twenty-year-old La-Z-Boy, but you already knew that. Take it back, if you want, because nothing has changed. You could knock down my house and build a mansion twice as big as Cortland Manor in its place, and that still wouldn't change anything. You can't buy me."

"I can buy anything I want. It's just a matter of how much it will take." His hand raises to within an inch of my face, but stops just short of touching. Then he twists a hank of my hair in his fingers and pulls hard enough to make me wince. "What the hell is this?"

His mood changes are giving me whiplash. "What?"

"Your hair. What the hell happened to it?"

"I straightened it. You know, that thing that pretty much every girl does when she dresses up. I know it looks nice, so fuck off."

I hate that he can make me feel self-conscious, because I

don't want to care what he thinks about anything. But my hair is a sore spot, the thing that has caused me more angst than anything else. Every time I look in a mirror, years' worth of insults run through my head.

Nappy.

Brillo pad.

All the times someone claimed not to be able to tell the difference between it and pubic hair.

And the one time I try my best to tame it, to become something approaching traditional beauty, Vin has to take the opportunity to tear me down a little further. It shouldn't bother me because I know he's an asshole, but it still does.

Except his tone isn't exactly mocking as he rubs the strand between his fingers. "I like it better the other way. This is boring as hell."

Is there a compliment buried in there somewhere? I just stare at him for a long moment as pressure builds in my chest. I'm too surprised for dissembling. "You *like* it the other way?"

He frowns, seeming to realize what he had said. "Just an observation that at least one thing about you isn't total shit, don't let it go to your head. Right now you look like the before picture from a makeover show for street hookers."

And there is the Vin Cortland I know and hate. "You've always been so good at buttering people up, Vin. Is my hair what you chased Jake away to talk about? Stalking just makes you seem desperate."

"You're confusing desperation with patience. You'll come around eventually. You always do."

I guess the marriage proposal wasn't a fever dream spurred by hunger. "Not this time. Not about this."

"Time will tell." He shrugs as if whether or not I'll marry him isn't even worth discussing. "Let's get back to this kiss. On a scale from creepy uncle to Romeo-and-Juliet-I'll-die-for-you-even-though-we-just-met. Where did we land?"

Somewhere in the vicinity of holding hands with your third-grade crush, but I don't tell him that.

"None of your damn business."

"Everything about you is my business." His palm shifts to cup my cheek, leaving a sliding trail of heat in its wake. "Maybe you need something else to compare it to, like the control for an experiment. Tell you what, if I kiss you and you don't feel anything, then I'll never bother you with anything again. Fake marriage proposals included."

The offer is tempting, even as a traitorous part of me protests. But there is also a glaring problem. "You don't kiss."

It's not just common knowledge, but a facet of teenage myth-making. Everyone knows that Vin Cortland doesn't kiss anyone. Ever. Not his father. Not his step-mother. Definitely not any of the girls who show up for his parties in the pool house. He might even draw the line at a peck on the forehead for his little sister.

"Definitely not on the mouth, because I know exactly where those have been," he agrees. "But I might be tempted to make an exception for somewhere else."

"I don't need to try a shit sandwich to know I wouldn't want to eat it." Bravado is easy to fall back on when you don't have any other defenses left. The little pride I have refuses to let him see that my knees are shaking. "And you can stop with whatever game you're playing. Jake is probably waiting outside."

"Jake is long gone. If he wanted to fight for you, then he would have. I'm not that much bigger, he might be able to take me if he had passion on his side. That's how I know your kiss wasn't worth shit."

"I just met the guy. There might be something between us if *you* stopped showing up."

Vin continues as if he doesn't even hear me. "And he's already gotten his ass kicked, which should make this personal. But he still just walked away."

"Because you threatened him!"

"Because he is a drooping pussy who isn't actually that interested."

I let out a frustrated noise. "God, you are such an asshole."

Vin sighs, the sound almost wistful. "I know, baby."

His hands are still on me, playing with my hair. He touches me almost absentmindedly, as if he has every right to.

This isn't a seduction. It's compulsion. And both of us would stop if we could.

But he always gives me plenty of time to say no, knowing I won't.

I can't decide which of us is crazier.

My eyes drift closed on their own when his hand teases at the hem of my dress. A shock of heat runs through me as his fingers stroke the sensitive skin just above my knee.

His gaze moves down my body as my face heats up.

"Now, about that kiss."

Even though I know I should, I don't stop him as Vin sinks to his knees in front of me. His upturned face is barely visible in the shadows, but white teeth flash as he smiles. Warm fingers tease up my thighs, impossibly hot against the cool skin.

Cortland Manor might be colder than death, but Vin burns like there is a fire lit inside him.

My skirt is bunched up in his hands, and he breathes across the sensitive skin on my upper thigh. "I'm going to wipe that kiss from your memory."

I fist my hands in his hair, urging myself to shove him away.

But I don't.

This is Vin like I've never seen him. On his knees. Anyone else in this position would seem like a supplicant, like the one without the power. But even kneeling at my feet, he is somehow still the one in control.

A spark of pleasure tightens my belly as his tongue teases at the seam where my hip and thigh meet. I breathe out in a soft sigh. His name catches in my throat, but I won't say it because that would make all of this real.

I struggle to remember what kind of underwear I'm wearing. So many of them have bits of elastic coming undone or tiny holes ripped in the fabric. Sexy panties are another indulgence that has no place in my life. Hopefully, he won't be able to tell how shabby they are in the dark.

Vin nips my skin with the edge of his teeth. The shock of pain makes me jump. "Stop thinking."

But I have to focus on something else, anything else. Because he is making me crazy.

I don't realize I've spoken out loud until he murmurs against my skin.

"Not crazy enough."

He shifts the crotch of my panties to the side, gliding one finger down my wet folds. My head falls back against the wall behind me as I stare up at the ceiling and try to remember that we're enemies.

Then he forces two thick fingers into me, excruciatingly slowly.

"Oh, God."

"It's Vin, actually. But I believe in freedom of religion."

His fingers push in and out of me, so deep on the upstroke that his knuckles grind against me. I take deep breaths through my nose in sharp gasps, wondering if I'll pass out. Then his thumb shifts higher to rub the thin strip of fabric covering my clit.

Stars burst across my closed eyelids.

"And now for that kiss."

His fingers are gone. Before I can mourn the lack of contact, he leans forward. My gaze shifts down, but I see only a mess of dark hair. He presses his mouth against me, flicking his tongue with the same rhythm as the sharp edge of a thumbnail that scratches against my clit.

The small bit of pain has me thrusting my hips forward. Vin's free hand grips my waist, pushing his thumb into the hollow bone of my hip and forcing me to be still. His tongue pushes deeper, but his thumb continues the same maddeningly slow rhythm, easing the pressure when I shift my hips to entice him into pressing harder. He just barely grazes me through the fabric, enough to keep me spiraling higher, but not send me over the edge.

He presses a closemouthed kiss against my clit through the soaked fabric of my panties.

Vin shifts away, and his fingers thrust inside me again, the movement almost leisurely. I look down the line of my body to find him staring at me, eyes narrowed and fierce as they land on my face.

"What do you want?" he asks.

I glare down at him, my expression enough of an answer. *What the fuck do you think?*

"Beg me to let you come."

The words come out in a hiss as he thrusts his fingers deeper. "Not on your life."

"What's the magic word?"

"Asshole."

"Maybe later." He places another gentle kiss on my clit through my panties, leaning away when my hips jerk toward him. I'm seconds from orgasm. Then he pulls his fingers out of me and cool air rushes over the wetness on my skin. "Only good girls who do what they're told get what they want. Remember that for next time."

Vin laughs at the expression of shock on my face as he rises smoothly to his feet.

My body is on fire. The inferno burns so hot it doesn't matter that the manor's thermostat is set to negative fifty degrees. His satisfied smile makes it clear that he has every intention of leaving me like this. That realization is like being doused with a bucket of cold water.

Passion isn't the only emotion that burns hot.

"There won't be a next time," I spit at him, shoving my dress back down to cover myself. My underwear is still pulled to the side, but I won't give him the satisfaction of watching me fix it. Let him think I don't care. "We're done."

He smirks. "We will never be done."

Pleasure is always pain, at least where Vin Cortland is concerned. Pleasure that curls my toes and pain that stabs as sharply as a knife in my belly.

Things were never supposed to be this way.

We were never supposed to be this way.

He won't stop, even when it hurts us both.

But that's what secrets do, infect everything until only sickness is left.

A look of surprise briefly crosses Vin's face when I shove him away.

"You can't seduce me, and you can't buy me. I don't care how much you think I owe you, no debt in the world is worth this. You don't own me."

"That's where you're wrong." His heated gaze burns through mine for a moment so charged it is indistinguishable from eternity. "We've tried carrot, let's see what you think of stick."

Vin has swept out of the room before I can think of a suitable response.

No one has ever been able to make me feel what Vin seems to arouse so easily. I hate him, even when I know he is a parasite burrowing underneath my skin.

I'll never be free of him.

Vin wasn't wrong about Jake, who is nowhere to be seen when I scurry into the darkened hallway. He must have returned to the party. Being abandoned by my date is about what I deserve at this point. I can't explain to Jake the hold that Vin Cortland has over me, that he has always had, because I struggle to understand it to myself.

The past keeps a stranglehold on the present, like creeping vines that never stop growing until everything else dies in darkness.

I take my time returning to the ballroom, because I recognized that look on Vin's face. Rejecting him is the same as throwing down a gauntlet at his feet.

And he has never backed down from a challenge.

It surprises me when I see Jake standing in the entryway, waiting for me.

He turns a concerned face toward me as I approach. "Are you okay? I saw Cortland come stomping down here a minute ago looking like a psycho. But when you weren't with him, I thought maybe he'd done something to you. You had me worried."

I just shake my head and smile, even though it feels more like a grimace.

But Jake wasn't worried enough to come back for me or refuse to leave me with Vin in the first place. I suddenly find his concern inexplicably annoying, though I know I shouldn't blame him for what Vin does.

That is precisely what Vin wants me to do, see Jake as

cowardly and weak. When really, I shouldn't expect the world from someone I barely know.

This is exactly what Vin does. He twists things, until up is down and lies are truth. Until the sweet guy isn't good enough because he didn't throw himself in front of a bullet.

Jake takes my arm as if nothing has changed. For him, maybe nothing has. We enter the ballroom just as the music crescendos with breathtaking drama that resonates through my body.

My gaze is drawn to the center of the room, as Vin obviously intended it to be. The crowd has parted so that only one couple stands together under the gigantic crystal chandelier. It's like a scene from a Disney movie.

Vin's back is to me as he pulls the girl in his arms closer against his body. From the garishly purple color of the dress, I can only assume it's Sophia. He twirls her around so their faces are in profile. When he turns his head toward the doors and sees me standing there, frozen in place, a malicious smile curves his lips. Something drops in the pit of my stomach, as if the ground has disappeared beneath my feet and I'm falling down into darkness.

He bends his head and kisses her.

The entire room lets out the collective breath they've been holding in anticipation. This is the sort of moment that people will still be talking about months from now. Vin Cortland never kisses in public, and he never links himself publicly to a girl.

Their kiss doesn't last long, but it's long enough. Sophia wraps her arms around his neck while I fight off the feeling that I've been punched in the gut. After less than a few seconds, Vin pulls her hands away and uses her wrist as leverage to pull her toward the far doors that lead outside.

I force myself to turn away as they pass within a few feet of where Jake and I stand. The triumphant look on Sophia's face is imprinted on my brain, burned into my eyes even when they close. I tell myself I don't care, that Vin can do whatever he wants as long as he stays the hell away from me.

But I'm honest enough to admit that's a lie.

It doesn't take a genius to figure out they're headed for the pool house where Vin hosts all his legendary parties. I wonder if he is going to finish with her what he started with me. The idea makes me feel dirty and inadequate.

It makes me feel used.

I tell myself I don't care. They're welcome to each other. I hadn't been lying when I told Vin that he wouldn't have a problem finding someone stupid enough to marry him. Sophia will fit in well as another gilded fixture in this cold, dark place.

Better her than me.

Jake squeezes my hand and guides me toward the dance floor after they're gone. His touch is respectful, but demanding. I imagine what his hands might feel like on other parts of my body, but that thought doesn't arouse anything more than mild interest. I know it would be nice, but not earth-shattering.

As much as I like Jake, there isn't any passion here.

Vin makes me burn, with hate and a dozen other things I wish I didn't feel.

But what good is pleasure when it is always accompanied by pain?

NINETEEN

Zaya

Jake doesn't seem to notice that my mind is somewhere else for the rest of the Founder's Ball. We dance and eat finger foods together, I even manage to smile and laugh at appropriate intervals. But my mind is on Vin and what he must be doing with Sophia.

I wonder if she even realizes that he is using her. For all I know, she doesn't care.

Or maybe I'm the one he's been playing this entire time.

What was it he had said? *I chose you because I knew you'd be easy to control.*

Sophia wouldn't know how to play hard to get if you gave her a script with lines to read, so Vin certainly doesn't need me.

I hate that the realization bothers me.

"Ready to go?" Jake smiles at me in the same gentle way he has since that first morning in the hallway at school.

I realize I've missed a good portion of whatever he last said, but nod anyway and return his smile.

He leads me to the door, obviously intending to give me a ride home. I'd gotten a ride here with my brother and a friend of his that managed to get their hands on a car, but Zion is long gone. I don't have any way to get back to the Gulch unless Jake takes me or I try to bum a ride with Amelia's family, if they have any room in their van.

But Jake's question, if I'm ready to leave with him, feels charged with an unspoken invitation.

He drives a gleaming Land Rover Defender that can't be more than a few years old, but shrugs apologetically when I stroke my hands over the plush leather interior and obviously marvel at the bells and whistles. It's probably a hand-me-down, from his mother most likely.

Suburban mom's in luxury SUVs that were originally intended for tours through the African savannah are a common sight on the Bluffs. This is a car for people who apparently need to always be ready for an off-road excursion on their way to the grocery store.

An expensive waste of resources for the self-indulgent.

But Jake is gracious enough to act embarrassed about the ostentatious vehicle. It reminds me of the kind of person who spends all day cleaning and when you arrive gushes *don't mind the mess*. I get the impression that he knows his family's money is something he should pretend not to care too much about.

"I had fun," he offers, taking my hand as he settles into the driver's seat.

I smile and squeeze his hand back, though I'm grateful when he pulls it away to put the SUV into drive. His palm is slightly clammy, sweaty like I make him nervous.

Jake is acting so sweet, and all I want to do is go home, crawl into bed, and stay there for the rest of the weekend. It isn't his fault that my mind has careened off into outer space. But I can't rewind the clock to an hour ago before I let Vin finger me in a dusty bedroom and then watched him saunter off with Sophia like it never happened.

Normally my restricted speech is a burden. But right now I'm grateful for it. If I can't tell Jake the truth, then it saves me from having to lie. He won't ask me any uncomfortable questions when he knows I can't provide the answers.

Because if I did speak, then I'd have to explain to him that this isn't going to work, and I'd rather put off the inevitable. Like a coward, I don't want to let him down when I have to be here for his reaction.

But it isn't because of Vin.

My focus needs to stay on getting out of this town and forging a future for myself as far from this place as I can get. Anyone that might tie me tighter to Deception needs to be abandoned, or ignored. For all of his kindness, Jake is another tether to this town that I don't want. When it's finally time to leave, I don't want anything holding me back.

Halfway down the cliff-side road, I realize he doesn't know where to go. Reaching for his phone, I plug my address into a navigation app and hold it up for him to see.

Jake makes a grateful sound, but barely glances at the screen as he drives toward the Gulch.

I can't decide if I should be flattered or freaked out that he already seems to know where I live.

The Land Rover slides smoothly up to the curb in front of my house, stopping right behind a black pickup truck. A shiny gold Cortland Construction logo is emblazoned on both its sides.

My house looks dark on the inside, so Zion isn't home yet, assuming he plans to come back tonight at all. The workers must have finished for the night by now, which means they left the truck full of supplies for when they return. I'm surprised Vin hasn't already called off whatever work he authorized they get done, but he'll likely get to it in the morning.

After Sophia is done sucking his dick.

I don't care. I don't care. *I don't care.*

Those words have become a mantra I say to myself over and over again in my head, hoping that at some point I'll actually believe it.

My thoughts distract me long enough that Jake has already shut his door by the time I realize I should get out. He leaps up onto curb and comes to my side, pulling the passenger door open before my fumbling fingers can find the handle in the dark. Like the true gentleman he is, Jake helps me out of the car and keeps his steadying hand on my elbow as we mount the steep dirt path leading up to the front door.

"Did a hurricane come through here?" Jake laughs awkwardly as he helps me over a pile of rubble from the excavation work.

I had met him at the ball, instead of having him pick me up, precisely so he wouldn't see any of this.

I can only imagine what he's noticing about our house. The listing foundation that makes the house look a bit like a boat about to capsize. Scrubby grass out front made entirely of barely tamed weeds. The general air of abandonment and neglect.

It makes me feel pathetic.

I unlock the door, relieved that Vin hadn't rekeyed it without bothering to tell me. The level of invasion into my life it requires for him to remodel my house without even consulting me first doesn't surprise me at this point.

That is the saddest thought I've had all night.

Jake does surprise me when he steps into the house after me and closes the door behind him. He catches my expression and gives me a lopsided smile.

"I thought we could hang out a little longer. Spending time with you is nice."

The look I cast him is curious and openly doubtful. You'd

think by this point he would be getting tired of putting up with all my baggage.

"It doesn't bother me that you don't talk," he says, anticipating my thoughts. "The silence is sort of nice, actually. I usually can't get past the awkward conversation stage with a girl, and we get to blow right past that. Although, I don't know where you get the willpower to never say anything to some of the assholes at our school."

I smile weakly because his words are meant to be funny, but the smile is more than a little sad.

"If you did talk to me, I wouldn't tell him." Jake takes a step closer. "Guy doesn't deserve to even look at you, much less treat you the way he does. I don't get why everyone in this town acts like he shits solid gold."

All it would take is for the Cortland's to pack up their money and their businesses for half the town to lose their only source of income. Almost everyone in Deception has worked for a Cortland company at some point, or has a family member that does. They own the only strip mall in the Gulch and the holding company that has majority shares in most of the real estate everywhere else in town. First Bank of Deception, another Cortland family holding, backs pretty much every mortgage.

You can't make a life in this town if you end up on the Cortland's bad side.

Jake will figure that out eventually, it's only a matter of time.

And then he will never speak to me again.

That is the only reason I don't try to make him leave. I want to appreciate the one friend I have at Deception High before this relationship evaporates like everything else good in my life. Even though we spent the last few hours pressed against each other while we danced, standing together in my dark and silent house feels somehow more intimate.

Maybe because there isn't anyone here to interrupt whatever happens between us.

Instead of attempting to answer without words, I hold my fingers to my lips and point to the living room. Even in the near-darkness, Grandpa's hospital bed shines a dull white. The machine feeding him oxygen hisses every few seconds in time with each slumbering breath.

A pang of regret shoots through me as I remember that comfortable setup is only a result of Vin's attempts at bribery. Now that I've rejected him, the expensive hospital bed and day nurse will go back wherever they came from.

But I won't be bought. Not for this or anything else.

Moving past the living room, I take Jake on an impromptu tour of the first floor of our house, pretending to check that the doors and windows are all locked. Even in the Gulch, nobody would bother trying to steal from us. Even with Vin's upgrades, there isn't anything in this house worth the effort.

I hesitate when we get back to the entryway, unsure of precisely what he wants from me.

And even if I were willing to speak, I probably still wouldn't ask him because I'm not sure I want the answer.

Jake leans against the wall next to a floating shelf full of worthless knickknacks: pottery projects Zion and I made in middle school and some pieces of raw quartz we found in the backyard. Unlike the entryway of Cortland Manor, there are no pictures of Milbourne ancestors hanging on the walls. Anything of value got sold off generations ago, and we'd lost possession of anything sentimental that wouldn't be refused by the pawn shop. There used to be a few pictures of Zion and I with our mother, but Grandpa had us take them down after she left because the reminder made him angry.

She didn't just leave her children without so much as a goodbye, but her father too.

Just like me, she stayed in Deception until she couldn't take it anymore and had to run away. I'll probably never know why she didn't take us with her.

A few years back, I'd tried searching for her online. I used to think the only way she wouldn't come back is if she couldn't. She obviously never left a forwarding address, but Google searches for her name always came up empty. I checked the obituaries of neighboring counties and ran a database search for death certificates, but nothing ever came of it.

If my mother is still alive, she has no interest in being found.

I shouldn't miss her, not after the mess she left for me to clean up, but I still do.

Even when I've lost all respect for her.

Perhaps sensing my unease, Jake doesn't try to go upstairs. But he does shift closer, eating up the small amount of personal space separating us.

"You look really pretty tonight. Your hair looks great." He pushes a gentle hand into my hair, fingers teasing at the painstakingly straightened strands. Without my hours of effort, his fingers would have caught in my curls. "I'm glad you decided to come with me to the Founder's Ball. I had fun, even with all that shit from Cortland. He really knows how to ruin a good time."

When he lowers his head to kiss me, all I want to do is push him away. The churn of emotion at the pit of my belly feels like physical sickness. I turn my head so his lips brush across my cheek, and even that small touch leaves me feeling cold.

"What's wrong?" he asks, realizing my hands on his shoulders are forceful enough to keep some space between us. "Are you okay?"

If I could explain it to him, I would.

It isn't an unwillingness to speak that makes that impossible, there just aren't words to accurately describe the turmoil of my thoughts. But instead I just shake my head and gesture at the door.

"You want me to leave?" He sounds incredulous.

I try to smile in apology, even as I nod and gesture again toward the door. I have no idea what I'm apologizing for, but he doesn't even notice.

His eyes have narrowed. "Seriously?"

Grandpa coughs in his sleep, and the oxygen tank hooked up to him to makes a sort of wheezing sound that echoes off the walls. Jake seems to remember where he is. He backs up a step, but glares down at me.

"Is this because of fucking Cortland? I knew there was something weird going on between the two of you."

I shake my head in sharp negation. I'm not lying to him, but I haven't determined yet if I'm lying to myself. Like always, Vin manages to sneak into moments that shouldn't have anything to do with him. But this is about me and Jake, about how continuing to lead him on would be cruel when there isn't anywhere for the two of us to go together.

"You know what, screw this. I don't know why I'm bothering. You're just a fucking tease."

With an angry curse, Jake pushes past me.

I don't watch him leave.

The door slams hard enough that I wince. If it hadn't just been repaired, that would have been enough to break it.

I stay standing there for another few minutes, just staring at nothing in the darkness, trying to decide if I've made a terrible mistake by letting him walk away.

A tease is someone who acts like it's a yes, but then still says no.

And I don't say anything at all.

But that's boys for you. They worry so much about whether or not a girl will say no, when all girls can think about is whether or not they'll listen when we do.

The screech of tires peeling out on the street feels like a nice counterpoint to the night. Jake won't be back, not now that I've ripped away the last few shreds of pride he managed to hang onto.

His reaction is what I deserve.

I check on Grandpa one last time, watching the steady rise and fall of his chest as he breathes more easily than he has in years. I wonder how much all of this equipment costs, if paying for it myself would even be within the realm of possibility.

My new phone is lit up on the desk upstairs. The dress I'm wearing obviously doesn't have pockets, and I'm so unused to carrying a phone that it didn't occur to take it with me to the Founder's Ball. Amelia and Zion are the only people who have the number, aside from Vin of course. But the screen is full of dozens of notifications for missed calls.

Most of the calls are from a blocked number, and there aren't any voicemails because I haven't bothered to set the voicemail up yet. The most recent call is from a number I recognize because I've dialed it many times before when Zion needed to check in with his probation officer. He would only do it if I picked up the phone, dialed the number, and shoved it into his face right before the other end picked up.

This is the number for the Deception Police Department, which can only mean one thing.

My brother has been arrested.

TWENTY

VIN

SOPHIA IS WAITING IN MY DRIVEWAY WHEN I LEAVE FOR school Monday morning. She leans against the door of my Maserati like I haven't broken other people's jaws for doing the same damn thing.

"What do you want?" I ask as I stride up, not bothering to look at her.

"Last night you said we could ride to school together." The simpering look on her face tells me she's lying through her teeth. I'm never drunk enough to black out, and I have no memory of saying anything that even sounds like riding together.

"I got a bunch of crap in the front seat. Sorry, no room."

"Please. I can't afford to be late again. I have Ms. D'onofrio first period, and she'll give me detention."

I shrug. "Not my problem."

"How am I supposed to get to school?"

She lives less than two blocks away and has her own car. Riding with me is a power move, not a necessity.

"I'm sure you'll figure it out."

Never one to take a hint, Sophia chases after me. Her too high heels clack against the pavement. "After last night, I just thought it would be nice to spend some more time together."

I regretted that kiss pretty much the moment I laid it on her. Her mouth tasted like lipstick wax and left me looking like I snarfed a glass of red Kool-aid.

I don't exactly feel bad for using her, because Sophia spends pretty much every moment of her day begging to be used. But the girl is like a venereal disease, one mistake and she never completely goes away.

When I climb in the driver's seat and close the door, she leans through the open window. If I drive off now, the car will take off her head.

"What?"

"Did you hear what happened in the Gulch last night?"

The engine starts with a satisfying rumble, and I give her a look that says she is moments from getting her feet run over. "Like I give a fuck."

She raises a micro-bladed eyebrow. "Even if it involves Zaya Milbourne?"

My fingers drum against the steering wheel. Little bitch knows she has me interested. "What happened? Something bad, I hope."

Platforms tapping against the pavement, Sophia tottles around to the passenger door. "I'll tell you all about it on the way to school."

I unlock the doors, not bothering to clear off the pile of workout clothes and other crap covering the seat so she is forced to do it herself. Once she has the door closed, I peel out of the driveway without waiting for her to get settled or buckle her seatbelt.

Sophia lowers the visor and checks her makeup in the

mirror then fluffs her hair. When she pulls a tube of lip gloss out of her bag, I lose my patience.

"Spit it out."

She purses her lips at her own reflection. "Do you think this cherry color works with my outfit? Maybe I should put on something with more pink in it."

"I honestly do not give even one individual shit. You have exactly five seconds before I get annoyed."

"God, you can be so mean." But she says that like it's a funny joke, gently slapping my arm. "Patience is a virtue, Vin."

I hate girls who hit. Let me raise my hands to them and see if they call it flirting. "If you want mean, I can shove you out at the next stoplight. Bet it would be fun to walk the rest of the way in those heels."

Sophia laughs, as if I'm not deadly serious. "You can be so silly sometimes."

It's almost refreshing how much she'll put up with to get close to me. I have no illusions she wants me for anything more than the power and position she thinks being attached to a Cortland will bring her. But the fact that she puts every ounce of pride she has aside in the pursuit always surprises me a little.

If only Zaya were this transparent. That would make my life a hell of a lot easier.

"Tell me what happened in the Gulch."

"I knew that would get your attention." She snaps the visor shut. "Someday, you're going to have to explain to me why you like messing with Zaya Milbourne so much."

My fingers tighten on the steering wheel. "Except, I don't."

A calculating look enters her gaze. "If you won't be sweet to me, then I won't tell you anything."

Sophia will see how easy it is to talk when I have both hands wrapped around her throat. I decide to change tactics, because she responds to threats by getting pouty. Flattery will get you everywhere with her.

"You looked gorgeous at the Founder's Ball, by the way. Was that a new dress?" I ask through grinding teeth.

"Oh my God, you noticed! It was an Alaïa that I got at the Neiman's in Newport Beach. I had to buy three different dresses because you were being so ridiculous and wouldn't just tell me what color you'd be wearing so we could match."

Sophia playfully slaps my arm again, and I resist the urge to grab her wrist and snap it in half.

"Well, you looked great." I wait for the insincere compliment to widen her smile. Her general air of smugness is something I hate at the best of times, but sometimes you just do what you have to do. "Now tell me what happened in the Gulch."

Taking a deep breath, like a performer about to reveal their greatest trick, Sophia leans closer. "I heard that like at least a dozen of the Gulch's usual suspects got scooped up by the task-force. The cops got them all on RICO charges."

I glance at her, confused. "On what?"

"RICO." At my still blank look, she just shakes her head. "They use it to take down big mafia guys and drug kingpins. If someone is part of a criminal organization, like a gang, then you can charge everyone with the same thing even if they weren't directly involved. One guy gets caught selling drugs, and everyone can go down."

I forget that her father is the Chief of Police. The dinner table small talk at their house probably gets real interesting. Maybe it's because Sophia doesn't seem like a real person to me, I find it difficult to remember that she is slightly more than the girl who will give me a blowjob whenever convenient. But let's be honest, she acts like that's all she wants to be.

But I don't actually care about any of this true crime shit.

"What does that have to do with Zaya?"

"Well, her brother is a little budding hoodlum, right? From what I heard, he got picked up with a bunch of other people. I have no idea what he actually did, but right now he is facing the same charges. Serious ones."

"Zion got arrested?"

"That's what I just said." She pops a piece of gum into her mouth. "It was bound to happen eventually. Trash is as trash does."

It doesn't sit quite right with me that she calls him that, although I'm not sure why I care. If Zion is trash, then by extension the rest of his family is, too. Trash is one of the nicer words people use when talking about the poor souls dying slow deaths in the Gulch. Usually it doesn't bother me, but for some reason today is different.

"Not everyone gets to be born with a silver spoon shoved up their ass."

Her laugh is derisive. "You're one to talk. Vin Cortland has never wanted for anything a single day in his life. It's one of your best qualities."

The whole Cortland empire is about to go up in flames. Perversely, I want to tell her that I'm a year from being broke just to see how she might react. She would probably dive out of the car while it was still moving to get away as fast as possible.

"So your dad says Zion is pretty screwed?" I ask instead.

"Not in so many words, I guess." She has her phone out and starts texting, her interest in this topic already waning. "But unless the Milbournes have a fairy godmother I don't know about, I'd say yes."

Someone with a functional soul would feel sympathy for the guy rotting in a jail cell and his desperate family, but all I can think about is how to take advantage of the situation. I'm not the one who put him there, but ignoring this would be colossally stupid. Her family is the only leverage that has ever worked on Zaya, and I'm not about to kick a gift horse in the teeth.

I might not be a fairy godmother, but Zaya is about to find out I'm the only one who can wave a magic wand over the steaming shitpile of her life.

TWENTY-ONE

Stress makes me oversleep, and I miss the school bus. Even with the three city bus transfers it takes to get to school, I make it right before the tardy bell rings.

Just in time to see Vin's shiny red Maserati peel into the parking lot with a giggling Sophia in the passenger seat.

It's pathetic that he thinks seeing her with him will make me jealous.

And even more pathetic that I feel a little bit jealous, even if I'd never admit it.

I don't want Vin Cortland.

If I say it enough times, that just might make it true.

But right now, I really need to talk to him. I refuse to believe that my brother's arrest is just some perfectly-timed coincidence. Vin must have something to do with it. He is going to fix this before I set him on fire.

Talking to him or anyone else while at school is strictly against the rules. That isn't what stops me. When Sophia gets out of the car, long legs wide open despite the fact that her skirt barely covers her upper thighs, she runs around the car to wrap her arms around Vin's waist.

I want to punch them both in the throat.

Turning away, I don't bother to wait and see if he returns the embrace or pushes Sophia away. Apparently, the guy who is known for never engaging in public displays of affection has conveniently decided to change his ways. Outside of the infamous parties he throws at his pool house, Vin Cortland doesn't do hugs and kisses. And even that is just him getting blowjobs from random girls while his friends play video games and drink.

But I don't care about any of that.

No, it isn't jealousy that makes me turn away, but the fact that I need to wait until Vin is alone. Sophia doesn't have any place in my business. She gossips like she gets paid for it and is perpetually short on cash.

I slam open the double doors, and the sound is loud enough to echo off the concrete walls. A handful of students milling in the hallway look to see who is making all the commotion. But when they realize it's me, all of them immediately turn away.

The forced isolation doesn't usually get to me, because I'm so used to it. But today, the cone of silence is just one more shitty thing I can lay at Vin's doorstep. He has spent the last four years doing his best to ruin my life, and so far he has been an unparalleled success.

By lunchtime, my anger has built into a raging inferno that won't be eased by anything less dramatic than seeing Vin's head mounted on a spike.

I want to rip his face off with my bare hands and dance in the blood spray.

He isn't hard to find.

Lunch finds him sitting at his usual table with his band of cronies and Sophia hugged up to his side. At this point, I don't even care that we practically have the entire school as witnesses.

Marching up to the table, I slam a sheet of paper down in front of him. The message on it is written in block letters with a permanent marker.

WE NEED TO TALK!

There are murmurs from students sitting at nearby tables, but hushed because nobody wants to miss whatever is coming next. I've just thrown a proverbial gauntlet at Vin's forehead, and he is not the type to lose face by turning down a challenge.

He glances down at the paper and then back up at me. "Can't you see I'm eating?"

Someone laughs as I glare down at him, but I ignore it. If he expects me to be the old familiar Zaya who weakly submits, then he has another thing coming.

If getting my brother arrested doesn't violate our fucking deal, then I don't know what does.

I snatch the lunch bag that rests on the table in front of him. Ignoring the gasps of shock from the peanut gallery, I march to the nearest trash can and slam it inside.

Returning to the table, I tap the note with my finger before crossing my arms over my chest and glaring down into his face.

Your move, asshole.

If the loss of his lunch bothers him, Vin doesn't show it. With a smirk, he shoves the paper away so it skitters across the table towards me and hits the floor. "Leave a message for my secretary. She'll pencil you in sometime next month."

Silently, I shove between Iain and Elliot, who surprise me by moving over to make room. Once seated, I lean forward so my elbows rest on the table and I tap the part of my wrist where a watch would be if I could afford one.

I hope the message is clear: *I'll wait.*

Whatever game Vin wants to play obviously involves pretending I'm not sitting directly across from him.

"Anybody catch the game last night? I swear the Dodgers are doing this on purpose just to hurt me."

Elliot takes a bite of his apple. "Don't forget you owe me fifty bucks. A bet is a bet, even if the game is fixed."

They fall into some indecipherable conversation about baseball that I don't even try to follow. But even as he shoots the shit with his friends, Vin doesn't take his gaze off my face.

One of us is waiting for the other to break.

Like always, Sophia can't keep her stupid mouth shut. "Since when do we let any old trash sit with us at lunch?"

My hands curl into fists on the table as the anger that has been simmering all day finally boils over. It isn't enough that I live in the gutter while she enjoys entirely unearned luxury, but she has to rub salt in my wounds every chance she gets.

Iain doesn't look up from the game system in his lap. "You're here."

If Sophia understands that was a dig, she doesn't show it. Instead, she leans across the table towards me. Vin's attention must have her emboldened enough that she speaks directly to me this time. "All the other hood rats are over there."

It doesn't even matter that she wouldn't know a hood rat if one stabbed her in the face. Or that most people in the Gulch are honest, hard-working, and just trying to keep food on their tables.

I've had exactly enough of her mouth.

Launching myself up, I nearly fly around the table. Sophia's blond curls are in my hands and I slam her on the ground before anyone can stop me. Like a pussy, she goes for my face with fingers that are bent like claws. I duck my head and bring my fist up hard into her chin, feeling a satisfying crunch even as pain explodes in my knuckles.

Her nails scratch at my face. I bat them away with one hand while the other punches her again, this time in the nose that everyone knows she had done the summer before freshman year.

There is a satisfying spray of blood as her nose bursts like a ripe tomato.

Sophia screeches like a wounded cat, and then someone is pulling me off her. I don't need to look to know it's Vin —no one else would dare put their hands on me just to break up a fight.

I kick out behind me in the hopes he'll let me go, hitting something soft. He grunts in pain, but doesn't release me. He has me completely off my feet with one hand wrapped around my waist and the other keeping my pinwheeling arms at bay.

Vin drags me out of the cafeteria to the sound of Sophia screaming that I'm going to be sorry if her face doesn't heal right.

Like that bitch needs another excuse to hit up a plastic surgeon.

Metal doors crash open, and then we're outside the school building. He doesn't put me down until we've crossed the parking lot and stop beside his Maserati.

"Get in," he snaps.

I spit at him. "Fuck you."

"Your mood is a bit violent for my tastes. Maybe later."

Opening the driver's side door, he forces me inside and easily dodges when I try to kick him in the crotch. I'm not playing games here — if I get half the chance, then I just might try to actually kill him. The gear shift pokes painfully into my hip as I tumble backward across the seats. Vin keeps shoving only until he has enough room to climb in behind me.

By the time I make it to the other side and reach for the passenger door, the car is already screeching backward out of the parking space.

"What are you doing?" I screech, reaching for the seatbelt as he takes the turn out of the school parking lot at breakneck speed.

"You wanted to talk, so talk."

"Here?"

"I figured you won't try to kill me if we're doing eighty down the highway, unless you're hoping to die with me."

Until today, I wouldn't have considered myself a particularly violent person. But beating the absolute shit out of him sounds like heaven right now. "God forbid, you just talk to me when I asked you, like a normal person. I'm sure Sophia is already sobbing in Principal Schneider's office. Thanks for getting me suspended."

He has the nerve to laugh. "If it comes to that, then you got yourself suspended. Nobody told you to give her a lesson in proper form for a basic uppercut. You'll have to tell me where you learned that someday."

The Gulch isn't exactly a safe place for a girl who spends all of her time alone. You learn what you need to learn.

"I'm not telling you shit."

"Except the reason you were stomping around the cafeteria like Godzilla and threw my lunch away. An explanation would be welcome anytime now, by the way."

That move in the cafeteria was supposed to make him angry, but he seems more amused than anything. Changing moods more frequently than underwear is just another way he likes to mess with me so I never know what to expect.

But the fight has drained me, and I suddenly don't have the energy to go back and forth with him.

"Did you have my brother arrested?"

He raises an eyebrow. "Why would I do that?"

"To blackmail me into marrying you," I snap, glaring at his profile. Even when I'm furious, it's hard not to notice that he looks like a Greek statue. "Because you're the kind of asshole who doesn't feel guilty about fucking with people's lives, and you know my brother is one of the few ways you can get to me."

"I'm flattered that you think I have that much control over police resources." Vin glances at me, his smile mocking. "Of course, if I did have something to do with it, coming at me like that might not be the best way to ask for help."

I glare at his profile, starkly illuminated by the midday sun. He looks like a fallen angel, come down to earth to wreak havoc on susceptible mortals.

"That isn't a *no*."

"Would you believe me if I said no?"

"Maybe."

"That isn't a yes."

I just shake my head, because I don't ever believe a single word that comes out of his mouth. "Are you going to help me get him out of trouble?"

"Is this the part where I ask what's in it for me?"

"Stop playing with me." My hand slams down on the dashboard, and I ignore the aching stab of pain in my palm. "Everything isn't a game."

"Oh, it is a game." He turns in the seat to look at me, ignoring the road as he stares me down. "And both of us are going to play. It's your move, by the way."

I look nervously out the windshield at the empty road ahead of us as he continues to watch me. "Will you help me?"

"Will you marry me?"

A romantic proposal if I ever heard one.

"You seemed pretty happy with Sophia." The words don't sound jealous in my head. But judging from the smirk on his face, they come out more strident than I intended. "Not that I care what you do with your dirty dick."

Vin opens his mouth to say something, probably along the lines of reminding me what I've let him do with the dick in question, but he shuts it again. He seems to consider his words for the barest moment.

"I wouldn't marry Sophia if she were the last woman on earth."

I know there are any number things he isn't telling me, but that at least sounds like the truth. "But you want to marry me?"

"Out of the currently available options, sure." He hesitates, but then shrugs. "But this is Deception, so that isn't really saying much."

"How romantic."

"This isn't about romance. It's a business transaction."

A pang of hurt accompanies his words, even though it shouldn't. I know who he is. "If this is all about business, then you shouldn't have any problem negotiating."

His smile of dark anticipation makes my knees go weak.

"Give me your terms."

"You get my brother out of jail, or at least get his charges knocked down to something that will have him out well before he dies of old age."

"Is that it?"

I force a deep inhalation of air into my lungs, preparing myself. "And if this is a business arrangement, which I agree is the only way it makes sense, then sex has to be off the table."

I expect him to fight me, but instead he just smiles. I feel reassured for about a millisecond.

"No."

I jerk back like I've been slapped. "What do you mean *no*?"

"I mean that your terms are unacceptable, but I'm open to making a counter offer." He navigates the car onto the exit for the coastal highway, and the ocean looms big and bright ahead of us. "I will do whatever I can to help your brother. But sex is definitely on the table. And in the car, the pool house, my parent's bed, even in the school cafeteria if the mood strikes us."

"That's disgusting," I scoff.

"Is it? I bet if I stuck my hands down your pants right now, you'd be wet and ready for me."

I clamp my hands together in my lap to stop them from trembling. "You don't get to talk to me like this."

"I'm Vin Cortland, sweetheart. I can do whatever I want."

My lips thin as I glare at his profile. "Then maybe you should just take me back to school, and we can forget all about it."

"Take a joke, Milbourne." He signals to exit for the beach, and the car slows down as we end up on one of the meandering roads that wind toward the ocean. "We are negotiating, after all. But if I give something up, then I'm going to want something else in return. What are you willing to trade if I kill the dirty talk?"

"No sex until after the wedding, then." I insist on it, not because it matters, but so I can feel like I still have some control over this situation that is quickly flying off the rails. There is a very thin line between a whore and trophy wife, but I'd still like to stay on the right side of it.

His smile is brief. "Done."

I wonder if I've fallen into Wonderland, because everything has suddenly turned upside down. This is not the conversation I wanted to have with him, and I hate that he managed to turn it into this. I'd been so angry with him, ready to tear him into pieces, and now we're talking about sex.

"I don't want to talk about this anymore."

"Unfortunately, that's not how a negotiation works. If you want some time to come up with a list, then you should say so."

His hands glide over the steering wheel with the same strokes he would use to explore the contours of a woman's body. From the heated look he casts me, the association is deliberate. "But just so you know, I'm already willing to offer you quite a bit. I even ate you out at the Founder's Ball. I never do that."

I want to ask him how he got so good at it without any practice, but manage to bite my tongue before the words spill out. This is surreal and not what I planned, but it also might be the most civil conversation we've had in years. I could almost pretend that the fragile friendship we used to have is still intact. If an uncomfortable sex talk gets Zion the help he needs, then I'm willing to put up with it.

And there isn't any other reason to engage with Vin worth mentioning.

"Then you stopped before I came," I scoffed. "Teasing is worse than nothing at all."

"Is that what has you so upset? I guess Sophia's face is as good an outlet for your sexual frustration as anything else."

"It's not sexual frustration, you dick. My fingers work just fine."

I freeze, unable to believe I just said that out loud.

Too late to snatch it back, because Vin already heard every word. His head slowly turns to face me, gaze intent on my face. I shift to glare out the window before he can see my blush.

"Is that so?" His voice turns low and seductive. "Did you think about me while you were bringing yourself off, wishing it was my tongue between your legs and not your own fingers?"

I shake my head, still refusing to look at him. "Just forget I said anything."

"Not a fucking chance." He grips the gear shift hard, watching me as his fingers stroke the leather.

I stare down at his hand, trying to forget how much better those strong fingers felt inside me than my own. "Don't get so excited. It won't be happening again – I've learned my lesson about expecting anything from you aside from disappointment."

"You couldn't be more wrong if you tried. Just like everything else about you, that hot little body belongs to me. Whether you're ready to admit it or not."

A burst of heat hits my belly. "Stop doing that."

"What?"

"Pretending like there is something more here than what there is."

His quizzical gaze passes over me before his attention returns to the road. "You must know that you're gorgeous. Sophia wouldn't hate you nearly so much if you weren't."

I hate him for saying that, because I refuse to believe this isn't just another manipulation. He doesn't actually mean the pretty words. Empty compliments in the hopes of getting what he wants.

And I'm weak enough that it might be working, at least a tiny bit. But if I allow him to burrow further into my life, then it won't be possible to get him out again. He will have the power to consume me. And when he finally grows bored and moves on, I won't be able to rebuild what he will have inevitably broken.

"You need to find another girl you can marry to save your inheritance. This isn't going to work."

"Are we back to negotiation? Tell me what would make it work for you."

"Anything short of you becoming a totally different person won't be enough. Please, just take me back to school."

"What kind of person?"

I turn to stare at his profile, midday sun setting his features aglow. "What?"

"You said I'd have to be a totally different person for this to work," he replied patiently. "I'm asking you to expand on that statement. This will probably be your only chance to say exactly what you think of me to my face with impunity. If I were you, I'd take advantage of the opportunity."

Vin's voice is mild, but I hear the warning there. Even though his features are relaxed, tension simmers just under the surface.

I take a deep breath. "How about the kind of person who wouldn't have his friends hold me down while he cuts me up?"

Whatever reaction I expected to that, it isn't the one I get. He just shrugs. "I have my reasons for that, but okay."

My hands ball into fists, and I resist the urge to wrench the wheel toward the guardrail. "What reasons could there possibly be?"

"I'll tell you if you want, but I don't think you'll like it."

I'm not sure what to say to that.

He drives slowly down the beach road and then parks the car in the nearly empty parking lot attached to the access boardwalk. This isn't a good spot for surfers and it's a school day, so the beach is probably deserted. Aside from any homeless people that might wander by, we are completely alone here.

The thought should scare me more than it does.

Screwing up my nerve after a minute of agonizing silence, I finally insist. "Tell me."

Instead of answering, he gets out of the car and goes around to sit on the hood. With a weary sigh, I shove open my door and follow him. Sand crunches under the thin soles of my sneakers as I deeply inhale air so salty it stings my nostrils.

When I come around the front of the car, he already has his vape pen in his hand.

"Well?"

He takes a pull and exhales a cloud of wispy vapor. "I cut you when you fuck up so you don't do it to yourself."

"What—"

I stop myself short. He can't possibly know I started cutting myself after my mother left, that I did it for years. Usually when I screwed something up or felt too much like the mistake my parents didn't want, but I stopped a few years ago.

After the first time he laid a blade against my skin.

"I read somewhere that people who cut use it as a coping mechanism, like a release valve. You weren't very good at hiding the scars. And they were always low on your arms, places where slicing too deep could mean the end. I would have told you to stop that shit if I thought you'd listen. Instead, I found another way." His smile is humorless as he takes another pull from the vape. "Just like everything else, if I do it, then it takes all the fun away."

This is why talking to him is a bad idea. Vin knows how to twist things, confuse me until I'm not sure if I remember parts of my own history correctly.

I hate it.

I hate him, even when I feel other things just as strongly.

"The kind of person I'm talking about wouldn't do that." If I don't steel myself against him, then I'll drown in the ocean of his personality. "It doesn't matter what the reason is."

"You know what also does damage. Nicotine. I read somewhere that one of these cartridges is the same as two packs of cigarettes. No matter how good it tastes, really makes me wonder what this shit does to your lungs." He takes another pull from his vape pen. "Let's call it an eye for an eye."

Does he smoke at times aside from when he is hurting me or being obviously self-destructive? I can't remember well enough to say.

A pang hits my chest that I try to ignore. I don't want to weaken where Vin Cortland is concerned.

But it almost sounds like he thinks he hurts me to save me from hurting myself even worse, and then punishes himself for doing it.

There is a twisted sort of caring in that, even though it's absolutely ridiculous.

And might even be another lie.

"You've never been nice to me, not even before we were enemies." At this point, I'm reminding both of us. I can't fall under the spell he is trying to cast. "You can't expect me to think that will change."

"You can't tell me what you want and then not even give me the chance to give it to you. Want to walk down the halls of the school holding my hand while chattering to everyone who crosses your path. Fuck it. Fine."

A tingling sensation starts up on the back of my neck. "And you'll do whatever it takes to help Zion?"

He gives a heavy sigh as if the subject has grown tiresome and collapses back against the windshield. "I already said I would."

I can't fight the impulse to say something about the bitchy elephant in the proverbial room. "I saw you kiss Sophia."

He glowers at the bright horizon. "Would have been hard to miss."

"Did you do more with her than kiss that night?"

"Why do you care?" His gaze sweeps over me as he asks. "You made it clear you weren't interested."

"And you put on that little display for my benefit, right? I want to know how far you took it, how much you're willing to use people when it suits you." I don't want to say out loud that I'm also asking because of jealousy, but that feeling is there. At least I can admit it to myself. "The kind of person who would treat a girl like that, even Sophia, isn't someone I can marry."

Vin settles back with his eyes closed, as if trying to say this conversation is boring him to sleep. "Nothing else happened, okay. I took her home right after we left. I just wanted you to think it was something more. Happy?"

He doesn't look at me, which makes it impossible to tell if he's lying.

"I guess."

"Anything else?" he asks, voice sardonic.

But I just shake my head. All of the anger has completely drained away at this point, leaving me resigned. "All I have to do is stay married to you for a year, and then we go our separate ways?"

He glares at the distant horizon. "That's it."

"Fine," I grouse, already regretting it.

Abruptly, Vin jumps to his feet. "Let's go."

He hustles me back into the car as if a fire has suddenly been lit under him. I don't understand the sudden rush as he guns the engine and pulls out of the parking lot.

"Where are we going?"

He looks at me like I'm an idiot. "To the D.A.'s office. Your brother isn't getting out of jail until someone talks to him."

TWENTY-TWO

VIN

A YEAR ISN'T THAT MUCH TO ASK.

I'll bring up the pregnancy requirement eventually. After I got her to agree to the marriage, Zaya seemed so on edge that broaching the topic now might destroy our fragile deal before we can even ink out a contract.

Eventually I can figure out the best way to tell her, when the time is right.

I'm not a complete monster, I'll make sure that she has everything she needs. She might enjoy playing Mrs. Cortland, assuming she quits the moping enough to enjoy anything. Aside from when I'm just trying to torture her, she has always managed to enjoy our time in the dark together.

We sit silently in the car as I drive to my uncle's office for the second time in as many days. I glance at her a few times, looking away before she catches me, if just to convince myself she's still there. Her body language is as tense as ever, but her gaze flits over my profile every few seconds when she thinks I'm not paying attention. Her impressive resolve is weakening, whether she wants to it admit to herself or not.

She said yes.

And she'll keep saying it until I have what I need.

I can't fight the triumph that surges through me at the thought. My inheritance is in reach with only a few hurdles left. Zaya has already promised me a year, and eventually I'll figure out how to broach the subject of having my kid.

I've already convinced her of this much, what's this one last thing?

It's not like I'd expect her to raise it, that's what nannies are for. I saw more of my nanny than I ever did my father or Giselle, and I turned out just fine.

Maybe I could even convince her to give it more than a year.

I force away the rogue thought as my fingers tighten on the steering wheel. That is the craziness talking, the impulse I seem to have for destroying things that were working just fine before. This isn't about love or any other fluffy emotions. Love is a weakness that opens your heart up to being ripped apart.

Zaya Milbourne betrayed me once, I'm not going to give her a chance to do it again.

I want to own her, possess every part of her, and I want everyone in Deception to see me do it. Then I'll toss her away when it's all over and done with.

Securing my inheritance is the glorious icing on the cake.

But it isn't about love.

"Are you okay?" she asks.

I force myself to look at her, finding her staring at me. "Fine."

The district attorney's office is busy because it's a Monday morning. That doesn't stop me from breezing past the reception desk like I always do.

"You can't just go back there," the secretary calls as she half-stands, but I hear the resigned note in her voice.

Because she knows as well as I do that yes, I can.

But Zaya hesitates, falling back by a few steps as she looks nervously around the crowded office. I grab her wrist and pull her after me, loving the little squeak of surprise she makes.

"You'll be a Cortland, too," I murmur just loud enough for her to hear. "Get used to the fact that normal rules no longer apply."

She makes a disgusted sound, but follows behind me as we push through the glass doors that lead to the offices. I can't help but notice she doesn't pull her hand away.

West is on the phone when we burst in. There isn't any surprise on his face, just resignation, as he waves at me to shut the door. He usually has the male equivalent of a resting bitch face, so it's an angry expression that passes over us as we step into the room. I have to drag Zaya over to the desk and push her down into the seat because she is so obviously intimidated.

People think that West only got his position through nepotism until they come face to face with him in a courtroom. The man is like a pit bull who grabs ahold of things and refuses to let go. I hope his mood is amenable today, but it's impossible to know for sure until he opens his mouth.

Zaya sits gingerly, tucking her hands underneath her thighs as if she worries we'll see them shaking. She shouldn't bother, West is amazingly perceptive when it comes to people. I've always been able to read her like a book, so he'll know her every secret at a glance.

West barks something into the phone that I can't translate because it's in advanced legalese, before slamming the down the receiver and turning to us. "The next time you bust in here like this, I'm having you arrested for trespassing."

I doubt the threat is a serious one, but who can ever really be sure? Slouching down in the chair like everything bores me,

I cross my arms over my chest. "That's no way to treat family, dear uncle. I always thought you enjoyed our time together."

"Smart ass." His narrow-eyed gaze swings away from me and settles on Zaya. "We haven't officially met, but I assume you're Zaya Milbourne."

She nods, eyes wide.

"So, you must be here about your brother."

Instead of answering, she hesitates and looks at me. It's interactions like this that make people see weakness and think they can just roll over her. But Zaya isn't afraid, she just won't commit to any course of action until she has thought through every angle. For now, that means letting me take the lead.

I've seen the core of steel inside of her every time I try to get her to do something she truly doesn't want to do.

"She saw the police report," I tell him. "It looks worse than it should. Zion isn't some cartel boss."

With an annoyed sigh, West reaches for the stack of files on his desk. "And you thought it made sense to come see the attorney prosecuting the case instead of maybe, I don't know, hiring him his own lawyer?"

Zaya has gone tense beside me, her eyes narrowing. I gently tap her knee, a reminder that this is under control. "

He can't even make bail. The public defender's office is a joke. C'mon Uncle West, this is ridiculous."

"I shouldn't be talking to you about this at all, especially without a defense attorney present," West points out, voice caustic. "You're lucky I like you, nephew. Anyone else would have been tossed out on their ass."

"We're already here. Spill."

"These are serious charges." West skims a few pages before shaking his head. "A group of young men were picked up on suspicion of committing a serious assault and robbery. Apparently, some or all of them held up a convenience store in the

Gulch, and the cashier was injured." He glances at Zaya before looking away. "Your brother runs with a very dangerous crowd."

"And that makes him guilty?"

My uncle glares at me, and I have a stab of sympathy for anyone who comes face to face with him in a courtroom. He returns his attention to Zaya. "My advice would be to hire the best defense attorney you can afford. This case will be going to trial, there really isn't any other option."

Zaya visibly deflates. I hate the stricken look on her face. It makes me want to do things that I never do, like protect people even when there isn't anything in it for me.

I lean forward. "But there isn't any evidence that Zion was actually there when the crime was committed."

West snaps the file shut. "I won't comment on an active investigation. All the men involved are in custody."

"Zion isn't a man." Zaya's voice is a touch louder than it should be, as if she is out of practice with modulating it. She winces slightly, but then squares her shoulders. When she continues, her voice is a little softer. "He's still underage."

Eyebrows raised, West glances down at the file. "So he is. The only one, in fact."

"That has to count for something," I reason. "Couldn't you at least get the case moved to juvenile court?"

West drums his fingers on the desk as he stares us down. "First of all, Zion requires an actual lawyer to represent him before he can get any sort of deal. Another teenager with a God complex doesn't count as effective counsel, just because he happens to be my nephew. Nothing is official unless you use the proper channels." His gaze moves from one of us to the other, drilling in so we know how serious this is. "That said, there is a diversion program upstate that is intended for juvenile offenders of serious crimes whom the state thinks are potentially good candidates for rehabilitation. It's new, still in the pilot stage, and like everything else in this world worth a damn, admission to the facility is pay to play."

My ears perk up at that, buying our way out of things is a Cortland family tradition. "You should have just said this is a money problem in the first place."

"Everything is a money problem," West says, voice droll. "But we're not talking about getting off scot-free, here, not with these charges. Juvenile offenders can be held in the system until they're twenty-three, so we're still talking about a significant amount of time, just better than twenty years to life."

Zaya's face is carefully blank. "Tell me more about this program."

"Blackbreak Academy is set up as much like a private school as it is a juvenile prison. Everyone there would otherwise be in the state prison system, but we hope this setup will encourage a lower rate of recidivism. If the participants complete the program successfully, then their records are expunged. It was only approved by the governor because most of their families are paying dearly for the privilege of keeping their children out of the regular system. Apparently, this fits the definition of a public-private partnership according to our state legislature."

West isn't exactly a bleeding heart, but it's obvious from his tone that he recognizes the fundamental unfairness of this particular opportunity.

From her pursed lips and sour expression, I can tell Zaya isn't happy with the idea of a system of justice based on the depths of your pockets, either. But this is the way the world has always worked, she just needs to get used to it.

"Sounds great—" I say.

She interrupts. "And Zion won't have to do anything?"

West shrugs. "If he's willing to testify against the other

members of his gang, that would help me convince the judge to allow diversion. This will be a hard sell, otherwise."

That doesn't sound like a deal breaker, but Zaya stiffens beside me. Then she shakes her head so violently it sets the tightly wound curls on her head quivering. "He won't do that."

I turn to her in shock. "Why not?"

"He won't testify against anyone, no matter what kind of deal it gets him. That just... isn't how things are done in the Gulch. He testifies, and he can't ever come back home."

"And that's worse than twenty-to-life?"

"The rules are different where I live, Vin. Most of us don't have the luxury of our big house on the mountaintop." Zaya's glare is hot enough to sear my soul. Her reaction is as much about Zion as it is about the two of us. "We don't have an uncle in the state attorney's office or a cousin that runs the largest bank in town or enough wealth to literally buy and sell a person's entire life. When we get in trouble, no one comes to bail us out."

"I'm here."

I can't believe those words just came out of my mouth. Even West glances at me with a raised eyebrow.

But Zaya just shakes her head. If she realizes what a watershed moment this is, she doesn't let on. "He will not paint a target on my back like that, not when he has to leave me behind."

"You won't be living in the Gulch, anyway. You'll be up on the Bluffs with me, safe and sound."

Zaya stares at me like she has never seen me before, the surprise on her face obvious. Did she really think that nothing would change, that I'd put a ring on her finger and then leave my wife wallowing in squalor?

"I don't want to live in Cortland Manor."

"It won't be the manor. I stay in the pool house."

She just shakes her head and abruptly stands up. "This is too much to deal with right now. I need to go."

"We're not done yet."

Ignoring me, she addresses West. "Thank you so much for your time, Mr. Abbott. Sorry for busting into your office like this." She holds up a trembling hand when I move to follow her. "You can finish without me. I'll take the bus back into town."

With an annoyed sigh, I collapse back onto the seat. That girl doesn't know how to do anything without a fight.

West looks amused when I turn my attention back to him. "You aren't going after her?"

"The buses only run on the hour – she'll be down there for a while," I say with a shrug. "I'll give her some time to calm down, and then I'll take her home."

He shakes his head. "You make it sound so easy."

"Zaya likes to play hard to get, but I always get what I want from her eventually."

"If you say so," he says with a laugh. "She's the one, huh?"

"Not as if I have a choice," I snap, suddenly annoyed. This situation might amuse him, but it's my fucking life we're talking about. "Grandpa Abbott made sure of that."

"He might be doing you a bigger favor than you think, even if it is from beyond the grave." West takes another file from the stack and opens it in front of him. "Get the Milbourne boy a lawyer and have them send me a formal plea offer. I'll see what I can do with Judge Prior. But Zion will have to testify, I don't see any other way around that."

"He'll do it, I'll make sure."

"Oh, to have the confidence of youth." Without looking up from the paperwork in front of him, West waves his hand toward the door. "Now get the hell out of my office, I have real work to do."

"Love you too, Unc."

He makes a farting sound with his mouth. "Shut the damn door behind you."

Zaya is sitting at the sad little bus stop when I stroll out of the building. She stares off into space, so absorbed in her thoughts that she doesn't see me coming. I smile when she visibly jumps as I sit down beside her.

"Let's go."

She glares at me. "I told you I'm taking the bus."

I relax against the uncomfortable metal bench. "Then I guess I am, too."

"Vin Cortland doesn't take the bus," she scoffs.

"Vin Cortland doesn't leave his fiancée by herself in a bad part of town to take the fucking bus." I watch the dip of her throat as she swallows hard. I'd laugh if this weren't so serious. The word *fiancée* scares me too, babe. "He also isn't a huge fan of talking about himself in the third person."

"Your car is here," she argues.

"And if it gets vandalized or stolen, I'm taking the cost to replace it out of your allowance."

Her eyebrows go up as her expression turns stormy. "My allowance?"

"Look, a bunch of things are going to change." I turn toward her on the bench, careful not to touch her. She reminds me of a spooked horse that is moments from kicking me in the face. "Behind closed doors, this is a business relationship, but it has to look real to anyone watching. I need the marriage to stand up to any challenges in court, and I refuse to let myself be embarrassed where the whole town can see it happen."

"Not embarrassing you is definitely on the top of my list of priorities," she replies sarcastically. "What does that entail exactly?"

"Moving out of the house that is falling down around your ears, for one."

Her lips thin into a frown. "And what about Grandpa?"

"There's a senior care home on the east side of town that would be a good fit for him." I hurry with the next point, trying to decide if she'll slap me when she hears it. "Another item on the agenda will be buying enough new clothes that you can burn everything you currently own."

Her eyes narrow, but the hand I expect to fly for my face doesn't move. "You're trying to *Pretty Woman* me. That's a little gross."

"Richard Gere hired a prostitute half his age, and he didn't even offer to marry her until she decided to leave him. Give me a little more credit than that."

I can tell from the expression on her face that she didn't expect me to get the reference.

A musing note enters her voice. "I could spend a thousand dollars on t-shirts and jeans, just to spite you."

She has no idea what Giselle's monthly credit card bills look like, but I let her have the minor victory. "That's tough, but fair. Go crazy."

Without her, there won't be any money at all. She can buy out an entire Nordstrom's for all I give a fuck. And as much as I hate her wardrobe, everyone else's reaction is what has me concerned. People in this town can be cruel, and marrying me will paint a target on her back bigger than Cortland Manor. As much as I've tortured her over the years, I feel perversely unwilling to allow her to be the butt of anybody else's jokes.

Her sigh is one of unwilling agreement. "How much do you think it's going to cost for Zion to be in this diversion program?"

"Doesn't matter," I reply with a shrug, because it really doesn't. "We'll pay whatever it takes. The hard part is going to be convincing him to go. That's on you."

"I was already planning to go see him tomorrow at the jail. It takes a few days before they allow visitors."

"We can go together. No more taking the bus like a single mom working minimum wage."

She cuts her eyes at me, but a small smile teases her lips. "You know one of those gave birth to me, right?"

"Nobody's perfect. Let's go."

I only realize belatedly just how many times I said *we* over the course of our conversation and how natural it seemed. The two of us have temporarily aligned in our goals, I already know that. But I didn't anticipate how easy it would be to wrap our priorities up together with a little bow.

Zaya is mine, which makes *her* problems the same as *my* problems.

Hopefully, she doesn't go running for the hills when the tide inevitably turns in the other direction.

I hold out my hand to her with every expectation she'll refuse to take it. To my surprise, she does and allows me to pull her to a standing position. I don't let go of her hand as we head toward the parking lot, and she doesn't yank it away. We hold hands all the way back to my car, which feels nicer than it should.

This feels like the start of something, even if I'm not sure what that might be.

I'm so used to holding a knife to her throat that I never thought it might feel good to stand at her back.

When I drive Zaya home in the afternoon, we don't do much talking outside of the barest pleasantries. She is practically as quiet as she was before I gave her voice back. Her fingers fidget nervously with the frayed hem of her shirt, avoiding my gaze when I glance over her.

I try to picture her in some cupcake-shaped wedding dress made with five times as much fabric as it needs. And she won't just be in a dress she hates, but standing up in front of hundreds of people who will be studying every inch of her for something to criticize.

It would be excruciating.

She seems nervous just sitting in the damn car with me.

I wonder if she's thinking about what it felt like to have my hands up her skirt while she was grinding on my dick.

I know I am.

And I bet she's trying to figure out whether I'll be sneaking into her room tonight, silent as a ghost but with the intent of something much more physical than spiritual.

Zaya hesitates as she gets out of the car, standing there with the door still open. "I guess I'll see you tomorrow."

I give her a polite smile, even as I resist the urge to grab her arm and yank her across my lap.

"Sure thing."

She needs to get that sweet ass inside the house so I can set the plans that have been percolating in my brain the entire way home into motion. We negotiated our terms, and I plan to follow them to the letter.

But that means I'm running out of time to get things set up before I burst like a half-corked, furiously shaken champagne bottle.

Confusion twists her features and she drums her fingers on the roof of my car. "Alright, then."

I love keeping her confused, more than I love almost anything else. She wants me to tell her what to expect next, but I won't do it. Sure, I could go in after her and finally relieve the tension that has been building between us for days.

The wait is making both of us edgy and overly full with pressure. We're balloons blown up too far that are moments from popping.

"I'll watch to make sure you get inside okay."

She frowns, then seems to realize she's still standing on the sidewalk staring at me. Her blush is the prettiest shade of burnished rose gold.

As she walks away, I lean back against the window behind me so she won't see the barely contained laughter on my face.

I know the look of someone who is burning up when I see it.

Zaya seems to realize that her hesitation says more than words ever could and hurries up the grassy embankment to her house. The car door slams hard enough to shake the car on its axels as she whips away. I watch her stomp up the wooden steps to her porch and unlock the door. It's not a surprise when she doesn't look back.

She's angry. But she has no idea how much I want to chase her into the house and fulfill sexual fantasies I didn't even know I had before I met her. The anticipation is killing us both, but I refuse to give in until the fire burning me stokes even higher in her.

I'm done with the full frontal assaults. Those are precisely what she expects from me. The name of the game is seduction, and I plan to win it.

Zaya will be on her knees and begging me before we're done.

Her face flashes in the small inset window after she locks the door, expression still confused and maybe even a little hurt.

I shouldn't get so much pleasure out of keeping her off balance, but I really do.

Whistling, I feel practically giddy as I put the Maserati in gear and ease out into the street. I can only hope Zaya will spend the next few hours stewing in repressed sexual need and crazed desire.

I'll be right there with her.

The wait is necessary. There are more than a few things on my to-do list and very little time to get them done. Pulling my phone out of my pocket, I'm already connecting with the receptionist for a gorgeous little bed and breakfast a few hours up the coast. When I'm done with that, the next call will be to good old Uncle West to ask for a simple prenuptial agreement that will result in my father slowly dismembering me if I don't get it signed.

Soon, there won't be anything else standing in our way.

The future Mrs. Vin Cortland has no idea what's coming for her.

TWENTY-THREE

TEN YEARS AGO

Cortland Manor was always frigidly cold. Even in the dead of winter, or whatever passes for winter in this part of California, the air-conditioner blasted so I could see my breath each time I exhaled. When I would grab my mother's arm to show her, she shushed me.

She had been working at the manor for a few months before she ever brought me with her on the job. I didn't really want to come, but she promised there would be someone here our age to play with.

Up until then, we'd only driven by the fanciest mansion in town, waiting in the backseat to drop her off at work. I pressed my nose against the window glass of Grandpa's ancient sedan while Mom scurried up the long driveway, tugging at the skirt of her uniform. They made her wear a stiff white dress with thick pantyhose underneath, and she never looked anything but uncomfortable wearing it.

I'd always wondered what it might be like inside the imposing stone structure that reminded me of something out of a fairy tale.

The kind of story with evil queens and desperate princesses locked in towers.

But I didn't know it would be like this.

Giant paintings of white men lined the massive stairwell, each one more imposing than the last. I couldn't help but feel like they were all glaring down at me like some dark interloper who didn't belong.

Mama pushed me forward when I would have otherwise stayed rooted to the spot.

"Go on, now," she urged, sharp voice echoing off the sky-high ceiling.

Zion was supposed to come with us, but he had refused. No amount of wheedling or threats could make my brother do anything he didn't want to do. But Mama gave into it instead of fighting him and let him stay at home to play in the street with his friends.

"At least he won't be making any trouble for me here," she'd said. "You know I need this job."

But she said it affectionately, as if his intransigence were something she valued. And maybe it was. The indulgent tone she used on him was never directed at me. It always seemed like the more I gave into what she wanted, the more things it occurred to her to ask of me.

I was always the quiet one, the agreeable one, the one who didn't argue.

Even when on the inside, I raged.

It wasn't lost on me just how much she needed this job. She thought I didn't see the bills spread out over the kitchen table, stamped with the words PAST DUE in bold red letters. I heard the whispered arguments between her and Grandpa at night when I was supposed to be asleep, about how long each one could go unpaid before the city came out to turn off the water or the heat.

She thought I was too young to understand, but I wasn't.

That was why I didn't bother to ask her why she was so insistent we come with her today. Or just me, since she let Zion stay at home.

Dodging responsibility had always been easy for him.

My plain shoes were silent on the marble floor, the soles so worn down I might as well have been barefoot. She hustled me through the house and toward the back, but my widened eyes took in every detail of this place that felt more like a museum than a home.

Ten bedrooms with en suite bathrooms. Oversized kitchen. Infrared sauna and saltwater infinity pool. Five-car garage filled with luxury imports. A full-size bowling alley in the basement next to the wine cellar. All of it tucked into a cozy 25,000 square feet of space.

Mama would list the accoutrements like a mantra, describing in detail all the spaces with a voice that sounded awed. I understood that taking care of this place was backbreaking work, and not just because she told me so at every possible opportunity.

But that first time, I followed her through the house feeling a bit like a lamb led to slaughter. Even if I didn't understand where that feeling had come from.

I wondered how many people must live here, given the abundance of space. As we turned the corner, I expected there to be a veritable army waiting for us, because this house seemed big enough to comfortably house an entire football team. But every room we passed was empty, each hallway cold and full of only silence.

Mama led me through the kitchen, past a counter laid out with trays of food that made my mouth water, and through a sliding glass door that opened out into manicured gardens. But she didn't give me a chance to appreciate the view of perfectly symmetrical hedges and neatly groomed flower beds, pulling me by my elbow down the path and away from the house.

Cortland Manor was built on the edge of a sheer cliff, and nothing compared to its views of the sea. The best spot was on the far side of the gardens where a small table had been laid out with fine china, perfectly sized for childlike fingers, set before a pair of wrought iron chairs painted white.

A boy sat at the stone table, glaring off into the distance where waves crashed against the rocky shore. I couldn't see the exact expression on his face, but unwelcome radiated from the tense set of his shoulders and the way he shifted away as we approached.

"Vincent? This is my daughter, Zaya. Remember, I told you about her." Mama's voice was hesitant, which surprised me. She never spoke to anyone else with this sort of respectful hesitation, this reverence. "Your mother thought it might be nice for you to play together."

"Giselle isn't my mother."

The whispered words were harsh and clipped, but Mama had already turned away to rush back toward the house.

My first thought was that his voice sounded so much older than he looked.

In fact, I'd assumed on first glance that he had to be significantly younger than me. His angular body was small with thin shoulders, but the gaze that narrowed on my face was heavy with the knowledge of a hundred years.

I approached the table, but didn't try to sit down. For some reason, it felt like I needed to wait for his permission.

Some indication that I was welcome.

But he didn't do what any normal boy of his breeding would and stand up to pull back a chair for me. Instead, he glared with obvious derision in his gaze.

"Why are you here?" he asked, voice caustic.

"To play." The words weren't even sarcasm, I just found myself repeating what Mama had said although I didn't have any idea what she'd meant. This boy definitely didn't seem like the playing type, and I really wasn't either. Plus, there didn't seem to be any toys or games around. "Whatever that means."

"I don't play with the help." The look he cast over me was cold, judgmental. "You should just go back in the house and clean something."

His words were obviously meant to be insulting, but I recognized that they lacked a certain amount of heat. He was saying what he thought was necessary to get me to leave.

Why did he want so badly to be left alone?

"What are you doing out here?" I asked, surveying the table. It was laden with plates of cakes, cookies, and little sandwiches with a creamy filling I didn't recognize. There was an elaborate tea set, but the cup beside him was full and untouched. My stomach rumbled, but I knew better than to eat anything without asking. Mama had been very clear about that. "Just sitting?"

"What are you doing here?" he snapped. "I told you to leave."

"I'm not very good at following instructions." Without waiting for an invitation that would clearly never come, I plopped down across from him at the metal table. Wrought iron dug into my backside, and I couldn't help but wonder why a family with so much money would buy a chair this uncomfortable.

"Hungry?" he asked, cold gaze passing over the spread of food. All of it was balanced on the serving platter in the same towering configuration it must have been in when it emerged from the kitchen. Not even one bite of it had been touched. He waited until I reached for one of the glistening cakes filled with buttercream. "Although you should know it's all poison."

I pulled my hand back as if I'd been burned, staring into his pinched and expressionless face. It was impossible to know if he was telling the truth. But the rumbling in my stomach wasn't something easy to ignore. As I stared into his cool blue eyes, the color of a crashing wave under storm-darkened skies, I picked up the sugary confection and brought it to my lips. Our eyes held as I took a large bite.

It tasted like burnt sugar and rich possibility.

A smile touched his lips, so brief I would have missed it if I hadn't been so rudely staring. But he didn't seem bothered by my inability to look away. If anything, just the opposite.

His face fascinated me in a way that I was too young to understand. It was all sharp angles and lines that seemed drawn by a too heavy hand. He was beautiful, but desolate at the same time. Cheeks hollowed beneath the dark circles under his eyes and his lips pinched painfully tight, even as he glared across the table at me.

I'd never seen anger like this in someone I had only just met. It should have made me want to run as fast as I could in the opposite direction. But instead it drew me in.

That was the first warning I ignored.

We sat in silence for longer than should have been comfortable, assessing each other like two combatants meeting across the battlefield. I told myself it was a battle I could win, even if I wasn't sure that was true.

"My brother and I like to play tag," I told him, finally breaking the long silence. Mama had told me to stay out here with this boy until she finished her work, and that was what I would do. But I wouldn't sit here in silence for hours and hours on end. "Do you like that game?"

His assessing gaze roved over me, but his expression gave absolutely nothing away. "Only if it's downhill."

It was only then that I looked down to see he wasn't sitting in one of the pretty wrought-iron chairs, but a different one. Dark metal spokes poking out from beneath the tablecloth.

He was in a wheelchair.

With an angry jerk of his arm, he wrenched the chair back so I could get a good view of what had been hidden beneath the long tablecloth. A blanket laid over his lap, but it was obvious at a glance that his legs were thin, muscles wasted from disuse.

When my gaze again rose to his face, his eyes were full of challenge. He dared me to pity him, to feel sorry for the boy that had to farm for playmates from among the *help*.

"Can you walk at all?" I asked.

He jerked his chair back to the table, hiding the gleaming metal of the wheels from my view. "Some days are better than others."

"Is today a good day or a bad day?"

A grimace curled his lip. "Every day is a bad day."

Inexplicably, I wanted that smile to come back to his face. I wanted to make him feel better, even though I knew he didn't deserve it. It was an urge that made no rational sense, but felt as natural as breathing.

"So is that a no on playing tag? I'll give you a rolling start."

That surprised a laugh out of him that transformed his face into something so lovely it was heartbreaking. But then the now familiar mask descended back over his features. "You're funny. But you know, if I tell my step-mother what you said, she'll fire your dumb mother and then it's back to the slums for you."

He was trying to make me angry on purpose, even if I didn't know why. If I let him accomplish it, this would never happen again.

"Tell her then. And you don't have to be rude." My voice was placid with only the barest trace of steel that I liked to imagine ran down my spine, even when I knew no one else could see it. "My family has been here as long as yours has."

"Longer. The Milbournes were first."

My head snapped up in surprise. "How do you know that?"

We didn't go to the Founder's Day celebrations anymore, and none of the other families had paid us any attention in years. The dusty little elementary school in the Gulch that I attended was different from the fancy one for the kids living in the nicer part of town. Deception only had one high school, so kids from both sides of town mixed there, but not any earlier.

"We've met once before, when we were little," he told me, studying my face as if he tried to reconcile whatever differences he saw. "You don't remember?"

I would have remembered a boy in a wheelchair. I would have remembered a boy with intense eyes and an angry smile. I would have remembered him.

"You're thinking about someone else."

"There aren't many girls around here that look like you." His gaze lingered on the riot of curly hair that my mother had struggled and failed to tame, then dropped to the skin of my arms that always tanned deep in the summer, no matter how much sunscreen she slathered on me. "I remember."

Vague recollections of my last Founder's Day sifted through my mind, but the memories were hard to recall. It had been years, and anyone I'd met that day existed in a very different world from me.

"No flowers?" An empty vase sat in the middle of the table. I stared at it for a long moment, wondering why someone would lay out a spread like this but neglect to arrange the flowers. My gaze fixed on the porcelain, white with veins of gray running through it like a piece of marble.

"Giselle planted those oleanders. Pick some."

I followed his gaze to the nearby shrubs that were a riot of color, pretty pinks and deep purples. The flowers were lightly scented, their aroma drifting on the wind in a way I didn't notice until I paid attention to it.

There was a sort of challenge in his gaze that I didn't understand. But I decided to rise to the occasion. Literally. Pushing up from the table, I went to the beautiful shrub, so large it was more like a tree. I reached forward to pick one of the blooms, and a shock of pain made me give a surprised gasp.

When I pulled back my hand, there was a streak of red across my palm.

I'd been cut.

"You've probably never seen oleander with thorns." Vin had managed to silently roll his chair behind me, so close that if I reached out he'd be close enough to touch. "There used to be roses here a long time ago. The flowers died, but the thorns are still there. Oleander just grows over them. Our gardeners won't pick them without shears." His voice was mocking. "Did I forget to mention that?"

My gaze moved to the laden table with its empty vase and then back to the broken boy who seemed determined to reject me before I could do it to him first.

Without understanding the impulse that drove me, my injured hand gripped the closest stem that wrapped around a thorny branch. My gaze focused on the beautiful flower, even as thorns dug hard into my skin, the pain enough that I never would have tolerated it if I wasn't trying to prove a point.

Eyes burning and vision blurred, I returned to the table and placed the single flower in the vase. A streak of blood remained on the porcelain as I pulled my hand away.

When I turned back to face him, there were tears in my eyes that I refused to let fall. My gaze returned to his expressionless face as I bunched the fabric of my skirt in my hand to stop the flow of blood.

"There."

He didn't say anything as he rolled the chair back to the table. But his gaze lingered on my injured hand as some unknown emotion moved behind his eyes.

When I came back the next day, there were two plates on the table.

Mama brought me to Cortland Manor every day for the rest of the summer.

Usually, Vin and I spent time together in the garden with its deceptively beautiful flowers. Sometimes we talked about things that didn't really matter, but sometimes we simply sat in companionable silence.

And every day I picked a thorny oleander and placed it in the vase, no matter how much it hurt.

TWENTY-FOUR

VIN

WEAKNESS OF ANY KIND IS AN UNACCEPTABLE CONDITION.

Maybe it was all the years I spent so weak that I could barely stand, but nowadays I get off on pushing my body to the limits of what it's capable of.

I get off on pushing everything to its limits.

But tonight, I'm distracted.

Iain drives a right hook toward my face that I don't dodge fast enough. Pain explodes on the side of my head and sets my ears ringing.

The pain focuses me, lets me see everything around me with startling clarity. When Iain takes what he thinks is a moment of weakness to get inside my guard, I'm ready for him. My arms wrap around his neck and bring his head down as I drive my knee into his cheek.

His ass hits the mat hard, and he lets out a low groan of pain.

"Okay, enough," he insists as I reach out a hand to help him up. "You're in some kind of mood today. Is it blue balls?"

"Never." I smirk. "Both my hands work just fine."

It's a repeat of the same thing Zaya said to me, which only makes me think of her.

Just a few more hours. As soon as West lets me know that the license and contract are ready to go, there won't be anything else standing in my way.

"Always keep it classy, Cortland."

My eyebrow quirks. "I might be a married man in a few hours. Not getting any is supposed to come with the territory."

Like always, Iain sees right through the thing I say to all the shit I'm not saying.

He probably knew what was up when I invited him to the deserted school gym for a few impromptu rounds. It's amazing how well a few solid hits to the head can clear out the cobwebs.

I've dabbled in almost every martial art under the sun in the last few years, but Iain is the only sparring partner I've ever had who will do his best to kill me when I ask him to. Every so often we sneak into the school gym after hours to beat the shit out of each other in privacy. Basketball and wrestling are over for the season, so the only people using it after school right now are guys on the volleyball team. Those pussies are easy to chase away.

Every so often, we'll bring in other guys but Iain will always drop everything for a match. He is the only one who likes fighting as much as I do.

And unlike Elliot or Cal, he doesn't get wound up about bruising his pretty face.

Giselle calls it barbaric on the occasions she catches sight of me with a broken nose or blackened eyes. My dad just shakes his head before his fleeting attention moves on to something else. Emma is the only one who ever bothers to ask how the other guy looks.

The answer: always worse.

Iain's face is expressionless as he unwinds the tape from

around his bleeding knuckles. "If you're sure that's what you want."

"I want my inheritance," I deadpan. "That's all this is about."

If I say it enough times, that might make it true.

"And what does the girl desperate to escape the slums think about an impending teenage pregnancy."

The real trick to being a good fighter is accepting the pain, maybe even looking forward to it just a little bit. The guy who flinches when he should brace himself and blocks when he should lunge has already lost.

I'm not afraid to take a few hits if it gets me where I need to be.

"I'll let you know when the topic comes up."

A brief expression of surprise crosses Iain's face before it returns to the perpetual mask of disinterest. "You really haven't told her yet? That's interesting."

"I barely got her to say yes in the first place." The lengths it took to get that yes from her are already a sore subject. "Don't worry about it. Zaya will do what I want her to do eventually. She always does."

"Getting her to play mute for a few years is one thing..." He snorts and just lets the words trail off with a shake of his head. If he ever indulged in humor, the dick would probably be laughing his ass right off. "I'm looking forward to watching this explode in your face."

"I'm not worried."

My best friend does laugh at me then, a single guffaw that rings off the rafters before he is back in control of himself. "You sure as fuck don't fight like you're not worried. I can't remember the last time you tried to break my jaw."

Was the stress of this really getting to me?

No. Zaya will do what I want. It just might take some time for me to figure out the best way to go about making it happen.

But the expression on Iain's face is more mocking than ever. He looks at me like he knows exactly what I'm thinking and finds it patently hilarious.

"What do you suggest I do then? If you know so damn much."

He seems to actually consider that for a moment. "No way you're getting that girl to agree to a baby. Not until she finishes her degree in accounting, or whatever the fuck, and is at least five years into her first cubicle job." His lips quirk again in what almost looks like a smile. Guy is just giddy today watching me squirm. "Probably not even then, if she has to have the kid with you."

"I assume all these words of encouragement mean you have a suggestion."

"More of an observation." He watches my face for a few seconds, as if trying to decide how I'm going to react to whatever it is he plans to say next. "The only way a girl like Zaya Milbourne gets pregnant is if it's an accident."

"I've never gotten near her without a condom."

"Condom. Safety pin." He holds up his hands and mimes jabbing one into the other. "Works like a charm, if you trust daytime soap operas."

My mouth opens and then closes again. It doesn't surprise me that Iain would think of something so devious.

Or that the freak watches soap operas.

What surprises me is that I'm actually considering doing it.

Then I come to my senses. I'm a bad guy, but this would be terrible even for me. "She would never forgive me."

"Because you care about that."

Considering the things I've done, that's a fair point. "I can't force her to carry a baby to term, and eventually she has to for the codicil to be fulfilled. She would just end the pregnancy."

"It's amazing to me that you can be this obsessed with a girl and not understand her at all." He easily dodges when I swing at his head. "Zaya's mother abandoned her when she was still in elementary school. All she wants to be is the opposite of what everyone in town says her family name makes her. She isn't going to get an abortion. The girl would never be able to live with herself."

"You think I should trick her into getting pregnant on the wild assumption that she will feel compelled to carry the baby to term."

"Essentially." Iain's expression changes as he turns toward the doors, moments before I hear a clatter in the hallway. "Someone's out there."

I shrug it off. Nobody around here is going to involve themselves in my business, much less go running back to Zaya telling stories. "I don't know if I can do that."

"I'm not telling you to do anything, just pointing out that you only have two options." He picks his gym bag off the ground and slings it over his shoulder. "Either tell her the truth and watch her walk away. Or make walking away from you impossible. I'm sure you'll make the selfless decision."

My bloody lip aches. I lick it clean as I watch him go, relishing the flash of pain from the cut.

Everything worth having comes with at least a little bit of pain.

TWENTY-FIVE

VIN

THERE IS ONLY ONE PERSON WHOSE OPINION OF MY upcoming nuptials matters to me at all.

Emma isn't just surprised to see me parked in the pick-up lane of her fancy private school, she acts like I'm a soldier who has been away at war. Her face lights up with hope when she sees the shiny red Maserati. When her gaze moves to where I'm leaning against the hood, she starts running down the hill, long hair flying out behind her like a banner.

I'd sent her driver and nanny away, letting them know I'd get my sister home myself. Emma isn't the only one who has an employee, not a parent, picking her up from school but the idea of it still bothers me. My Maserati stands like a blood stain on white silk among the orderly rows of town cars and sedans.

"Are we going for milkshakes?" she asks as a greeting, coming to a stop just before running right into the side of the car.

"Or tacos?" I ask because I know it's her favorite.

"We had tacos in the lunchroom today." She pauses, thinking about it for a second. "But that doesn't matter."

"We can do whatever you want." I open the passenger door and raise the seat so she can climb in the back. "I'll even try to find a place that has milkshakes and tacos."

"That's gross." She hesitates with her hands on the frame. "Do I have to sit in the back?"

"It's the safest part of the car, so yes."

"Nanny Oona lets me sit in the front when she picks me up from school."

"Are you trying to get Nanny Oona fired? Because this is how you do it."

With a dramatic sigh, Emma flops into the back and slings her scruffy pink backpack onto the seat beside her. The bag looks like it's spent the last ten years buried underground. Like all her supplies, I know it was purchased this school year, so it's shabby appearance is deliberate. Emma probably dragged it through the dirt to hide the offensive color.

If Giselle isn't careful, her daughter is going to grow up dressing all in black with Goth makeup just out of spite.

"You can't protect me from everything, you know," she whines as I settle into the driver's seat.

"We're gonna agree to disagree on that, kid. I'm watching your every move until you're thirty."

She raises a blonde eyebrow. "And what happens then?"

"That's when you're allowed to date. And the upstanding young fellow I choose can pick up where I've left off."

"You are so stupid, even for a dude."

"I love you, too, bubblegum. Now, buckle up." I gun the engine and swing out of the pick-up line, waving to the stay-at-home moms who glare at me as we drive by. "Where are we going?"

"*Sweethaus* for milkshakes, and then you're taking me to *Ricardo's* for the all-you-can-eat taco bar."

"You got it." I don't even care that she's trying to be difficult because she thinks I treat her like a baby. And I definitely do, because I'm going to protect her from the entire world while I still can. "Are we doing double chocolate or Rocky Road with extra marshmallows?"

Emma crosses her arms over her chest, expression smug. "Both."

"Done."

The drive-through at *Sweethaus* is full of the after school crowd, and I spend the time listening to Emma describe all the drama going on within her friend group. She has already forgiven me for being heavy-handed, but I know more moments like that are coming. Her thirteenth birthday is only months away, and it's already obvious she will grow up to be a heart-breaker. As much as I want to lock her away so she never meets a guy anything like me, I'm reasonable enough to know that the countdown on her childhood is running out.

But for now, she is still a girl who gets excited about having milkshakes with her big brother, and I'm going to take advantage of that for as long as possible.

"I can't be friends with Lily anymore, because she has gone totally boy crazy," Emma tells me as I hand her one of the milk-shakes. "All she wants to talk about is kissing. It is so gross."

Thank fuck for that.

Over tacos, I finally broach the topic that compelled me to butter her up with her favorite foods. "There's something I need to talk to you about."

Emma takes a huge bite of her taco and replies with her mouth full. "Did you get somebody pregnant?"

"Jesus."

"It wasn't that Sophia girl, was it? You being with her seems a little sad, I don't know why."

I put down my own taco before I crush it in my fingers. "No one is pregnant. And this has nothing to do with Sophia."

"I heard dad saying something about babies the other day and I know Mom isn't pregnant, because she refuses to ever go through that again." She shakes her milkshake and then slurps up a large mouthful. "What is it, then? Must be something big if we did *Sweethaus* and *Ricardo's* in one day."

This girl is too smart for her own damn good. Or mine. "Some things are happening, and I want you to hear about it from me first."

Emma just stares at me, expressive blue eyes that are big as a porcelain doll's give absolutely nothing away. She learned her poker face from me, so there is no way to know how she might react. "And?"

"And I have to get married."

She blinks. "To Sophia?"

"God, of course not. To a girl I don't think you've ever met. Her name is Zaya."

"Why?"

"It's complicated legal stuff, but we'll lose a bunch of money if I don't. When Dad married my mom, there were a bunch of rules that her father insisted on making. Me getting married is one of them."

Lifting the cover off her cup, Emma stirs what's left of her milkshake before looking back up at me. "Are you mad about it."

"I was, but I'm getting used to the idea." The world has tilted on its axis, and now up is down, right is wrong, and Zaya Milbourne is the next Mrs. Cortland. "Are you upset about it?"

"Nah." Emma lifts the cup to her mouth and tilts it up to slurp out the last bit of milkshake. When she sets it back down, there's a ring of chocolate around her mouth. "As long as you and her move into the house with me so I'm not alone all the time."

A pang of unease shoots through me. That house is like an

altar to all of my worst memories. Every time I'm within its walls, an itch starts up under my skin, and it's hard to breathe. "I'll let her decide."

"You're not usually nice like that to girls." With her fingers, Emma picks up the last bit of meat and cheese that had fallen from her taco and pops it in her mouth. "Do you love her?"

Every time I try to pretend that my sister is still just a little girl, she hits me a with a gut shot. I can't lie to her, because she'll see right through it. But I can't tell the truth, because I haven't figured out what it is yet. "No idea."

"I think it's going to work out," she says, with all the certainty of a girl still in middle school. "She's like Cinderella, and you're Prince Charming. It can't possibly go wrong."

Except, Prince Charming didn't climb into Cinderella's window, hold her down, and fuck her like a whore before the ball.

Maybe in the German version, who knows. The Brothers Grimm got freaky as hell with some of those stories.

"You'll like her," I finally say, even though I have no way to know whether or not it's true, but realize I'm nearly positive it is.

"If you do, then I know I will."

But that's the problem with leaving parts of your life to chance — you can never be certain what might be coming for you next.

TWENTY-SIX

I wake up with the not so unique feeling that I'm being watched.

But unlike every other time this has happened, it isn't fear that shivers down my body when I sit up.

Vin sits in the corner of the room where he has so many times before. Even though only the whites of his eyes are visible in the darkness, I know he's staring straight at me.

The air between is charged with electricity, evidence of the coming storm.

I tried really hard not to let it bother me when he left me on my doorstep this afternoon, not even bothering to look back as he jumped into his car to drive away. The urge to invite him in had come up my throat like bile and been swallowed back.

The peace between us is fragile and probably temporary.

Our relationship, no matter how good it feels at times, isn't actually real.

I need to remember that, even when his smile widens and heat races over my skin. When he smiles, I can almost convince myself that we are something different than we are.

It would be a lie.

But it's hard to remember that when his eyes flash in the dark and he stands up from the chair.

I wait for him to decide what he is going to do, but it quickly becomes clear he has no interest in climbing into bed with me. He doesn't make a move toward me, even once I've completely sat up and we're just staring at the outline of each other's faces in the dark.

When he finally speaks, his voice is suddenly loud in the dark and silence.

"Are you ready to go?" he asks.

I struggle out from under the comforter that seems too heavy on my overheated body. "Go where?"

His lips quirk, but he gives nothing away. "It's a surprise."

"It's also the middle of the night and we have school tomorrow."

"Like I give a shit. You shouldn't either because there's barely a month left of senior year." He holds his hand out to me. "Let's go."

The smart part of me wants to ask what he has planned that requires leaving my bed in the middle of the night, but if he had any intention of telling me, then he already would have. No, my only option is to go with him willingly or put up a fight.

"I'm not dressed," I point out, half-rising from bed.

His gaze skims over my bare legs beneath the sleep shirt that hits me well above mid-thigh. "You have five minutes."

Vin sweeps out of the room, not even bothering to turn on the light.

I want to fight him, regain some of the power I lost when I agreed to all this. He can take his mysterious nighttime adventure and shove it up his ass. Whatever he has planned can't be more important than my education.

But eventually, curiosity wins and I climb out of bed.

There isn't anyone else in the house. Less than an hour after I got home, medics in starchy white uniforms arrived to transport Grandpa to the care home. I was happy to see him go, because I know it means he'll get the care he needs, but it was strange to fall asleep in an empty house.

None of the neighbors will come running if I scream. There isn't anyone or anything to stop Vin from doing whatever he wants with me.

At least, that's the excuse I give myself as I pull on a wrinkled pair of shorts and follow him out my bedroom door.

Vin isn't outside where I expect him to be when I reach the bottom of the stairs. Instead, he is in the small office off the living room that is so crowded with boxes and plastic trash bags full of junk that the beaten up desk inside is impossible to reach.

"What are you looking for?"

Vin doesn't bother to look up as he rifles through the filing cabinet. "Your birth certificate."

"What do you need with that?"

He shuts the drawer hard enough that the cabinet almost tips over with the force of it. "You're a smart girl, I'm sure you can figure it out."

Pressure swell ins my chest, making it difficult to breathe.

I've always hated guessing games, because the surprise is never the one I want. "Just tell me."

The look on his face is almost pitying, as if he hears the note of tension in my voice and assumes it is spurred by fear. Pulling out a manila envelope from a drawer in the desk that I could have sworn should be locked, he makes a triumphant sound as he dumps the contents onto the battered surface of the desk.

I know this situation is rapidly spinning out of control, but it was stupid for me to worry about that. Standing awkwardly a few feet away from the fully stocked kitchen, on the floor that no longer creaks because Vin had presumptuously had it repaired, I have to admit that none of this has ever been under my control.

But I still want to hear him say it.

"What do you need my birth certificate for, Vin?"

He looks up in surprise, as if only just realizing he hadn't bothered to answer my question the first time. His full lips turn down in a frown, preparing himself for resistance.

"We're getting married today."

I EXPECT VIN TO DRAG ME TO VEGAS.

Just like Sin City, everything about our arrangement screams trashy and fake with a veneer of slime.

And greed.

I've been bought and paid for, no different than the escorts who work the clubs on the strip.

But Vin doesn't drive us in the direction of the place where the sanctity of marriage goes to die. Instead, he takes Highway One up the coast, which gives me little idea of where we're headed. Most of California is to the north of us.

Even though it was still dark outside when he woke me up, it isn't as early in the morning as I originally thought. Predawn light has escaped over the horizon, casting the sky in pretty pinks and blues that blend with the receding darkness like a painting done in ombre.

I could almost enjoy it if I weren't terrified.

The first time I ask him where we're headed, Vin cranks up the radio and sings loudly along to some top 40 ballad. I'm shocked that he knows the words, but not enough to forget I want an answer.

When I turn off the radio and start to ask again, he rolls down all of the windows. My words are lost to the rush of air that spins up my hair into a knotty mess and makes it look like I just stepped out of a wind tunnel.

The third time, when it finally becomes clear that under our new paradigm he has to work a little harder to shut me up, Vin casts me a look that is darkly sensual.

He finally speaks for the first time since we got in the car.

"What will you give me if I tell you?"

I strive to keep my voice flat, uninterested, even as it feels like I'm locked in a cage with a wild animal that also has the key hanging from its neck. "I don't do road head. It's the best way I can think of to die in a fiery car crash."

"Why does your mind always go to something sexual?" he drawls, voice faintly mocking. "And you could at least give me a chance to act like a gentleman. I would take care of you first."

One of his hands teases at the hem of my shirt until I slap it away.

"Yeah, that sounds much safer."

His eyebrow raises in obvious challenge. "Is that the only problem? Say the word, and I'll pull this car over right now."

"We have a deal." I clamp my thighs together to keep them from shaking. "You wouldn't let me take sex off the table, but we agreed it won't happen again until after the wedding."

His tone is mild, but I hear the touch of mockery in his voice. "What does a few hours really matter?"

"It matters to me."

"So if I wait five minutes and then stick a finger inside that pretty little pussy, you won't be wet for me?"

I fight off a shiver. "Wanting something physically isn't the same as wanting it in any other way."

Vin makes an agreeable sound, but smirks at the empty road ahead of us.

My consent has always been an assumption with him, and I only have myself to blame for that.

Because he has been crawling into my bed at night since the end of sophomore year. Because the only thing we've ever had between us is anger, hatred, and sexual tension that burns hotter than a grease fire.

I've never taken a guy wanting to fuck me as any particular compliment. Maybe it was growing up in the Gulch and seeing how men act when they feel emboldened to ignore the rules of society, but most guys will stick their dick into almost anything. Just because a guy doesn't want to show a girl off, doesn't mean he won't crawl into her bed in the middle of the night and whisper anything he thinks she might want to hear if it gets him what he wants.

Nobody should be proud of what only happens in the dark.

But this playfulness is something new. Bantering with me and flaunting us together by driving through the nicest parts of town with me in the passenger seat is something new.

Vin is acting like we have a relationship outside of the deal that needs to stay purely business. His teasing makes me feel desirable. It makes me feel normal. I've already said yes to this ridiculous arrangement, so he doesn't have to offer me anything else. It almost makes it possible to convince myself he treats me this way because he likes it.

Because he likes me. Like he used to.

The small part of my heart that hasn't already turned to dust isn't strong enough to resist him.

And I have to resist him.

Because the moment I give him a way to hurt me, he will be compelled to use it.

"Maybe I'm not so sure I want to go through with this, after all." Maybe I was testing him, or myself, but I suddenly felt a perverse need to show him I can't be so easily controlled. "If you aren't going to hold up your end of the deal by keeping your hands to yourself, then I don't see why I should bother with mine. You won't be touching me again."

The car comes to a screeching stop abruptly enough it gives me a slight case of whiplash.

Without bothering to apologize, Vin throws the Maserati into reverse and flies backwards down the highway toward the exit we had just passed. The transmission grinds with a screech of metal as he peels out down the ramp in a way that has me gripping the handle of my door as I brace for what seems like an inevitable crash.

He pulls onto some random two-lane road lined with massive redwoods, going double the posted speed limit. When he finally rips off the road into a small clearing so the brush conceals us from view, my heart is in my damn throat.

"What the fuck, Vin—"

The metal buckle of his seatbelt hits the glass window from how forcefully he yanks it to the side. He moves more quickly than should be possible in the small space as he lunges for me.

I manage to get my own belt undone and reach for the door handle just in time to hear the locks go off.

The second I use to search for the latch is all it takes for him to land on top of me. One of his hands captures both of mine and presses them to my chest. He uses the other to pull my legs onto the seat so my back presses against the door and I'm completely underneath him.

His lower body straddles my legs. The thick length of him presses against my thigh — even through his pants I can tell he is rock hard.

"Say that again," he growls.

The sound resonates through my body and goes straight to the aching part of me that is just as wet as he said it would be.

I glare up at him, ignoring the storm brewing in those toxic blue eyes. "What. The. Fuck. Vin."

"Nope, not that." He bends his head and nuzzles my neck, his voice practically a purr. "Back up just a step."

But I refuse to answer, not when he is so ready to turn my words against me.

His mouth is close enough to kiss, but that isn't what he does. He bites my lip hard enough that I taste the tang of blood.

I swallow it down and try to remind myself that pleasure from him always comes with pain. That should turn me off, should make me want to shove him away and insist that he drive me back home.

Instead, my traitorous legs fall open enough that he can press himself more firmly against me.

He slams his hips against me, squeezing my ass with his bare hand and forcing the abrasive fabric of his jeans against my sensitive skin that only has a loose strip of cotton shielding it from the world.

"Fuck, I love these shorts," Vin says on a groan, practically talking to himself. His attention returns to my face. I recognize that look in his eye. It's the one he wears when he is willing to do anything to prove a point, even if it degrades us both. "I think you said something about me not touching you again."

He has always relished his ability to turn my own body against me. And I let him, not because I have a problem denying him what he wants, but because I haven't figured out how to deny myself.

He has always had that power over me and has never hesitated to use it.

His jean-clad hips ride me through our clothes. I feel the roughness everywhere: on my thighs, my belly and the sensitive bud of my clit.

Which seems to be entirely the point.

Blood streaks across my lip as his mouth shifts across my chin and down the line of my jaw, kissing and biting so hard I should be concerned he'll leave marks. Then my tongue dips out to lick the blood clean, abrading the cut he left there, and I no longer care.

With his face still buried in my throat, Vin blindly frees himself from the confines of his jeans, seeming heedless of the dangers of a zipper undone too quickly. I feel the soft skin at the head of his cock rub against my thigh, even though I can't see it.

"No fucking without condoms." I strengthen my voice enough that he'll know I'm drawing a line in the sand. After a year, I can walk away from this, but not if I'm saddled with a baby. "That's non-negotiable. I can't get pregnant."

His head shifts to rise above mine, close enough that I feel the rush of air against my mouth as he speaks. We were practically kissing, but just short enough for it not to count.

Vin and I never kiss.

This is the first time I can remember thinking that I wish we did.

I want to kiss him hard enough to make him bleed.

"No fucking without condoms," he repeats, as if reciting a lesson from his favorite teacher. But he doesn't stop rubbing himself against me. He has pushed my shorts aside so my soaked panties are the only barrier between us. "Anything else? This is your last chance to negotiate before you say *I do*. We're signing a prenup before the ceremony."

He punctuates his words by pressing his thumb down on my aching clit, leaving me lightheaded.

I can't think past the ache, and he knows it. My mind whirls for something else to demand from him, but all my mind can process is how much I need to come. Now isn't the time to discuss the finer details of our contractual obligations to each other. He knows it, and that's precisely why it's only coming up right now.

I just shake my head, barely able to form words. Negotiating isn't an option, much less reasoning through anything more profound than how good it would feel if the hard cock rubbing against my thigh pushed all the way inside of me.

"I guess that means we have a deal." His voice is almost conversational. The only hint that we aren't just having a civil discussion about a contract is the slightly breathless quality of his voice. Otherwise, he acts like he isn't holding me down in the front seat of his Maserati while cars trundle by on the road that is only a few yards away. "Now, about that touching I'm not supposed to do."

My shirt has hiked up in our brief struggle until the hem of it floats around my ribcage. His free hand shoves the hem higher until my chest is exposed. I don't typically where a bra when I sleep, and it hadn't occurred to me to put one on before we left, though it probably should have.

When he pushes the shirt up so it bunches around my neck, my entire chest is exposed.

"So perfect..." he murmurs, before his head lowers and licks across one taut nipple.

Using his hips as leverage, Vin pushes at one of my legs until it spreads wide enough that he can get up on his knees. My thighs drape over his hips, so obscenely wide that anyone walking by would see everything that wasn't hidden by the thin strip of my underwear.

Even though his cock is free in all its glory, he doesn't try to move my underwear aside. Instead, he grinds against me through the sopping cotton, creating a channel for himself that forces the fabric taut against me.

"What are you doing?" I gasp.

A lick on my neck leaves a trail of heat. "Fucking you without a condom."

He shifts his hips so the head of him enters me through my panties, creating a burning pressure. I buck off the leather seat. My hips thrust against his, even as I beg him with the frantic sounds that escape my throat to put an end to the torture.

The pressure from the hand he has wrapped around both of mine and pushing against my chest keeps me still. That still doesn't stop me from thrashing frantically beneath him, chasing the sensations to oblivion and beyond.

Dry humping hadn't been cool even at kissing parties in middle school, but today it's more than enough to make me feel wound up tighter than a spinning top.

All he has to do is let me go, and I'll spin off into outer space.

Fingers move up my chest. He doesn't hold back with his nails, digging into the skin as they trace a sharp pattern around one breast. When he squeezes one nipple hard between his thumb and index finger, twisting it harder than should feel good, fireworks shoot off inside of my head.

"If I can make you come like this, then I'm shoving my dick down your throat next chance I get. No condoms required for that." He doesn't wait for me to agree. Which is good, because I'm not sure what I would say if forced to respond.

Because I am about to come just like this. I'm going to come on the sleek cock grinding over my clit, and there isn't anything that can stop it.

"I don't have to be inside you to fuck you. Because I am always inside you. We crawled inside each other's skin ten years ago, and we'll never tear ourselves apart again, even when all we feel is hate." He punctuates the last word with another harsh thrust of his hips. The tip of his dick pushes past my entrance again through the fabric of my panties. "Don't come, or you'll prove me right." His voice is mocking, even as he grinds down harder. "Don't come. Don't come."

The angry words are meant for both of us.

Vin leans so close that the tip of his nose pushes against mine. The brilliant blue of his eyes fills my vision, drowning me. His eyes alone almost take me over the edge.

For a brief and shining moment, I forget all about who we are and all the history that makes peace impossible.

I have the insane thought that I can float away on that deep blue sea of his gaze.

But then his hand pushes underneath the curve of my ass and slips past the edge of my underwear. I only have a millisecond to wonder if he will really do it before a single finger pushes past the tight ring of muscle at my rear entrance.

The intrusion hurts, but in a way that feels like the preface to something more. I just don't know yet if that more is a good thing or a bad one. His first stroke is tentative, hesitant. But the moment he feels my spasming hole relax the smallest bit, he forces that finger inside until it disappears to the second knuckle.

My orgasm explodes out of me with a pained cry. The aftermath of it leaves me shivering underneath him. It only takes a few more strokes against my slit for him to let out a groan of his own.

Vin gives a low groan above me. Jets of warm liquid shoot onto my bare belly, just missing the fabric of my shirt and pooling into the divot of my belly button.

It's only when I finally catch my breath enough to wipe myself off with a handful of napkins from the glove compartment, straighten my clothes, and sit upright on the clammy leather seat that I realize how thoroughly he managed to distract me from getting an answer to my question.

I still have no idea where we're going.

TWENTY-SEVEN

VIN

WHEN WE FINALLY REACH THE VINEYARD, I SEE IN HER eyes an understanding of why I've been so cagey.

I need her not to get the wrong idea about this, because it isn't what she thinks.

But I see the question in those limpid brown eyes. Why would I bring her all the way out here?

The picturesque seaside vineyard looks like something out of a Hallmark movie. A gorgeous lodge is nestled at the center of acres of wine country. It's beautiful, and not the sort of place you come for anything short of luxury. A quick hop over the Nevada border to some dingy chapel would have served the exact same purpose, but here we are.

Explaining myself to her would require having an explanation in the first place. If I can't make myself understand the wild urges driving me, then I'd like to avoid making myself look like a fool. Especially in front of the girl who has always seen a little bit too much of the truth I prefer to hide.

I'd love to find the pieces of her that grow like a cancer inside me so I can finally cut them out for good.

I'm still trying to figure out how the hell to do that.

Zaya's eyes stay glued on the view out of her window, probably so I don't see the blush still staining her cheeks or the orgasm-blasted haze in her eyes. Our little encounter hadn't done anything to ease the tension growing between us. If anything, it was like smelling something mouthwatering in anticipation of a feast.

All we managed to do was whet our appetites.

When we pull off the highway and onto a winding road that leads to a long gravel driveway, I watch out of the corner of my eye as some of the tension leaves her body.

There are special places in the world where it's almost impossible not to feel at peace. Anna's Vineyard is one of those places, and that plays a huge role in me dragging us out here on a whim. As much as I hate to admit it, I don't want my wedding — despite it being the quickie kind with only a legally mandated witnesses and no fanfare — to be something embarrassing.

Even if everything else comes crashing and burning around me, at least I won't have to feel grossed out when I think back to my wedding day.

It doesn't really matter that this union is faker than the peace between us.

I remind myself that this is all about getting what I want. The happier I can make Zaya in the short term, the more likely I am to keep enough of my inheritance to avoid living in the Gulch in the house right next to her.

The look she casts me now is exactly why I didn't warn her about this beforehand. She looks at me like I'm something different than the monster she always thought I was.

She's wrong.

"We have to hurry." I mean to sound brusque, but the words come out too softly to be anything by cajoling. I'm losing my edge. "Iain is already waiting for us so he can get back to Deception before baseball practice."

"Iain is here?"

She sounds wary, and I can't exactly blame her. Iain is my best friend, but sometimes he even scares me a little.

"We need a witness."

For our damn wedding ceremony.

Zaya just stares at me as we drive slowly past trellises heavy with grapes, rolling hills, and clear blue skies on the horizon. This place offers tours, but we're the only visitors right now. It's early in the morning and a weekday, which is a deliberate choice on my part. The whole point of this is to avoid a crowd.

"Are we actually getting married today? If this is some sort of trick, I really don't have any more energy left for it."

"I told you what the fuck we're doing. No need for tricks when you're going to do whatever I want anyway."

That makes her angry, which is precisely the point. When she's pissed off and calling me an asshole, which she proceeds to do for the rest of the way through the vineyard, it's easier for me to remember who she is and who I am.

We aren't in love, we aren't even friends. No matter how much I enjoy screwing her, it won't ever be more than that. Whether she has a ring on her finger or not.

I thought getting off would temper the edge of tension tightening every muscle in my body. But jerking myself off against her hot little body has only made things worse. My skin is so tight it feels like it belongs to someone else. I should be loose and relaxed after coming in my fucking jeans like a middle schooler who just discovered porn for the first time, but I'm tenser than if I just spent the last week at a monastery. We need to get this over with so I can be inside of her. For real, this time.

Sex is something I understand. Good sex doesn't require

emotions or deeper meaning. But each time I put my hands on her, it gets easier to imagine doing it for significantly longer than a year. I have to remind myself over and over that she will eventually walk away.

Or run, if she's as smart as I think she is.

"You didn't think to ask me if I'd want somebody here besides Iain McKinley?" she snaps.

"Not really."

I also didn't ask her if she minded missing school since we'll be spending the night. I don't particularly care, so it's easy to assume that she doesn't, either. I'm paying for the privilege of her agreement, no matter how much she might want to pretend like her opinion matters for any of this.

Apparently, she disagrees.

"You are so damn high-handed." Anger narrows her eyes and purses her lips in a way that highlights the sharp angle of her cheekbones. The more pissed off she is, the prettier she gets. "The more you try to bully me, the more I want to say no on principle, you ass."

"Say no, then. Tell me exactly where to shove my money and my offer to change your fucking life." My hand slides along her slim thigh, ignoring her attempts to push it away. I barely need to slip under the hem of her skirt to feel the raging inferno between her thighs. "Then give me about thirty seconds to change your mind."

Her eyes narrow, but she doesn't rise to the bait. Smart girl.

"I'm not getting married in my pajamas. If you think I'm going to stand up with you at an altar looking like this, then you've lost your goddamned mind."

Without bothering to respond, I reach behind me and pull a dress bag out of the back seat then dump the whole thing on her lap. It might be a little wrinkled from the drive, but nothing that should embarrass her. It wasn't a joke when I told her I'd thought of everything.

I've probably spent too much time thinking through this.

Suddenly sobering, I force myself to remember I've had to literally buy her attention. Just like every other girl who has ever been in my life. Zaya is doing this for money, nothing else.

"Next time you run your mouth, remember why you're doing this." I keep my voice cold and remote, as if doesn't matter to me at all what she decides to do. "You want to keep Zion out of prison and your grandfather eating something other than dog food. Play along, or I'll take back all my toys and find someone who will actually appreciate them."

She plays at the zipper of the dress bag, obviously resisting the urge to look at the dress inside. Her lips thin, and I almost see the start of what looks like tears in those overly large eyes.

Maybe both of us need the reminder.

Zaya pulls herself together and shoves open her door before the car has even rolled to a complete stop. "Let's get this over with."

ZAYA MAKES A BEAUTIFUL BRIDE. EVEN WHEN SHE IS ONLY wearing a white silk dress that I picked up at the last minute and her face bare of makeup. Bridezillas who spend months stressing over their perfect day could eat their hearts out.

I open my mouth to say that, but then shut it again.

If she were actually my fiancée, then I might pay her the compliment, like the type who actually means it when they say *as long as we both shall live* at the altar. But it would just be a waste of time on the girl I bought and paid for.

That isn't how we talk to each other, even when the words taste like poison on the tip of my tongue just begging to be spat out. Everything about this is temporary, no matter how pretty it looks from the outside.

But I could still see myself wanting her forever.

Which makes absolutely no fucking sense.

Iain is already waiting at the altar with a bored expression on his face. He has on the sport coat I begged him to wear, with board shorts on bottom and no shirt underneath. The only reason he agreed to come out here was because the surf is breaking in bombs along the north coast and he can get in a few rides before going back to Deception.

Despite his apparent lack of interest in the proceedings, I chose Iain for the specific reason that he won't try to talk me out of any of this. He has always been an any means to end type of guy, which is probably why we get along so well.

He won't stand in my way, even when I might be self-destructing.

Zaya stands up next to me at a makeshift altar and is shaking like a leaf. An archway has been set up in an open area at the center of the vineyard. Honeysuckle hangs down from it to sweeten the air. It might as well be swamp gas for all that she seems to notice.

Neither of us are enjoying this.

It was probably a bad idea for me to try and make this nice. The pretty facade just serves as a reminder that there isn't any substance under all this fanfare.

The ceremony itself is brief and anticlimactic. The justice of the peace that I paid double to get out here at the last minute recites the same speech he has probably used a thousand times before.

When it's time to exchange rings, Zaya's mouth falls open when I shove a rock the size of a goose egg on her finger. The thing is older than I am, some family relic that can be traced back over several generations of Cortland wives. It seemed like a better idea to whip out some old artifact than to pick out something new that I would just want to return when this is all over.

Even Iain seems surprised when he sees it, eyebrows raised as I shove the thing on Zaya's finger. He won't say anything, not about this or anything else, but that doesn't mean he approves. Iain lives in a house made of spun glass, so he isn't about to go around throwing stones.

I didn't have the ring sized, and she has to squeeze her hand into a fist to keep it from slipping down to her knuckle.

"It's beautiful," she murmurs, voice barely audible.

As if it matters.

But from the looks on their faces, I wonder if I might have made a mistake. Maybe I should have grabbed some gaudy thing from the jewelry store at the mall. I assumed it would be too much to pick out a ring specifically for her, but handing over a family heirloom might be sending a message I didn't necessarily intend.

Too late now.

"You may now kiss the bride," the justice intones softly, as if any part of this charade is worthy of gravity.

Both of us freeze like we've been splashed with frigidly cold water and then dropped unceremoniously in Siberia.

Zaya and I don't kiss. Ever.

I don't kiss anyone.

It started as an unspoken rule that grew into something infamous and is now a matter of gospel. Girls have placed bets in the past over whether they could get me to stick my tongue down their throats. Never happened.

That show at the Founder's Ball with Sophia was the notable exception, but I only did that because regardless of how much it skeeved me out, it was worth the benefits. The look on

Zaya's face when she caught sight of us will be my fondest memory for years to come.

But this isn't about jealousy or power plays.

Even though there are only four of us standing here, and no one in the empty lawn chairs spread out on the grass, the silence stretches uncomfortably long. Iain vibrates slightly behind me, and I don't need to look to know it's from suppressed laughter.

I turn to Zaya, assuming she'll be looking down at her own feet in shame.

Instead, she boldly stares right at me. The expression on her face is frankly exasperated, like I'm a little kid about to throw a fit because I don't want to eat my vegetables. She doesn't look afraid of my reaction, but like she pities me.

"Don't worry about it," she says to the justice of the peace, dramatically rolling her eyes as if they're both in on some joke. "We can just skip that part."

When the justice nods in sympathetic understanding, I want to punch the man right in the throat whom I begged to drive out here at dawn.

Zaya is in my arms before the justice has a chance to pronounce us anything. She stares up at me in obvious shock, and I relish seeing that look on her face. I give her half a second to pull away before I jump over my line in the sand and then blow up the whole beach.

She doesn't even look away.

I kiss her like I want to suck the soul out of her body. If this were a real wedding, I'd be embarrassed by us both. But the only people here to see this are my best friend and a justice of the peace who probably got ordained over the Internet. No one who matters will ever find out about this, but I'm still determined to make it count.

My mouth owns hers, a prelude to what I'm going to do

with the rest of her body. Her mocking smile evaporates as quickly as it formed. The pressure of my mouth won't let her do anything but part her lips with a gasp. I bend her over my arm, forcing her body backward in a way that looks romantic but can't possibly be comfortable.

If I let go of her, she'll fall. I hope she's smart enough to understand the lesson in that.

Her small hands grip my shoulders. Nails dig into my skin even through my dress shirt, but I ignore them. My tongue forces its way halfway down her throat until I inhale the sound of protest. She tastes like resistance and spun sugar, even though I woke her up in the middle of the night.

What started out as an attack quickly turns sensuous. I tease at her lips with mine, even as my tongue invades every corner of her mouth. I kiss her like she belongs to me.

Because as of this moment, she does.

When I finally release her, I have to hold on to her shoulders for a few seconds before Zaya can stand on her own. I make a point of keeping the look of triumph on my face when she looks up at me.

She glares at me, but keeps her mouth clamped shut.

The justice seems taken aback, but quickly recovers. He doesn't meet my gaze as he fumbles for the bible in his hands.

"I now pronounce you man and wife."

I CAN TELL ZAYA THINKS I'M GOING TO THROW HER OVER my shoulder and carry her off to the nearest bed when the ceremony ends.

So I take her to breakfast instead.

The lodge attached to the vineyard is empty of other guests, but the hostess at the front greets us warmly and seats us at a table all the way in the back.

Surprise blooms on her face when the waiter places a prosecco and aperol spritzer in front of her before melting away into the background.

She picks up the glass and takes a careful sip before screwing up her face and putting it back down again. "How much did you pay them not to card you?"

I don't bother to lie to her. "My father saved this place from bankruptcy with a low-interest loan a few years ago. I can do whatever I want here."

She gives me the same annoyed look she always does when I spout off something about my charmed life that she finds offensive.

Spoiler alert, sweetheart: people only say that money can't buy happiness when they don't have enough of either. Sure, you can be sad and rich, but that is a damn sight better than being anything else and poor.

"One of these days, you're going to want something you can't buy." She picks up the croissant in front of her, then sets it down again without taking a bite.

"Doubt it."

"Not everything is for sale."

"You were."

That reminder doesn't sit well, if her glare is any indication. Then her face clears, and a mocking smile curves her lips.

"Except you're renting, not buying." She smirks at me. "I wonder what people will say when they find out that Vin Cortland has to pay for it."

I want to shove something in that smart mouth. My dick, for starters.

"People can say whatever the fuck they want," I comment, keeping the anger at bay as I flip open my menu and pretended to study it. "And as soon as we're done with breakfast, I plan to get my money's worth and then some."

"There goes my appetite," she sneers. The plate clatters on the linen tablecloth as she pushes it away.

I just stare at her for a moment over the rim of my glass. We're playing a game, I remind myself, and she doesn't even know how many pieces I have on the board. "Finish your drink."

Still glaring at me, Zaya makes a point of pushing the cocktail away.

Fine. I prefer her sober and clearheaded for what comes next. She needs to remember every second of me shoving my dick down her throat.

I drain the drink for her and stand. "Let's go. Our room should be ready, Mrs. Cortland."

She scowls but doesn't respond.

Our deal is done. She already signed the marriage certificate under my watchful eye, and it will get filed with the county clerk as soon as we return to Deception.

Her hand hangs limp in mine as I pull her up from the table and toward the stairs. The ring on her finger digs painfully into my palm. I could have kept this marriage secret, signed some paperwork, and never told a soul about it, but instead I put the same ring on her finger that my many many times great-grandfather brought to the New World for his virgin bride.

I marked her. Made it clear to the whole world that she belongs to me.

It bothers me how much I like it.

TWENTY-EIGHT

I ALWAYS THOUGHT I WOULD HATE IT IF VIN EVER kissed me.

But I was wrong.

He drags me up the wide wooden staircase with a single-minded intent, barely seeming to notice the beautiful furnishings or warm sunlight filtering through the bay windows that dominate the second floor. We pass about a half a dozen rooms but don't see any other people as he tugs me toward a set of double doors at the far end for the hallway.

Honeymoon Suite is etched onto a little gold placard above the lock.

The doors swing open so violently I'm convinced the wood will crack.

But as soon as we're alone in the room, the frenzy fades away. He takes in the room with an unreadable expression, dropping my hand as if it burned him.

A trail of red rose petals leads to a massive four poster bed. Rose petals are also scattered across the bedspread. Someone clearly butchered an entire garden to accomplish the task. An uncorked bottle of champagne sits in a bucket of ice on the nightstand next to a bowl of bright strawberries, the same red of the rose petals.

With a disgusted sigh, Vin rips off his suit jacket and tosses it in the general direction of a nearby chair. "I'm taking a shower."

He doesn't wait for me to answer and stalks away. I hear the slam of a door and the sound of rushing water.

Gingerly, I sit on the edge of the bed and brush the petals to the floor. My gaze immediately moves to where my hands clench in my lap, drawn like a moth to a flame to the stone that has glittered on the edges of my vision since it was shoved on my finger.

The ring I'm wearing feels a bit like having a cowbell hanging from my hand. Traditional setting. Clearly an antique, but polished until it shines. A diamond the size and shape of a robin's egg.

It's the sort of ring that Mrs. Vin Cortland would wear, like a dozen women probably have before her.

I'm surprised he would give me something so obviously expensive and clearly of sentimental value, though probably not to him. Vin doesn't care about anything as silly as family legacies, but people are going to assume things when they see this ring on my finger. This isn't a ring you use for a fake marriage that is only for the money.

It's the ring you give someone who will bear your name for the rest of your life.

I had barely even read our prenuptial agreement, barely skimming it for mention of the $100,000 and that it would be mine after only a year. Part of me wanted to pour over it in great deal, just to annoy him. But what do I really have for him to take away? It seemed better to just get it all over with as quickly as possible.

Iain hadn't said so much as a word to me during the entire the ceremony and left as soon as it was over. I used to think that Vin's best friend hated me as much as he did, but I realize now that Iain doesn't care enough about anyone to hate them.

The guy is practically a reptile.

But even he seemed surprise when Vin pulled out the ring, his gaze resting on it for too long before his piercing gaze rose to my face. I don't know what expression he saw there, but it made him shake his head and look away.

I never thought I'd be on the same page as Iain McKinley, but here we are.

Everything about this has been unnecessarily over the top. The grand gestures made sense in the beginning when Vin was trying to convince me to agree to this ridiculous arrangement. He didn't have to drag me out to wine country and book us into a honeymoon suite.

The skirt of my dress spreads out around me on the bed and I rub the smooth silk between my fingers before letting it drop. This isn't fancy enough to technically be a wedding dress, but it is white and elegant in its simplicity, nothing that would embarrass if anyone saw us standing together on that altar. He didn't have to do that either. He could have dragged me to the courthouse in sweatpants and still made it to school in time for first period. That would have amounted to exactly the same thing.

Why would he do this?

If I didn't know Vin, if he were literally anyone else, then the only conclusion I could draw is that he cares about if I feel used. That he wanted to make some virtue out of this necessity so I won't feel like a whore spreading her legs for a meal ticket.

Because he cares.

Except I know Vin doesn't care about anyone but himself, and he hates me.

But a guy who is only filled with hate wouldn't take the time to pick out a dress or book a honeymoon suite. That guy wouldn't give me a ring that should rightfully only be worn by the woman he actually wants to marry. For real.

Forever.

Ever since I agreed to this, he hasn't just been nice. He has taken the time to figure out what I need before I've even asked for it. Anticipating me. Making this as painless as his prickly personality will allow instead of robbing me of any dignity I have left like I assumed he would.

I can almost convince myself we could be something more than we are.

A strange feeling builds in my chest, pressure that makes my heart ache. There has always been a link between Vin and I, but until this very moment I imagined it as some sickly and twisted thing that burrowed into my chest like a knife.

But it isn't pain that makes my heart race and robs me of breath.

It feels like hope.

And maybe even a little bit of love, because sometimes I see in him the boy I used to know.

There was a time when we didn't hate each other. When I was his only friend, the only one who ever saw him at his weakest. He let me past the hardened shell that is all the rest of the world gets to see, so I know somewhere in there is a beating human heart.

I wish I didn't remember, but I do.

Ten Years Ago

I LIKED THE OUTSIDE OF CORTLAND MANOR MUCH BETTER than the inside.

The moment we pulled up to the driveway, I sucked in a huge breath. I wouldn't let it out until I had hurried through the massive foyer, past the kitchen, and out the French doors that lead into the gardens.

I wouldn't breathe until I was back outside again.

Vin hadn't been in the wheelchair for very long, and there were good days when he was able to walk. He really wanted to make sure I knew that.

Mama said he had been able to walk when she first started working at the manor, but she didn't know exactly what was wrong with him. Something to do with a weak heart, maybe. She got annoyed if I asked too many questions and would change the subject.

I used to wonder if it was the house itself that made him sick. The air inside the manor was so cold that it burned my lungs if I inhaled. It felt like poison. Even then, I knew something about that couldn't be right.

But it wasn't the air I should have worried about.

At some point, instead of already waiting outside at the garden table, the tea set and tray would be sitting on the edge of the counter in the kitchen, waiting for me carry it out.

I held my breath as Mama explained it, fidgeting from one foot to the other while my lungs burned. I had managed to convince myself that something terrible would happen if I took even a single breath inside of the manor. What started as a child's game had morphed into a true phobia.

"There is medicine for him in this cup, so make sure that one goes to Vin."

Vin never drank or ate anything in the garden, until I started bringing out the tea. That first day, he warily eyed the cups as I set them on the table. But when I sat down and took my first sip, so did he.

"It's bitter," he complained. Then dipped the frosted cookie in the tea to sweeten it.

Mine didn't have a bitter aftertaste, but I assumed that had to be the medicine Mama mentioned.

For weeks that summer, every day it was the same.

Eventually, she no longer had to remind me. Rushing into the kitchen, I would scoop up the tray and carry it outside, exhaling a desperate rush of air the moment I passed through the French doors.

The black cup was for him and the white one for me.

One day, things were different. When I raced for the kitchen, the tray wasn't on the counter waiting for me like it should have been. Mama grabbed the back of my shirt and held me back when I tried to run outside without it.

She made me wait while she made up the tea. I fought so hard not to breathe, chest burning as I silently begged her to hurry. It would have cost too much of the little air I had left to speak. It seemed like it took so much longer than it should to pour hot water into the delicate ceramic pot and drop little bags of tea into each cup.

I wouldn't remember until later how odd it was that Vin's medicine was in an unlabeled bottle kept under the sink. Mama seemed to hesitate before pouring a generous amount of it into the black cup without bothering to measure. Then she adjusted the cups on the tray once. Then twice. Then again.

I wanted to scream at her to hurry up, but all I could focus on was how badly I needed to breathe.

It took too long for her to finish preparing the tray. I didn't have any choice but to inhale a lungful of frigid air that did nothing to relieve the burning in my lungs. My hands shook when Mama finally gestured at me to take the tray outside.

I should have known then that something terrible was about to happen.

Vin smiled as I approached with the tray. I couldn't have known it, but it was the last smile I would see on his face for a very long time.

In hindsight, I wish I had appreciated it more.

Instead, I rambled about how annoying Mama was being, barely giving him a chance to respond. I didn't have anyone else in my life to complain to. Zion was more interested in hanging out with the neighborhood than spending time with his sister and Grandpa rambled more than I ever could, so there was no getting in any words edgewise.

Vin said something nice and took a gulp of his tea.

Then his face changed, eyes widening like he just saw something that scared the hell out of him.

Then he collapsed onto the table, knocking aside the plate of tiny cookies.

I laughed, thinking he was messing with me. Then I said his name a few times, each one more strident than the last. His face was the color of skim milk, pale and faintly bluish.

When I screamed for Mama, she didn't come.

The Cortlands were away, a day trip out of town. Vin had been left with a Ukrainian nanny who barely spoke any English and didn't even seem to realize I was in the house with him. Instead of calling an ambulance, she panicked and bundled us both into her own car. I was too small for the front seat, barely able to see over the dash, but Vin was sprawled across the backseat.

He wasn't breathing by the time we got to the hospital.

Vin Cortland's heart stopped beating for two and a half minutes.

They eventually brought him back, but a lot of people would say that necessary organ never started back up again.

The doctors said the damage was consistent with poisoning. That was how I first learned that the beautiful oleanders lining the pathways of Cortland Manor's gardens are toxic. Perfectly safe from afar, but the leaves secrete a poison. When consumed, enough of them can stop a grown man's heart.

They asked if I had ever seen Vin eat the flowers. Maybe we had played with it, like kid's do when they scavenge the yard for ingredients to make mud pies. Pretend play that had turned unknowingly, and accidentally, dangerous.

I didn't answer the question. I didn't answer any of their questions. At first, I was too shocked to do anything but stare up at the intimidating men in their white coats looming over me, insistent and impatient.

My throat squeezed shut, and all I could manage was a whimper.

They ran tests on me too, just to be sure, but I was healthy as a horse.

Later, when I finally found the words to speak, no one bothered to ask me any questions.

The nanny drove me home and dropped me off without bothering to see me to the door. She had just been fired, so had better things than me to worry about.

My mother was gone.

She must have been in a hurry, but her belongings were packed up so thoroughly that it was hard to say she had ever lived there at all.

A postcard arrived from her a few weeks later. *Sorry* written on it in big block letters, scribbled so hastily that it barely even looked like her handwriting.

It would be years before I stepped foot in Cortland Manor again.

Grandpa told me when Vin got out of the hospital because

he'd heard from the butcher who delivered meat to the Bluffs. For years, I would wonder why she did it. Had it been some strange sort of accident? Or had she hoped to swoop in and save him to the relief of the Cortland family, but somehow miscalculated?

I'll never know.

The next time I saw Vin Cortland was on our first day at Deception High. He was bigger than I remembered

"Who did it?"

He had snapped the question as a crowd gathered. They might not have known precisely what was going on, but recognized the start of a fight when they saw one.

My throat froze in the same way it had with the doctors. So many years had passed. I almost had myself convinced that I had imagined most of it. Grandpa always said that Mama would come back eventually. She had never been good at sticking with anything. Not her education, or relationships, or jobs. Why would motherhood be any different?

But I knew the truth. She ran away from what she did.

Vin looked at me like he wanted to grind me into dirt. And the longer I stayed silent, the more anger filled his eyes.

His reputation from middle school preceded him. People already whispered about the rich boys from the Bluffs who did whatever they wanted and got away with it.

The VICE Lords.

And he was the worst of them.

Vin's lip had twisted in a sneer. "If you can't tell me what I want to know, then maybe you shouldn't speak at all."

But even when I opened my mouth to speak, no sound came out.

She did it.

She did it.

She did it.

I couldn't do it. I couldn't turn on my own mother even after what she did.

Even after she left me.

I had a few friends from middle school, the ones who hadn't dropped out before we reached freshman year. But none of them were willing to stand with me, not with Vin Cortland on the other side.

Maybe he meant it to be an idle threat at first, even a joke. But it didn't matter. Words passed from Vin Cortland's lips to the ears of pretty much everyone in town.

Eventually, I got so used to the silence that I forgot how to exist with anything else.

The truth might set you free, but guilt is a cage that has been welded into place. There isn't a key in the world that might unlock it.

I won't ever be able to escape it.

TWENTY-NINE

VIN

I SCRUB AT MY BODY WITH THE EXCRUCIATINGLY HOT water and rose-scented soap. Like I can wash away whatever part of Zaya feels like its stuck to my skin.

It was fucking stupid of me to set all this shit up. I told the vineyard staff to make it nice, but I didn't know that would mean covering literally everything in roses. I have no idea what stupid urge drove me to make things nice for her, but I need to get my shit together.

We aren't in love. This isn't some tragic story about star-crossed lovers. We have a deal, and we just need to put up with each other until the deal is done.

No more of this romance shit.

I hear it when the door opens, but initially assume that the latch didn't catch and a gust of wind blew against it. But when the shower curtain parts and a slim body slips in behind me, the last thing on my mind is the breeze.

"What the fuck?"

"I don't want you to use all the hot water," she says lightly. "My hair takes forever to wash."

Which does nothing to explain why she is shoving herself in behind me butt naked.

"This place has dozens of rooms. They don't *run out* of hot water."

She snaps the curtain shut. "Thanks for the bit of trivia. I clearly don't know as much about luxury accommodations as you do."

Her tone is sarcastic, but teasing. Miles away from the moody anger I saw downstairs.

I have no idea what to make of this.

"I got here first."

She shrugs and reaches for a bottle of rose-scented shampoo. "I know you never learned to share in kindergarten like the rest of us, Cortland. But it's never too late for a lesson in the basics."

If any other girl looked at me like this, opened up her hot mouth to smart off like this, I'd bend her over and smack her ass a few times. I can practically hear the wet slap of flesh because the water on her already heat-reddened skin will hurt that much more.

I've got a *lesson* for her. It's hard as a rock and about to be inside of her.

For about a minute, I try to ignore her. I scrub my face and rinse it off in the water spray where I can't see her naked body or hear anything aside from my own thoughts.

I feel her eyes follow me like a burning on every inch of skin her gaze touches. It lingers on my chest and the flat plane of my abs before coasting down to my dick that is so hard it's almost painful.

When I lean back and swipe the water from my eyes, Zaya is still staring at my dick.

I wonder if I've fallen down a rabbit hole in Wonderland, or maybe Earth had an alien invasion when I wasn't paying attention and Zaya got body snatched. Those are literally the only explanations I can think of for this surreal situation.

Especially when she turns, giving me an unfiltered view of her luscious ass and looks coquettishly over her shoulder. "Will you get my back?"

No matter how much weight this girl loses, and she has already lost way too much, that ass never changes. Round. Soft. The perfect size to fit inside my hands if I want to pick her up, spread her legs, and force her down onto my cock.

I force those thoughts away as I reach for the soap. When my hands glide over the sharp lines of her back, all I can think about is gripping that flesh in my hands as I sink inside of her.

My shower gel coated hands skim over her back. Her smooth, dark skin feels even softer under the water than it does normally, glistening and flushed from the heat. Every time I look at her, I discover something new.

Like the way that curls in her hair tighten and define before she has even stuck her head under the water, twisting like some living thing. I used to sit behind her in English class and would study the back of her head, trying to count how many different types of curl I could find there. Each one is entirely unique, like snowflakes. Beads of water catch on her eyelashes, making her look like some seductive water nymph emerging from the waves.

Even if I spent the rest of my life studying every facet of her face, I'd probably never lose interest.

It's been a long time since I've seen her naked, especially in the light with no part of her hidden away. Yes, I've fucked her. Eaten her out. Held her down and dragged my dick across the soaked lips of her pussy through her panties, whispering filthy things into her ear, until we both came.

But I've never just looked at her like this, especially without any timeline to stop doing it.

We have hours here. Days, if we want them.

Plenty of time for all the things I want to do to her.

When her back is cleaner than any piece of skin should rightfully ever be, I lean forward to whisper in her ear. My murmur is barely loud enough to be heard over the rush of water from the showerhead.

"You have about thirty seconds to get out of here before I fuck you up against the wall."

Her smile widens as she backs toward the spray of water. "It takes longer than that to rinse my hair out."

Before she can say anything else smart, I press my lips hard against hers.

I can count on two fingers the number of times I've kissed a girl, unless you want to count pecking Emma on the forehead when she was a baby. Both times were about Zaya, because everything has always been about her, even when I refused to admit it.

Once was to make her jealous.

Twice was to make her mine.

But I only kiss her now because I want to taste her again. Her scent suffuses my senses, warm cotton laid in the sun with just the lightest hint now of roses. If I had known kissing her would be like this, I might have started doing it sooner.

Zaya melts against me. Her body fits against mine like a matching puzzle. My hand wraps around her slim waist to pull her closer to me. Everything about her is soft, yielding. I don't sense any of the resistance that has characterized every other encounter we've ever had. Usually, I have to compel her responses, force her to accept what her body craves, even when her mind screams out protests.

There is no hesitation here.

My hands settle over her breasts, stroking and punching until her breaths come in desperate gasps. I force my tongue in her mouth, just as I twist one taut nipple between my fingers so I swallow her low moan.

She breaks our kiss. "You did my back, let me do your front."

The diamond glitters on her finger underneath the spray of water. She keeps adjusting it back down since the ring ends up closer to her knuckle because it needs to be resized. I didn't do that, because it seemed liked a step too far considering the temporary nature of all this, but now I'm rethinking that.

I don't have a choice but to release my hold on her as she sinks to her knees in front of me. The water spray hits me square on the chest, burning hot but still soothing compared to the fire raging inside of me. My hands push into the strands of her hair, curls slippery from the conditioner she hasn't washed out. I pull a curl out with my fingers, watching it spring back when I let go.

Her hair is momentarily fascinating.

Until her slim fingers wrap around my dick and she sucks the tip of it into her mouth.

It stands up so stiff that she doesn't need to do anything to keep it straight, but that doesn't stop her hand from running up and down the length of me. Her cheeks pucker from the effort she puts into sucking me off. My eyes roll back into my head with the effort it takes not to come down her throat after the first minute.

Zaya could lick me like a lollipop, and it would still be the best blow job I've ever had. Because it's her mouth. And her hands. It's just her.

She pulls back enough to lick her lips before sliding them slowly back over the sensitive head of my cock. Her hands work harder, both of them twisting down my shaft. My thighs twitch and I almost lose my balance. I have to hold on to the little towel bar on the wall to keep from falling to my knees and taking her down with me.

As nice as it might be, I don't want to come down her throat. Not this time, at least.

I yank her to her feet, catching her when she slips on the soapy floor and stumbles against me. Kissing her hard again, just because I can, my hands grip her ass and mold her body against mine.

Her leg lifts to balance on the shower ledge, grinding her herself against my upper thigh. The heat of the water is nothing compared to the furnace of her cunt against my skin.

I think about how easy it would be to slip inside of her without any barriers between us. Later, I could blame the heat of the moment and manfully insist on dealing with any potential consequences.

But she is smart enough to anticipate my thoughts, even if she doesn't realize it.

"Condom," she gasps against my mouth. "I think I have one in my purse."

Her hips pull far enough away that I feel a rush of cold.

"Let me get it."

My toiletry bag is on the counter, totally innocuous. She can't know that the strip of condoms coiled up in the side pocket have already been prepared with the edge of a safety pin. She won't know that they won't provide the protection she thinks.

And I'm not going to tell her.

I hate myself more than a little bit as I sheathe my still cock and step into the shower. She stands there waiting for me, body lushly welcoming and an invitation in her smile.

When my mouth opens again, and I almost tell her the truth. The urge to drop down on my knees and beg forgiveness is overwhelming.

Then her thigh hooks over my hip. She squeezes my cock in her hand and urges my hips forward until I am posed at her entrance.

Any ability for rational thought flees and the words die on my tongue.

Pushing inside of her feels like finally coming home after a lifetime of wandering.

I push her back against the tile wall of the shower. Her passage clenches around my cock, gripping harder than a fist. It only takes a few strokes before I feel the sharp fluttering of her approaching orgasm.

My hands form a shelf under her ass so I can lift her feet off the floor. Using her back against the wall for balance, I slam into her over and over again. Zaya begs me to fuck her harder, faster, fisting my hair and pulling on it hard because she is losing control of herself.

I'm right there with her.

Her eyes roll back into her head and her pussy clamps down on me like a vice when she comes. A silent cry parts her lips. I cover her mouth with my own, taking everything she has to give. Her whimpers, her screams, her very breath.

She is too far gone to tell any difference when I explode inside her.

I've always liked watching Zaya sleep. Nobody needs to tell me how weird and creepy that is, but it is what it is. The first few times I climbed into her room, it was just to stare at her sleeping face. I think I hoped that she might whisper her secret into what she thought was empty air and I'd finally get the answer I've been waiting for since we were children.

It became something different the first time she woke up to

see me sitting there. I had to pretend that I hadn't climbed up the trellis outside and hung from my fingers until I could level my foot up on the window sill, just because I wanted to study her face in the only moments when she seemed at peace.

So I made it about sex, because that was easier than telling the truth.

We've always had everything but truth between us, so what was one more lie.

But I no longer have to think of excuses to watch her sleep. I carry her from the shower to the bed, and she is already asleep by the time I lay her out on the blanket. To be fair, I woke her up in the middle of the night to bring her here, and not everyone needs as little as sleep as I do.

When she rolls over and lets out a little sneeze before burrowing into the downy comforter, I nearly wake her up to fuck her all over again. Instead, I let her rest while she still can.

I don't bother trying to sleep, because there isn't any point. Instead, I surf Reddit on my phone and respond to the handful of text messages I've been ignoring. The oldest one is from my father:

Is it done?

My response is only one word.

Yes.

He hasn't asked me for any details about the money I've spent or the plans I've made to get Zaya's compliance, and I haven't offered any. I get the feeling he'd rather not know what I'm doing, because he doesn't want to feel compelled to get involved. That has always been the way of things. Whenever some uppity administrator at school tried to force me to heel by threatening parental interaction, they quickly learned that for every ten messages they left with my father's secretary, maybe one would get returned. Even that was a stretch.

We'll expect you for dinner tonight.

And that's what I get for not ignoring him. As stupid as it sounds, I had this idea that I could keep these two very different facets of my life completely separate. I doubt she wants to be inside Cortland Manor any more than I do. I angrily push out a reply and close the messaging app. I hate that I'm supposed to be available to everyone in my life at all times. Sometimes, I just want to cut myself off from the world.

The next time I look up from the screen, Zaya is awake and staring at me.

She opens her mouth. Before she can say anything, I hear a loud rumble from under the sheet coming from the general vicinity of her stomach.

Her face flushes with embarrassment.

"I've already ordered lunch," I laugh, thoroughly amused. I keep forgetting how cute she manages to be without trying.

Her shy and grateful smile sends a stab of warmth through my cold heart.

Zaya attacks the tray before the room service guy can even finish setting it down on the small table. The fact that she refused breakfast is a testament to just how annoyed she had been with me earlier.

She eats with a single-minded intensity, systematically demolishing the Montechristo sandwich as I watch in amazement. When I snag a french fry from her plate, she practically slaps my hand away.

"You eat like you've spent time in prison."

"And you eat like someone who always knows the next

meal is coming." The dull point of her butter knife stabs at the back of my hand when I go for another fry. "Steal anything else off my plate, and I'll shank you."

"Are you really threatening me over a fry?"

"Five fries. You've taken five fries. Keep your hands off." A small smile teases the corner of her mouth, but her tone brooks no argument. She might just stab me over a side dish. "If you wanted french fries, then you shouldn't have ordered that sad little salad."

I glance down at my plate full of freshly-picked arugula and heirloom tomatoes.

"Calm down, Shawshank. The rest is all yours." Shaking my head, I hold my hands up in surrender. "Though I do feel compelled to point out that bottomless french fries are only a phone call away."

Zaya starts at that, as if only just realizing there is more food where this came from.

I know she doesn't want me to pity her, so I keep my face carefully blank.

The tension leaves her expression as she takes a furious bite of her sandwich. "Then leave mine alone and order some for yourself."

If she eats like this at dinner with my parents, Giselle is going to have a field day. "We're leaving soon to head back."

Food gone, she leans back in her chair and just stares at me as I stand up from the table. The robe I wrapped around her after we got out of the shower gapes open in the front, exposing the smooth expanse of her chest. My gaze narrows on one almond-colored nipple just peeking out past the terry cloth.

"We're not spending the night?" She almost sounds disappointed.

Aside from the dinner date with my damn parents, there is a laundry list of things we need to accomplish for this marriage to hold any water. Our marriage license needs to be filed at the courthouse, and West wants a copy of the prenuptial agreement as soon as possible. Not to mention, I figured she would want to go see her brother as soon as possible.

"Is that a problem?"

"No," she replies hurriedly. "I just thought...you know what, never mind."

Her dress is draped across the foot of the bed. I toss it in her general direction without looking at her. "Get dressed. We're going."

Her balled up robe hits me hard in the face. With a force of will that almost brings me to my knees, I keep my head turned away.

That lasts for about fifteen and a half seconds.

When I finally chance a look at her, not only is she still naked, but posed with her hips jutting forward so my gaze is automatically drawn to the part of her I can't stop thinking about.

Smirking at whatever look is on my face, she finally pulls the damn dress over her head.

I don't know how the hell I'm going to make it through the next year without losing my mind. The game has changed, and Zaya just scored another point.

THIRTY

"Oh, hell no."

I hold the dirty receiver away from my face so it won't touch my skin, but Zion's voice is still loud enough to practically burst my ear drum.

Visiting Zion at the Justice Center is even less fun than I thought it would be. Luckily, they haven't transferred him to the county jail because he's underage, but this place still sucks. I spent an hour in the visitor's waiting room watching the parade of stricken family members come in and out, trying not to cry from the stress of it all.

My idiot of a brother should be grateful he isn't completely on his own.

"You really don't have a choice," I reply with an aggrieved sigh. "Unless you want to spend all of your best years behind bars."

"So I should just trade one prison for another?" Zion glares at me through the thick glass separating us, his anger and frustration palpable.

Those are the emotions he uses to hide his fear.

"It's more like private school than a jail. You'd be able to get your diploma and take some college classes. Might even be the best thing that ever happened to you, if it gets you out of Deception." I can't decide which of us I'm trying to convince. The thought of sending him away makes my heart ache, but I can't consider the alternative. "You might even like it, everyone else there will be a juvenile delinquent."

He makes a rude sound with his mouth. "You mean the kind who shoplift from fancy department stores to get back at their rich absentee parents? Where do I sign up?"

"If you don't take the deal, then you're going to adult prison. You really expect me to believe the people in there are any better?"

Zion shakes his head. "My crew is at county."

"Your crew is why you're here in the damn first place."

"I told you these charges are trumped up. I'm innocent."

"And since when does that ever matter for people like us?"

I read the whole story on my phone during the ride back to Deception. Three masked men burst into the Gas and Sip, demanding all the cash in the register. One of them pistol-whipped the cashier and the gun went off, killing the poor guy. All three of the suspects fled the scene, but a witness caught the license plate of their getaway car. That car was picked up a few hours later with four people in it, Zion included. My brother swears up and down that he wasn't in that convenience store and had no idea what they'd done when he hooked up with his friends later in the night. The police maintain that he could have been in the car to act as a getaway driver, which would make him just as culpable.

Someone has to go down for this. The Deception police aren't exactly motivated to look any further than my brother and his shitty friends. Even I wondered if Zion could have been involved when I read the story. The only thing that makes me believe him is that he has never been able to lie to me, even when we were kids.

Living in a place like the Gulch turns everyone into something dark and twisted eventually. You either become the aggressor or just more collateral damage. If Zion weren't sitting behind this glass now, something else would have brought him here eventually.

Zion curses into the phone. "This is bullshit."

"And if your *crew* is so tight, why aren't any of them saving you from this? If they know you weren't there, why not just say so?"

"Because that would mean admitting they *were* there. Don't be an idiot."

I raise my eyebrows. "Which means they're okay with you going down for a crime that they committed. These definitely sound like true friends to me. Remind me to put them on our Christmas card list this year."

He just shakes his head, looking defeated. "You just don't understand how this works."

My brother looks like shit, though I don't tell him that. His eyes are bloodshot with dark circles underneath, like he hasn't slept at all since he got here. Maybe he hasn't. A splash of blood stains his beige jumpsuit right on the chest, like drips from a nosebleed. It makes me wonder if someone has roughed him up, which might explain why he doesn't want to talk.

"I understand that you have a chance to save yourself. And nobody else is stepping up to do it."

His fist grips the receiver on his end, so hard that I wonder if the plastic will crack. He slumps against the wall beside him. "You don't know what they'll do to me if I talk."

"I know what will happen if you don't. According to Vin's uncle, they have enough evidence to nail you to the wall. There won't be any walking away from this, no matter what happens."

"Vin, huh?" Zion's glare is strong enough to peel the paint from the walls. "He already managed to worm his way into this, I see. Guy works fast."

I haven't told him about the marriage, mostly hoping it never comes up at all. By the time his sentence is served, a year will be long past and I can pretend that Vin Cortland never existed.

"Without Vin, there wouldn't be any deal at all. Don't be stupid about this."

My brother doesn't know that Vin is waiting for me outside. I managed to convince my new husband not to come in with me, but that means he planted himself in the coffee shop across the street, watching the door of the Justice Center like a hawk so he'll know the moment I walk back out. He told me that if I tried to take the bus home, he'd put me over his knee and spank my bare ass.

I can't decide if I want that to be a real threat or not.

When I showed him the article, pointing out that I could have been the one working at the Gas and Sip that night, his only response was, "Good thing you don't work there anymore."

Vin is still the same autocratic asshole he's always been, but I don't understand this sudden desire to protect me. Obviously, he doesn't want me dying before he gets his inheritance, but my reputation seems to matter to him as much as my safety does. I don't get the impulse that has him suddenly acting like the hero in a romance novel. Although I have to admit it feels nice to have someone looking out for me, instead of the other way around. But I shouldn't let him lull me into a false sense of security. He might be on his best behavior right now, but it won't last.

It never does.

Vin is truly a force to be reckoned with when he deigns to

turn on the charm, but eventually something will piss him off and we'll end up back where we started.

His whims are too unpredictable to trust.

As if reading my mind, Zion murmurs. "I don't trust the fucking Cortlands, and you shouldn't either."

"Trust has nothing to do with it," I snap. "Look, your lawyer is going to meet with you this week with the paperwork ready to sign. You have until then to decide. But your only choices are to rot in prison until you're forty, or testify and go to this cushy diversion program. The judge has already said that you'll be transferred on the same day you testify so the assholes here won't get a chance to touch you."

"Fuck." His head drops against the glass. "This is too much."

"Nothing is ever easy. Not for us."

One of the guards raps his knuckles against the door, letting me know we have less than a minute left. "I have to go soon. I put some money on your commissary and you need to call me if you need anything else."

His gaze narrows on my face. "Where are you getting the money for all this? Lawyers aren't cheap, and I already heard it isn't a public defender on my case."

Zion is not going to want to hear where the money came from or why it's coming. "We can fight about the details later. Just focus on getting through this."

"Please tell me this isn't what I think it is."

He thinks I'm whoring myself out to save him. Maybe I am, even if we've put a prettier label on it. "You made the front page of the paper, so I suggest you hold on to whatever stones you're planning to throw. We'll talk about everything later. I love you."

"Love you, too," he says with a sigh. "Even though I don't want you fucking up your life to save mine."

"No need. I fuck my life up all on my own for no good reason at all."

I put down the receiver without waiting for a response, because I don't really want to hear whatever he would have said next. Zion has always let his frustration at our circumstances get the best of him, like railing against the universe is going to change anything. He thought that acting out would show the world how much he doesn't care, but that just has him facing a possible life sentence for a crime he almost certainly didn't commit.

Life isn't fair. And sometimes you have to deal with the devil to get your due.

THE RIDE BACK TO DECEPTION WITH VIN IS QUIET, BUT not exactly awkward.

Neither of us talk much, probably because anything else we say might break the strange spell that has been cast over us. Knowing that I'm his wife, even though it's temporary, has changed things. Kissing him changed things.

Throwing myself at him, initiating sex for the first time ever, has changed things.

I know Vin has to feel it, too, even if I'm not stupid enough to ask him. We're at a place where we can actually enjoy some aspects of each other's company. That's the most we've had between us in years.

I'm not going to ruin it with talk.

My elbow is on the arm rest, which puts my arm close to his when he grips the shifter to switch gears. Every so often his fingers gently stroke the back of my hand, smoothing along my skin.

He seems lost in his own thoughts, making me wonder if he even realizes he's doing it.

I really don't want to have dinner with his family. His parents seem nice enough, if distant, but they aren't the problem.

Being inside Cortland Manor kicks up an itch under my skin that I can't scratch. My flesh feels like it's gone too tight on my bones until I'm all dried out and practically dead. I managed the annoying sensation during the Founder's Ball, but that was only because I had Jake there to distract me.

I still feel more than a little bad when I think about Jake. I can only imagine the look on his face when he finds out that Vin and I got married.

If he even finds out, at all.

It isn't like Vin ever made it clear whether we're going public with all this crap or not. He had us elope to wine country with only his closest friend to serve as a witness. Nobody has to know about any of this for it to be legal.

I'll just be his dirty little secret.

Except, we're on the way to dinner with his parents. He publicly sent work crews in to fix up my house and battered down the door of the district attorney's office to get my brother out of trouble.

That isn't how you treat a secret.

I shouldn't care, either way. We made a deal. It would be stupid of me to expect — to want — anything else.

I'll let him pay my way through school, keep my brother out of prison, and set my Grandpa up somewhere with appropriate medical care. All of that is worth a year.

And the way he sets my body on fire won't be anything more than a fringe benefit.

Cortland Manor is almost completely dark when we pull into

the long circular driveway, one large window brightly lit on the far side of the house where the dining room is located. Even from the outside, the place reminds me of a mausoleum at the best of times.

But it's even worse in the dark.

I've only ever gone in through the front door, so I suppress a fearful shiver as he navigates the car toward the pitch black rear of the house. Anything not illuminated by the Maserati's headlights is sunk into darkness. Intellectually, I know there aren't any monsters hiding in the palm trees and wax myrtle that mark the property line of Cortland Manor.

I don't breathe again until the motion-activated floodlights come on and light up the long garage.

Vin navigates the car into the only open space. As the lights continue to come on, one by one, I count the cars that fill the garage that has at least double the square footage of my entire house. All of the vehicles are sporty and expensive – I don't even recognize some of the shiny emblems on their hoods.

I'm almost surprised that I've only ever seen him with the Maserati. He could drive a different luxury car every day of the week and still not be back where he started.

"How much money is in this garage?"

He blinks, probably surprised to hear my voice after hours of silence. "I've never counted. A couple million, maybe."

Considering that only a few miles away in the Gulch children are going to bed hungry, this is more than a little sickening.

"Must be nice."

"Dad is a collector. Most of these don't leave the garage more than once a year."

"He collects... cars?"

Vin shrugs. "Pretty common thing around here."

Common among the self-important assholes on the Bluffs who have more money than they know what to do with.

"Awesome."

"You don't sound impressed."

There isn't any point in lying. "I'm not."

"Me neither." He loops his arm around my back and pulls me toward the door. "I much prefer collecting women."

On that note.

His family is already waiting for us in the formal dining room. The long table is big enough to seat at least a dozen people, but they cluster on one side with his father at the head. Place settings glitter like oyster shells in the light, but no food has been served.

They've been waiting for us.

Vin introduces me as if we haven't been living in the same town our entire lives. I've encountered his parents many times before, not that it means I know them at all. Duke Cortland barely looks up from the open laptop he has next to him on the table. While his stepmother doesn't look up from her phone, lazily swiping with one manicured finger.

His little sister is the only one who actually looks at me when she returns my greeting.

My expression of silent entreaty doesn't escape Vin's notice, but he just shrugs. When I glare at him, all I get in response is a placid expression.

"Emma, this is Zaya." He says it breezily, as if I'm just a friend that he brought home from school.

Not his wife.

I'm not sure what to think about that as I sit down next to Emma.

A silent maid serves the food, placing a plate of something vaguely green and unrecognizable in front of me before disappearing.

"We're gluten and dairy free," Emma pipes up helpfully as she catches my expression. "Want me to pass you the salt?"

I accept it, gratefully. But I doubt there is enough salt in the world to make whatever this is palatable. It's a real shame for people to have this much money and still eat food that isn't fit to feed livestock.

"Emma here is a little too interested in sweets," Giselle says as she puts down her phone. Her own plate has a significantly smaller portion than everyone else's, which can't possibly be an accident. "You'll have to share your secrets for keeping such a trim figure, Zaya."

It's amazing what a starvation diet can do for you.

I bite my tongue on a sarcastic remark. Emma is a perfectly healthy girl. With her blonde hair and round cheeks, she looks fresh off a photoshoot for Gap Kids.

Vin clearly agrees with me, if the death glare he levels at his stepmother is any indication. But he doesn't bother to say anything to Giselle and instead addresses his sister. "I've got some ice cream in the pool house, if you want something that doesn't taste like the devil's ass crack."

Emma smiles, just as her mother makes an annoyed sound, "Enough, Vin!"

"No dairy or gluten?" His voice is conspiring as he leans over Emma's plate to peer at her serving. Judging from his sister's smile, they're used to being on the same side against Giselle. "C'mon, this might as well be Auschwitz."

Despite all appearances to the contrary, I was actually raised with some manners.

"It tastes wonderful, Mrs. Cortland." I bring a forkful of limp green sludge to my mouth and take a bite. About ten seconds later, I have to fight the urge not to spit it back out. If Giselle notices the expression on my voice, she doesn't comment.

I have literally been so hungry that it felt like my stomach was wrapped around my spine. I still probably wouldn't have eaten whatever the hell is on this plate.

Duke finally speaks without bothering to look away from his computer screen. "I hear congratulations are in order."

I raise my eyebrows as I glance at Vin. I guess none of this is a secret from his parents.

"Signed, sealed, and delivered," Vin comments nonchalantly.

"We'll need to plan for an official ceremony. Soon, for the sake of appearances. I can book the chapel relatively soon, likely by the end of the month. But it will be more difficult to find a venue for the reception on such short notice, so perhaps we'll do something on the beach. Let people think it's a matter of taste, rather than haste."

My wild-eyed expression flies to Vin, who has his fist clenched around a water glass. The last thing I want to do is stand up in front of the entire town and pledge my troth to the guy who tortured me for years. Judging from the look on his face, he doesn't want that either.

"Marriage is already legal," he says, using the same low voice that has had people all over Deception shaking in their boots since he was fourteen years old. "I'm filing the paperwork tomorrow."

But Duke doesn't seem to be listening. He taps out a few letters on the keyboard before speaking again, not so much as sparing his son a glance. "Cortlands do not elope. Appearances matter, you know that. I'm sure Giselle would be happy to take care of the planning details"

I shake my head so hard I feel a little lightheaded. Giselle's smile is more than a little forced when she agrees.

"I would be happy to plan everything." Her voice is saccharine, but there is a brittle note underneath the sweetness. "Do you have any preferences, Vin? The oleander is blooming and would look lovely in the centerpieces."

Vin abruptly stands. "Thanks for dinner."

He grabs my wrist. I briefly resist, but at the look on his face decide it's probably better to just go along with him. I'm sure as hell not going to eat any more of the food.

"This was lovely," I call over my shoulder as he hustles me out of the dining room.

I'm glad he doesn't let go of my hand as we leave the house and are plunged into darkness. The pathway to the pool house is barely lit and I would probably head in the wrong direction if Vin wasn't leading the way.

"Are you guys behind on your light bill, or something?" I grouse.

"Giselle thinks that lighting the house attracts vandals or thieves. Most of the outside lights have been switched off."

I wonder if he ever feels afraid out here alone in the dark.

The pool house is smaller than I thought it would be, less like a cool bachelor crash pad and more like an abandoned flop-house people sneak into when they want to get high. There are beer cans and empty liquor bottles littering every surface. Dirty clothes are piled up in the corner, and I recognize a shirt that he last wore weeks ago.

"I thought you guys had maids."

Vin makes a beeline for the fridge. "They're on orders not to come out here. Giselle says she doesn't want them finding drugs and reporting me."

"When did you move out of the main house?"

"Some time in middle school, I think. Definitely by freshman year."

I bet that was Giselle's decision, too. It doesn't seem like there is much love lost between Vin and his stepmother, with his father too oblivious to notice.

I never would have thought it possible for me to feel pity for Vin Cortland.

"You mind if I clean up a little?"

He turns back from the open refrigerator, a strange expression on his face. "Sure, knock yourself out."

His gaze follows me as I start filling the trash can with empty cans and other trash. No way am I carrying any laundry back to the main house in the dark, but I gather it all into the hamper and push that into the corner of the bedroom.

The bed has clean sheets on it, so at least Vin's lack of fastidiousness doesn't extend completely beyond the pale.

When the room is slightly less of a biohazard, I collapse onto the leather couch. I'm exhausted, but somehow still wired. Vin settles next to me with two beers and a plate with several slices of pizza on it.

"Leftovers from the weekend." He sets the load down on the table. "Better get used to takeout if you want to eat around here."

I take a bite of pizza and nearly come on the spot. "You could have warned me about the green machine. That food looked like it had already been eaten."

"Don't worry. Thankfully, family dinners are a rare occurrence."

The pizza goes quickly. It doesn't escape my notice that he lets me have the last piece, even though I've already had more than him.

"You're trying to fatten me up," I comment.

"Whatever works. I don't want you passing out from hunger the next time I fuck you."

The words shimmer between us.

I set down my plate on the narrow coffee table. Vin is already reaching for me before it drops from my fingers, and it lands on the wooden surface with a clatter. He doesn't give me the chance to check if the plate has broken.

Vin kisses me hard and forces me back against the leather couch. My legs spread wide as he settles between them, his mouth never leaving mine as his body shifts over me.

The already hard kiss turns biting before he pulls back to look at me. His hands run up my ribcage to my breasts, until one of them wraps around my neck. "You married me, Zaya. That makes you mine." His mouth presses against my neck until I feel the sharp edge of his teeth. "Every inch of you is mine. I decide when you eat. When you sleep. When you come all over my fingers."

To punctuate his point, his other hand slips under my dress. I didn't have a change of underwear at the vineyard and I wasn't about to put the old ones back on, so I'm not wearing any. Nothing is there to stop his fingers from pushing inside of me. My own hands are trapped beneath my body, so I can't stop him from ruching my dress up around my hips.

His tongue traces a line down the flat plane of my belly. He still has a hand pressed against my throat, not too hard, but enough that I won't forget it's there.

Holding me.

Controlling me.

"Vin..." His name is a plea, but I have no idea what I'm asking him for.

"Tell me the truth, Zaya." He shifts so his mouth rests just above mine. The hand he has over my throat presses down harder. "Tell me why you never fought me off when I crawled into your bed at night. Tell me why every time I've touched you, you've been wetter than diving into an ocean wave. Tell me you've always wanted me to own you."

"I've always wanted you," I breathe out on a sigh, not realizing until I say it that it's the truth. My throat pushes harder against his hand when I swallow back any more words that sound like love. I know he doesn't want to hear them, and I'm too aroused to decide if I'm only thinking them because his fingers are teasing at my clit. "You have always owned me."

"I've spent so much time thinking up ways to hurt you, and now I have you here with me and my mind won't stop whirling with possibilities. I want to hurt you." The harsh words are completely at odds with the slow plunge of his fingers in and out of me. They pull out to tease at the top of my opening before pushing in again. The sensation he creates is as far removed from pain as anything can be. "It takes everything I have not to break you in half."

He broke me a long time ago. It's only now that he has ever tried to put me back together. But I will always be the rag doll knitted together at the seams. His broken doll.

I can't handle any more talk, not when it leaves a feeling like broken glass in the pit of my stomach. Vin will never be able to love me, not after everything that has happened. Allowing myself — even for a moment — to treat this as anything by temporary will just lead to more pain.

And I've had enough of that to last a lifetime.

I manage to free one hand and press my palm over the back of the hand he holds to my throat. "Then hurt me."

Without warning, he slaps me hard on the pussy.

My hips buck off the couch. He shoves those same wet fingers in my mouth to stifle a desperate cry. The pain is gone as quickly as it appeared, but the shock of it leaves me gasping.

Vin pulls away just long enough to roll on a condom that practically appears out of thin air. He is back on top of me before I have the chance to decide if I want to be the dozenth girl that he has fucked on this couch.

Next thing I know, my face is buried in the couch and my

ass is in the air. He grips my hips and buries himself inside of me again with enough force that it nearly bowls us both over.

He slaps my ass once. Then twice. Then again and again, until each strike matches the rhythm of his thrusts and my backside blazes with heat.

And pain.

Tears prick my eyes, nose burning, as he fucks me. The spanking isn't that painful, it shouldn't be enough to make me cry. But the tears come anyway, starting out as a few drops that quickly becomes a wracking sob.

If anything, crying seems to make him rougher. He doesn't ask if I'm okay, doesn't hesitate when I make desperate noises underneath him. But I'm moving with him. My hips rock back to meet each one of his thrusts, even when it means that the tip of him bottoms out inside me, striking hard against my womb in a way that could be either pleasure or pain.

The pain is a release I didn't know I needed.

"You like this?" he asks. The words are completely unnecessary considering that he must feel my flesh shivering around him with impending orgasm. He slaps my ass again. "Show me how much."

I say the only thing that seems to make sense. "Harder."

Vin takes me precisely at my word.

His hands clench tight on my inflamed skin as he pounds into me as hard and as fast as he can. I come like an explosion that sends every particle of my consciousness shooting off into space. I come apart under his hands, every piece of me shaking and quivering with my need for him.

Vin collapses on top of me with a low groan. His mouth moves over my back, peppering soft kisses along the skin as I float in a dreamlike haze. Maybe this is a dream. I'm going to wake up in my own bed to see him sitting there in the dark, rage and hate in his eyes.

His hands are anything but hate-filled as he gently lifts me in his arms and carries me to the bed. He lays me gently down in his bed, a place I never in my life thought I would be, and pulls the blanket up to my chin.

He shuts off the light, but doesn't climb into bed with me. "Sleep."

I'm dimly aware of the fact that I've never heard of any girl spending the night in Vin's bed, not even Sophia.

I wonder if I'm the first.

My hand pushes out from under the covers. I hold it out to the shapeless form that I can barely see in the dark.

I don't have to see his face to sense the hesitation.

He doesn't move for a long time, likely hoping I've fallen asleep, but he doesn't say no. I'm still surprised when he crosses the narrow room and climbs into bed beside me.

It has been the longest day of my life, but sleep is elusive. When I wake up, yesterday will have been my wedding day. I'm not ready for tomorrow, when the reality of it finally comes crashing down on me.

The diamond on my finger glints in the meager light, reminding me I no longer know who I am anymore.

My breath is slow and even, but I'm still awake hours later when his arm drapes over my waist and he settles against my back. His lips tickle the back of my neck. I resist giving any reaction that might make him pull away.

I've never been so completely broken apart.

I can only hope that at some point he plans to put me back together.

THIRTY-ONE

I EXPECT THE WORLD TO FEEL DIFFERENT WHEN I WAKE UP in the morning.

It surprises me when everything seems almost exactly the same. Then I remember where I am. I'm not in the bed of my cramped little room, or inside the house that is my family's last earthly possession in a world that has clawed everything else away from us. Instead, I'm in the pool house of Cortland Manor, next to a guy who is the worst cover hog I've ever encountered.

This morning, I wake up as Vin Cortland's wife.

But it feels like something more should be different. Because I am not the same. The Zaya Milbourne who existed a few weeks ago never would have agreed to any of this.

It should scare me more how quickly things can change, especially the way that I feel.

Now that we're married, there might finally be cracks in the wall that has stood between us for the last ten years, letting the smallest amount of light through. That isn't enough for me to think the past is actually behind us, but it gives me hope I might be able to walk away from this with my soul intact.

There isn't a name for the emotion that wells up in me as I climb out of bed: a mix of fear and anticipation.

Fearcipation?

The thought makes me smile to myself, which surprises me again. Even in my own mind, there has rarely been room for playfulness or cheer. Every day of my life up to this point has been a slog to get from one moment to another without collapsing under the weight of it all.

Vin has always been part of the worst of that, but even he isn't powerful enough to be responsible for it all. He didn't lose the Milbourne fortune or cast us down into the muck in the Gulch. He didn't force my mother to pack her bags and run because she couldn't face the things she had done.

Vin Cortland had nothing to do with whatever made my last name synonymous with the dirt underneath people's shoes, even if he has taken advantage of it. Any well-meaning adult could have stopped him from tormenting me, but no one in this town ever cared enough to make the attempt. And I know from experience that he has his own demons.

Already, I'm trying to rationalize the fact that I've said yes.

But today is the first day I can remember that I haven't woken up with what feels like the weight of the world on my shoulders. My grandfather is under better care than he has ever had in his entire life. Down in the Gulch, Grandpa will be out of bed and doing laps around the living room in his walker with the help of a physical therapist. Just seeing him walking is enough to make me forgive the horrible things Vin has done to me over the years.

Maybe one day, I'll even forgive myself.

A social worker is already scheduled to come out and evaluate him for placement at the senior care home. Zion is days from getting out of Deception and away from the worst influences in our town with the chance to end up on a much better path than he ever would have been on otherwise.

In a year, I'll be free. With enough Cortland cash lining my pockets to go anywhere and be anything I want. If Vin hadn't come along with the deal, I would say it's too good to be true.

But I can handle anything for a year, even Vin. What is one year in exchange for a lifetime in which nothing would have changed?

I've gotten acceptance letters to UCLA and UC Santa Barbara, both close enough that I could possibly commute from home with a car to avoid paying for campus housing. But that doesn't matter, because neither of them offered me any financial aid. Without access to my mother's financial records, they couldn't offer me an aid package. Since Grandpa never adopted me, I have to submit her information.

Just one more thing to add to the list of all the ways she screwed me over by leaving.

But Mrs. Vin Cortland doesn't need financial aid. She can write a check and pay for all four years of school at once.

Vin seems less concerned about the abrupt change in his routing. He is apparently the polar opposite of a morning person. His eyes don't open all the way while he gets dressed, and it takes two cups of coffee for him to even seem to realize that I'm there.

When he catches me watching him, he just glares and gestures for me to follow him out the door, which he slams shut behind us.

Definitely not a morning person.

Neither of us speak until I notice we're driving in the opposite direction of Deception High. "Where are we going?"

"We have an errand to run before school."

We're headed back toward the nicer shopping district in town. "What kind of errand?"

"The kind you'll find out about in less than five minutes if you just shut up and wait."

"Oh look, you're being a jerk just for the fun of it. It must be a day that ends with Y."

"Whatever else you got, get it out now." Vin pulls the car into a parallel space along a nearly deserted street lined with designer shops. He pushes the gearshift into park and turns to me with a mocking smile. "The next step is slapping Duct tape over your mouth, which might raise some eyebrows around here."

There are a few people drinking cappuccinos outside a French bakery on the corner, but aside from that we're the only ones here. "All the shops are closed."

"Not for me."

With that cryptic remark, he grabs my arm and half-drags me down the street toward an upscale boutique a few doors down from where we parked. On the glass window, *Le Clotherie* is etched in white script with *Hours by Appointment Only* inscribed underneath.

I hesitate at the door, but Vin shoves it open as if he has every right to bust inside. When he turns and locks it behind us, I experience a trill of nervousness.

"For privacy," he murmurs, catching the expression on my face. "Wouldn't want someone to walk in off the street and ruin the *Pretty Woman* moment."

Before I can think of a suitable response, he gently pushes me through a gossamer curtain and into the back of the space.

A chicly petite older woman with midnight skin and hair so aggressively white that it had to be a fashion choice not to use dye when it went gray comes out from behind a rack of clothes.

"*Monsieur* Cortland, *mon petit crotte.* I am having too

much happiness when you call. It has been too long. I have not seen you since you were *un enfant*." She comes forward with her arms wide and wraps her arms around Vin in a giant embrace that I am shocked to see him return. "I was so happy to get your call."

This is the only time I've seen him accept non-sexual affection with an audience. I expect the sky to fall at any possible moment.

I wrack my brain for what little I remember from the French class I took sophomore year.

"Did she just call you a little shit?" I ask him sotto voce, when the woman steps back.

He grimaces. "Apparently it's a term of endearment, so shut up."

"And let me look at you." The woman grabs my hands and spreads them wide. "You must be the special girl I have been told about. We must take very good care of you. I am Adelphine Turay, and this is my shop. Vin has known me for his whole life. His mother used to come here for her entire wardrobe. She was my favorite customer, only I had the privilege of dressing her."

Vin's mouth has thinned into an unhappy line when I risk a glance back at him. He doesn't let anybody talk about his mother, as if he wants to forget she ever existed.

Adelphine doesn't seem to notice his frown, or simply doesn't care. "Sit here while I bring out the racks. What refreshment do you prefer: coffee, tea, lemon water?"

"Bourbon?" Vin mutters.

She waves her hand at him, but the smile on her face is indulgent. "Coffee for you, bad boy."

I collapse into a fabric-covered chair, exhausted just from watching her twirl around the room. "Tea would be great. Thank you."

"So polite, not like the other prissy misses I see all day." She pats my hand before turning to Vin, her tone changing to one that is more motherly but still gently chiding. "Take care of this one so I am seeing her again."

"That's up to her, isn't it?"

There's something in his voice that makes me turn to look at him. But Vin picks up a fashion magazine and opens it up. "Casual female nudity. God, I love the French."

"Those designs are Algerian, my heart." Adelphine sweeps back in with our drinks before I can say something caustic back to him. She waves me toward a raised platform at the center of the room. "Undress."

I look at her in pained shock, realizing there aren't any dressing rooms back here. My gaze swings back to Vin, who has put down the magazine and regards me with eyes full of both challenge and anticipation.

"Go on," Adelphine encourages as she drapes a measuring tape over her shoulder. "You Americans can be so prudish. You are married, non?"

I raise my eyebrows at Vin in obvious question. He had acted like our quickie ceremony in Sonoma was meant to be a secret.

"Where do you think I got your wedding dress?" Vin's smug grin makes it clear that he expects me to embarrass myself by making some protest.

I remind myself that it isn't as if he hasn't seen all of me before.

A sudden surge of bravado moves through me. If he wants to play games, then I'm already dressed and out on the field.

Gripping the hem of my t-shirt, I pull it over my head, only faltering when it catches in my hair.

"Need any help?" Vin calls from across the room, laughter in his voice.

"No," I snap back at him. My pants hit the floor on top of my shirt, and I'm left standing in my bra and underwear on the platform. Heat suffuses my skin, and I force myself to stare at a spot on the wall above Vin's head.

Adelphine clucks over me like a mother hen, measuring my bust, waist, and hips as she makes marks on a little pad of paper. "So wispy like a fashion model. The selection we have will be *tres bien* for you."

I can already see that it was a calculated move on Vin's part to bring me here. Adelphine is so personable and moves so quickly that I don't have the chance to gainsay her on anything. I try on a dozen outfits in the space of thirty minutes, each one more perfect for me than the last. She seems to understand that comfort is more important to me than style, even while ensuring I still look like someone with refined taste.

The last outfit is a midnight blue tunic dress with billowy sleeves. Tiny red flowers are stitched on the waist and trail down the sleeves. It looks very dreamy California summer without trying too hard. A pair of strappy sandals made of thin gold rope complete the outfit.

When I risk a glance at the price tag dangling across my wrist, I nearly swallow my own tongue.

My mouth opens to say something, but Vin beats me to the punch.

He steps up next to me, head only rising to my shoulder while I'm still standing on the dais, and waves Adelphine away as she approaches with another dress laid over her arm. "We'll take everything she tried on already. School starts in twenty minutes."

I glare at him. "How much is this going to cost?"

He pinches me lightly on the hip before I can pull away. "Why? Keeping track of how much you're worth."

"I really don't feel comfortable with all this." I'm not sure if I'm talking just about the clothes, or something else.

"No backing out now, you already signed the contract." His hand stays on my hip as he turns back to Adelphine. "Thank you for everything, Mama Turay. I knew we could count on you. Zaya is going to wear this one out. Go ahead and trash everything she came in wearing. Or rip it up if you're cleaning service needs extra rags for scrubbing the bathroom."

"The hell are—"

Vin comes steps up onto the platform and covers my mouth with his free hand as he smiles widely at Adelphine. "You mind writing up the bill for me real quick?"

"Of course." I don't miss that she gathers up my discarded clothes into her arms before disappearing into a backroom.

As soon as she leaves, I sink my teeth into his palm. Vin pulls his hand away with a muffled curse. "Now you're making that lovely woman your accomplice?"

"She knows how to read a room. And a bigger bill is good for all of us."

"This isn't what I agreed to," I grind out through clenched teeth, pulling away from him. "You don't get to play dress up doll with me."

"We negotiated, remember? It's your fault for not taking this off the table when you had the chance. I don't want people seeing you in rags."

Those familiar feelings of inadequacy are rising back up. "Just because clothes are from discount stores, doesn't make them rags."

He sighs, obviously exasperated. "It does when they have holes and ripped seams because they were already well-used when you got them. This doesn't need to be as hard as you're making it. Let's pretend you're a brand new Zaya, one that wears nice clothes, drives a car with advanced safety features, and does what her husband tells her to do."

"Is she married to a brand new Vin?" I glare down at him. "Because that's the only way I see it working out."

A calculating smile twists his lips. He takes a step back off the platform so I tower over him and his face is level with my waist. "I like you in dresses, by the way. They provide easy access."

His hands slide up my thighs, and I slap them away. "Maybe the new Zaya isn't the type of girl who believes in public displays of affection."

"Maybe the new Zaya is whatever type of girl I want her to be." His hands grip my thighs as he lifts me up. My hands go around his neck by reflex so I don't tip over backwards. He backs up toward the chair and sits down, tightening his arms around me when I attempt to pull away. "Maybe I'll have her right here in the middle of my godmother's store."

"Stop it. She's going to come back..." His lips touch my neck, and the words turn into a soft sigh. My hands press against his chest so I can feel the steady beat of his heart against my palms. "You can't do just do whatever you want."

"Watch me." His mouth nips a trail along my jaw until his lips brush against my ear. "This doesn't have to be hard. We can make it so simple and so easy. Just enjoy ourselves for a year without turning everything into a fight."

"Vin—"

He presses a finger against my lips, silencing me. "The next time I get you alone it's going to be just like this, with you in one of these fucking dresses. Only no one's going to be there to stop me from pulling your panties aside and plunging up into you. Then I'm going to fuck you so slowly that you'll be begging me to let you feel every inch."

My hips grind down against him, only the thin fabric of my

panties and his jeans separating us from each other. Part of me wants him to rip off these brand new clothes and screw me right here in the middle of *Le Clotherie*.

I need to know that this situation makes him as crazy as it does me.

Gripping his hair with my fingers, I force his head closer to mine. I kiss him softly, just because I can. "Do it."

There is a creak of floorboards behind us, and Vin has me back on my feet about one second before Adelphine sweeps back through the thick black curtain. The knowing look on her face makes me wonder if she made the noise on purpose.

She drops half a dozen bags onto the floor next to Vin and hands him a bill to sign. Taking it back, she kisses him gently on each cheek. "Be good."

Then she grips my hands and presses her cheek against mine in an air kiss. "Make him work for it. That boy needs a challenge."

Blushing, I back away from her. It is weird as hell to be hugging Vin's godmother when my panties are soaked. "I'll do my best."

"We're going to be late." Vin picks up the bags and hustles me out of the shop. I barely have time to say goodbye to Adelphine as he pushes me out the door.

As he cheerfully loads the bag in his trunk, whistling to himself, I try to figure out which part this is on the rollercoaster of our relationship. He pings so quickly from one extreme to another that I can barely keep up with him.

Then I ask myself why I'm trying so hard to figure this out. Whatever exists between us has always been beyond reason. This temporary peace doesn't mean that anything has fundamentally changed.

I'll enjoy the peaks, because the inevitable plunge will come in its own time.

THIRTY-TWO

VIN

I've never slept as well in my life as I did last night.

Not that Zaya would know that. I was up before her and sitting on the couch with my vape in one hand and my phone in the other by the time she rolled out of my bed.

My bed.

I thought I would hate having her in my bed, even if it had been my idea for her to stay with me in the first place. Leaving her alone in that dilapidated old house wasn't an option. Not that her grandfather would provide much defense against a home invasion, but at least he was lucid enough to be a witness. Her brother is still sitting in jail and her grandfather is in the care home, not that he would be up to providing much defense.

But the minute that the lowlifes down in the Gulch realized she was in that house all by herself, Zaya would be a sitting duck. Bringing her to the manor is the only option that makes sense, doesn't mean I was looking forward to having her invade my space.

I woke up curled around her as dawn sent pink streaks of

light through the curtains, only realizing then that it had still been dark when I closed my eyes. Usually, I can manage fifteen or twenty minutes at a time before something startles me awake.

But last night I slept like a baby, at least for a few hours.

Zaya seems oblivious to my thoughts as she fidgets in the passenger seat of my Maserati, pulling at the hem of her dress. Her gazes shifts to the display every so often to check the time, obvious impatience written into every line of her body.

She runs for the double doors as soon as I pull into the parking lot, the tardy bell clanging over the loudspeakers. The girl cares a hell of a lot more than I do about being late.

My phone rings, and I lean back in the seat as I answer it, so I can watch her ass as she races up the stairs.

It is a very nice ass.

My father's voice comes over my phone's tinny speaker. "How is it going with the Milbourne girl?"

Oh, just a little bit of dry humping before school while my godmother waited in the other room.

"Fine."

"I didn't bring up the pregnancy codicil at dinner, because I wasn't sure what you had already discussed. Is she agreeable?"

I'm surprised he's asking, because I sincerely doubt he wants the unvarnished truth. "We just need to work out some of the details."

My father lets out a relieved sigh. "Giselle tells me that the Shore Club had a cancellation, so we can hold the reception there, but that means the ceremony will need to be moved up to three weeks from now. Hopefully, enough of our friends can make it that the turnout will be appropriate. A few of my business partners and their wives already have the date penciled in."

Penciled in? He makes my wedding sound like a round of golf. If it wasn't fake, I might be offended.

"We really don't have to go through with this," I hedge. "Everything is already legal as it is."

"Someday you'll understand the sacrifices required to be who we are. You are a Cortland."

I'm already marrying a girl that I'm pretty sure tried to kill me when we were kids. And after compelling her into a fake marriage, I'm going to trick her into carrying my child. There isn't anything more Cortland™ than that.

"Like I give a shit."

"Watch your language."

The phone dangles from my fingers as I see Principal Friedman coming out the main doors, on the lookout for people smoking or playing hooky. I wonder if Zaya got to class on time, if she felt good walking down the halls in an outfit that highlights her beauty instead of hiding it.

I wonder if anybody has said anything about the giant rock on her finger.

"Dad, I've got to go. We'll talk about this later."

I hang up before he can respond.

My relationship with my father has always been...*interesting*. I hate to call it complex, because that implies there are multiple layers when it has always been aggressively superficial. But it's not precisely distant. He cares in an absent way, spending most of his time working or living the life on public display that is expected of the Cortland patriarch.

To hear him tell it, my father married Giselle because he wanted me to have a mother. But my earliest memories are of nannies and frigidly cold rooms in a deserted mansion. Giselle is smart enough not to act like a stereotypical evil stepmother, but I never got the impression that she married my father out of a desperation to play the nurturing mother. The glitz of constant parties and events seems to have been a much greater allure.

Along with all the money, of course.

I used to take it personally until I saw her dealing with Emma in pretty much the same way. If she treats her own biological kid like little more than a fashionable accessory, what chance did I have?

My father's words echo in my head. *You are a Cortland.*

I don't give a fuck about 99% of the people in this town. But I also don't want to set my little sister up for ridicule. Especially when she's in those tender middle school years where everything is *oh my God, so embarrassing*!

The thought of some big to-do in front of the entire town, only to get a quickie divorce a year later, just seems tortuous. An actual wedding ceremony means inviting a whole bunch of people who won't be the least little bit happy to see me walking down the aisle.

Like sharks scenting blood in the water.

My asshole friends are waiting for me with grins on their faces when I get to the cafeteria at lunch. Cal is holding a snack cake from the vending machines with an unlit candle stuck into the center of it. Elliot is holding up a sad sheet of notebook paper with *CONGRATULATIONS?* written on it in block letters.

I glare at Iain. "You fuck."

He just shrugs, not looking the least bit repentant. "You know I don't keep secrets."

Elliot claps me on the back hard enough that I have to catch myself on the edge of the table as I sit down. "Never thought I'd see the day."

"You haven't seen shit," I reply, slouching in the chair. "The ceremony is in a few weeks. I'm sure Giselle will have someone get in touch about your matching cummerbunds."

"This is actually happening." Cal is incredulous. He runs through girls like there's a Guinness record for screwing he hopes to beat before he dies. If it was a choice between tying himself down to only one for a year and the poorhouse, Cal would be drowning in pussy while living under a freeway overpass. "I'll admit I got a laugh when Iain first told us, but I didn't actually think you were serious."

"I'm serious about keeping my inheritance."

But the words ring hollow even to my ears. In the beginning, this was entirely about keeping the Cortland fortune where it belongs. I hated that it was Zaya whom I had to convince to help me, hated her more than I normally did, even though I knew it wasn't her fault that she was the only girl from a Founding family of legal age.

I want to believe that only the money matters, but still find my gaze scanning the cafeteria for her face. I'm already thinking about when she'll want to visit her grandfather at the care home. Whether I should pick out a car for her so she isn't tempted to take the bus anywhere again, or if it would make her happier to go the dealership herself and pick something out.

I find myself wanting to do things just to make her happy, not because I'm getting anything out of her in return.

"Have you seen the rock on Zaya's finger yet?" Iain asked the other two, voice mild. "It's a Cortland family heirloom."

If looks could do damage, Iain would be bleeding on the floor. He might still be later when I get my hands on him.

Cal let out a low whistle. "You gave Zaya Milbourne Gram Gram's ring. Who are you, and what the fuck have you done with Vin?"

"Piss off."

"You haven't even heard the best part," Iain drawls. "He only has a year to—"

I kick Iain hard enough in the shin that I think the bone

might have broken my toe. He doesn't react to the pain, but stops talking long enough for me to divert us to something else.

"I only have to last a year. Zaya walks away with money for college, and I get to keep my inheritance." My annoyed gaze tracks around the table. "Is there anything else you assholes need to know, or can I tell my stepmother to add you to the headcount?"

"Count me in for a plus one," Cal says.

I resist the urge to roll my eyes. "Who?"

"Who cares?"

That isn't even worthy of a response. I look at Elliot. "You in?"

"Of course," he replies immediately. "I'll even stop making fun of you, if just so Zaya doesn't overhear and think she's the one I'm laughing at."

"You won't be laughing when I break your jaw."

He guffaws, if just to prove a point. "Hell yes, I will."

One of these jerks will be my best man. If that isn't a sign this marriage is doomed, nothing is.

THIRTY-THREE

Zaya

News of my elopement is all over school by second period, if I'm judging by the way people openly stare at me in the halls. Their gazes linger on the designer dress and practically bulge when my ring catches in the light.

I've never felt as much like a zoo animal on display as I did when I stepped foot inside Deception High this morning.

Then I notice that something is different.

Most of the looks aren't hostile. If anything, people scurry out of my way like there will be consequences if they don't. The silence is there like it always has been, but now it's respectful instead of deafening.

Vin has still marked me. But instead of being a pariah, now I belong to him.

Every so often, though, I catch a smile or a nod from someone who has never given me either for years. I nearly run into a bay of lockers when a girl from my P.E. class murmurs a quick *Hi, Zaya* as she passes me.

Then one of the football players dives to catch a football in mid-air before it can hit me in the back of the head.

When I look up at him wide-eyed, he thanks me for the invitation.

Too stupid to put it together, I ask what invitation he's talking about.

"To your wedding, of course."

Giselle Cortland works fast, I have to give her that. Apparently, sometime this morning a save the date went out on social media with a promise that formal invitations would arrive by the end of the week. My fake wedding is gearing up to be as big as Founder's Day, with most of the town planning to attend.

It didn't seem to matter to anyone that the invites were coming at the last possible moment.

For the first time ever, I have a partner for the lab experiment in Physics as opposed to working alone like I normally do. People who had spent years pretending I don't exist, suddenly find time to compliment my outfit or greet me as if we were long-lost friends.

This should all make me angry, this reminder of all the things Vin has taken away from me over the years. Instead of angry, it all just makes me feel weird. Like I'm getting a glimpse into someone else's life while wearing their skin, making the world around me seem both completely familiar and entirely alien.

And when I think about him, it isn't anger that stirs in my belly and robs me of breath.

As if I need another reminder that I'm in the midst of doing the dumbest thing I've ever done: falling in love with him.

When I get distracted in class and drop a beaker so it shatters to the floor, three different people rush over to help clean it up. It takes a beat too long for me to thank them. I'm still not used to being allowed to speak to anyone.

Part of me expects Vin to jump out from behind a lab table with murder in his eyes.

Then I remember again that I let him marry me yesterday.

I'd already decided not to eat lunch today, and I never willingly skip a meal. But that's where Vin will be, holding court with his friends at his usual table in the cafeteria. The minute that I set foot inside, every single eye in the room will be on us, raptly watching, waiting to see what we say or do. Even with our newfound peace, hanging out with Vin and his friends while the whole school watches is not how I want to spend any amount of time.

I'm not used to this much attention, even when it's good. I think I might be going more than a little crazy from it. Being invisible had its perks from time to time — at least I didn't feel like everyone was watching me like they're desperate to see what I might do next.

Briefly, I consider going to the library, but I don't want to run into Jake. I've never seen him eat lunch in the cafeteria, so that has to be where he goes. We haven't spoken since he stalked out of my house the night of the Founder's Ball, and something tells me we never will again.

Can't exactly blame him.

It's almost a reprieve to hide in the upstairs girl's bathroom after third period. Nobody ever comes up here, because the air-conditioner blew out after the winter and never got fixed. The slatted windows near the ceiling are the only source of ventilation.

Only burnouts come to this bathroom because they'll claim any empty place to use for getting high, but they also won't skip lunch. With the pipes dried out from disuse, it smells like sewer gas and ditch weed pretty much all the time.

I should have the place to myself for at least twenty minutes.

A burst of hot fetid air greets me as the wooden door creaks open. The smell isn't so bad if you only breathe through your mouth.

Clearly, I'm willing to trade a lot for peace and quiet right now.

It takes a second for me to realize I'm not alone. Someone is crying in the last stall. I try to catch the door before it bangs shut, but I'm not quick enough. The sound echoes off the tile, and the sobbing immediately cuts off.

"Who's out there," a familiar voice demands.

It's too late to sneak out of the bathroom, although if I run fast enough I might make it out in time. But my indecision costs me. The stall door slams open, and the only other person pathetic enough to hide out in the bathroom stumbles out.

Sophia Taylor.

Her blue eyes are bloodshot with smudged eyeliner. Her lipstick is spread across her face like she just swiped at it with the back of her hand. She looks like the horror movie version of a cheerleader, moments from spinning her head around in a full circle.

Alarm crosses her face when she realizes it's me, then anger.

"What the hell are you doing here?"

The old me would have turned tail and run. But a lot has changed since the last time Sophia and I faced off. "Hiding from everyone, obviously. You?"

Sophia opens her mouth like she's about to say something, and then the expression on her face changes. Whatever words she planned to say are about to be accompanied by vomit.

I get close enough to the stall that I can see her bent over the yellow-tinged water, heaving her guts out. A very small part of me feels pity, but mostly I watch with clinical interest as she hurls chunks into a toilet that might not even flush when she's done.

"You're not pregnant, are you?"

It's supposed to be a joke, but the tear-stained face she turns toward me is bleak.

"Oh shit, you actually are?"

"Fuck off, Milbourne."

I bite my tongue on a snappy response, something along the lines of how that's what got her into this mess in the first place. As much as Sophia deserves to be knocked down a bit, I can't think of anything worse than getting pregnant in high school. I know from experience what happens to women who end up with kids they never should have had in the first place.

The self-proclaimed queen of Deception High has never looked quite this pathetic. I should revel in it after everything she's done to make my life miserable, but looking at her just makes me tired. There has been more than enough misery spread around this place over the years, I'm not going to add to it.

"Can I get you anything?" I ask. "Water or something."

Sophia swipes the back of her hand across her mouth. Judging from the state of her lipstick, this isn't the first time that she's mopped herself up today. Makes me wonder how much time she spent in here, crying and puking.

Her voice comes out in an incredulous croak. "You're really not going to say anything else? Even my own friends wouldn't be able to resist a few catty remarks if they saw me like this. If anyone should be just loving this right now, it's you."

She isn't wrong. I can't deny that the part of me designed for schadenfreude is kicking up its heels at seeing her kneeling on this dirty floor while crouched over a toilet bowl.

"Graduation is in, like, three weeks," I point out. "We're all going to go off to college, get jobs, or whatever. We never have to think about the shit that happened in high school ever again. Bygones are bygones, and all that crap."

"That doesn't really work when you're pregnant." She groans and retches again, but nothing comes out. Her stomach must be empty. "I'm going to be thinking about high school every day for the next eighteen years. At least."

"You have other options..."

She glares at me. "Not if I want to live with myself."

I understood that, if I didn't get anything else about her. Getting pregnant before I'm ready might be my worst nightmare, because I know what I would feel compelled to do if that happens. My mother turned her back on me when I needed her, I couldn't bring myself to do the same thing.

I look away from her, unable to keep anything but pity on my face when I know she doesn't want to see that.

"Congratulations on your *engagement,* by the way."

Nobody knows that Vin and I eloped. Giselle spun the ceremony she has planned as an actual wedding, not a vow renewal, probably for the sake of appearances. The end result is the same, so it seems silly to quibble about the details.

The way that Sophia watches me is like an injured animal that's been trapped in a corner. Gone is the sexy and confident bitch who has ruled our school since freshman year. I always assumed that she and Vin would end up together, like that was the natural order of things. Looking down at her, it's hard not feel a bit like a usurper. As if I've done something to create such a dramatic reversal in our fortunes.

Except I haven't done anything to Sophia, not even when she rightfully deserved it.

"If you don't need anything, I'm going to go." I back towards the door. "Good luck with everything."

Her voice stops me, the tone almost threatening.

"You're not going to ask me who the father is?" Her gaze drops to the ring on my finger, eyes narrowing with anger and a strange sort of sadness. "Considering recent history and who you're about to marry, I'd think that would be your first question."

Tension shimmers in the air between us.

My heart freezes.

"Is it Vin's?"

I wait for her to say yes, because why else would she have brought him into this conversation in the first place. I still remembered what it had felt like when he kissed her at the Founder's Ball, then swept away with her into the night to do exactly the sorts of things that result in unwanted pregnancy.

All I need her to do is confirm for me that Vin is exactly what I always thought he was.

And then I would tell him exactly where he could put his deal, along with any of the bourgeoning feelings I've been trying to deny.

I can't love someone who would do this to me.

"I stopped taking my birth control a few months ago after Danny and I broke up. I'd been spending so much time with Vin at the pool house, and he never seemed interested in any of the other girls there." Her glare is full of angry heat, but for the first time I realize it might not all be aimed at me "We fooled around so many times that I had myself convinced it would eventually lead to more. I've gone down on him before, but never anything that could lead to this." Sophia points an accusing finger at her belly. Her eyes have narrowed on my face. But now the anger is gone, replaced by hurt and self-recrimination. She looks absolutely defeated. "When he asked me to go with him to the Founder's Ball, I just knew that he was planning to make us official." "When he kissed me in front of everyone, it was like something out of a fairy tale. Then he shut the door of the pool house in my face and told me to find my own way home."

That sounds like a typically asshole move on Vin's part. I

won't try to defend what he's done, but my mind sticks on a very specific part of what she said. "So the two of you have never..."

"Not all the way. It was like he was saving himself, or something."

"Oh." My mind whirls at that. Vin's parties have been legend for years — I always assumed that he was sticking his dick into anything that moved. "I don't know what to say."

Sophia isn't done as she stares me down, makeup destroyed and clothes rumpled. "I really wanted to lie to you, make you think I'm carrying his baby to drive some sort of wedge between you. But you two have always had something crazy and special, something I couldn't touch no matter how much I tried. And I did try. But I want better than this." Seeming almost wistful, her hand touches her belly for the briefest moment. "I have to be better than this."

"Thank you."

Her expression is droll. "Don't thank me, Milbourne. You're the one stuck with him now, and it only takes one mistake to fuck up your whole life."

Before I can decide how to respond, she is already shoving past me toward the door.

Another three weeks go by like I'm living in someone else's dream.

Vin seems to consider it his mission in life to make me as comfortable being the new Mrs. Cortland as I possibly can be. Even though I know it's just because he wants to ensure I hold up my end of our deal, it's hard not to just let myself enjoy it.

I won't let him buy me a car, not when there are already dozens sitting in the garage at Cortland Manor. But he is also always there to take me where I need to go, so it seems like a moot point, anyway.

Every day, we attend Deception High where we exist in this surreal bubble of attention for a few hours that makes it nearly impossible for me to focus on schoolwork. And every night, we go back to the pool house and fall into his bed together.

The bed he has never shared with anyone before, not even Sophia Taylor.

I still feel a shiver of premonition when I think about her. She hasn't come back to school since that day I found her in the bathroom, probably because she assumed that her business would be all over Deception by the next day. Because if our situations were reversed, I'd walk into school to find blue and pink streamers decorating my locker and people holding out their bellies and laughing when I walked by.

But I haven't told anyone, and I won't. Sophia doesn't have to worry about that, though I don't have any way to reassure her.

She is living my nightmare, the one I wouldn't wish on even my worst enemy.

It gets easier to forget about that under Vin's dedicated attention. Although I've become as militant as possible about contraception, reminding him about condoms pretty much every chance I get. He promised to take me to a clinic for the pill, but they're booked out a few weeks for new patients.

The same thing that happened to Sophia will not happen to me.

When I finally tell Vin about what she told me on the way home from school, his reaction is to burst into guffaws of laughter.

"That is rich." He just shakes his head. "I always knew she'd end up with three kids and slinging diet shakes to the other PTA moms on Facebook. She got there a littler earlier than I thought, but still."

Vin seems patently unconcerned with Sophia's potential fate, which only makes me feel sorrier for her. She would kill me if she knew I had come close to anything approaching pity.

I drum my fingers on the armrest, trying for a severe expression that utterly fails. "What if she said you're the father?"

He laughs so hard that he nearly cries.

"Is she the fucking Virgin Mary now?"

I tell myself that I don't actually care what Vin has done in the past. In fact, I don't care what he does now. Our marriage is fake, and we're only being so nice to each other because we both get something out of it.

Lie detector determines that was a lie.

"Obviously not, but I think you know that. And if you don't remember that day in health class, it only takes one time."

"One time is still too many where Sophia is concerned. In fact, I've only ever had sex with one girl."

He says it casually, not like a bomb being dropped in between us.

I just stare at him. "I'm not an idiot, Vin."

"What do you want me to say? I've done stuff with other girls, just not that."

"I saw you leave with her after the Founder's Ball," I splutter.

"And if you'd stuck around for another five minutes, then you would have seen me slam the door of the pool house in her face." His hands are squeezed tight on the steering wheel, but that is the only sign of any tension in him. "For some reason, I wasn't in the mood for a shitty blow job that night."

"You're making me feel sorry for her."

"Sophia only gets exactly what she asks for," he grumbles. "The rumors of my sexual proclivities are just that. Fucking rumors. Sorry to ruin any of the fantasies, but I mostly spend my nights getting blackout drunk and hanging out with my friends."

Unless he was sneaking into my room in the middle of the night.

Of course, no one but us has ever known about that, which means the rumors never had a chance to spread.

No one has ever known about us. Except us.

Every time that I thought he came crawling straight from someone else's bed into mine, I hated myself for giving in. The compulsion driving him was always obvious, but I assumed he was obsessed with hurting me because of what I'd done. I always thought that it was just another bit of punishment to make me complicit in my own destruction, to remind me that I would always be less than nothing in his eyes.

Now I realize it might have been something else entirely.

I have to look out the window as the million-dollar houses of the Bluffs drift past my blurry vision. My tears are worthless, but that doesn't stop them from coming. In that moment, all I want is to take back the past and tell him the truth about what my mother did.

I kept silent to protect the person I loved.

Turns out, I was wrong about which love I needed to protect.

I can't say that the feeling slams into me all at once. My heart is like the metaphorical frog in a pot of water slowly being heated to a boil. I should have jumped out right from the very beginning, but the heat came on so slowly that I didn't notice it until much too late.

My heart is on fire, and I don't have anyone to blame but myself.

I love him, and he will never feel the same way about me.

Vin doesn't seem to notice my struggle to pull myself

together as he hums along to the radio. I desperately want to tell him, to spew out proclamations of desperate love that will ensure he steers this Maserati off the nearest cliff. Vin might like to screw me, but he has made it very clear that the only thing I will ever be to him is a means to end. You don't hate someone for ten years and then suddenly abandon it for the opposite emotion.

I can't ever tell him how I feel.

Instead, I ask, "Who do you think the father of Sophia's baby is?"

"Someone who I hope is smart enough to run like hell."

THIRTY-FOUR

VIN

I'm not sure when I decided that Zaya and I are permanent.

I keep telling myself that it's just the novelty of having someone to play house with that has me twisted up. It would be a struggle to remember the last time anyone used the oven in the pool house for something aside from drying out weed, if ever. But Zaya is obsessed with her newfound ability to prepare meals using more ingredients than what comes in boxes from the food bank. All those years without a mother seemed to have primed her for playing happy homemaker.

She cooks, she cleans, and she sucks my dick like it's the absolute highlight of her day.

But as much as I like a gorgeous and willing girl to come home to, it's more than that.

When she smiles at me, I feel a pressure in my chest that makes it difficult to breathe. Any time she manages to wake up before me in the morning, which has been happening more and more often these days, I find myself rolling over to inhale the pillow where she slept. It always smells like the conditioner she uses, vanilla milk and plumeria.

I've bought about a dozen bottles of the stuff so she isn't tempted to switch to anything else.

Fast forward a year when she has a newborn baby in her arms and a more comfortable life than she has ever dreamed of, it won't matter that we started with a lie. It won't even cost her anything. A baby might delay the start of her future, but she can still go to college. I'll have a nanny sit in class next to her if that's what she wants.

I can give her everything she never had – it would be stupid for her to walk away.

I've never been able to take my eyes off her. It used to be because I was thinking of more and more creative ways to torture the truth out of her. But it's hard to care about the past when the future is punching me in the face.

When I watch her now, it's only because I struggle to tear my gaze away.

Getting her pregnant started out as only an obligation, something that needs to happen for me to keep my inheritance. But I find myself watching her for signs of morning sickness or tenderness in her nipples, although sucking on those until they're hard as almonds on her chest has always been a favorite pastime. Even though I've managed to put a few pounds on her, she is still skinny enough that a baby bump will probably be obvious pretty early.

Even in my own head, it's hard to call it love. There are too many other emotions wrapped up between us for me to put a name to just one. If love is forgiving her for trying to poison me when we were kids and never giving me reason why she did it, then we can call it that.

Also obsession, possession, and any emotion that involves never letting her go.

A few years after it all happened, I read the medical report. There was enough concentrated oleander in my blood to represent thousands of flowers. Something like that doesn't happen by accident. The poisoning had to have taken place over weeks, with a higher dose on the day that I finally collapsed. My weak heart had nothing to do with poor genetics and everything to do with the effects of all the oleander being slipped into my food.

A poisoning that started when Zaya became my childhood playmate.

But if I can forgive her for that, then she can forgive me for playing a dirty trick on her womb.

Maybe someday, I'll convince her to finally tell me why.

Although I'm not sure I really want to know.

The day of our wedding ceremony dawns bright and clear. Harsh waves crash on the silky sands of the Shore Club, and the water is too frigid for even a toe dip, but the beach is there to look at and not to swim in.

That water is cold enough to stop your heart after only a few minutes.

There is a nice metaphor in there for the rich people of this town, pretty on the outside but deadly when you get too close.

Giselle has truly outdone herself, which isn't precisely a compliment. Hundreds of white wooden folding chairs are decorated with gauzy bows, forming a semicircle around a raised altar that has to be the result of about a hundred hours of illegal labor. Almost everyone in town has RSVP'd, and this is shaping up to be an event that puts even the Founder's Ball to shame. Everything, from the decorations to the view, is like something from a manic chick's Dream Wedding Pinterest board.

It's perfect.

And I can't wait for it all to be over.

Giselle spirited Zaya away early this morning when I was still barely awake. My stepmother insistent that we do the full pre-wedding workup, everything from hair to makeup to sitting in a dressing room and sipping champagne with Giselle's vapid friends for a few hours. Apparently, I'm not allowed to see her until she walks down the aisle because of some bullshit related to bad luck.

The fact that we're already legally married doesn't seem to have filtered through the haze of Giselle's wedding planning.

Iain is standing up as my best man, with Elliot and Cal behind him as my other groomsmen. Zaya's bridesmaids are a few random daughters from families on the Bluffs, handpicked by Giselle based on their dress sizes and coloring.

God forbid that the wedding photos embarrass us.

When the music starts up, I'm almost grateful that my stepmother insisted on hiring a full orchestra to play. The Bridal March wouldn't have the same power coming from a tinny loudspeaker.

Emma comes first, dressed in a pink confection of a dress and flinging handfuls of flower petals in every direction.

But at the sight of Zaya walking down the aisle, it doesn't matter that my friends are snickering behind me and the closest bridesmaid is surreptitiously checking her phone.

I don't care about anything except for how beautiful she looks.

Her hair is done up in a twist with gentle curls framing her face. The one thing I insisted on was that the stylist Giselle hired not do anything to straighten it. Her dress is a creamy ivory, fitted at her slim waist and flowing into a full skirt that makes me desperate to find out what might be underneath it.

If there is a garter on her thigh, I am definitely tearing it off with my teeth.

The music swells just as she steps up beside me.

"You look like you've seen a ghost," she murmurs in my ear.

"Or an angel."

"Shut up." She rolls her eyes, but the blush on her cheeks makes it clear that she appreciates the compliment.

"You know how I feel about dresses – can't wait to get up under this one."

She stifles a giggle just as Father Mackerly begins the service.

This time it feels like second nature to gently kiss her when we're pronounced man and wife for the second time in as many months. The surprised gasps and appreciative murmurs from the crowd don't even faze me. I wonder how many people just lost bets on whether or not I'd actually go through with this.

I have never given less than a shit about what people think.

My hand grazes the flat plane of her belly over stiff lace as she pulls away from me, mind whirling over the possibilities. Up until now, all of this felt like playing pretend.

Now, it's real.

We have about five minutes to enjoy congratulations before Zaya is being whisked away again by the wedding planner. Apparently, she has another dress to change into for the reception, because this hasn't already been enough of a circus.

She casts me an apologetic smile as her hand slips out of mine. I still feel the heat of her against my palm even once she disappears from sight. I take a glass from a passing waiter to calm my damn nerves.

I try to mingle without looking like the only place I want to be is upstairs and between my wife's legs. My friends have already claimed their bridesmaids and have melted away to seal the deal. Nothing unwads panties like a wedding reception. The stink of marital bliss must be some sort of aphrodisiac.

I check my watch again, shocked to find that less than a minute has passed since the last time I looked at it.

Someone bumps hard into me from behind, and champagne splashes my suit.

"Looks like you do always do get what you want."

I turn to see Jake Tully of all people, looking like he has spent the better part of the day drowning in hard liquor. The sour smell of it wafts off of him. My gaze takes in his wrinkled suit and bloodshot eyes. "Someone has been taking advantage of the open bar, I see."

"Fuck off, Cortland." He swipes the sleeve of his suit jacket against his runny nose, leaving a trail of snot on the fabric. Hopefully, that shit isn't a rental. "And congratulations, for now at least. Something tells me I'll eventually end up with your leftovers again. Third's time the charm."

The anger on his voice is for more than the ass beating he got on the first day of school or whatever happened at the Founder's Ball. It only takes a minute of mulling it over before something clicks into place for me. "You and Sophia."

"She came running to me after you dumped her, probably thinking that it would make you jealous or some shit. I wanted to get back at you, too, so it seemed like a fun time. A few more times after that just for fun, and now my life is over." Jake gropes for my glass, and I let him take it. Hopefully, a few more gulps of champagne will be enough to get him to pass out somewhere. "You know, I didn't believe it when people said getting in your way would only mess me up. Guess this is what I get for not listening. Whatever demon owns your soul definitely puts in long hours."

I almost feel sorry for him. Almost. Nobody told him to

stick his dick where it doesn't belong. "Just because Sophia is pregnant, doesn't mean she'll stay that way."

"With the way my luck is going, I'm not taking bets." He eyes me over the rim of the champagne flute as he drains it, tipping the glass upside down for the last few drops. "But maybe I'm not the only one whose luck has run out."

Something in his tone makes me wonder if the guy is as drunk as he seems. He looks at me like he would like nothing better than to pound me into the dirt, even if he knows better than to try.

I resist the urge to shove him away when Jake stumbles past me. This is my wedding, after all, it wouldn't look good if I got into a fistfight during the reception with a guy drunk off his ass. He can be as pissed off as he wants to be, I'm the one who just married the girl he wants.

But something about his last words leave me cold. Misery loves company, and he has enough of it to drag us both to the bottom of the ocean.

THIRTY-FIVE

I'M ALONE WITH AMELIA IN THE DRESSING ROOM. SHE IS the only addition to the proceedings that I insisted on. Giselle hung around long enough to insist that I change into the pale blue dress she left hanging over the door. My bridesmaids are long gone — apparently, whatever she bribed them with wasn't enough to get more than the ceremony.

"I can't believe you're married," Amelia says as she collapses into a plush chair.

Giselle wouldn't let her be a bridesmaid if she wore a homemade dress and her parents wouldn't let her out in public in anything as scandalous as silk and chiffon. I'd seen the Makepeace's in the last row of seats during the ceremony, dressed like they were ready for a barn-raising. Getting married made me slightly less of a Godless jezebel in their eyes, which is probably the only reason they allowed Amelia to attend in the first place.

She managed to slip away from her parents' watchful eye when they struck up a conversation with Father Mackerly about mortal sin. Perfectly appropriate conversation for a wedding.

There hasn't been anyone else that I can tell the entire truth. Grandpa's dementia has gotten so bad the he barely knows what day it is, and Zion has already been transported to his diversion program, which won't let me so much as contact him for the first year. I've had to sit here with only the voice in my head to remind me I'm not going completely insane.

"It's all fake."

Amelia's eyes widen into saucers as I tell the whole sordid story. Her mouth falls open when I mention the part about Vin and I eloping to wine country and playing house together for the last few weeks. Since she's homeschooled, Amelia wouldn't have seen firsthand the things that went on at Deception High, even if she heard of them. When the story is done, I put into the words the one thing that I never have before.

"I think I might love him."

She just shakes her head, fanning herself as if suddenly overheated. "Do you think he feels the same way?"

"Vin has never been this nice to me, but I keep telling myself it's just so I'll keep my end of the deal."

"Except the marriage has been legal for weeks, and he still moved you into his house," she points out. "He definitely didn't have to do that or buy you a new wardrobe. Stuff like that isn't what you do when you're keeping it strictly business."

"If you say so," I murmur, even though my heart sings.

"I saw that kiss he just laid on you. Vin Cortland has got it bad." Amelia picks up a lip gloss and dabs it on her lips then makes a puckering kiss at the dressing table mirror.

I want to believe her so badly that I can barely stand it.

My gaze moves to the tall window, where I can barely make out waves crashing outside in the growing darkness. The reception will go on well into the night if Giselle has anything to say about it, but I'm already looking forward to what will come after.

If my first wedding night was good, I can only hope the second will be even better.

There is a loud banging on the locked door.

Amelia looks amused when I turn to stare at her with wide eyes. "I think I know who that is."

But when she gets up to open the door, it isn't Vin who bursts into the room.

Jake freezes in the doorway when he catches sight of me.

I didn't even realize he had been invited.

When I open my mouth to asks what the hell he wants, he blurts out a question before I have the chance.

"Are you pregnant?"

"What the hell?" I'm not sure if I should be offended at his concern or not. "That isn't the only reason people get married, you know."

"I heard him talking about it with that other sociopath he hangs out with, Iain or whatever his name is. Vin was practically bragging about how he was going to trick you into getting pregnant by poking holes in condoms. All so he could get his inheritance." The words are slurred but clear as Jake leans against the wall for support. His eyes are bleary as he stares across the room at me. It doesn't take a field sobriety test for me to know he is moments from collapsing in a drunken stupor. "Please tell me that you haven't fucked him yet."

Anger rises in me as I stare at him. This guy hasn't spoken to me in weeks, and now he shows up to ruin my wedding. "Which time? Vin and I have been screwing since sophomore year."

"You bitch." His expression turns furious. "So you'll put out for Cortland, but not for me? I always knew you were a little slut."

The words slam into me with enough force that it robs me of breath. But Amelia doesn't suffer the same frozen reaction. She leaps up and hustles Jake out of the room, sending him stumbling in the corridor before she slams the door shut.

"Jealousy sure does strange things to people." Amelia turns back to me with her eyebrows raised. "You mind telling me what that was all about?"

"No idea." My voice is breezy, even as I feel a stab of pain in the pit of my stomach. "Jake was drunk."

But I have condoms in my purse that I grabbed from Vin's bedroom. I didn't have any idea where the night would lead us, and I wanted to be prepared.

That's almost laughable if what Jake said is true.

While Amelia frantically asks what I'm doing, I rifle through my bag for the condoms. I hold one up to the light and squint at it. In the very center of the outlined circle is a tiny hole in the foil, only visible when it catches in the light.

A hole that is the exact size and shape of a safety pin.

Amelia's face is pinched with worry. "When was the last time you had your period?"

My periods have never been regular. Thank stress, intermittent starvation, or just plain old body chemistry, but I'm not in the habit of bothering to keep track of them. I've gone months in between before, so the delay isn't something I would normally worry about. "I'm not sure, but that doesn't mean anything."

She bites her lip. "There's a drug store right down the street. I can be back in five minutes."

"No, really..."

But Amelia is already heading resolutely for the door. "Five minutes, okay. Don't move."

It actually takes seven for her to get back. I know that because I find myself counting every second as I stare at the floral-patterned wall. The pregnancy test comes in a little box that should rip apart easily under my fingers, but I struggle to get it open because my hands are shaking.

Amelia waits in the other room while I hover over the toilet to pee on the little stick.

It only takes another minute or so for my fate to be sealed.

Two little pink lines waver in my vision as I struggle not to pass out.

The bathroom door bangs open and crashes against the far wall. I don't need to look up to see who it is. His presence sucks all of the air out of the room until I find it impossible to breathe.

"Why am I pregnant?"

The expression on his face is all the confirmation I need of his guilt. He doesn't seem surprised as he stares down at me.

Just resigned.

Amelia peers at me over his shoulder, expression puggish like she is more than willing to manhandle him out of the room if necessary.

Vin doesn't so much as glance back at her. "Because I needed to be sure that I would get what I want."

I wrack my brain for an explanation for this that makes the glittering future I imagined still even remotely possible. But the only one that makes sense to me is the one in which Vin Cortland is a selfish piece of shit who has been playing me this entire time.

"And that's all that has ever mattered to you, isn't it? Getting what you want. My feelings have never been on the radar." I feel a sensation like my body is dropping over a cliff. The ground is rushing up to meet me, but there won't be any waking up from this nightmare just before I hit the ground. "You could have chosen anyone for this. Why would you do this to me?"

"It had to be you," he admits. "I can't inherit anything

unless I marry a daughter from a Founding family. You were my only option. And you have to be pregnant within a year, or my inheritance disappears." He sees the look on my face, and more words rush out. "That's how it started, but this has all become so much more than that. I was only doing what I thought I had to do. I've never lied to you about anything else."

Vin has always hated me. It would take a complete moron to think he was capable of feeling anything else where I'm concerned. It was only a matter of time before we went right back to being enemies.

I muster all of the bravado that I don't feel. "What if I had just gotten rid of it?"

"You wouldn't do that." Vin reaches out to stroke my cheek, and I pull away before he can touch me. If I let him touch me, then I might let him convince me that he hasn't been laughing at my naivety for the last two months. "You would do yourself in before you harmed an innocent baby."

The sense of despair that washes over me is unlike anything I've ever felt. Darkness creeps in on the edges of my vision, a tide threatening to pull me out to sea. Even when I realized that my mother had no intention of ever coming back or that the first time Grandpa forgot my name wouldn't be the last, nothing compared to this.

Staring into Vin's pinched face, I realize that I still love him. Desperately.

And he will only ever see me as a means to an end.

I would rather die than feel this way for even one more minute.

"It was my mother who tried to kill you when we were kids. She always put this medicine in your tea, but I didn't think anything of it until the day you collapsed. I never said anything until now, because I wanted to protect her. I should have learned my lesson about protecting people who don't give a shit about me."

Vin must see something change in my eyes, some indication of the direction of my thoughts. He grabs for me, but I dodge around him as Amelia lets out a cry of alarm.

The door to the bridal suite is open, so there isn't anything to slow my headlong rush into the hallway. My bare feet pound against the hardwood, painful enough to slow me down under any other circumstances. But right now, I run like the hounds of hell are chasing me. I have no idea where I'm going, just that it has to be somewhere far away from here.

Impending darkness is the shadow dogging my every step.

Dark clouds swirl on the horizon. A distant storm rapidly approaches the shore. The crash of ocean waves is louder than ever as I walk down the deserted beach. I've spent my whole life with the world on mute, and now I'm hearing it all for the first time.

Silence has been my only defense against the world's cruelty for so long that the noise is more than I can bear.

My whole life has been driving toward this moment, forcing me closer and closer to the edge of the cliff until I don't have any choice but to jump.

I've never really felt like I belonged anywhere, certainly not here where I've never been more than the town trash. Even my family is only bits and pieces with no glue holding it together. My own mother couldn't bear to stay with me, not for any longer than she had to. Dementia has freed my grandfather of his bad memories and saved him from the pain of missing me. My brother is gone, and he won't be coming back.

No one left will miss me if I'm gone, at least not for long.

Shocking cold hits my toes as I step into the surf, a bitter mismatch for the warmth in the air. The water here is always frigid. It takes a brave soul to step into it without protection and hope to make it back out.

I've never been anything close to brave.

The idea of being done with all of it brings a surprising lightness to my step, a stark contrast to the crushing despair that has always been my constant companion. In death, there won't be fear or pain.

There won't be anything at all.

I've always feared the ocean, a strange thing for someone who was born in spitting distance of the water. Growing up, trips to the beach were more frequent than visits to the grocery store. I'd never understood how anyone could look at the infinite water, the waves crashing hard enough to break bone, and see anything but death.

Just more evidence I was never meant to survive in this world.

As a kid, my mom used to tell me stories of people being washed out to sea by the tides, unable to make their way back to the shore. Even the strongest swimmers eventually grow exhausted fighting the undercurrent. She described in detail the lashing waves during a storm that could tear apart fishing boats in a matter of minutes and suck the pieces down to the bottom, too deep to be recovered.

Darkest ocean is the final frontier, harder to reach than walking on the moon.

I've dreamed about what it might be like to give my body over to the sea. I'd called them nightmares until I realized that the real nightmare began the moment I opened my eyes.

Water churns around my ankles like the phantom hands of death, so cold it burns my skin. I take another step forward and the frigid surf splashes against my knees, weighing me down as water seeps into the long train of my dress.

Some girls gently pack their wedding dresses away like priceless antiques — mine will be a death shroud.

I shiver at the creeping chill, knowing it will only get worse. The most excruciating moment will come when the water rises to my chest, just above the level of my heart.

It's always the heart that can least take the cold.

My hand drifts down to touch the still flat plane of my belly. I imagine a touch of heat there, the tiniest spark of life, but it isn't enough to call me back. And I refuse to bring anyone else into this world who might experience the same pain I have.

A voice echoes through the distant canyon, familiar even over the sound of crashing waves that is so loud it's nearly deafening.

It's too late.

It has always been too late, even from the very beginning.

I force myself further into the water, because I'm running out of time. If my nerves give out now, I won't get this chance again. Padded restraints and the double locking doors of a psychiatric ward are all that await me. My supposed husband would rather leave me somewhere to rot than lose his meal ticket. I'll never be out of someone else's sight again.

This is my only opportunity.

"Don't do this, Zaya. Please!"

Vin is already on the beach, but far enough away that I can't make out his face under the night sky. The only light out here is from a full moon hiding behind dark clouds. I don't need to be close to know it's him. No one else would stride down the sand of a public beach like he owns the entire world.

I turn away to face the endless black of a dark horizon. There may be distant lights from our small town behind me, but I can no longer see them. All I have to do is take a few final steps into oblivion, and it will all be over. I wade further into the water, licking cold creeping up my thighs and then my waist, forcing myself to take painful steps forward even as my heart pounds in my chest.

"Zaya," he calls again, voice sounding more desperate than I've ever heard it.

He can't see me in the dark, might even walk right past and never know, as long as I don't say a word. But that doesn't stop him from shouting his promises into the wind, begging me to give him another chance to prove himself.

Vin has never broken a promise to me, because I've never expected him to make any.

I don't want to believe it's possible for him to change. Belief requires hope. And hope forces you to pick yourself up so life can kick you right back down again.

I don't have the strength left to hope.

Eventually, he'll go away and I can finish this.

Except I underestimate both his vision and the flash of my off-white dress against the dark water. His feet slap on the shallow water as he starts toward me, but he still isn't close enough to reach me in time. I just have to force myself to move fast enough.

He shouts my name, screams it, until his throat sounds like it is going hoarse.

Soon he'll be on top of me, grabbing me, forcing me out of the water and back to the shore. If I'm going to choose, then it has to be right now. The time for indecision has long passed.

I have to make a choice.

Stay and fight, give him the chance to build me up so he can tear me down all over again.

Or let it all just float away with the tide, taking a lifetime of pain away with it.

I have to decide.

THIRTY-SIX

VIN

I PUSHED TOO HARD AND FOR WAY TOO LONG. THERE ISN'T any excuse except that I'm the biggest asshole who has ever lived.

Not to say that I haven't had my reasons for it. But it's hard to make the past matter when you're confronted with the reality of your future.

In the beginning, I convinced myself that keeping secrets would be the best thing for both of us. The less she knew, the easier it would be for me to control her. But I didn't understand what I stood to lose.

And now I've lost everything.

Waves crash around me with destructive force. The wind is so howling that it steals my voice and carries it away to the sky. I pray that I'm not too late, even though I don't deserve to have any prayers answered at this point.

I don't deserve her. I don't deserve anything.

But I've never been one to worry too much about what I deserve. I've always taken what I want when I want it, regardless of the consequences. There isn't any reason to change my ways now, not when it means I have the chance to save her.

I'm going to save her.

From herself. From me. From the world, if I have to.

I'll tie her to the bed and keep her there for the rest of her life, if that is what it takes to keep her alive.

I'm barefoot because I kicked off my shiny loafers to run faster. Bits of coral and stone dig into my skin. Sharp enough to cut, but the physical pain is a distant thing. If I have to run a hundred miles across hot asphalt covered in broken glass to save her, then that is precisely what I'm going to do.

I scream her name again, even though I know she wouldn't hear it if she was standing only a few feet away. The darkness and the angry sound of crashing waves are enough to hide any number of sins.

Hers and mine.

For the longest time, I wanted to break her. Tear her into bits so I could examine every piece until I figured out exactly what fascinated me so damn much. I succeeded, but she isn't the only one who has been broken.

In the beginning, this had mostly been about the money. And maybe a little bit about how much I got off on forcing her to be what I want. Everything seemed to make so much more sense back then — even the worst of what I've done seemed justifiable.

But now, I'm just disgusted with myself.

King of Deception.

Vice Lord.

The guy who has never heard the word no.

My reputation is as big as the waves crashing onto the beach and as powerful as the undertow threatening to pull us out to sea. I tell myself I'm more than the things people say about me, but I'm not convinced that's true.

Maybe it has never been true.

I see a dark shadow in the meager light, and I fight through the water toward it, driven by instinct.

Everything about her is dark. Her hair. Her eyes. Her thoughts, at least the ones she shares with me. But that didn't stop her from becoming the only spot of light in my otherwise colorless world.

And I let all of my worst impulses nearly destroy her.

When I squint, there is the barest outline of a figure moving through the waves. The white dress is what gives her away. She has gone far enough out that the water has to be past her waist.

I'm running without a conscious awareness of what I'll do when I reach her. Like every other interaction we've ever had, I'm operating on an instinct I've never fully understood.

As I chase her into the water, I realize I would give anything to rewind the clock to a time before we became what we are.

Before tragedy robbed me of a real childhood.

Before I stole her voice.

Before fate and bad luck forced us together.

Before secrets and lies drove us apart.

Before it all went wrong.

I follow her into the sea like I'd follow her to the ends of the earth if that is where she leads me. Even if it is impossible to go back, I can move forward. Into tomorrow. Into the future. Whatever place she chooses to go.

Even death.

If she throws herself on the mercy of the gods, then I'll jump off the cliff after her.

At this point, it's only a question of who gets to her first.

Oblivion or me.

THIRTY-SEVEN

I WAKE UP WITH SUNLIGHT STREAMING ONTO MY FACE AND a restraint on my arms tying me down to the hospital bed.

My body feels like it just got run over by a truck.

I'm only awake for a few minutes before a nurse bustles in to check my vital signs and remove the restraints. Clearly, they only had me tied down in case I woke up and tried to kill myself again.

Did I try to kill myself?

They ask me that question enough times that you think I'd have a clearer answer. I remember feeling a blackness descend over my mind, so deep that I couldn't see any way out of it that didn't involve just being done with all of it.

All of it meaning...life, I guess.

But with the sun shining brightly on my skin through the window and several locked doors between me and Vin, it was getting easier to see the forest for the trees.

I don't want to die. I just want to be as far from Deception as it's possible to get without actually leaving planet Earth.

Eventually the doctor comes in, pleasant-faced but eager to

get to the point. He explains that I nearly drowned and that I was technically dead when they brought me in. My heart had to be restarted at some point.

I guess Vin and I have that in common.

"*What happened?*" he asks.

But he really means, *Did you do it on purpose?*

And I don't have an answer that will satisfy any of us. They won't let me go until I assure them that I've returned to sanity, although I'll have to be here at least a few days for monitoring.

I say all the right words, like an intelligent person would. It seems silly to ask someone if they're suicidal when anyone who truly is would never admit to someone who might stand in their way. I guess the better question is *can we still save you?*

The answer is yes, at least for now.

But I made it clear from the moment consciousness returned that I don't want them to let Vin anywhere near me. Even with the faintly coercive nature of my hospital stay, I still get a say in who comes to visit. There isn't anyone that I particularly want to see.

Especially Vin Cortland.

He doesn't try very hard to get in, according to the nurses. As soon as they told him that I wasn't going to see him, he stormed off without so much as a backwards glance.

That's what I get for falling in love with a monster.

My hand keeps straying to my belly, and I don't realize it until I find my palm stroking there, searching for any hint of a developing bump. I know I'm not far enough along for anything to be physically different, but my mind can't focus on anything else.

How can something be so barely real and also entirely destructive?

No matter what empty promises Vin made, college is off the table. The $100,000 he promised me won't be enough for paying tuition and raising a child, especially since I wouldn't have time to work on top of all that. Vin would probably help if I asked him, or took him to court if necessary, but I'm not going to do either of those things.

As far as I'm concerned, he has ceased to exist.

Just like my dreams. Those have shattered like shards of glass, and I don't have the will left to gather them all up and glue the pieces back together.

I barely have enough will left to keep myself alive.

But it isn't just me anymore, is it?

My palm presses hard against my belly again, pushing until it almost hurts. I just need to feel something, a stirring or a lump of tissue, anything to prove this is real.

With a start, I remember that my mother was in her last semester of high school when she got pregnant with me. I count up the months in my head, only to realize that she would have had to be exactly as old as I am when she conceived, practically down to the month.

Like mother, like dumbass daughter.

Everything I have ever done has been in the hopes of breaking the legacy that she left for me. And she had actually managed the one thing that I couldn't.

Finally escape Deception and never look back.

But I'm not the same as my mother, for all the good it will do me. I won't be able to abandon a life that I created, no matter how difficult it will be to stay. And if I'm lucky enough to have a girl, she will never be tempted to sell her soul for a better life. I'll provide for her the life that I always dreamed of having.

A new sense of determination washes over me as I think about it. All the PTA meetings that my mother never bothered to attend, the afternoons when I would get home from school to a dirty house because she was still asleep in bed, how she never managed to hold down a job for more than a few months.

What she did to Vin was just the culmination of a lifetime of terrible decisions. Maybe it was jealousy or some desire for Vin to stay weak so she could keep her job taking care of him. I'll probably never know, and I don't really care about the reason anymore.

She had been a perfect example of all the things that are the polar opposite of motherhood. I shouldn't expect anything she has ever done to make sense to me.

I'm going to be everything she wasn't.

I'm going to be everything for this baby she refused to be for me.

I'm going to be the kind of mother I deserved to have.

Something good will come out of the twisted wreckage of whatever it is we used to be. Something new and innocent, born a freshly blank slate that will know from the moment it enters the world that it has its mother's unconditional love.

I'll turn Zion's old room into a nursery and enroll in night classes at the community college. My job at the Gas and Sip is almost certainly still waiting for me, and I can probably convince Amelia to help out with babysitting. If Vin has even the tiniest bit of his soul left, then he'll keep his promises. Grandpa can stay in the care home, and Zion will stay at a place that actually cares about rehabilitation.

This baby and I can make it on our own.

Lightness fills my chest for the first time since I woke up in the hospital. It amazes me that I could so easily flip that switch in my brain, but I've gone from dreading the thought of what this new life would mean for my future to embracing it.

A nurse comes in with a handful of pills in blister packages, rattling off long confusing names as she pops them into a plastic cup.

"Are all of those safe to take when your pregnant?"

She looks up at me in obvious surprise. "You're pregnant?"

"Tested positive yesterday."

"We should have that on file, I don't remember seeing it." Brows furrowing, she leaves the cup of pills on the table and goes to a computer terminal in the corner of the room. She pecks at the keyboard a few times while mumbling to herself. "The damn techs should have drawn enough blood for a full panel. Results need to be cleared before any orders get put in." Her sigh of relief is palpable. "Nope. We always run a pregnancy test with the full workup, blood not urine because that's the only way to be sure. You are definitely not pregnant."

Her words hit me like a punch to the gut. "I took a test yesterday. Did I lose the baby because I went into the water?"

The smile she gives me is gently reassuring. "No, honey. Your hCG levels would still be elevated if you had a miscarriage that recently. It takes weeks for them to go back to normal." The nurse returns to the side of the bed and holds out the pill cup to me, giving it a little shake. "Word of advice, always double check those drug store tests. Peeing on a stick is great and all, but they're not always 100% accurate. Consider yourself lucky it was a false positive this time and not a false negative."

Not pregnant.

I sit with that realization for a moment, feeling a unique sense of desperate relief and keening loss.

Nothing good could possibly have come from this twisted situation, and it was stupid of me to think that anything could.

Definitely not pregnant

I start to cry when the words bang off the insides of my skull.

But I can't say if they are tears of relief or pain.

THIRTY-EIGHT

VIN

Zaya wasn't breathing when I pulled her out of the water.

Her body was colder than death, which might be what saved her life. The frigid water acted like the mundane version of cryostasis, slowing her heart and diminishing her body's need for oxygen so her brain didn't burn out.

An ambulance was already waiting on the beach when I stumbled out of the water with her limp body cradled in my arms. I likely have Amelia to thank for that. If Zaya survives, then I need to remember to send her friend a fruit basket.

The wait at the hospital might be the most excruciating hour I've ever experienced. I remember learning about Einstein's Theory of Relativity in a science class at some point, but there is no greater object lesson then watching a clock on the hospital wall practically tick backwards.

One hour might as well be half a lifetime for all I can tell the difference.

I know there are people filtering in and out around me. My parents come for a bit, but didn't stay very long. Iain doesn't say anything as he slouches in the uncomfortable plastic seat next to me, but just rolls his eyes when I tell him to go if he wants.

It doesn't escape my notice that there isn't anyone there for Zaya. Her brother is still locked up, and her grandfather is too far gone to understand what might be happening.

She doesn't have anyone but me.

And I drove her to the point of suicide.

I'm not usually the type to go around analyzing my own behavior, but I've heard enough about the feeling to recognize guilt. I've just never had the opportunity to feel it in the way I do now.

It surprises me how little I feel about the revelation that it was her mother who poisoned me. I might be surprised later, when the shock of all this wears off, but it's hard to care about anything aside from Zaya's life being on the line. And it didn't sound like she had any explanation for why her mother would want to kill me, and a reason is all I ever wanted.

Until I married her.

Now, it's hard to remember that I ever wanted anything aside from Zaya.

If she dies, I'm not going to be able to live with myself. We might as well have a suicide pact at this point, because the minute her coffin gets lowered into the ground, I'm throwing myself in after it.

But fear will make you crazy.

Everyone else leaves after a few hours except for Iain. His head rests against the back of the seat, looking so relaxed that I might assume he is sleeping save for the fact that his eyes are wide open and staring.

"This is your fault," I grouse.

"That's the grief talking." His voice is mellow, which means he probably smoked a dab before coming to the hospital.

"Nobody makes Vin Cortland do what he doesn't want to do, remember?"

"Poking holes in the condoms was your idea."

"As if you wouldn't have thought of something equally diabolical if given enough time. At best, I'm your accomplice." Iain glances at me briefly, before returning his attention to the ceiling tiles. "To be fair, if I thought you'd caught actual feelings for the girl, then I might have given you different advice."

Just because I'm ready to admit things to myself doesn't mean I'm ready to let the rest of the world in on it. "You don't know what the fuck you're talking about."

"Okay, man." He lifts his head again, gaze taking in the crowded waiting room before sliding up and down my tense form. "I think the asshole doth protest too much."

Before I can think of a suitably barbaric response, a nurse with a clipboard calls out my name.

Iain's dry laugh is easy to ignore as I bound to my feet and rush over to her.

"Vincent Cortland?" At my nod, the nurse checks something on her clipboard before looking back up. "Zaya Milbourne is awake."

"Cortland," I correct automatically. "Zaya Cortland."

Then exactly what she said finally filters through the frenzy in my mind.

Zaya is awake, which means she isn't dead.

The sense of relief I feel is so keen that it weakens my knees. I have to grip the back of a nearby chair to keep from falling over. Thankfully, it's bolted to the floor.

When I move to stride toward the double doors, the nurse stops me with a hand on my chest.

"She doesn't want to see you." She sounds apologetic, but her gaze is resolute. "This kind of thing happens sometimes, people go into shock. We'll be keeping her for a couple of days, so you might want to come back."

"I'm her husband," I snap.

"Patients always have the right to refuse visitors, including family." The nurse backs away, keeping her gaze on me like she thinks I might dive past her. "Your wife is on the third floor. You can try calling the unit tomorrow."

She turns on her heel and strides away before I have a chance to argue anymore with her.

Iain sidles up next to me "Third floor is the psych unit. It's where they put the people who try to off themselves."

I don't bother to ask him how he knows that.

Under other circumstances, I would have barreled after that nurse like a steamroller and forced the staff to allow me in to see Zaya or suffer the consequences.

Except I know I've finally found a situation I can't bully my way through. Even if I forced my way into to her room and insist she talk to me, I won't be able to force my way into her heart. And that is exactly what I plan to do, no matter how long it takes.

I'm going to make this right, even if it kills us both.

It's amazing what you can do when money is no object.

I only have to make two phone calls, one to a private investigator and another to the bank for a wire transfer, to get a last known address.

The drive to LAX is completely silent, because the rush of my own thoughts is enough of a distraction at the moment. My anachronistic love for girl power pop songs is legendary, but I need to be alone with the maelstrom inside my own head.

This isn't a problem that Taylor Swift can fix.

But two hours of total silence can do a lot to keep things in perspective.

The gate agent raises an eyebrow when I buy a ticket for the next flight to Portland without so much as a carry-on bag. It probably doesn't help that I'm still dressed in my tuxedo from the wedding, although only the wrinkled pants and stained shirt are left, I realize. My uselessly expensive suit jacket disappeared somewhere.

Probably the hospital waiting room, if I had to guess.

The agent's gaze rests on the loosened bowtie hanging around my neck for a beat too long, but she still sells me the ticket. And she doesn't alert the TSA, because I make it through security without any problems.

The wait isn't long until boarding, but I spend the next hour pacing up and down past the same gift shop. If I actually stop to think about what I'm doing, then I might realize what a bad idea this is.

Zaya and I will never have a future if we can't come to terms with the past.

Which is why I'm going to find her piece of shit mother.

I'm the first one on the plane, having paid three times the normal rate for a first class ticket so I could jump off as soon as we landed without waiting for the rest of the herd.

Why is it that people only seem to remember they have luggage in the overhead bin when the aisle clears in front of them?

The stewardess offers me a beverage before takeoff, but I wave her away, practically vibrating in my seat. A businessman in a tailored suit sits in the seat next to me. He tries to strike up a conversation, but my glare is enough to shut him up.

If I open my mouth again, it will only be a scream of rage and frustration that comes out.

I've never been to Portland, not that I plan to see any of it. This isn't a pleasure trip, after all. But it's only after the plane lands, as I walk out of the airport and end up under overcast skies even grayer than my mood, that it really hits home for me what I'm doing.

I don't expect Zaya to thank me for this, definitely not at first and maybe not ever. But it needs to be done. Without knowing what drove her mother to do what she did, Zaya will always wonder if she is walking down the same path toward inevitable destruction. That question — *why?* — will continue to hang over everything until we get an answer.

We both need to know why.

I plug the address I got from the PI into my phone. The five-minute wait for my Uber feels like at least that many hours. I practically sprint out from under the awning to get to the car. The sky opens as I step out onto the curb, drenching me in the time it takes to climb into the backseat.

The driver raises an eyebrow in the rearview mirror as I wring out the bottom of my shirt with a curse.

"Bad night?"

"Year, maybe. Just drive." I pretend to find something very interesting on the lock screen of my phone so he won't speak to me again. "I'll tip you the cost of the ride if you can beat the estimated arrival time by at least ten minutes."

The driver peels out without another word.

I expected the neighborhood to be a shithole, but we drive onto a street that makes the crappier parts of the Gulch look palatial. Rows of boarded up houses, empty storefronts, and broke down vehicles line either side of the broken pavement. The driver slows down to maneuver around potholes deep enough to double as in-ground pools.

"You want me to wait?" the driver asks as I climb out of the car, sounding like he wants to do precisely the opposite.

I wave him away impatiently. Concerns for my own safety aren't exactly at the forefront of my mind at the moment. Zaya might even be better off if I get shot by some random lowlife and left bleeding to death in the street. Our marriage is legal, and at this point she stands to inherit everything if I kick the bucket.

My destination is the only house on the block that still appears occupied. There is a rusted out tricycle on the front lawn next to a deflated kiddie pool. I have to bang on the door after it becomes obvious the bell is nonfunctional.

I hear noises on the other side, the scrabble of bare feet across hardwood and the shriek of a baby that is quickly hushed.

My heart sinks. If Zaya's mother ran off to start a new family, it might be better not to have found her at all. The last thing I want to do is cause her even more pain on top of everything else.

Before I can decide whether to stay or to walk away and pretend that this impromptu trip never happened, the door swings open.

A woman stands in the doorway with a baby on her hip. Another child, slightly older, peers at me from between her legs.

Something is immediately off. It's been almost a decade since I last saw her, but I still remember Zaya's mother. This woman is about half a foot shorter. The blonde hair would be an easy thing to change, but not the color of her skin.

Zaya's mother is white. This woman definitely is not. I'd say Phillippino if I had to take a wild guess.

"You're not Julia Milbourne."

THIRTY-NINE

Vin must have the charm of a demon, because every nurse on the staff seems to be complicit with his attempts to visit me.

The one who brings me my afternoon meds sounds gently chiding. "That poor boy hasn't left the waiting room all day. Don't you think you should at least let him visit, so you can tell him in person to piss off?"

I close my mouth on a recommendation that she do something similar. It isn't her fault that Vin is really good at pretending not to be an asshole, at least for small periods of time. He is probably having a grand old time playing the worried husband, clutching his hands in the waiting room and refusing to leave until he gets the chance to profess his undying love.

More likely, he just wants confirmation that I'm going to stay pregnant long enough for him to get his inheritance, because he doesn't know that there isn't any baby.

And there never will be, at least not for us.

Fighting back sudden tears, I urge myself to focus on the

anger and not the sadness. It actually would be nice to tell Vin Cortland precisely what I think of him before I make it clear that I don't ever want to lay eyes on him again.

"Fine, send him in."

The nurse pats me gently on the shoulder before whirling out of the room to deliver the good news.

But it isn't Vin that peers around the doorway of my hospital room.

Iain watches me carefully, as if he isn't quite sure I won't try to jump out the nearby window.

Or throw something at him.

The first option isn't possible, but I'm strongly considering the second.

"What the hell do you want?"

His expression remains placid. "Can I come in?"

I have a feeling that Iain could skin a cat alive and have that same blank look never leave his face for a minute. "It's a free country."

"Debatable. None of us is really free, even if we try to convince ourselves we are." He pushes off the wall and comes to the edge of the bed, staying just out of reach. "But I think you already know that."

"Did he send you?"

We both know who I'm talking about.

"Nope. He'd probably try to hurt me if he found out." Iain tips over an empty blister package on the table with one finger. "They giving you anything good?"

"Magnesium to keep my heart from stopping again and diuretics so my kidney's don't have to work so hard," I bite out. "That sound good?"

"Not really. It does sound like running into the ocean after dark is a pretty stupid idea. Do they think you still might die?"

"I'm getting discharged this afternoon, so probably not." I

roll my eyes as I shift uncomfortably in the bed. They did give me something for the pain in my chest where I got shocked by the defibrillators a few hours ago, and it makes my whole body itch. "Thanks for stopping by, Iain. Send my regards to whatever vampires gave birth to you."

But he doesn't move so much as an inch.

"I heard about the pregnancy." At the look on my face, he quickly adds. "Vin tells me everything. The Deception gossip network hasn't gotten ahold of that juicy bit of news yet."

My hands clench into fists, imagining that I'm squeezing them around Vin's neck. "You're not going to congratulate me?"

He shakes his head. "It was my idea, you know."

"What was?" I ask with an annoyed sigh.

"The whole poking holes in condoms thing." He actually has the grace to look ever so slightly abashed. "I figured by the time the truth came out, you guys would have been together long enough that it wouldn't matter."

"You're a dick."

"Tell me something I don't know."

I glare at him, wishing the nurses had left something heavy in reach for me to bash across his skull. "I'm not pregnant. False positive, apparently."

"Too bad."

"Excuse me?"

"You and Vin are good for each other when one or both of you has your head out of your ass long enough to realize it."

I just stare at him, too shocked for anger. "Vin has been torturing me for years."

"To be fair, you did try to kill him when you guys were kids."

Clearly, Vin doesn't tell him everything. If what my mother did isn't common knowledge yet, I'm not about to change that. "That isn't an excuse for everything he's done since."

"Vin Cortland has been obsessed with you for years. You should have seen his face when he realized that the pretty girl from the Gulch that all the guys were talking about freshman year was Zaya Milbourne. He almost knocked my teeth out once when I mentioned you have a nice ass." Iain's voice is matter-of-fact, like I can take the compliment or shove it up my ass and it wouldn't matter to him either way. "Why do you think any guy who gets within five feet of you is putting his life on the line? Vin made you off-limits for anyone but him."

"So what? You're saying Vin Cortland has secretly been in love with me since freshman year?"

"He's been in love with you since elementary school. You don't get this obsessed over a girl that you don't care about. Vin isn't the type to work out his keen sense of betrayal in a healthy way. He was raised by an absentee father and a narcissistic social climber. For him, love has *always* been the same as suffering. Feelings aren't his forte."

I let out a humorless laugh. "But they're yours?"

He shrugs. "Just because I don't have the capacity to feel something doesn't mean I don't know the name for it, or how to recognize it when I see it. Vin has it bad, he always has, which explains the vast majority of his behavior over the years."

I get that hollow feeling in my chest again, like a hole waiting to be filled with something besides pain. "That isn't an excuse for anything he did."

"I'm not excusing him. Walk away from him and never look back if that's what you want to do. But do it with some honesty." Iain starts backing out of the room. This is more words than I've ever heard him string together before, which explains the exhaustion written across his face. "Both of you walk around like open wounds, bleeding your shit all over the place. Either let the injuries you inflicted heal, or get the fuck away from each other."

I TAKE A CAB TO CORTLAND MANOR, ARGUING WITH myself the entire way there.

It's crazy that I would even consider giving Vin a chance to explain himself. After so many lies and secrets, I shouldn't ever want to see him again.

But here I am.

Letting Iain into my room was a bad idea. Now that the smallest seed of doubt has been planted, I can't get the idea out of my head. I've spent the last few hours replaying every interaction Vin and I have ever had for some hint that I had gotten them wrong. And all I see is anger and hatred.

Then I think about the last few weeks, when I saw a side of Vin I never knew existed.

I tell myself I just want to hear him say it. I need to hear directly from him that Iain is full of shit and that he has never loved me.

Otherwise, the possibility will haunt me for the rest of my life.

Because I have always loved him, even when I hated him.

It's completely dark when the cab finally winds its way up the long private road leading to Cortland Manor. There are no lights to use to navigate, and my heart is in my throat as I rush down the stone pathway.

The pool house is deserted when I get there, no sign that Vin has been there since we left before our vow renewal, which was almost three days ago now.

I don't have any choice but go into the main house.

Cortland Manor is as silent as the grave and only slightly warmer. When I call Vin's name, my voice echoes off the walls before fading away into more silence. I take the stairs two at a time and yell for him again when I get to the second floor.

Giselle appears in an open doorway at the end of the hall.

"I'm so sorry no one came to the door to greet you. Most of the staff is off for the week after working your reception." She approaches me slowly, bright red nails caressing the wooden banister. "If you're looking for Vin, I haven't seen him since last night. I hope there isn't any trouble in paradise."

Trouble in paradise might be the understatement of the year. "You don't have any idea where he is?

"Last I heard, he was going to visit you in the hospital." Her gaze travels up my body, taking in the hospital scrubs I had to put on since the emergency room staff cut my wedding dress off of me. "I assume that you're fully recovered."

"Getting there, thanks. I'm going to call around and see if anyone has seen Vin. Maybe I should ask Duke."

She shakes her head. "He's away on business."

I'm about to turn away when something occurs to me. "Do you remember my mother?"

Her lip quirks. "Vaguely. I wouldn't say we ran in the same circles."

"She worked for you, right?"

"She did," Giselle replies slowly. "But that was years ago. She never came back to work after Vin's accident. Of course, we would have had to let her go even if she had. Accidental ingestion or not, you expect more from the people caring for your children."

"Yeah, of course." I don't know what drives me to ask her about this. But the more I think about it, the stranger it seems that none of them ever suspected my mother of being involved with his poisoning. She had been Vin's nanny at the time, after all. "Did they ever figure out how Vin got the oleander in his system?

Instead of answering, she moves to a small end table near the top of the stairs and opens the drawer. "It's really too bad that Julia decided to leave town. Considering she was the one there at the time, these seem like better questions to ask her. It's a shame that she hasn't ever come back to Deception."

"Julia never came back because you killed her." Vin says from below us. His voice startles me so much that I stumble on the last step when I turn to see him standing below us in the entryway. He bounds up the stairs and comes to a stop right behind me. "Isn't that right, mother dearest?"

When I turn back to Giselle, she pulls a gun out of the drawer and points it at my chest.

FORTY

VIN

My heart is in my throat when Giselle pulls the gun.

"Point it at me," I insist, looming closer to make myself as large of a target as possible. "I'm the one you've always wanted dead, right?"

I let out a harsh breath of relief as the gun swings toward me.

"No..." Zaya cries out, but I silence her with a harsh movement of my hand.

This is between me and my stepmother, Zaya is just collateral damage.

"I tracked your mother down," I say conversationally, not taking my gaze off of Giselle's face. Even though I'm ostensibly speaking to Zaya, my words aren't really meant for her. "Or at least, I tracked down the woman who has been using your mother's identity. She's an illegal immigrant who bought Julia Milbourne's social security number ten years ago and has been using it ever since. The white woman in expensive clothes who sold it to her insisted it was high quality, because the person that the identity belonged to was dead. It's amazing what people will tell you when they think you're an immigration agent."

Zaya's body is frozen behind me. "I don't understand."

"My father didn't tell me about the restrictions on my inheritance until recently, which almost certainly means that Giselle didn't know about it, either." I stare down the woman that had taken the place of my mother when I was still an infant. She was supposed to care for me as if I was her own. And instead, she'd paid someone to poison me. "Emma wasn't born yet, and Giselle didn't have any way to ensure her hold on the Cortland fortune with me standing between her and the jackpot. She thought with me out of the way that all money would eventually go to her. I can only assume that my father would have been next if her plan had worked."

"What does this have to do with my mother?"

"Giselle couldn't poison me on her own, that would have looked suspicious. So she paid your mother do it, taking advantage of the destitute and desperate. I'm guessing Julia regretted what she had done when I collapsed and it looked like I might actually die. She probably threatened to go to the cops, so Giselle killed her and made it look like she just skipped town."

My stepmother's face has contorted into something monstrous. "Julia screwed up when she didn't give you enough oil of oleander to kill you. She only made things worse when she threatened to tell your father everything. I didn't have a choice."

"What's your plan here, Giselle?" I position myself so as much of my body as possible is between Zaya and the gun pointed at us. "The police won't believe that you killed us both on accident."

"This one was just released from the psychiatric unit after

she tried to drown herself in the ocean." Giselle gestures with the barrel of the gun at Zaya, who clenches her fists in the back of my shirt. "I'm thinking she showed up here raving like a crazy person, then shot you right before she killed herself. I found that pregnancy test you left in the bathroom at the Shore Club. Now that she's pregnant, your inheritance stays with the Cortlands. Even if you die."

My heart pounds painfully in my chest as she raises the gun and points it directly at my heart. There is a vanishingly small chance that I can rush her, but that would just leave Zaya defenseless, and Giselle won't miss at this distance. As her finger squeezes down on the trigger, I have a moment of perfect clarity. I am going to die standing in between the woman I love and a monster.

There are worse ways to go.

Then a blur of pink and white rushes past me.

Giselle goes flying, the combination of surprise and the force of Emma crashing into her enough to knock the gun from her hand and make her stumble back toward the stairs. Her arms pinwheel wildly as she tries and fails to gain purchase. The sky-high heel of her designer shoes, the ones that it makes no sense to wear inside the house, catches on the top step, and she finally loses her fight with gravity.

She hits each step on the way down, her body contorting in a way that no person should until she hits the hardwood floor at the bottom, her neck bent at an impossible angle. Her eyes are wide and fixed as they stare up at the ceiling, a small trail of blood leaking from the corner of her mouth.

Emma's voice is barely a whisper in the silence.

"Is she dead?"

I HIDE THE GUN BEFORE WE CALL 911.

The police believe us when we tell them that it was an accident, that we all saw Giselle stumble and fall down the stairs.

They don't seem to notice that Emma stays huddled in the corner while she stares at nothing at all. It's probably easy to mistake her behavior for grief and not something else entirely. I'm going to get her bundled off to the best psychologist money can buy at the earliest opportunity, but for the moment it's better that she doesn't say anything at all.

Zaya surprises me with how smoothly she tells the story, crying real tears when she talks about searching for a pulse on my bitch of a former stepmother and not finding one. Lying to the cops must be something kids learn early in the Gulch.

But it doesn't take long for the facade to break down after the police finish taking our statements and leave. I make her lay down on the couch in the living room while the paramedics zip Giselle's body into a black bag and carry it away.

I call my father to tell him the sanitized version of what happened, but he doesn't pick up. This isn't exactly the kind of thing you leave in a voicemail, so I hope I get a chance to talk to him before he hears about it on the news.

Right now, I have more important people to think about.

Emma lets me shuffle her off to bed, still looking lost and shell-shocked. She hasn't spoken a word, not even after the cops left. I'm just praying that things are different in the morning.

Zaya has fallen asleep, exhaustion and emotion robbing her of the ability to stay conscious. I stand there and watch her for a few minutes, marveling at how much younger she looks in sleep.

I still remember the day I met her, the tiny girl with wild hair and a stained dress who never seemed at all intimidated by me. I'd gotten used to other kids cozying up to me because of the Cortland name and fortune, but Zaya had never seemed to care about any of that.

She is still too light in my arms when I pick her up. The weeks I've spent trying to fatten her up have only gone so far to overturn a lifetime of never getting enough to eat. I carry her up to one of the guest rooms, because I don't want to leave Emma alone inside the house.

With Giselle gone, I might not ever sleep in the pool house again.

Zaya feels too good in my arms, like it's the place she is meant to be. But that's only because she's unconscious. Once she wakes up, we'll go right back to being enemies sighting each other across a battlefield.

Maybe I can lock her in the room until I convince her that there is something real between us.

She's alive, which means I still have a chance.

Hope threatens to crush my heart into dust as I mount the stairs one by one. The same stairs that had broken Giselle's neck less than an hour ago. It bothers me a bit that I don't feel much more than relief at the reminder my stepmother is gone, if just for Emma's sake.

But the woman got what she deserved. We all do, eventually.

Zaya comes suddenly awake when I lay her down on the bed, kicking and fighting like her life depends on it. Her crazed eyes shift to my face and she immediately stills, staring up at me like I'm some demon who has materialized out of the ether to torment her.

"Vin?" On her lips, my name sounds like a wish. There is so much yearning in the sound that I can barely take it. "Please..."

I kiss her before she can say anything else, fully expecting her to shove me away. She doesn't just kiss me back, her hands come around my neck and pull with the weight of her entire body until I'm laying over her.

"Please what? Tell me what you want." I cup her cheeks with my palms, the warmth of her skin seeping into me. Cortland Manor has always been too cold, but now I feel heat like a furnace burns inside her body. "I would give you anything."

"Even love?" The manic disorientation of sleep is gone from her gaze. She stares up at me like she sees right through me, like she sees everything I've ever tried to hide from her and the rest of the world.

Love. I've never used that word with anyone. Not my father, because he wouldn't want to hear it. Not with Giselle. Maybe once with Emma when she was already asleep and wouldn't hear it.

Love is terrifying. It makes you weak because it gives you something to lose.

"You are the air that I breathe. You always have been, even when I hated you," I say, staring down into her eyes as I watch for any reaction to my words. "I don't care about the money or the family legacy. I would burn this town to the ground and never look back, if it means I get to have you. I love you so much that it fucking hurts."

"No one is suggesting arson." Her small smile plows into me and sucks the air from my lungs. "I've always loved you, I think. Even when you hated me."

"I never hated you as much as I hated myself." My hands coast over her body, tracing the curves of her hips and over the flat plane of her stomach. "I'm so sorry for everything. I let the anger twist me up until I became a monster, but I never stopped wanting you. Loving you. I don't care about the inheritance. The money is just another noose tied around my damn neck. We don't need it."

"Really?" Her disbelief is obvious. She laughs when I tickle her hard in the ribs, but doesn't try to roll away. "You have no idea what it's like to be poor."

"I know what it's like to be without you. Anything else is just details." It isn't a lie. Money is a tool, a means to an end. I've had it before, and I'll manage to get it again. The only thing I can't stand to lose is her.

"I'm sorry, too. For going in the water..." she trails off, voice stricken.

Zaya had tried to escape. Escape, because I drove her past the point of desperation. She hadn't been running towards death so much as she had been running away from me.

I will never give her a reason to run again.

"You don't have anything to be sorry for." I press another kiss against her full lips. It's still hard to believe that she's mine. I might have thought I owned her before, but I had no idea. "But if you really want to make it up to me, I have a few ideas."

"I'm not pregnant, by the way."

I briefly consider lying and immediately abandon the idea. "Iain told me. It's a relief, honestly. Babies shouldn't come into the world already burdened with their parents mistakes."

She grips my forearms and pulls me closer, pressing her lower body against mine. Her expression is playful. "No more holes poked in condoms?"

"I'll take you to the clinic first thing in the morning," I promise, trying for contrite with the wide smile on my face. "In the meantime, I can think of dozens of things we can do that won't make a baby. Care for a demonstration?"

Zaya giggles as I duck my head to press a kiss against her stomach with every intention of moving lower. Her fingers tangle in my hair, forcing my head up so I can look her in the eye.

"I love you," she says again, and my heart sings.

"I would have chased you into the deepest ocean,

Milbourne. It doesn't matter how fast you run or how far you go, I will always follow after you." The words are an incantation, invoking whatever dark diety might be listening. "You're in my head and in my heart. My blood only flows for you. Forever."

And I kiss her like I mean for this to be forever, because I do.

EPILOGUE

Zaya

Perfect isn't supposed to exist in real life.

Correction, in *my* life.

But I don't have any other word to describe what it's like to be Vin Cortland's wife.

My brother is safely away at Blackbreak Academy, far from the criminally sophisticated friends he made in the Gulch. It will be up to him whether or not he decides to make anything of himself.

I call Grandpa every Sunday and listen to him gush about the care home as if it's the first I'm hearing it. Apparently, there is another resident named Gladys that he has been making eyes at for the last few weeks. I hope that works out. The important thing is that someone makes sure he takes his medication every day and eats three meals, which is more than I ever managed on my own.

Everything is wrapped up tighter than a Christmas gift.

The door of our tiny apartment slams shut, which is always how Vin announces his return home.

"Kitchen," I bellow, hoping he hears me over the blare of some pop song playing on his phone.

That man has the worst taste in music, but I manage to love him anyway.

Vin eyes me appreciatively from where I'm standing at the stove. For him, the paisley printed apron I'm wearing might as well be lingerie. Maybe it's because he never had a real mother, but watching me pretend to be a housewife is the sexiest thing he can imagine.

"What's for dinner?" he asks, wrapping his arms around my waist and pressing himself against my back. "Something smells delicious."

His tone makes it clear that it isn't only the food that he's talking about. I try to push him away, but it's like shoving a brick wall. "The roast is going to burn if you don't keep your hands to yourself."

"Let it burn," he growls against my neck, nipping the skin hard enough to make me gasp.

"First lesson on not being rich is that you don't let food go to waste."

Vin licks the sensitive spot behind my ear. "Is the second lesson that you have to make your own fun? Because all the best things I can think of right now won't cost a dime."

Vin fits in to life in Los Angeles the same way he fits in everywhere else, like the world was designed with him in mind. He managed to get himself enrolled in classes at the last minute, probably with a sizable donation involved. Most of his coursework is at the business school, because he needs to figure out how to rebuild the Cortland fortune after it disintegrates.

I assumed the thought of being cut off financially would bother him, but he has taken it completely in stride. It doesn't escape my notice that all it would take to right the ship would be a pregnancy, a real one this time, but he hasn't brought it up in months, and I'm starting to think he never will.

He was true to his word about getting me on the pill, going as far as to remind me to take it every day. As if I'm the kind of girl who would forget something like that.

"I am not burning this dinner, doesn't matter what you do. This beef cost almost twenty dollars."

"And maybe all I want to eat is you." He nuzzles my neck again and bites down on my earlobe, just hard enough to leave a sting that he soothes away with his tongue. "Did you take your pill today?"

He doesn't know that I stopped taking the birth control pills months ago. Just like I didn't know that poking holes in condoms is so easy, it makes you wonder how the things are at all effective in the first place.

There are test results in a manila envelope on the table. I just have to figure out the best way to let him know what they say.

His hands roam over my body, making it easy to forget that our dinner is sizzling on the stove in front of me. Switching the knob to low, I turn in his embrace and wrap my arms around his neck. "You have ten minutes before this burns."

Vin smiles at me in a way that is frankly carnal. "With the way you come, I only need five."

He carries me away as I laugh.

VIN

I've been spending money like there is no tomorrow, because there isn't.

Zaya's tuition at UCLA is paid in full for the next four years. I gave the landlord of our apartment as much money upfront as he would take. My unfettered access to the Cortland fortune is on a ticking clock, and I intend to take full advantage.

The codicil requires that she be pregnant within a year of our marriage, and we're ticking over into month eleven. Another few weeks and the money will be out of my hands forever.

I've been trying really hard to decide what I think about that, but it's been easier not to think about it at all. The money itself doesn't mean anything, but I do sometimes wonder how I'm going to take care of her. There is a pressure to being a husband that I hadn't anticipated.

Zaya is mine, which means all of her needs are, too.

Nothing else seems important when my head is buried between her legs and she writhes against my tongue.

If someone had asked me six months ago if I was willing to give up everything I had for Zaya Milbourne, I would have laughed in their faces.

Now, it doesn't feel like I'm giving anything up at all.

When she has come enough times to forget that our dinner is burning on the stove, Zaya stares up at me with wet eyes.

"Are you really willing to be poor with me forever?"

"I'm willing to be pretty much anything, as long as it's with you."

She rolls her eyes, but I can tell my response makes her happy. "We're still in the honeymoon phase, though. What happens in ten years when you wake up in a shitty apartment with no money in the bank and hate me for it?"

"For starters, our honeymoon period happened sometime around the 3rd grade. As far as I'm concerned, our first wedding anniversary might as well be our tenth, considering everything we've been through together." My voice is stern, but I can't stop the gentle way that I cradle her face so she can't turn away when I glare down at her. "You don't have to convince me that I'm giving up too much to be with you because I've known what you're worth from the very beginning. I would give up billions of dollars before I let you walk away from me. Do you get that, or do I need to pound you into this mattress a few more times before it all becomes clear?"

She gasps in surprise when I push into her without a condom on, but doesn't push me away. Instead, her legs rise to wrap around my back until I don't have any choice but to sink into her and stay there.

The sex is unhurried even as the stench of burning meat fills the air. I don't need her to tell me that she loves me, not when she is letting perfectly good food go to waste in favor of fucking me.

I come with a force that bends my spine, right after she does. It's only belatedly that I realize my mistake.

"Oh shit, sorry." I roll off of her with a groan. The pill isn't one hundred percent, neither are condoms for that matter, but the combination seems to be enough. "You want me to run down to the drug store for a morning after pill?"

Instead of seeming upset, Zaya sits up in bed and just stares at me for a long moment. "Are you sure you're okay without the money?"

At the moment, my only focus is her bare tits, because the sheet has fallen to bunch up around her waist. "I'm sure."

She continues to stare at me. "If you did have your inheritance, what would you want to do with it?"

The easy answer is that I would carry her off to some place nice and keep her chained to my bed until we both died of exhaustion. But I get the feeling she wants to hear something more than that.

"I've always wondered what Deception would be like if

someone invested in it," I respond with a shrug, wondering why the hell she is so interested in a hypothetical. "Cortland Construction only builds in the parts of town that are nice. But the Gulch might not be so bad if someone put some money into it. The mines closed a long time ago, but there are still plenty of people willing to work. We could create jobs if we really wanted to, instead of just taking them away."

Zaya's eyes are shiny, but there is a soft smile on her face. Still naked, she jumps out of bed and runs for the kitchen. "I have something for you."

Thoroughly confused, I wait until she races back in with a manila envelope in her hand. She hands it to me with a flourish.

"What am I supposed to do with this."

She rolls her eyes. "Maybe try opening it."

I rip open the envelope, and several sheets of paper fall out onto my lap. The first page is clearly test results, but I can't make heads or tails of the jumble of letters and numbers.

Then I pick up the smallest piece. The paper is thin and mostly black with a blurry shape outlined in white.

It's a sonogram.

My mouth opens and closes again as my vision blurs.

"I went to the clinic this morning. Doctor says I'm maybe eight weeks." Her voice is soft and her gaze never leaves my face, as if gauging my reaction. "It's too early to tell, but I'm hoping for a girl."

I have Zaya in my arms before I even make the conscious decision to reach for her. "Are you sure about this?"

Her smile is tremulous. "If you are."

I've never been more sure about anything in my life.

The money I worked so hard to keep is finally mine, just as soon as I realized that I didn't care about having it anymore.

I whisper against her mouth. "I'll eat burnt steak every day if it means I get to be with you. I don't want to have it all."

She smiles as she kisses me. "That's exactly why you're going to get it."

And I do.

THE END

Thank you so much for reading!

Want more of Zaya and Vin?
Join my mailing list for a steamy second epilogue 🔥🔥🔥

https://BookHip.com/JDMAPG

Ashley Gee is a romance author and part-time adult. She lives in Indiana with her husband, two children, two cats, two dogs and partridge in a pear tree (okay not really!).

She doesn't enjoy long walks on the beach because the sand gets everywhere but can often be found binging Netflix and drinking wine from Kroger. Her books feature brooding boys and the girls who bring them to their knees. And the one thing she loves more than anything else is talking about herself in the third person.

www.ashleygee.com